DOCTOR DOLITTLE

VOL. 3

The COMPLETE COLLECTION

READ ALL OF
DOCTOR DOLITTLE'S ADVENTURES!

Doctor Dolittle
The Complete Collection, Vol. 1
The Voyages of Doctor Dolittle
The Story of Doctor Dolittle
Doctor Dolittle's Post Office

Doctor Dolittle
The Complete Collection, Vol. 2
Doctor Dolittle's Circus
Doctor Dolittle's Caravan
Doctor Dolittle and the Green Canary

Doctor Dolittle
The Complete Collection, Vol. 3
Doctor Dolittle's Zoo
Doctor Dolittle's Puddleby Adventures
Doctor Dolittle's Garden

Doctor Dolittle
The Complete Collection, Vol. 4
Doctor Dolittle in the Moon
Doctor Dolittle's Return
Doctor Dolittle and the Secret Lake
Gub-Gub's Book

DOCTOR DOLITTLE

VOL. 3

The COMPLETE COLLECTION

Doctor Dolittle's Zoo * Doctor Dolittle's Puddleby Adventures
Doctor Dolittle's Garden

HUGH LOFTING

Aladdin
NEW YORK LONDON TORONTO SYDNEY NEW DELHI

ALADDIN

An imprint of Simon & Schuster Children's Publishing Division
1230 Avenue of the Americas, New York, New York 10020
First Aladdin edition November 2019
Updated text copyright © 2019 by Christopher Lofting
Doctor Dolittle's Zoo copyright © 1925 by Hugh Lofting
Doctor Dolittle's Zoo copyright © 1953 by Josephine Lofting
Doctor Dolittle's Puddleby Adventures copyright © 1925, 1926, 1950, 1952
by Josephine Lofting
Doctor Dolittle's Garden copyright © 1927 by Hugh Lofting
Doctor Dolittle's Garden copyright © 1955 by Josephine Lofting
Cover illustration copyright © 2019 by Anton Petrov
All rights reserved, including the right of reproduction in whole or in part in any form.
ALADDIN and related logo are registered trademarks of Simon & Schuster, Inc.
For information about special discounts for bulk purchases, please contact Simon & Schuster
Special Sales at 1-866-506-1949 or business@simonandschuster.com.
The Simon & Schuster Speakers Bureau can bring authors to your live event.
For more information or to book an event contact the Simon & Schuster
Speakers Bureau at 1-866-248-3049 or visit our website at www.simonspeakers.com.
Cover designed by Karin Paprocki
Interior designed by Mike Rosamilia
The text of this book was set in Oneleigh Pro.
Manufactured in the United States of America 0719 FFG
2 4 6 8 10 9 7 5 3 1
Library of Congress Control Number 2018959982
ISBN 978-1-5344-4897-1 (hc)
ISBN 978-1-5344-4896-4 (pbk)
ISBN 978-1-5344-4898-8 (eBook)
These titles were previously published individually with slightly different text and art.

CONTENTS

Doctor Dolittle's Zoo

— 1 —

*Doctor Dolittle's
Puddleby Adventures*

— 249 —

Doctor Dolittle's Garden

— 513 —

DOCTOR DOLITTLE'S ZOO

WRITTEN & ILLUSTRATED BY HUGH LOFTING

Contents

	Prologue	5
1	A Message from Dab-Dab	9
2	The Adventurer's Return	14
3	The Surprise Party	21
4	The New Zoo	29
5	Animal Town	37
6	Poverty Again	44
7	The Badger's Tooth	51
8	The Puddleby Gold Rush	57
9	The Mouse Code	64
10	The New Learning	71
11	The Rat and Mouse Club	78
12	The Mooniversary Dinner	85
13	The Hotel Rat	92
14	Leery, the Outcast	99
15	The Volcano Rat	106
16	The Voices in the Earth	113
17	The United Rat States Republic	120
18	The Museum Mouse	126
19	Professor Foozlebugg's Masterpiece	132
20	The Prison Rat	143
21	A Rat's Pilgrimage	150
22	The Stable Mouse	159
23	The Cunning of Lucifer, the Jackdaw	170

24 Moorsden Manor   179
25 The Fire   186
26 The Leather Boxes   193
27 The Watchdogs   199
28 The Scrap of Parchment   205
29 The Coming of Kling   210
30 The Mystery of Moorsden Manor   216
31 The Dog Detective   223
32 Old Mr. Throgmorton   227
33 The Secret Cupboard   231
34 The Wild Ride of the White Mouse   236
35 Our Arrest   242

PROLOGUE

"POLYNESIA," I SAID, LEANING BACK IN MY chair and chewing the end of a quill pen, "what should you say would be the best way to begin another book of Doctor Dolittle's memoirs?"

The old parrot, who was using the glass inkpot on my desk as a mirror, stopped admiring her reflection and glanced at me sharply.

"Another!" she exclaimed. "Is there going to be *another* Dolittle book?"

"Why—er—yes," I said. "After all, we are writing the Doctor's life and we haven't nearly finished yet."

"Oh yes, I quite see that," said Polynesia. "I was only wondering who decides how many books there shall be."

"Well, I suppose—in the end—the public does," said I. "But tell me now: How would you begin?"

"Thomas Stubbins Esquire," said she, screwing up her eyes, "that's a very difficult question to answer. There is so much of interest in the life of John Dolittle that the problem is what to leave out, rather than what to put in. Already I see gray hairs showing at your temples, Tommy. If you try to write down everything the Doctor did, you'll be nearly my age before you've finished. Of course, you're not writing this book for the scientists exactly, though I confess I often think since you are the only person so far—besides the Doctor—to talk animal languages at all well, that you ought to write something sort of—er—highbrow in natural history. Usefully highbrow, I mean, of course. But that can be done later perhaps. As you said, we are still engaged on the story of the great man's life. . . . How to begin? Humph! Well, why not go on from where we all got back to Puddleby River inside the giant sea snail—you remember?—after our journey under the ocean?"

"Yes," I said, "I thought of beginning there. But it was more *how* than *where*—I mean, the things to leave out and the things to put in; what parts to choose as the most interesting."

"Ah!" said she. "Yes, that's the problem. How often have I heard the Doctor himself say those very words as he was packing his little black bag to go on a voyage: 'What to leave out and what to put in? That's the problem.' I've seen him spend half an hour wondering over his razor—whether he should pack it or not. He said a broken bottle did just as well, once you had learned how to use it. You remember how he hated a lot of baggage. He usually decided to go without the razor. But Dab-Dab and I were so scared he'd cut himself with the broken glass, we always secretly opened the bag later and slipped the razor in before starting. And as he never could remember which way he had decided the problem, it was all right."

"Indeed," said I. "But you haven't answered my question yet." Polynesia pondered a moment.

"What are you calling the book?" she asked presently.

"*Doctor Dolittle's Zoo,*" I said.

"Humph!" she murmured. "Then I suppose you ought to get on to the zoo part as soon as possible. But first I think you had better put in a little about your own homecoming and your parents and all that. You *had* been away nearly three years, you know. Of course it's sort of sentimental. But some people like a little sentiment in their books. In fact, I knew an old lady once who simply loved books that made her weep. She used to—"

"Yes, yes," I said hurriedly, seeing that the old parrot was drifting into another story, "but let us keep to the point."

"Well," said she, "I think this would be the best way: you read it all out aloud to me as you put it down, and if it starts to get tiresome you'll know because you'll see me dropping off to sleep. You will have to keep it bright and lively, though, for as I grow older I find it harder and harder to stay awake after lunch—and I've just had a big one. Have you got enough paper? Yes. And the inkpot is full? Yes. All right. Get along with it."

So taking a new quill pen and sharpening the point very carefully, I began:

A Message from Dab-Dab

I T SUDDENLY OCCURRED TO JOHN DOLITTLE that in the excitement of getting back he had not said good-bye to the snail who had brought us through this long and perilous voyage and landed us safely on our home shores. He called to us to wait and ran down the beach again.

The farewell did not take long; and presently he left the great creature's side and rejoined us. Then for a few moments the whole party stood there watching, with our bundles in our hands, while the giant snail, half-hidden in the mists that writhed about his towering shell, got under way. Truly, he seemed to belong to this landscape—or seascape—for his long, gray body looked like a part of the long, gray sandbar on which he rested. With easy muscular motion, so fluid and smooth that you could not tell how he moved at all, his great hulk slid out into deeper water. And as he went forward he went down, and down, and down, till only the top of his shell's dome, a dim gray pink in the colorless sea, could be seen. Then, without sound or splash, he was gone.

We turned our faces toward the land, Puddleby and home.

"I wonder what supplies Dab-Dab has in the house," said the Doctor, as we formed into single file and, following Jip, began to pick our way across the boggy marshland. "I hope she has plenty to eat. I am thoroughly hungry."

"So am I," said Bumpo.

At that moment, out of the wet, misty air above our heads two handsome wild ducks curved fluttering down and came to a standstill at John Dolittle's feet.

"Dab-Dab asked us to tell you," said they, "that you're to hurry up and get home out of this rain. She's waiting for you."

"Good gracious!" cried the Doctor. "How did she know that we were coming?"

"We told her," said the ducks. "We were flying inland—there's a pretty bad storm over the Irish Sea, and it's headed this way—and we saw you landing out of the snail's shell. We dropped down at the house to let her know the news. We were awfully glad to see you back. And she asked would we return and bring you a message— she herself was busy airing the bed linen, it seems. She says you're to stop in at the butcher's on the way home and bring along a pound of sausages. Also she's short of sugar, she says, and needs a few more candles, too."

"Thank you," said the Doctor. "You are very kind. I will attend to these things. You didn't take long getting there and back; it doesn't seem to me as though more than a minute had passed since we landed."

"No, we're pretty good flyers," said the ducks; "nothing fancy, but steady."

"Didn't you find the rain a great handicap?" asked the Doctor.

HUGH LOFTING

"Dab-Dab asked us to tell you that you're to hurry home."

"No, the rain doesn't bother *us*," said the ducks, "though some of the land birds are very badly hampered by wet feathers. But, of course, for all, the going is a little slower in rain on account of the air being heavier."

"I see," said the Doctor. "Well now, let us be getting along. Jip, you lead the way, will you, please? You can pick out the firm ground so much better than the rest of us."

"Look here, you fellows," said Polynesia, as the ducks prepared to take wing. "Don't be spreading the news of the Doctor's arrival too fast, will you? He's only just back from a long and tiresome journey. You know what happens when it gets known that he's home: all the birds and beasts of the countryside come around to the back door with coughs and colds and whatnot. And those who haven't anything wrong with them invent some ailment just to have an excuse to call. He needs to rest up a bit before he starts in doctoring."

"No, we won't tell anyone," said the ducks. "Not tonight, anyway, though a tremendous lot of wildfowl have been inquiring for him for ever so long, wondering when he was going to get back. He has never been gone so long before, you see."

"Humph!" muttered Polynesia, as the ducks, with a whir of feathers, disappeared again into the rainy mist above our heads. "I suppose John Dolittle has to give an account of his actions now to every snipe and sandpiper that ever met him. Poor man! How dare he be away so long! Well, such is fame, I suppose. But I'm glad I'm not a doctor myself. Oh, bless this rain! Let me get under your coat, Tommy. It's trickling down between my wings and ruining my disposition."

If it had not been for Jip's good guidance we would have had a hard job to make our way to the town across the marshes. The light of the late afternoon was failing. And every once in a while the fog would come billowing in from the sea and blot out everything around us, so that you could see no farther than a foot before your nose. The chimes of the quarter hours from Puddleby church tower were the only sounds or signs of civilization to reach us.

But Jip, with that wonderful nose of his, was a guide worth having in a place like this. The marsh was riddled and crossed in all directions by deep dykes, now filling up like rivers with the incoming tide. These could very easily cut off the unwary traveler and leave him stranded at the mercy of the rising waters. But in spite of continuous temptation to go off on the scent of water rats, Jip, like a good pilot, steered a safe course through all the dangers and kept us on fairly solid ground the whole way.

Finally we found he had brought us round to the long, high mound that bordered the Puddleby River. This we knew would lead us to the bridge. Presently we passed a hut or two, the outposts of the town. And occasionally in the swiftly flowing water on our left we would see through the lifting mists the gray, ghostly sails of a fishing boat coming home, like us, from the sea.

HUGH LOFTING

"Jip was a guide worth having."

The Adventurer's Return

A

S WE CAME NEARER TO THE TOWN AND THE lights about Kingsbridge twinkled at us through the gray mist, Polynesia said:

"It would be wiser, Doctor, if you sent Tommy in to get the sausages and went around the town yourself. You'll never get home if the children and dogs start recognizing you. You know that."

"Yes, I think you're right, Polynesia," said the Doctor. "We can turn off here to the north and get around onto the Oxenthorpe Road by Baldwin's Pool and the Mill Fields."

So the rest of the party went off with the Doctor, while I went on into the town alone. I was a little sorry not to have been present at John Dolittle's homecoming, I must admit. But I had another thrill that partly made up for it. Swaggering across Kingsbridge, alone, I returned to my native town a conquering adventurer from foreign parts. Oh my! Christopher Columbus just back from his discovery of the New World could not have felt prouder than I, Tommy Stubbins, the cobbler's son, did that night.

One of the little things that added to the thrill of it was that no one recognized me. I was like some enchanted person in the Arabian Nights who could see without being seen. I was three years older than when I had left, at an age when a boy shoots up and changes like a weed. As I swung along beneath the dim streetlamps toward the butcher's on High Street, I knew the faces of more than half the folk who passed me by. And I chuckled to myself to think how surprised they'd be if I told them who I was and all the great things I had seen and done since last I trod these cobblestones. Then in a flash I saw myself back again on the river wall, where I had so often sat with legs dangling over the

"I knew the faces of more than half the folk who passed."

water, watching the ships come and go, dreaming of the lands I had never seen.

In the market square, before a dimly lighted shop, I saw a figure that I would have known anywhere, seen from the back or the front. It was Matthew Mugg, the Cat's-Meat-Man. Just out of mischief, to see if he, too, would be unable to recognize me, I went up the shop front and stood, like him, looking in at the window. Presently he turned and looked at me. No. He didn't know me from Adam. Highly amused, I went on to the butcher's.

I asked for the sausages. They were weighed out, wrapped, and handed to me. The butcher was an old acquaintance of mine, but

"It was Matthew Mugg."

beyond glancing at my old clothes (they were patched and mended and sadly outgrown), he showed no sign of curiosity or recognition. But when I went to pay for my purchases, I found to my dismay that the only money I had in my pockets was two large Spanish silver pieces, souvenirs of our stormy visit to the Capa Blanca Islands. The butcher looked at them and shook his head.

"We only take English money here," he said.

"I'm sorry," I said apologetically, "but that is all I have. Couldn't you exchange it for me? It is, as you see, good silver. One of these pieces should be worth a crown at least."

"Maybe it is," said the butcher. "But I can't take it."

He seemed sort of suspicious and rather annoyed. While I was wondering what I should do, I became aware that there was a third party in the shop interested in what was going on. I turned to look. It was Matthew Mugg. He had followed me.

This time his eye (the one that didn't squint) fixed me with a curious look of half recognition. Suddenly he rushed at me and grabbed me by the hand.

"It's Tommy!" he squeaked. "As I live, it's Tommy Stubbins, grown so tall and handsome his own mother wouldn't know him, and as brown as a berry."

Matthew was, of course, well known to the tradesmen of the town—especially to the butcher, from whom he bought the bones and odd pieces of meat he fed to the dogs. He turned to the shopkeeper.

"Why, Alfred," he cried, "this is Tommy Stubbins, Jacob Stubbins's lad, back from furrin parts. No need to be worried about *his* credit, Alfred. He's shopping for the Doctor, I'll be bound. You brought the Doctor back with you?" he asked, peering at me anxiously. "Don't tell me you came back alone?"

"No," I said. "The Doctor's here, safe and sound."

"You're just in, eh?" said he. "Tonight, huh? John Dolittle couldn't be in this town long without my knowing it."

"Yes," I said. "He's on his way up to the house now. Asked me to do a little shopping for him. But all the money I have is foreign."

I said this with the superior air of an experienced traveler, raising my eyebrows a little disdainfully at the obstinate butcher, whose stay-at-home mind couldn't be expected to appreciate a real adventurer's difficulties.

"Oh well, Alfred will let you have the sausages, I'm sure," said Matthew.

"Why yes, that's all right, Tommy," said the butcher, smiling at my airs. "Though we ain't exactly a money exchange, you know. But if you had said at first who you were, and who the sausages were for, I'd have charged them to the Doctor without a word—even though his credit hasn't always been of the best. Take the meat—and tell John Dolittle I'm glad he's back safe."

"Thank you," I said with dignity.

Then, with my package beneath one arm and Matthew Mugg firmly grasping the other, I stepped forth into the street.

"You know, Tommy," said Matthew, as we set off in the direction of the Oxenthorpe Road, "all the years that John Dolittle's been returning from voyages he ain't never got home once without me to welcome him the first night he got in. Not that he ever tells me he's coming, mind you. No, indeed. As often as not, I fancy, he'd rather no one knew. But somehow or other I always finds out before he's been in the town an hour, and right away I'm up there to welcome him. And once I'm inside the house, he seems to get used to me and be glad I'm there. I suppose you seen an awful lot of adventures and strange sights and things since I saw you last?"

"Yes, Matthew," I said. "We saw even more than I had thought or hoped we would. We have brought back notebooks by the barrow-load and a collection of wonderful herbs that were gathered by an South American naturalist—frightfully valuable and important. And—what do you think, Matthew?—we came back inside the shell of a giant sea snail who crawled along the bottom of the ocean with us all the way from the other side of the Atlantic!"

"Oh well," said Matthew, "there be no end to the strange things Doctor John Dolittle's seen and gone through. I've given up talking about his voyagings and strange doings. Down in the taproom of the Red Lion I used to tell about his travels—of an evening like, when folk enjoy a tale. But never no more. It's like this business of his speaking animal languages: people don't believe you, so what's the good?"

We were now some half mile along the Oxenthorpe Road and within a short distance of the Doctor's house. It was quite dark. But in the hedges and the trees all about us I could hear birds fluttering and chattering. In spite of Polynesia's request, the news had already spread, in that mysterious way it does in the animal kingdom. The season was still cold and few more than the winter birds could be found in England now. But round about the famous Little House with the Big Garden they were gathered in thousands—sparrows, robins, blackbirds, crows, and starlings—to welcome the great man back, prepared to sit up all night just to see him in the morning.

And it occurred to me, as I walked up the steps and opened the little gate at the top, that such was the great difference between

HUGH LOFTING

"People don't believe you, so what's the good?"

this strange popularity and friendship that the Doctor enjoyed and that of ordinary human society: with some friends, if you were away three years, it would mean you'd find yourself forgotten when you returned. But with John Dolittle and his animal friends, the longer he was gone the greater the welcome and rejoicing when he came home again.

The Surprise Party

S A MATTER OF FACT, I DID NOT ENTIRELY miss witnessing the Doctor's homecoming. When Matthew and I entered at the kitchen door we found an air of mystery in the house. We had expected, of course, an enormous amount of noise—greetings, questions, and so forth. But there wasn't a soul even visible besides the Doctor himself—and Dab-Dab, who promptly berated me for taking so long getting the sausages.

"But where is Gub-Gub?" the Doctor was asking as we came in.

"How on earth should I know, Doctor?" said Dab-Dab. "He'll turn up presently—and the rest of them, no doubt. Have you washed your hands for supper? Please don't leave it to the last moment. The food will be on the table in five minutes. I'll want you to help me, Tommy, with the sausages. By the way, Doctor, we're going to have supper in the dining room."

"In the dining room!" cried John Dolittle. "What on earth for? Why don't we use the kitchen as usual?"

"Not big enough," grunted Dab-Dab.

I suspected from an odd look in the housekeeper's eye that there was some surprise in store. And, sure enough, when the dining room door was opened, there it was. The whole crowd of them—Gub-Gub, Too-Too, Swizzle, Toby, and the white mouse—all in fancy dress. It was a surprise party given in the Doctor's honor.

The dining room was a funny old stately chamber that the Doctor had closed up years and years ago—in fact, it had not been used since his sister Sarah had left him. But tonight it was gaily decorated with colored papers, ribbons, and evergreens. The animals were all in their old pantomime costumes, even the white mouse was wearing a tiny waistcoat and pants in which he used to appear in the famous Dolittle Circus of bygone days.

Now, with the Doctor's appearance at the door, the noise which we had missed began in earnest. Barks, yelps, and squeals of greeting broke forth. But there was very little disorderly behavior, for apparently a regular program of entertainment had been arranged. The meal was most elaborate, the table piled high with fruits and dainties of every kind. Between courses, each one of the animals who had stayed at home had some performance to give. Gub-Gub recited one of his own food poems, entitled "The Wilted Cauliflower"; Toby and Swizzle gave a boxing match (the stage was the middle of the table) with real boxing gloves tied on their front paws; and the white mouse showed us what he called "The Punchbowl Circus." This took place in a large glass bowl, and was the most thrilling thing of its kind I have ever seen. The white mouse was ringmaster, and he swaggered about on his hind legs with a tiny top hat made of paper on his head. In his troupe he had a lady bareback rider, a clown, and a lion tamer. The rider

HUGH LOFTING

"Gub-Gub recited one of his food poems."

was another mouse (using a cutlet frill for a ballet skirt), and she rode a squirrel for a horse—the fastest mount I ever saw. The lion tamer was still another mouse, and his lion was a large rat dressed up with strings on his head for a mane.

Taken all in all, the Punchbowl Circus was, I think, the greatest success of the evening. The white mouse had even, in a way, made himself up. With some heavy black grease paint, which Swizzle, the old clown dog of the circus, had lent him from his own private makeup box, he had waxed his whiskers together so that they looked exactly like the long, ferocious mustachios of a regular ringmaster. The lady bareback artist leapt through paper hoops, the mouse

"The ringmaster of the Punchbowl Circus"

clown (also made up with a red and white face), threw somersaults, and the rat lion roared savagely.

"I don't know how on earth you all managed to get the show ready in time," said the Doctor, tears of laughter running down his cheeks at the antics of the mouse clown. "It's better than anything I ever had in my circus. And you only knew I was coming half an hour before I got here. How did you do it?"

"You'll soon see how it was done if you go upstairs, Doctor," said Dab-Dab severely. "It was Gub-Gub's idea. They turned the house inside out to get the costumes and the ribbons and they turned the garden upside down to get the evergreens. Tut! Such foolishness! And just when I needed every one of them to help me put the house in proper order against your coming."

"Oh well, never mind, Dab-Dab," said the Doctor, still laughing. "It was worth it. I never enjoyed anything so much in all my life. We can soon get the house straightened out. You have Stubbins and Bumpo and me to help you now, you know."

"Yes, and I don't know where I'm going to put Bumpo to sleep, either," said Dab-Dab. "None of the beds we have will fit him."

"Well, we'll manage," said the Doctor. "If the worst comes to the worst, we can put two mattresses together on the floor."

"And now, Doctor," said Gub-Gub, "your part of the performance begins. We want to hear all about your travels since you left here."

"Yes, yes," they all cried. "Begin at the beginning."

"But, good gracious!" cried John Dolittle. "I couldn't tell you our complete diary for three years in one evening!"

"Well, tell us some of it," squeaked the white mouse, "and keep the rest for tomorrow night."

So, lighting his pipe, which, with the tobacco jar, Chee-Chee brought down off the mantelpiece, the Doctor began at the beginning—the tale of his travels. It was a wonderful scene—the long dining room table packed all around with listening faces, animal and human. The Doctor's household had never, to my knowledge, been so complete before: Bumpo, Matthew Mugg, myself, Dab-Dab, Gub-Gub, Chee-Chee, Polynesia, Jip, Too-Too, Toby, Swizzle, and the white mouse. And then, just as he was about to begin, there came a thud at the window, and a voice said:

"Let me in. I want to listen too."

It was the old lame horse from the stable. He had heard the

noise, and, realizing that the Doctor had arrived at last, had come across to join the party.

To Dab-Dab's great annoyance, the double French windows that opened onto the garden were unlatched and the old lame horse invited to join the party. The good housekeeper did insist, however, that I brush his hooves clean of mud before he was allowed in onto the carpets. It was surprising to see how naturally he took to such unusual surroundings. He passed through the room without upsetting anything and took up a place between the Doctor's chair and the sideboard. He said he wanted to be near the speaker, because his hearing wasn't what it used to be. John Dolittle was overjoyed to see him.

"I was on my way out to your stable to call on you," he said, "when supper was announced. You know how particular Dab-Dab is. Have you been getting your oats and barley regularly since I've been gone?"

"Yes, thank you," said the old horse. "Everything's been quite all right—lonely, of course, somewhat, without you and Jip—but all right otherwise."

Once more the Doctor settled down to begin his story, and once more he was interrupted by a tapping at the window.

"Oh, goodness! Who is it now?" wailed Gub-Gub.

I opened the window and three birds fluttered in—Cheapside, with his wife Becky, and the famous Speedy-the-Skimmer.

"Bless my soul!" chirped the Cockney sparrow, flying up onto the table. "If anybody ever broke into this 'ouse 'e'd deserve all 'e could pinch. That's what I say. Me and Becky 'as been pokin' round the doors and windows for hours, lookin' for a way in. Might as well try to get into the Bank of Hengland after closin' time. Well, Doc, 'ere we are! The old firm! Glad to see you back. Me and the missis was just turnin' in up at St. Paul's when we 'eard the pigeons gossipin' below us. There was a rumor, they said, that you'd got back. So I says to Becky, I says, 'Let's take a run down to Puddleby and see.' 'Right you are,' says she. And down we come. Nobody can't never—"

"Oh, be quiet!" Too-Too broke in. "The Doctor is about to tell us of his voyage. We don't want to listen to you all night."

"All right, Cross-eyes, all right," said Cheapside, picking up a crumb from the table and talking with his mouth full, "keep your feathers on. 'Ow long 'ave *you* owned this 'ouse, anyway? Hey, Speedy, come over 'ere where it's warmer."

HUGH LOFTING

"All right, Cross-eyes"

The famous swallow—champion speed flyer of Europe, Africa, and America—modestly came forward to a warmer place under the branching candlesticks. He had returned to England a little earlier this year than usual, but the warm weather that had tempted him northward had given way to a cold snap. And now in the brighter light near the center of the table we could plainly see that he was shivering.

"Glad to see you, Doctor," said he quietly. "Excuse us interrupting you like this. Please begin, won't you?"

The New Zoo

S O, FAR INTO THE NIGHT, JOHN DOLITTLE TOLD his household the story of his voyage. Gub-Gub kept falling asleep and then waking up very angry with himself because he was afraid he had missed the best parts.

Somewhere around two o'clock in the morning, although he was not more than half done, the Doctor insisted that everybody go to bed and the rest of the adventures be put off until tomorrow night.

The following day was, I think, the busiest day I have ever seen the Doctor put in. Everybody and everything demanded his attention at once. First of all, of course, there were patients waiting at the surgery door: a squirrel with a broken claw, a rabbit who was losing his fur, a fox with a sore eye.

Then there was the garden, the Doctor's well-beloved garden. What a mess it was in, to be sure! Three years of weeds, three years of overgrowth, three years of neglect! He almost wept as he stepped out of the kitchen door and saw the desolation of it

HUGH LOFTING

"Patients waiting at the surgery door"

fully revealed in the bright morning sunlight. Luckily the country birds who had been waiting all night to greet him helped to take his mind off it for a while. It reminded me of the pictures of St. Francis and the pigeons, as the starlings, crows, robins, and blackbirds swarmed down about him in clouds as soon as he appeared.

Bumpo and I, realizing how deeply affected he was by the sad state of his garden, decided to put our shoulder to the wheel and see what we could do toward cleaning it up. Chee-Chee also volunteered to help, and so did a great number of smaller animals like field mice, rats, badgers, and squirrels. And, despite their tiny size, it was astonishing to see how much they could do. For example, two families of moles (who are usually a great pest in a garden) dug up, after the Doctor had explained what he wanted, the entire herb bed next to the peach wall and turned it over better than any professional gardener would have done. They sorted out the weeds from the herb roots and gathered them into neat piles, which Chee-Chee collected in his wheelbarrow. The squirrels were splendid as general clean-up men. They collected all the fallen twigs and leaves and other refuse that littered the gravel walks and carried them to the compost heap behind the potting shed. The badgers helped by burrowing down and pruning the roots of the apple trees underground.

Then, in the middle of the morning Too-Too, the accountant, wanted to go into money matters with the Doctor, so that Dab-Dab might see how much she had to keep house with. Fortunately, the Spanish silver we had brought back from the Capa Blancas (largely out of Bumpo's bet, which the Doctor didn't know anything about) looked, when changed into English pounds, as though it should keep us all comfortably for some months at least without worry. This was a great relief to Dab-Dab, though, as usual, she kept an anxious eye on any new schemes of the Doctor's, remembering from the past that the more money he had, the more extravagant he was likely to be.

It was a funny sight to see those wiseacres—Too-Too, Polynesia, and Dab-Dab—putting their heads together over the Doctor's money affairs while his back was turned.

"But, look here," Polynesia put in, "the Doctor ought to make a lot of money out of all these new and precious herbs of Long Arrow's, which he brought back."

"Oh, hardly," said I. "You'll probably find he'll refuse to profit

HUGH LOFTING

"Putting their heads together over the Doctor's money affairs"

by them at all. In his eyes they are medicines for humanity's benefit; not things to sell."

And then, in addition to all the other departments of his strange establishment that claimed the Doctor's attention that morning, there was the zoo. Matthew Mugg was on hand very early to go over it with him. Not very many of the old inmates were there now. Quite a number had been sent away before the Doctor left, because he felt that in his absence their care would be too ticklish a job for Matthew to manage alone. But there were a few who had begged very hard to remain, some of the more northerly animals like the Canadian woodchucks and the minks.

"You know, Stubbins," said the Doctor as we passed down between the clean, empty houses (Matthew had in our absence really kept the place in wonderful condition), "I have a notion to change the whole system of my zoo."

"How do you mean?" I asked.

"Well," said he, "so far I had kept it mostly for foreign exhibits—rather unusual animals—though, as you know, I always avoided the big hunting creatures. But now I think I'll give it over almost entirely to our native animals. There are a great many who want to live with me—many more than we can possibly manage in the house. You see, we have a big space here, over an acre, altogether. It used to be sort of a bowling green hundreds of years ago, when an old castle stood where the house is now. It is walled in—private and secluded. Look at it. We could make this into a regular ideal Animal Town. Something quite new. You can help me with the planning of it. I thought I would have several clubs in it. The Rat and Mouse Club is one that I have been thinking of for a long time. Several rats and mice have asked me to start it. And then, the Home for Crossbred Dogs is another. A tremendous lot of dogs—of no particular breed—call on me from time to time and ask if they can live with me. Jip will tell you all about it. I hate to turn them away, because I know many of them have no place to live—and people don't want them because they're not what is called pure-bred. Silly idea. Myself, I've usually found that the mongrels had more character and sense than the prize winners. But there you are. What do you think of my idea?"

"I think it's just a marvelous idea, Doctor," I cried. "And it

"I think it's just a marvelous idea!"

will certainly relieve poor old Dab-Dab of an awful lot of worry. She is always grumbling over the way the mice eat the pillow slips in the linen closet and use the fringes off the bath towels to make their nests with."

"Yes," said the Doctor, "and we've never been able to find out who the culprits are. Each one, when I ask him, says *he* didn't do it. But the linen goes on disappearing just the same. Of course, myself, I'm not very particular if a pillow slip has an extra hole in it or not. And bath towels don't *have* to have fringes. But Dab-Dab's awfully pernickety. Her linen closet—

gracious!—for her it is the same as the garden is for me: the most important thing! . . . Well now, Stubbins, supposing as soon as we get some of these poor old fruit trees into shape you plan out the new zoo for me. Get Polynesia to help you. She's full of ideas, as you know. Unfortunately, I've got my hands more than full already with the surgery and the writing up of the notebooks we brought back (I'll want you to help me on that, too)—to say nothing of Long Arrow's collection. Otherwise I could work with you on the first layout of the zoo. But you and Polynesia can do it between you. By the way, consult the white mouse about the quarters for the Rat and Mouse Club, will you?"

Well, that was the beginning of the new Dolittle Zoo. It was, of course, a thing that interested me tremendously, and I felt very proud that the Doctor had entrusted such a large measure of the responsibility to me. But I had very little idea, at the outset, into what an enormous institution it was to grow. "Animal Town" or "Animal Clubland" is really what it should have been called, instead of a zoo. But we had always called that part of the garden the zoo, and that name persisted.

But if it wasn't a regular zoo to the ordinary public's way of thinking, it was very certainly Doctor Dolittle's idea of one. In his opinion, a zoo should be an animals' home, not an animals' prison. Every detail of our zoo (as with the first one the Doctor had shown me long ago) was worked out with this idea foremost in mind, that the animals should be made comfortable and happy. Many of the old things were kept the same. For example, the latches to the houses were all on the inside, so that the animals could come in and go out when they chose. Latchkeys were given out (if a tenant wanted one) when a house or room or hole was let. There were certain rules, it is true, although the Doctor was not fond of rules, but they were all drawn up to protect the animals against one another, rather than to enslave them or cut off their liberty in any way. For instance, anyone wishing to give a party had to notify his next-door neighbor (they were very close, of course); and no tenant was allowed to sing comic songs after midnight.

Animal Town

ONE OF THE GREATEST DIFFICULTIES THE Doctor had in all his dealings with the animal kingdom was that of keeping anything secret. But then, I suppose, when we remember how hard it is for people to keep secrets, that need not be so surprising. Polynesia, as soon as I told her about the idea of the new zoo, immediately warned me.

"Keep this to yourself, now, Tommy, as long as you can. If you don't, neither you nor the Doctor will get any peace."

I certainly kept it to myself. But nevertheless the news leaked out somehow that John Dolittle was reorganizing and enlarging his zoo in order that a lot of new animals might live with him. And then, exactly as Polynesia had prophesied, we were pestered to death morning, noon, and night with applications. You would think that all the animals in the world had been waiting the whole of their lives for a chance to get into the Doctor's household.

He at once had it announced that as I was to be the assistant manager of the new zoo, all applications must be made through me.

But even so, of course, while that did relieve him of a good deal of annoyance, a great many animals who had known him a long time applied to him directly for a home in the new establishment.

And then we had quite a difficult time sending away some of the old tenants. The Doctor had found that for many foreigners the climate of Puddleby was quite unsuitable. There were a pair of beavers, for example, who had been sick a good deal and quite noticeably out of condition almost the whole time. But they were so attached to the Doctor that although he had often suggested sending them back to Canada, they had always politely but stubbornly declined. However, on the Doctor's return this time he found them in such poor health he decided it would be kinder to be firm.

"Listen," he said to them, "you may not know it, but this climate is very, very bad for you. It is either not cold enough or not dry enough—or something. I can't have you throwing your health away like this out of mere sentiment. You've *got* to go back to Canada."

Well, the beavers just burst into tears, both of them. And it was not until John Dolittle had promised them that they should come back after two years—if at the end of that time they still wanted to—that they were consoled and consented to go.

It was part of my duties as assistant manager to secure the beavers' passage back to Canada. This was no simple matter, as you can easily imagine, because, of course, I could not just hand them over to anyone. I spent several days around the docks of Tilbury before I found a ship's steward whose references for honesty and reliability were such as to satisfy the Doctor. For a certain sum of money he agreed to take them to Halifax on his ship's next voyage to Nova Scotia and to let them go at the mouth of a river well outside the limits of the town.

HUGH LOFTING

"'Listen,' he said to them."

Not only were there many applications from single animals and families for accommodations in our zoo, but as soon as it got abroad that John Dolittle was going to set up his long-promised Rat and Mouse Club, every other species of animal on earth, it seemed to me, sent committees to him to ask couldn't they have a club, too.

"I told you what it would be like," said Polynesia, as she and I were pondering one day over a map of the new zoo that I had laid out. "If the space you had was ten times as big you couldn't accommodate them all."

"But look here," said the white mouse (it was most amusing to see how important he had become now that he was being consulted in the Doctor's schemes), "suppose we set out on your drawing here all the different establishments, private houses, flats, hotels, clubs, and whatnot, then we can see better how much room there is left and how many clubs we can have."

"Yes," I said, "that's a good idea, because once we get the zoo running it will be very hard to dig things out and change them around afterward. The animals would very naturally object to that."

"And then I think we ought to have some shops," said the white mouse. "Don't you?"

"'But, look here,' said the white mouse."

"Shops!" I cried. "What on earth for?"

"Well, you see," said he, "by the time we're finished it will be like a town anyhow—an animal town—with a main street, I suppose, and the houses and clubs on either side. A few shops where the squirrels could buy nuts and the mice could get acorns and grains of wheat—don't you see?—it would liven things up a bit. Nothing cheers a town up so much as good shops. And I think a restaurant or two where we could go and get our meals if we came home late and hadn't time to raise our own supper—yes, that's a good notion—we should surely have a restaurant or two."

"But who are you going to get to run these shops?" asked Polynesia. "Stores and cafes don't run themselves, you know."

"Oh, that's easy," laughed the white mouse. "I know lots of mice—and rats, too—who would jump at the chance to run a nut store or a restaurant—just have a natural gift for business, especially catering."

"Maybe, for the rats and mice," said Polynesia. "But they're not the only ones in the zoo, remember. This isn't just a rat and mouse town."

"Well, I imagine it will probably separate itself into districts anyway," said the white mouse. "You won't forget, Tommy, that you've promised us the top end, near the gate, for our club? I have that whole section laid out in my mind's eye complete. And it is going to be just the niftiest little neighborhood you ever saw."

Well, after a tremendous amount of planning and working out, we finally got the new zoo going. The list of public institutions with which it began was as follows: The Rabbits' Apartment House (this consisted of an enormous mound full of rabbit holes, with a community lettuce garden attached), the Home for Crossbred Dogs, the

Rat and Mouse Club, the Badgers' Tavern, the Foxes' Meeting House, and the Squirrels' Hotel.

Each of these was a sort of club in its way. And we had to be most particular about limiting the membership because from the outset thousands of creatures of each kind wanted to join. The best we could do for those who were not taken in was to keep their names on a waiting list, and as members left (which was very seldom) admit them one by one. Each club had its president and committee who were responsible for the proper organization and orderly carrying on of the establishment.

As the white mouse had prophesied, our new animal town within the high walls of the old bowling green did naturally divide itself up into districts. And the animals from each, while they often mingled in the main street with those from other quarters of the town, minded their own business, and no one interfered with anybody else.

This we had to make the first and most important rule of the Dolittle Zoo: All hunting was forbidden within the walls of the town. No member of the Home for Crossbred Dogs was allowed to go ratting—in the zoo. No fox was permitted to chase birds or squirrels.

And it was surprising how, when the danger of pursuit by their natural enemies was removed, all the different sorts of animals took up a new, freer, and more open kind of life. For instance, it was no unusual thing in Animal Town to see a mother squirrel lolling on her veranda, surrounded by her children, while a couple of terriers walked down the street within a yard of them.

The shops and restaurants, of course, were mostly patronized by the rats and mice, who had a natural love for city life, and the majority of them were situated in the section at the north end of the enclosure, which came to be known as Mouse Town. Nevertheless, at the main grocery on a Saturday night we often saw foxes and dogs and crows, all mixed up, buying their Sunday dinner from a large rat. And the mouse errand boys who delivered goods to the customers' houses were not afraid to walk right into a bulldog's kennel or a fox's den.

"Buying their Sunday dinner from a large rat"

Poverty Again

OF COURSE IT WOULD BE QUITE TOO MUCH TO expect that with lots of different kinds of animals housed in the same enclosure there would be no quarrels or disputes. It was in fact part of the Doctor's plan to see what could be done in getting different creatures who were born natural enemies to live together in harmony.

"Obviously, Stubbins," said he, "we can't expect foxes to give up their taste for spring chickens, or dogs their love of ratting, all in a moment. My hope is that by getting them to agree to live peaceably together while within my zoo, we will tend toward a better understanding among them permanently."

Yes, there *were* fights, especially in the first few months before the different communities got settled down. But, curiously enough, many of the quarrels were among animals of the same kind. I think the badgers were the worst. In the evenings at their tavern they used to play games. Neither the Doctor nor I could ever make out what these games were about. One was played with stones on a piece of ground marked out with scratches. It was almost like drafts or checkers. The badgers used to take this game quite seriously—the badger is rather a heavy type of personality anyway. And there seemed to be championships played and great public interest taken in the outcome of matches. Frequently these ended in a quarrel. And in the middle of the night a frightened squirrel would come and wake me or the Doctor and tell us there was a fight going on in the Badgers' Tavern and the whole town was being disturbed.

In the end, at the white mouse's suggestion (he was more proud and important than ever, now that he had been elected the first mayor of Animal Town), this led to the Doctor instituting the Zoo Police Force. Two dogs, two foxes, two squirrels, two rabbits, and two rats were elected as constables, with a bulldog for captain and a fox as head of the Secret Service. After that, woe betide any quarrelsome member who tried to start a brawl in the Badgers' Tavern! He promptly found himself being trotted down the street under arrest to spend the night in the town jail.

One of the first arrests to be made by the zoo police was that of poor Gub-Gub. Having noticed that the vegetable garden attached to the Rabbits' Apartment House was promising a nice harvest of early lettuce, he made a descent upon it one night secretly. But the chief of the fox detectives spotted him and he was handcuffed (or trotter-cuffed) before he could say Jack Robinson. It was only on the Doctor's forbidding him entrance to the zoo compound for the future and going security for his good behavior that he was dismissed the following morning with a caution.

"Next time," said His Honor the Mayor (the white mouse who was acting as magistrate), "we will give you six days' hard labor in the rabbits' garden—with a muzzle on."

HUGH LOFTING

"Next time we will give you six days' hard labor."

Besides the Rat and Mouse Club, of which I shall speak further later on, the other more important department in the new zoo was the Home for Crossbred Dogs. This was an institution that Jip had long pestered John Dolittle to establish. Ever since the days of *The Canary Opera*, when Jip had tried to run a Free Bone kitchen for dogs in the East End of London, he had been hoping that the Doctor would discover a way to give all the strays and outcasts of dogdom a decent home. Now, in the seventh heaven of contentment, he, with Toby and Swizzle, was very busy working out the details of the new club.

"Now some dogs," said Jip to me, "like to live in kennels—

prefer to be private, you know—and others like to live in houses. So we'll have to have a lot of kennels and at least one good house."

Thereupon he persuaded me and Bumpo to build a house according to his, Swizzle's, and Toby's directions. Toby, always a fussy, bossy little dog, had a whole heap of ideas, mostly for the benefit of the small dogs who were to come. You would think they were surely the most important. And when we finally had it finished, I am bound to say the Dogs' House was quite an unusual building. All doors were made to open just with a lift of the nose-latch and a push. The fireplaces were built especially wide, so that at least a dozen dogs could find room to lie in front of each one. All sofas (of which there were many) were made low enough so that the smallest dogs could jump up onto them with ease, and were furnished with special oilcloth upholstery and cushions, so that they could be easily cleaned if they got muddied up with dirty paws. Drinking bowls were to be found in every room. It was against the rules to leave bones lying around the floor, but a bone-rack (rather like an umbrella stand) was provided for the members near the front door. And here the dogs could leave their bones on going out and find them again on coming in—if they hadn't been borrowed in the meantime.

Meals were served in a special dining room, where dishes were set out on very low tables; and a grand sideboard buffet with steps to it, where members could go up and make their own choice of cold meats, was an important and popular feature. This department— the supplying of bones and meat to the dogs' kitchen—Matthew Mugg took charge of. Matthew considered himself an expert in dogs and this side of the zoo held great interest for him.

Then there was a special sort of dogs' gymnasium, which Jip called the Roughhouse Room. It had trapezes, balls hung on strings, and other special apparatus for dog exercise and dog gymnastics. And here wonderful wrestling contests, tug-o'-war matches, tag games, and sham fights were staged almost every night. The Doctor, Bumpo, and I were often invited down to see these sports, which were very good fun to watch, as were also the races and leaping contests that Jip arranged in the dogs' gymnasium.

The Home for Crossbred Dogs was, I think, one of the happiest institutions that John Dolittle ever established. Of course, as the Doctor had said, there was to begin with a long list of dogs who had always wanted to be attached to his household. Among these, almost the first to turn up at the club were Grab the bulldog

"The leaping contests in the dogs' gymnasium"

and Blackie the retriever, whom John Dolittle had rescued from Harris's animal shop a long time ago.

But in addition to this class there was the much greater number of Jip's friends and acquaintances. Naturally a very charitable dog, Jip loved to go out and hunt round the streets for homeless vagabonds. Every day he would bring home one or two, till very soon the club had about as many members as it would hold. And even when the Doctor told him he would have to stop, he would, if he found a particularly deserving case, as he called it, sneak in with him after dark and see that at least he got a square meal off the sideboard buffet and a night's lodging. From the outside, the gate to the zoo could only be opened by a secret latch. This was worked by pulling a string carefully hidden in a ditch. All members of the zoo were specially instructed in this by the Doctor and made to promise not to give the secret away. And I am bound to say they were very conscientious about it. During the whole of the zoo's career no outsider ever learned the secret of the gate. But when Jip brought his "deserving cases" home after dark, he always made them turn their backs while he pulled the secret latchstring.

As soon as it became known in dog society that John Dolittle had formed a club, many dogs who had perfectly good homes of their own just left them and came here—for no other reasons than that they preferred living with the Doctor and because they loved the gymnasium and the good company. And more than one angry owner called at the Doctor's house and was all for having him arrested because, he said, he had lured his dog away from him.

Of course the cost of the upkeep of the new zoo was considerable, especially for the supply of food for the Home for Crossbred Dogs. And about six weeks after it had been established, Dab-Dab and Too-Too came to me, both looking very serious.

"More than one angry owner called."

"It is just as I thought it would be," squawked Dab-Dab, throwing out her wings in a gesture of despair. "We are already practically at the end of our money again. I don't know how many thousand pesetas it was you brought back with you, but it's nearly all gone. Too-Too and I have been going over accounts and we calculate we have about enough to last for another week. Jip has no sense. The Doctor is bad enough himself, goodness knows, the way he spends money—just regardless. But nobody in the world would be rich enough to keep all the stray mongrels Jip has been bringing in the last few weeks. Well, here we are, penniless again. I don't know what we're going to do, I'm sure."

THE SEVENTH CHAPTER

The Badger's Tooth

O F COURSE, WHEN I WENT (WITH DAB-DAB, Too-Too, and Polynesia) to the Doctor to report the condition of the family bank account he, as usual, took the matter very lightly.

"Don't bother me with such things now," he said. "Some money will come in somehow, I have no doubt—it generally does. I'm dreadfully busy."

But though we managed to collect a few pounds that were due him from people who published his books on natural history, that did not last us long. And soon we were as badly off as ever. Dab-Dab was terribly angry and kept insisting that the Doctor get rid of the zoo, which was almost as expensive to run as all the rest of the household put together.

But John Dolittle was right; something did turn up, and, curiously enough, it turned up inside the zoo itself and saved that institution from extinction as well as the Dolittle household from bankruptcy. This is how it happened: one night, just as the Doctor

"We went to the Doctor to report."

was going to bed after a hard day's work with his new book on oceanography, a member of the Badgers' Tavern knocked on the door asking to see him. He said he had a terrible toothache and wanted the Doctor, if he would, to look at it at once. This, of course, the Doctor did. He was very clever at animal dentistry.

"Ah!" said he. "You've broken a corner off that tooth. No wonder it hurts. But it can be fixed. Open your mouth a little wider, please. . . . That's better—why, how curious! Did I ever fill any teeth for you before?"

"No," said the badger. "This is the first time I've come to you for treatment of any kind. I'm very healthy."

"But you have gold in your teeth," said the Doctor. "How did that come to be there if you haven't been to some dentist?"

"I'm sure I don't know," said the badger. "What is gold?"

"Look, I'll show you in the mirror," said the Doctor. "Stubbins, give me that hand glass, will you, please?"

I got it and brought it to the Doctor, who held it in front of the badger's face while he pointed to a place in his teeth with a small instrument.

"There," said John Dolittle, "you see that yellow metal sticking between your teeth? That's gold."

"Oh!" said the badger, peering into the mirror, very pleased with his own handsome reflection. "I and my wife were digging a hole out by Dobbin's Meadow and we chewed up a whole lot of that stuff. That's what I broke my tooth on."

Polynesia, who was in the surgery at the time, was more interested in this statement of the badger's than was the Doctor. She flew across the room and from one of her hanging rings she peered into the animal's open mouth where John Dolittle was at work on the broken tooth. Then she came back to me and whispered:

"Well, of all things! He's been eating gold. *Eating* it, mind you—and us as poor as church mice. Tommy, we will speak with this gentleman as soon as the Doctor has done with him."

John Dolittle did not take long over making his patient comfortable. In spite of his pudgy fat hands he had the quickest and nimblest fingers in the world.

"I have put a dressing in your tooth that will stop the pain for the present and you'll have to come back and see me again tomorrow," he said as the badger closed his mouth and waddled down off the table. "You must be careful what you chew up when you're digging holes. No teeth will stand biting on metal, you know—not even yours. Good night."

As the patient left the surgery, Polynesia made a sign to me and we followed him.

"Where did you say you were digging this hole?" asked Polynesia as we walked beside him toward the zoo enclosure.

"Over near Dobbin's Meadow," said the badger; "just a bit to the north of it. We were tunneling into a bank—as much for exercise as anything else. It was a cold day. But we did hope we might find some pig nuts. Also, we need a refuge hole or two up in that direction. Some of these dogs the Doctor has here in such numbers now are getting entirely too cheeky. They never touch us while we are in the zoo, it is true, but if they get wind of us when we're outside they think it is funny to chase us all over the landscape. Our committee down at the Badgers' Tavern thought we ought to have a refuge hole up in that neighborhood."

"What is a refuge hole?" I asked.

"Oh, it's just a public hole," said he. "We have them stuck around all over the place. But we all know where they are. They're just holes where any badger can take refuge if chased by dogs. We dig them very deep and sometimes provision them with food in case the dogs should besiege us for a long time. We have to protect ourselves, you know. Our pace is slow."

"Well now, look here," said Polynesia as we reached the zoo gate, "Tommy and I would like to make an appointment with you for tomorrow morning early—very early. We want to see this place where you broke your tooth. Suppose we meet you at the north end of Dobbin's Meadow at, say, five o'clock."

"All right," said the badger. "But that isn't early for me. This time of year it has been broad daylight for more than a quarter of an hour by five. We don't go by the clock, you know; we go by the sun. We prefer to travel before dawn. I'll meet you there at daybreak."

The following morning Polynesia had me out of bed and dressing by candlelight before the roosters had given their first crow.

"But don't you see, Tommy," said she, in answer to my sleepy grumbling at this unearthly hour for rising, "it's frightfully important that we get there and do what exploring is necessary before there are people about."

I found it hard to be enthusiastic so early, even over the prospect of discovering gold.

"But what are you expecting to find?" I asked. "Do you fancy that old badger has run into a mine? There aren't any gold mines in England."

"I've no more idea than you have," she said impatiently. "But just because no gold mines have been discovered so far, that doesn't mean that none ever will be. The fact remains that that blessed animal ran into gold of some kind, or he wouldn't have it sticking in his teeth. Hurry up and get your coat on. I think I see the dawn beginning to show in the East."

Downstairs Polynesia made me collect a spade from the tool shed and the Doctor's mineral hammer from his study before we started away through the chilly morning twilight for Dobbin's Meadow.

The old badger was there, sure enough, waiting for us. And he promptly lumbered off alongside a hedge to lead us to the place where he had dug the hole. This, when we came to it, proved not to be in the Dobbin property at all, but on the other side of the hedge, in a wide-open piece of heath-land, known as Puddleby Common. It was territory I knew well. Many a time I had hunted over this semi-wild region for birds' nests, mushrooms and blackberries.

"The badger was there, waiting for us."

The Puddleby Gold Rush

"THIS IS LUCKY," WHISPERED POLYNESIA AS WE came to a halt before the hole that the badger had dug. "Puddleby Common, public property—don't you see, Tommy? Even if anyone does see us digging here they can't stop us. Just the same, we must not give the show away. Get your spade now and go to work."

I was still very sleepy. But little by little the fascination of hunting in the earth for treasure took hold of me. And before long I was working away as though my life depended on it, and, despite the chill of the morning air, the perspiration was running down my forehead in streams and I had to stop often and dry it off.

We had explained to the badger what we were after, and his assistance was very helpful. He began by going down to the bottom of the hole and bringing up several shapeless pieces of gravelly metal. These, when I cut into them with a penknife, showed the soft, yellow gold of which they were composed.

IUGH LOFTING

"Before long I was working away as though my life depended on it."

"That's the piece I broke my tooth on," said the badger, "and it is the last of it. Is the stuff any good?"

"Why, my gracious!" said Polynesia, "of course it is. That's what they make money out of—sovereigns. Are you sure this is all there is? If we can get enough, we have made the Doctor a rich man for life."

The badger went back and dug the hole still deeper, and with my spade I cut away the bank all around and leveled out tons of gravel, which we searched and raked over diligently. But not another nugget could we find.

"Well, just the same," said Polynesia, inspecting the array of pieces that I had laid out on my open handkerchief, "we have a tidy little fortune as it is. Now let's get away before anyone sees what we've been up to."

When we told the Doctor about it at breakfast he was much more interested in it from the geological, the scientific point of view, than he was from that of money or profit.

"It is most extraordinary," he said, examining the specimens I had brought home in the handkerchief. "If you had found old gold coins it would not have been so surprising. But these look like nuggets—native gold. Geologically, this is something quite new for England. I would like to see the place where you found it."

"In the meantime," said Dab-Dab, "leave these nuggets with me, will you? I know a safe place to keep them till we can turn them into cash."

When the Doctor set out with me and Polynesia to examine the place where the gold had been found, Jip and Gub-Gub, though they had not been invited, came along too.

Our prospecting exploration was very thorough. We searched the whole length of that gravel bank, digging and sifting and testing. Gub-Gub caught the fever, and Jip, too. They burrowed into the slope like regular prospectors, Gub-Gub using his nose as though he were digging for truffles and Jip scraping out the earth with his front paws the way he always did when he was going after rats.

But we found no more gold.

"It's very puzzling," said the Doctor, "very. Quite a geological mystery. This is not really gold-bearing gravel at all. And yet that gold is exactly as it would be found *in* gravel—in nugget form. The only explanation I can think of is that it was dug up elsewhere by some very early miners and then buried here for safekeeping."

"Gub-Gub used his nose as though he were digging for truffles."

But if we were not successful in finding a real gold mine, we were successful in starting a prospecting boom. By the time the Doctor had finished his survey of the ground it was quite late in the morning. As we left the Common and started on our way home we noticed that one or two people had been watching us. Later we questioned Matthew Mugg and Bumpo, who had accompanied the expedition, and they swore they never told anyone. Nevertheless, it apparently leaked out that gold had been found in a gravel bank on Puddleby Common. And by four o'clock that afternoon the place was crowded with people armed with picks, shovels, garden trowels, fire tongs—every imaginable implement—all hunting for gold.

The whole of Puddleby had gone prospecting mad. Nursemaids with perambulators left their charges to bawl while they scratched in the ground with buttonhooks and shoehorns for gold. Loafers, poachers, peddlers, the town tradesmen, respectable old gentlemen, schoolchildren—they came from all ranks and classes.

One rumor had it that the Doctor had discovered a lot of ancient Roman goblets, made of gold, and several old saucepans and kettles were dug up by the prospectors and taken away to be tested to see what they were made of.

After the second day the poor Common looked as though a cyclone or an earthquake had visited it. And the town council said they were going to prosecute the Doctor for the damage he had brought to public property.

For over a week the gold boom continued. People came from outside, real mining experts from London, to look into this strange rumor that had set everyone agog.

Gub-Gub, who of all the Doctor's household had the prospecting fever the worst, could hardly be kept away from the Common. He was sure he had found his real profession at last.

"Why," said he, "I can dig better holes with my nose than any of those duffers can with a spade—and quicker."

He kept begging to be allowed to go back to continue the hunt. He was so afraid these other people might any minute discover a real mine, which ought to be the property of the Dolittle household.

"You need not be worried, Gub-Gub," said the Doctor. "It isn't a mineral-bearing gravel at all. The gold we got came there by accident. The badger was probably right—there is no more than just that little hoard, which must have been specially buried there ages and ages ago."

But Gub-Gub, while the boom continued, was not to be dissuaded, and his mining fever got worse rather than better. When the Doctor would not allow him to go back to the Common (he went several times secretly at night), he consoled himself by prospecting in the kitchen garden for mushrooms. He even brought his new profession to the table with him and went prospecting for raisins in the rice pudding.

By whatever means the gold had come, Dab-Dab was very pleased that Polynesia's businesslike attention had secured it all for the Doctor. Left to himself he would most likely not have profited by it at all. The town council insisted that he give it up as Crown

"Prospecting for raisins in the rice pudding"

property. And this he willingly consented to do. But the wily Matthew Mugg consulted an attorney and found that under ancient law the finder was entitled to half of it. Even this sum, when the gold was weighed, proved to be quite considerable.

"Well," sighed Dab-Dab, "as the Doctor would say, 'It's an ill wind that blows nobody any good.' That old badger breaking his tooth was a stroke of luck. It was just in time. I really didn't know where the next meal was coming from. Now, thank goodness, we shan't have to worry about the bills for another six months, anyhow."

The Mouse Code

THERE HAD BEEN A GOOD DEAL OF ANXIETY for some time past in the various departments of the zoo over Dab-Dab's constant demand that the Doctor close the whole place up. Seeing how expensive it was to run, her argument sounded reasonable enough, and the members had all felt a bit selfish over continuing their clubs and other institutions when the cost was such a burden to the Doctor.

So with the news that half of the treasure found on the Common had been awarded to John Dolittle by the courts, the greatest rejoicing broke out in Animal Town—all the way from the Home for Crossbred Dogs at one end to the Rat and Mouse Club at the other. Even the timid Pushmi-Pullyu, who had now made his home within the peaceful, pleasant retirement of the zoo enclosure, joined in the jubilation, as did what few foreigners we still had, like the Russian minks and the Canadian woodchucks. I never heard such a pandemonium in my life. The information was brought to the zoo about suppertime by Toby and Swizzle. Immediately a demonstration began in every quarter. All the citizens spilled out of the clubs onto the main street cheering, or making noises which to them were the same as cheering.

"The Doctor's rich again!" passed from mouth to mouth, from door to door. The mixture of barks, squeals, grunts, and squawks was so extraordinary that a policeman, passing on the Oxenthorpe Road outside, knocked at the Doctor's door and asked if everything was all right.

A little later the animals began organizing parades and went traipsing up and down the main street of Animal Town singing

"'The Doctor's rich again!' passed from mouth to mouth,
from door to door."

what they called songs. The white mouse, as mayor of the town, was in charge—frightfully important—and he suggested, as it was now quite dark, that Mousetown have a torchlight procession. He asked me to get a box of those very small candles that they put on birthday cakes and Christmas trees. Then he insisted that I fix up a banner with "Hooray! The Doctor's Rich Again!" on it in large letters. And fifty-four mice and fifty-four rats formed themselves up, two by two, each pair carrying a candle, and they marched round Mousetown from eight o'clock till midnight, singing the most extraordinary songs you ever heard. Every once in a while they would come to a halt and yell in chorus: "Hooray! The Doctor's rich again!—Hooray! Hooray!"

A little extra excitement was added when one pair of torch-bearers had an accident with their candle and set light to the Squirrels' Hotel. And as that building was largely made of dry leaves it not only burned to the ground in no time at all, but very nearly set the whole zoo in flames as well.

However, no one was injured (the squirrels were all out celebrating), and after the entire town had formed itself into a fire brigade, the blaze was quickly put out. Then everyone set to on the work of reconstruction and the Squirrels' Hotel was rebuilt in a night.

"It was a grand occasion," declared the white mouse when it was all over. "And the bonfire was almost the best part of it."

Indeed, the white mouse was naturally of a cheerful, pleasure-loving disposition. And after the success of this first celebration he was continually wanting to organize club parties, city fetes, processions, and shindigs of one kind or another. This, while the Doctor was always glad to see the animals enjoying themselves, could not be encouraged too far, because a lot of noise was usually a most important part of Animal Town festivities. And although the zoo stood well within the Doctor's own land, the racket which the Home for Crossbred Dogs made on these occasions could be heard miles away.

Many new and interesting features developed quite naturally in the zoo, for example, the Animals' Free Library. Shortly after I had visited my parents on our return from abroad, the Doctor had asked me to try to organize and arrange the tremendous quantity of material that he had collected and written on animal language. He had one whole bedroom above his study simply packed with books, manuscripts, notes, and papers on this subject. It was all in great disorder, and the task of getting it straightened out was a heavy one.

But Polynesia and the white mouse helped me. We got Matthew Mugg to make us a lot of bookcases. And after a week of sorting and cataloging and listing, we had arranged the extraordinary collection in something like order. I think it was a surprise even to the Doctor himself, when we finally invited him into the little room above the study and showed him the bookshelves running all round the walls, to realize what a tremendous amount of work he had done on the science of animal languages.

"Why, Doctor," squeaked the white mouse, gazing round the shelves, "this is a regular animal library you have here! It ought to be down in the zoo, where the animals could make use of it, instead of here."

"Yes, there's something in that," said the Doctor. "But most of these writings of mine are only *about* animal languages—dictionaries and so forth—very few are actually storybooks written *in* animal language. And then besides, so few of you can read, anyway."

"Oh, but we could soon learn," said the white mouse. "If you got one or two of us taught we could quickly teach the rest. Oh, I do

*"'Why, Doctor, this is a regular animal library,'
said the white mouse."*

think an important institution like the Rat and Mouse Club ought
to have a library of its own. Yes, indeed!"

Well, in spite of the objection that the Doctor had advanced,
the white mouse stuck to his idea of an Animal Public Library for
the Dolittle Zoo. He pointed out that so far as the rats and mice
were concerned (and the dogs, badgers and squirrels, too, for that
matter), there was nothing they enjoyed so much as stories.

"I would be delighted to do it for you," said the Doctor, "but
in rat and mouse talk, for instance, there are no characters—there
is no written language."

"But we can soon invent one, can't we?" asked the white mouse. "Why, there must have been a time when there wasn't any human written language. Listen, Doctor, you invent a sign alphabet for mice—simple, you know—we don't want any physics or skizzics to begin with—and teach it to me. I'll promise to teach the whole of the Rat and Mouse Club in a week. They're awfully keen about learning new things. What do you say?"

Of course such a suggestion, one might be sure, would always interest John Dolittle, who had given so many years of his life to animal education. He at once set to work and with the white mouse's cooperation devised a simple alphabet in rat and mouse language. There were only ten signs, or letters, in all. The Doctor called it the Mouse Code, but Polynesia and I called it the Squeaker-B-C, because it was all in squeaks of different kinds, and each letter had two different meanings, according to how you let your squeak fall or rise at the end.

Then came the business of printing and binding the books. This the Doctor turned over to me as soon as he had established the alphabet or code. Of course, the volumes had to be terribly, terribly tiny in order that even the young mice could read and handle them with ease. The white mouse was most anxious that the young folk should be able to take advantage of the new education. What we called our "Mouse Octavo" size of book was just slightly smaller than a penny postage stamp. The binding had to be all hand-sewn and only the finest thread could be used. The pages were so small I had to have a watchmakers' magnifying eyeglass to do my printing with, which was, of course, also all hand work. But no matter how tiny the letters were made, they were none too small for mouse eyes, which can pick out single grains of dust with the greatest ease.

HUGH LOFTING

"Our 'Mouse Octavo' was slightly smaller than a postage stamp."

We were very proud of our first book printed in mouse language. Although it was mostly the work of the Doctor, I, as printer and publisher, felt just as important as Caxton or Gutenberg as I put the name of my firm into the title page: "Stubbins & Stubbins. Puddleby-on-the-Marsh" (I didn't know who the second "Stubbins" was, but I thought it looked better and more businesslike that way).

"This is a great occasion, Tommy," said the white mouse as we officially declared the edition (one copy) off the press. "The first volume printed in the mouse code! We are making history as well as books."

The New Learning

S THE WHITE MOUSE HAD PROPHESIED, THE new education was taken up with great enthusiasm by all classes of rat and mouse society. The famous and truly rare first imprint from the press of Stubbins & Stubbins did not survive to be handed down to posterity. It was torn to shreds in the first week by the zealous public, who thronged the Animal Public Library in the Dolittle Zoo.

For the white mouse had insisted that the book be put into the library, and that institution officially opened with great pomp and ceremony. This was an occasion also for another of his favorite celebrations. But the more serious purpose was to attract public attention in Animal Town toward education and reading generally.

But the rats and mice continued to be the most keen to learn for themselves. There was a mystery about this new art that appealed to their natural inquisitiveness. The others—dogs, badgers, squirrels, foxes, and rabbits—were quite content to be read to aloud. And for the first part of its career the Public Library chiefly did duty as a general recreation room where the white mouse read aloud every afternoon to a mixed and motley company.

The demand for books in the mouse code was enormous. The public, curiously enough, seemed to be very keen about poetry—especially comic poetry. The institution of the Public Library and of the Rat and Mouse Club Library (which was established a little later) seemed to encourage this art tremendously. And many rats and mice who had had no idea of being poetic heretofore suddenly, with the new education, blossomed forth into verse.

It became the custom at the restaurant in Mousetown (they called it "The Stilton Cheese") for rat poets to get up and recite their own ballads to the assembled diners. The audience expressed its opinion of the verse by hooting or cheering. If the poet had a good voice he often sang his ballad, and when it was well received a collection was usually taken up for him by the proprietor. An eggshell was used as a hat and it was passed round among the tables and the public dropped acorns or grains of barley into it instead of money. Nearly all the mouse poets wrote in a cheerful vein, and their comic songs were usually the most popular. Often around suppertime, if the Doctor and I passed near the zoo wall, we would hear shrieks of high-pitched, squeaky laughter; and then we would know that some comic ballad monger was singing his latest lampoon to the company at The Stilton Cheese.

Another thing that greatly encouraged the new zest for education was the mouse magazine that the Doctor established. It was called "Cellar Life," and was issued on the first of every month. This, too, was a semi-comic periodical, and besides giving the latest news and gossip of the zoo, it contained jokes and funny pictures.

Now, on the mantelpiece of the Doctor's old waiting room,

HUGH LOFTING

"Some ballad monger singing his latest lampoon"

disused ever since he had given up his practice, a miniature had always stood. It was a tiny portrait painted on ivory of John Dolittle as a young man, and for years it had never been moved from its place between the Empire clock and a Dresden china shepherdess. But one day the miniature disappeared and no one could account for it. The Doctor asked Dab-Dab, and that good housekeeper said she had seen it the previous day when she had given the waiting room its weekly dusting, but had no idea at what hour it had disappeared nor what could have become of it.

The Doctor asked Jip, Too-Too, Chee-Chee, Polynesia and me, but none of us could throw any light on the mystery. John Dolittle valued the picture only because his mother had had it painted by a well-known artist the year he had graduated in medicine. However, he had a great many things to keep him occupied, and after a few more inquiries, which met with no better success, he dismissed the matter from his mind.

It was about two weeks after the opening of the Animal Public Library that the white mouse called on the Doctor one evening, when he and I were busy with a new book he was writing on deep-sea plants.

"I have two things I would like to speak to you about, Doctor," said the mayor of Animal Town, gravely stroking his white whiskers. "One is, I would like to have a book written—in the mouse code, of course, a textbook on mouse traps. We need it—especially for the new generation. Young boy and girl mice wander off from the nest as soon as they get big enough. And before they've had time to learn anything about the world at all, they get caught in the first trap that entices them with a piece of moldy cheese."

"All right," said the Doctor. "I think that can be done—if Stubbins here can make the pictures of the traps small enough to go into a mouse-octavo volume."

"Oh, it could be done in rat-quarto if necessary," said the white mouse. "This is a textbook, you see. And we are going to make it compulsory for all parents who are members of the club to read it aloud to their children. The accidents from traps this last month have been just appalling. I would like to have every known kind of mouse and rat trap shown. It should be a complete work. Of course, I will help with the writing of it. You will need an expert, an old hand, to describe what the traps smell and look like from a mouse's point of view."

"Oh my gracious!" put in Dab-Dab, who was listening down by the fire. "Then we'll have the whole world overrun with mice. It is too bad we haven't got a few good mouse traps in my linen closet."

"Yes, but you wouldn't like it if there were duck traps there as well," the white mouse responded, his whiskers bristling with indignation.

"Well now, what was the other thing you wanted to see me about?" the Doctor asked.

"The other thing is also very important," said the white mouse. "I've come on behalf of the house committee to invite you and Tommy here to our club's Mooniversary Dinner."

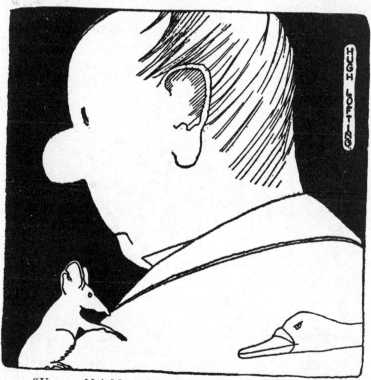

"You wouldn't like it if there were duck traps there as well!"

"*Mooniversary,*" the Doctor murmured. "Er—what does that mean?"

"Yes, it's a new word," said the white mouse, rather proudly. "But then all languages have special words, haven't they, which the other languages haven't? So why shouldn't the mouse code have a word or two of its own? It happened this way: the house committee was having a meeting and the Railway Rat—he's one of the members, lived in a railway station, decent fellow, but he smells of kerosene—the Railway Rat got up and proposed that since the club had now been going on successfully for some time we ought to have an anniversary dinner to celebrate."

"The Railway Rat got up."

"You're always celebrating," muttered Dab-Dab from the fireside.

"Then," the white mouse continued, "the Hansom Cab Mouse—he's another member, lived under the floor of an old cab, knows London like a book—he gets up and he says, '*Anniversary* means a year. The club hasn't been going for a year. A year's a long time in a mouse's life. I suggest we call it the Club's Mooniversary Dinner, to celebrate our month's birthday, not our year's birthday.'

"Well, they argued about it a good deal, but the suggestion was finally accepted—that our celebration banquet should be called the Mooniversary Dinner. Then the Church Mouse—he's another member, lived in a church, awful poor, fed on candle wax mostly, kind of religious type, always wants us to sing hymns instead of comic songs—he gets up and he says, 'I would like to suggest to the committee that the Mooniversary Dinner would not be complete without the presence of Doctor John Dolittle, through whose untiring efforts' (he rather fancies himself as a speaker, does the Church Mouse—I suppose he's heard an awful lot of sermons)—'through whose untiring efforts,' says he, 'for the welfare of rat and mouse society this club first came into being. I propose we invite the Doctor to the Mooniversary Dinner—also that strange lad called Thomas Stubbins, who has made a very good assistant manager to the Dolittle Zoo.'

"That motion was carried, too, without any question. And they chose me to come and present the club's invitation. The dinner's tomorrow night, Doctor. You won't have to change or anything. Wear just whatever clothes you happen to have on. But say you'll come."

"Why, of course," said John Dolittle, "I shall be delighted—and I'm sure Stubbins will, too."

The Rat and
Mouse Club

ITHOUT DOUBT THE RAT AND MOUSE Club was the only building of its kind in the world. At the beginning the clubhouse had been no more than two and a half feet high; but as the list of members had been enlarged, first from fifty to three hundred, and then from three hundred to five thousand, it became necessary to enlarge the premises considerably.

At the time when the Doctor and I were invited to attend the Mooniversary Dinner the building was about the height of a man and just about as broad—and as long—as it was high. The architecture was very unusual. In shape the clubhouse was rather like a large beehive, with a great number of tiny doors. It was fourteen stories high. The upper floors were reached by outside staircases, in the manner of Italian houses. In the center of the building, inside, there was a large chamber called the Assembly Room, which ran the entire height of the structure from ground floor to roof. Ordinarily this was used for concerts, theatricals, and for the general meetings

HUGH LOFTING

"The architecture was very unusual."

of the club when all the members came together to vote on some new proposal or to celebrate birthdays or occasions of importance. The whole thing was thus a sort of thick, hollow dome, in the shell of which were the living rooms, furnished apartments, private dining-saloons, committee rooms, etc.

The entrances were all very small, of course—just big enough for a rat to pass through. But for this special occasion the white mouse had gotten the badgers to dig a tunnel down under the foundations through which the Doctor and I could reach the Assembly Room inside.

When we arrived at the mouth of this tunnel we found the white mouse and a regular committee on hand to greet us. Moreover, every doorway, all the way up the building, was thronged with rat and mouse faces waiting to witness the great man's arrival. After the white mouse, as president of the club, had made a short speech of welcome, we began the descent of the tunnel.

"Be careful how you go, Doctor," I said. "If we bump the top of the tunnel with our backs we're liable to throw the whole building over."

Without mishap we reached the Assembly Room where there was just about space enough for the two of us to stand upright, very close together. The white mouse said he wanted to show the Doctor over the clubhouse. But of course as none of the rooms, except the one in which we were standing, was big enough for a man to get into, being "shown over" the building consisted of standing where he was and peering through the tiny holes called doors. Some of the rooms were along passages; and one could not see into them directly from the Assembly Room. But to provide for this, the white mouse had asked me to bring the Doctor's dentist's mirror, so he could poke it down the passages and see into the rooms around the corners, the same as he would look at the back of a person's tooth.

John Dolittle was tremendously interested in examining the tiny rooms that these highly civilized rats and mice had designed, set out, and furnished for themselves. For this building with all it contained was (excepting the few things that Bumpo and I had done for them) entirely their own work. The chief mouse architect—he was also the stonemason—was on hand and he took great pride in pointing out to the distinguished visitor the whys and the wherefores of all the details of design.

While the Doctor was poking round among the passages and holes with his tooth-mirror, he suddenly got quite excited.

"Why, Stubbins," he cried, "come and look here. I don't know whether I'm dreaming or not. But isn't that a human face I see down there. Look in the mirror. It reminds me of myself."

I looked into the mirror. Then I laughed.

"No wonder it reminds you of yourself, Doctor," I said. "It *is* yourself. That's the missing miniature of John Dolittle as a young man."

At this moment I heard the white mouse, who had left us for a moment, scolding the architect in whispers behind the Doctor's back.

"Didn't I tell you," he said furiously, "to miss the Committee

HUGH LOFTING

"'Didn't I tell you?' he said furiously."

Room and show the Doctor the Ladies' Lounge instead?—
Blockhead! Now we'll lose our best painting."

"But how did the miniature get here?" asked John Dolittle.

"Well," said the white mouse, "we didn't exactly steal it,
Doctor. It was the Prison Rat's idea—he's one of the members,
has always lived in jails, sort of an unscrupulous customer but has
a great sense of humor and knows no end of interesting stories,
crime stories. Well, as I was saying, it was his idea. We were
having a meeting about the layout of the new Committee Room
and how it should be furnished and decorated. You see, although
it's small, it is in a way the most important room in the club.
All the big decisions are made there. And someone got up and
said we ought to have a picture on the wall over the president's
chair. Then the Church Mouse arose and said, 'Brethren,' says
he, 'I think we should have a motto there, some message of good
counsel, like, *Love One Another.*' 'Well, I don't,' said the Prison
Rat, short like. 'We can love one another all we want without
boasting about it or writing it up on the wall.' Then the Railway
Rat gets up and says, 'No, we ought to have a picture there. We
don't want any sloppy mottoes. We want something cheerful.
Let's put up one of the comic pictures out of *Cellar Life.*' At
that the Prison Rat gets up again and says, 'I believe in being
lighthearted, but I think a comic picture is hardly the thing—
not—er—dignified enough for our Committee Room. What
we ought to have is a portrait of the founder of our club, Doctor
John Dolittle—and I know where I can get one, the right size
to fit that place.' So the motion was carried—and so was the
picture, by the Prison Rat, who went up to your house that very
night and—er—borrowed it off the mantelpiece in your waiting-

room. Will you want to take it away again, Doctor?"

"No, I don't suppose so," said John Dolittle, smiling. "It looks very well where it is. And it is quite a compliment that you want to keep it there. I will gladly present it to the club, provided you will take care of it. But you had better not let Dab-Dab know."

"You may be sure we won't," said the white mouse. "And now, Doctor, if you and Tommy will take your seats I will call in the members who are all waiting for the signal to assemble. We had to keep the hall clear till you got seated because, as you will see for yourself, there isn't very much room."

Thereupon the Doctor and I sort of folded ourselves up and sat down in the cramped space to this strangest banquet table that ever was laid. Our chairs were empty biscuit-tins borrowed from the Home for Crossbred Dogs. The table was egg shaped, about three feet across and five feet long. The dishes, tiny little messes of cheese, nuts, dried fish, fried bread crumbs, apple seeds, and the kernels of prune stones were all gathered in the center of the table, leaving a large outside ring clear for the diners to sit on. For in Mousetown one always sat, or stood, on the table at mealtimes, even in the best society.

As soon as we were seated the white mouse gave a signal somewhere and then a very curious thing happened: hundreds and thousands of rats and mice suddenly poured out of holes all around us, squeaking and squealing with glee.

"You must excuse them, Doctor," whispered the president, as a dozen rats ran around John Dolittle's collar and down his sleeve onto the table. "Their manners are not usually so atrocious. I expected a rush for the places nearest to you—it is a great honor for them, you know; they want to boast that they sat beside you—that's why I kept them out till you were seated. Every single member of the club bought a ticket for the dinner— five thousand, you see, as well as some extra guests from out of town. So you mustn't mind a little crowding."

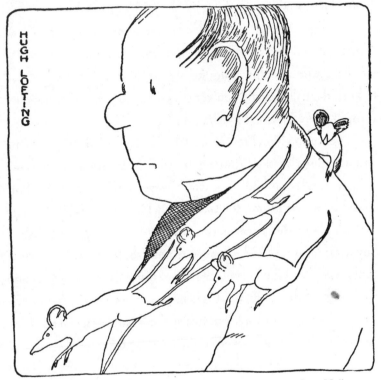

"Ran around the Doctor's collar and down onto the table"

THE TWELFTH CHAPTER

The Mooniversary Dinner

THE MOONIVERSARY DINNER WAS A VERY great success. Of course neither the Doctor nor I could say afterward that we had dined heartily. There were a vast number of dishes, it was true; but the plates were only walnut shells, and clearly it would need a tremendous number of helpings of that size to make a square meal for a man. The drinks were served in acorn cups.

However, the banquet was so interesting and unusual in other respects, neither of us noticed very much whether we were hungry or not. To begin with, it was quite a novel sensation to be dining, shut up in a room into which we only just fitted, with five thousand rats and mice. Once we got seated and the scramble for places near the great man was over, the members were very well behaved. There were two sets of waiters, one on the table and the other off the table. Those on the table carried the dishes from the center to the diners, who had seated themselves in a ring about twenty deep around the edge. The other lot were kept busy

HUGH LOFTING

"The drinks were served in acorn cups."

swarming up and down the legs of the table, running between the kitchen and the Assembly Room to replenish the supply of such dishes as ran out.

"More apple seeds up!" the head waiter on the table would yell. And a couple of mice down below would hustle off to the kitchen where the cooks would give them an eggshell full of apple seeds to bring to the table. It was all excellently managed. The kitchen staff was kept very busy; for although a mouse or rat may not eat a great deal at one meal, when you have five thousand diners to feed, it means considerable work.

At one of the upper doorways a small mouse orchestra played

tunes throughout the dinner. Their instruments were invented by themselves and consisted of drums of different kinds and shapes and harps made by stretching threads across nutshells. One mouse had a straw that he played in the manner of a flute. Their idea of music was rather peculiar and very faint—indeed with the enormous chatter of squeaky conversation going on all around they could hardly be heard at all.

When the last course had been finished the white mouse knocked on the table for silence. Immediately the chorus of conversation died down and several members shooed the waiters who were making a noise clearing away the walnut shells and acorn cups. Finally, after the door into the pantry had been stopped up with a banana skin to keep out the clatter of the washing up, His Honor the Mayor, First President of the Rat and Mouse Club, cleared his throat with a dignified cough and began a very fine after-dinner speech.

I was sorry afterward that I had never learned shorthand so that I might take down the white mouse's address word for word; for it was in its way the most remarkable I have ever listened to.

He began by telling the Doctor on behalf of the whole club how glad they were to see him seated at their board. Then he turned back to the vast throng of members and sketched out briefly what John Dolittle had done for mouse civilization and what it was to be hoped his efforts would lead to in the future.

"The majority of men," said he, "would never believe it if they were told of the general advance, organization, and culture that this club, through Doctor John Dolittle, has brought into rat and mouse society." (Cries of, "Hear, hear!") "This is the first time in history that our great race has been given a chance to show what it could do." (The white mouse pounded the table with his tiny fist and grew quite earnest and eloquent.) "What has our life always been heretofore?" he asked. "Why, getting chased, being hunted—flight, concealment, that was our daily lot. Through the Doctor's farsightedness the rat and mouse peoples have here, in Animal Town, been able to think of other things besides keeping out of the jaws of a dog or a cat or a trap. And, I ask you, what has been the result?"

The president paused and for a silent second twirled his white whiskers, while his spellbound audience sat breathless, waiting for him to go on.

"This is the first time in history."

"Why, this," he continued, waving his hand round the lofty walls of the Assembly Room, "this great institution called the Rat and Mouse Club; your education; the education of your children; all the things that our new civilization has given us, these are the results that John Dolittle has brought into rat and mouse society by removing the constant anxiety of our lives and giving us comfortable peace and honest freedom in its place. I, myself, look forward—as, I am sure, you all do—to the time when rat and mouse civilization shall be at least on a level with that of man; to the time when there shall be rat and mouse cities all over the world, rat and mouse railway trains, steamship lines, universities, and grand opera. I propose that we give the Doctor, who has honored us with his presence here tonight, a rising vote of thanks to express our appreciation of all he has done for the welfare of rats and mice."

At the conclusion of the president's speech a great tumult broke loose. Every single one of the five thousand members sprang to his feet, cheering and waving, to show that he agreed with the sentiments of the speaker. And I could see that the Doctor was quite affected by the extraordinary demonstration in his honor.

There was a slight pause during which it became quite evident that the guest of honor was expected to make some kind of an address in reply. So rising with great care lest he wreck his hosts' clubhouse, John Dolittle made a short speech that was also received with great applause.

Then followed a considerable number of personal introductions. Of course the Doctor knew many members of the club personally. But hundreds of rats and mice who had never met him were now clamoring to be presented to the great man.

Among those who came forward there were some very

interesting characters. First there were those whom the white mouse had already spoken of to the Doctor: the Prison Rat, the Church Mouse, the Railway Rat, and the Hansom Cab Mouse. But besides these there were many more. They did not all live permanently at the club. Several used to drop in there two or three times a week, usually in the evening, and then go back again to their regular homes around midnight. And there were some who came from quite a long way off, attracted by the reputation of this extraordinary establishment that was now getting to be known all over the country.

For instance, there was the Museum Mouse who had made his

"The Prison Rat and the Church Mouse"

home in a natural history museum up in London and who had traveled all the way down from the city (the Railway Rat had put him on a freight train that he knew was coming to a town near Puddleby) just to be present at this important banquet. He was a funny little fellow who knew a whole lot about natural history and what new animals were being stuffed by the museum professors. John Dolittle was very interested in the news he brought with him from the scientific world of London.

Then there was the Zoo Rat who had also come from London especially for the occasion. He lived in the Zoological Gardens in Regent's Park and boasted that he had often been into the lion's den—when the lion was asleep—to steal suet. There was the Teahouse Mouse, the Volcano Rat, and the Icebox Mouse (who had very long fur, which he had specially grown from living constantly in cold temperatures). Then there was the Ship's Rat, the same old fellow who had warned the Doctor at the Canary Islands about the rottenness of the ship he was traveling in. He had now retired permanently from the sea and come to settle down in Puddleby to club life and a peaceful old age. There was the Hospital Mouse and the Theater Mouse and several more.

Of course, with so many, it was only possible for the Doctor to talk a few moments to each. But as the president brought them up and briefly told us who they were, I realized that an assembly of rats and mice could be just as interesting, if you knew about their lives and characters, as any gathering of distinguished people.

THE THIRTEENTH CHAPTER

The Hotel Rat

WHEN MOST OF THE INTRODUCTIONS were over the Doctor surprised me (as he often did) by his remarkable and accurate memory for animal faces. Out of the thousands of rats and mice who were all staring at him in rapt admiration he suddenly pointed to one and whispered to the white mouse:

"Who is that rat over there—the one rubbing the side of his nose with his left paw?"

"That's the Hotel Rat," said the white mouse. "Did you want to speak to him?"

But the rat in question had already noticed the Doctor pointing to him and, most proud to be recognized, came forward.

"Your face is very familiar," said the Doctor. "I have been wondering where I saw it before."

"Oh, I'm the rat who was brought to you half dead, you recollect? About four years ago. My two brothers had to wake you up at six in the morning. It was an urgent case. I was quite unconscious."

"'Your face is very familiar,' said the Doctor."

"Ah, yes," said the Doctor. "Now I remember.

And you were taken away again the following morning before I was up. I never got a chance to talk to you. How did you come to get so badly smashed up?"

"I was run over," said the rat, a faraway look of reminiscence coming into his eyes, "by a perambulator containing two heavy twins. It happened—well, it's a long story."

"I'd like to hear it," said the Doctor. "After dinner is a good time for stories."

"I would gladly tell it," said the Hotel Rat, "if the company has time for it."

At once a little buzz of pleased expectant excitement ran through the big crowd as everyone settled down to listen in comfort. There is nothing that rats and mice love more than stories, and something told them that this one would likely be interesting.

"It was about five years ago," the Hotel Rat began, "that I first started living in hotels. Some rats say they're dangerous places to make your home in. But I don't think, once you get used to them, they are any more unsafe than other places. And I love the changeful life you meet with there, folks coming and going all the time. Well, I and a couple of brothers of mine found a nice old hotel in a country town, not far from here, where the cooking was good, and we determined to settle down there. It had fine rambling big cellars; and there was always lots of food lying around, from the oats in the horses' stables across the yard to the scraps of cheese and bread on the dining room floor. With us another rat came to live—a very peculiar character. He was not quite—er—respectable, as people call it. None of the ordinary rat colonies would let him live with them. But I happened to save his life from a dog once; and ever after that he followed me around. Leery, he was called. And he only had one eye.

"Leery was a wonderful runner. They said he cheated at the races. But I never quite believed that part of his bad reputation, because with a wind and a lightning speed like his, he didn't have to cheat—he could win everything easily without. Anyway, when he asked me could he live with us I said to my older brother, 'Snop,' I said (my brothers' names were Snip and Snop), 'I think there's a lot of good in Leery. You know how people are: once a rat gets a bad name they'll believe anything against him and nothing for him. Poor Leery is an outcast. Let's take him in.'

"'Well,' said Snop, 'I suppose it will mean that most of our

"Leery, the Outcast"

friends will refuse to know us. And Leery surely is a tough-looking customer. He's only got one eye, and that's shifty. Still, I don't care about society's opinions. If you want to have him with us, Snap' (that was my nickname in the family, Snap), 'take him in by all means.'

"So Leery became part of our household in the little old country-town hotel. And it was a very good thing for me he did, as you will see later on. Now there was one subject on which Leery and I never agreed. He was quite a philosopher, was Leery. And he always used to say, 'Rely on yourself—on your wits. That's my motto.' While I, I always pinned my faith to the protection of a good hole. You know there are an awful lot of dangers around a hotel—any number of dogs, two or three cats at least, plenty of traps and rat poison, and a considerable crowd of people coming and going all the time. The hole I had made for myself (it joined up with those of my brothers, but it only had one door that we all used) was the nicest and snuggest I have ever been in. It was alongside the back of the kitchen chimney and the bricks around were always warm from the fire. It was a wonderful place to sleep winter nights.

"'Well, Leery,' I would say, 'myself, I always feel safe when I get back to the home hole. I don't care what happens so long as I'm in my own comfortable home.'

"Then Leery would screw up his one shifty eye and blink at me.

"'Just because it's familiar to you,' he said—'because you know everything in it and love everything there, that doesn't mean it's a safe place, or a protection, at all.'

"'Well, I don't know, Leery,' said I. 'In a way it's like a friend, one who will help defend you.'

"'Oh, fiddlesticks!' said he. 'You got to carry your defense with you. A good hole won't save you always. You got to rely on yourself; that's my motto—Rely on your wits.'

"Now, there were two cats living at the hotel. Mostly they'd snooze before the parlor fire. They got fed twice a day. And of course we hotel rats knew their habits and their daily program hour by hour. We weren't really afraid of them because they were lazy and overfed. But about once a month they'd decide to go on a rat and mouse hunt together. And they knew where our holes were just as well as we knew what their habits were.

"Well, one day the Devil got into those two cats and they went on a rat hunt that lasted for three days. We got word that they were out on the warpath from one of our scouts—we had scouts on duty day and night, of course we had to, with all those dogs and cats and people around. And from then on we took no chances on being caught too far from a hole of some sort. But my own policy, as I told you, had always been to count on reaching my own hole. I didn't trust any others—not since I dived into a strange hole one day to get away from a dog and found a weasel in it who nearly killed me. However, to go back: late in the afternoon, returning home I ran into both the cats at once. One was standing guard over the hole and the other made for me straightaway. I kept my head. I had been chased lots of times before but never by two cats at once. There was no hope of my getting into my hole, so I turned about and leapt clear through the open window into the street."

The Hotel Rat paused a moment to cough politely behind his paw; while the whole of the enormous audience, who had experienced the thrill of similar pursuits themselves, leaned forward in intense expectation.

"I landed," he said at length, with a grimace of painful recollection, "right under the wheels of a baby carriage. The rear wheels passed over my body; and I knew at once that I was pretty badly hurt. The nursemaid gave a scream—'Ugh! A rat!'—and fled with the carriage and babies and all. Then I expected the cats would descend on me and polish me off right away. I was powerless; my two back legs wouldn't work at all, and all I could do was to drag myself along by my front paws at about the speed of a tortoise.

"However, my luck wasn't entirely out. Before the cats had time to spring on me a dog, attracted by the commotion, arrived on the scene at full gallop. He didn't even notice me at all. But he chased those two cats down the street at forty miles an hour.

"I leapt clear through the open window."

"But my plight was bad enough in all conscience. I didn't know what was wrong, only that I was in terrific pain. Inch by inch, expecting to be caught by some enemy any moment, I began to drag myself back toward the window. Luckily it was a sort of cellar window, on a level with street. If it hadn't been, of course I could never have got through it. It was only about a yard away from the spot where I had been injured, but never shall I forget the long agony of that short journey.

"And all the time I kept saying to myself over and over, 'The hole! Once I'm back there I'll be all right. I must reach the home hole before those cats return.'"

Leery, the Outcast

"MORE DEAD THAN ALIVE," THE HOTEL RAT went on, "I did finally reach my home hole, crawled to the bottom of it, and collapsed in a faint.

"When I came to, Leery was bending over me.

"'Ah, Snap,' said he with tears in his eyes, 'this is one place where your philosophy doesn't work.'

"'What's the matter with me?' I asked. 'What's broken?'

"'Both your hind legs,' said he. 'We've got to get you to Doctor Dolittle, over to Puddleby. Your home hole is no help to you this time.'

"My two brothers were there, Snip and Snop; and the three of them put their heads together to work out a way to get me to the Doctor's. They found an old slipper somewhere that they said would do for a stretcher or a sort of sleigh-ambulance. They were going to put me in it and drag it along the ground."

"What, not all the way to Puddleby!" cried the Doctor.

"No," said the Hotel Rat. "They had done some scouting

HUGH LOFTING

"Leery was bending over me."

outside. All the rats in most of the colonies around had heard about the accident and had helped with their advice and in any other way they could. And a farm wagon had been found loaded with cabbages, standing in an inn yard down the street. It was going to Puddleby first thing in the morning. Their idea was to drag me to the yard in their shoe-ambulance, hide me among the cabbages, and at Puddleby watch their opportunity to get me across to your house.

"Well, everything was in readiness and they had me tucked up in the ambulance when Leery comes running back from the mouth of the hole, swearing something terrible.

"'We can't go yet,' he whispered. 'Those horrible cats have

come back and they've mounted guard outside the hole. They know well enough we've only got one entrance. I nearly walked right into their paws just now. We're nicely trapped! Give me the open, town or country, any day.'

"So, there was nothing to do but to wait. My legs were getting worse and worse all the time, and I had an awful high fever. Leery got me mad by keeping on talking about relying on yourself.

"'This shows you,' says he. 'What's the good of a fine hole now? We want to get out of it and we can't. You've got to rely on your wits, on yourself. That's my motto.'

"'Oh, be quiet!' I cried. 'Such a comfort you are to have at a sick bed! My head feels red-hot. Pour some cold water over it. You'll find a thimbleful over there in the corner.'

"But if Leery's bedside manner was not as cheerful as it might be, just the same, in the end, he saved my life—and nearly lost his own in doing it. The best part of a day went by and those horrible cats still kept watch at the mouth of the hole. I was so bad now that I was only conscious in short spells—and even then sort of delirious with fever.

"In one of my clear moments after Leery had been watching me for a few minutes he turned to my brothers and said:

"'There's only one thing to be done. Those cats may stick on at the mouth of the hole for another couple of days. Snap can't last much longer. If we can't get him to the Doctor soon, it's all up with him. He saved my life once, did Snap. Now's the time I can pay back the debt—or try to. I'm going to give those cats a run.'

"'What,' cried my brothers, 'you mean to try and draw them off!'

"'Just that,' said Leery, winking with his one shifty eye. 'I'm the fastest rat in the country. If I can't do it, no one can. You pull the shoe up to the mouth of the hole and stand ready. In a little while it will be late enough so the streets are nearly empty. I'll give them a run right round the town. Get Snap down to that inn yard. There's a cart full of cabbage leaves there every morning just about daylight. If I'm lucky I can keep those two mean brutes busy till you've had time to get him in among the cabbages.'

"'There are two cats, remember,' said my brothers. 'Watch out! If you get caught we'll be one less to get him to the Doctor's.'

"Well, they drew my shoe-ambulance up to within about three inches of the mouth of the hole. Then Leery, one-eyed outcast, champion runner and faithful friend, went up to the entrance. The light of the streetlamps, coming in through the window, shone down into the hole and lit up his ugly face. You could see, too, the shadows of those beastly cats, waiting—waiting with the patience of the Devil.

"It was indeed a dramatic moment. Leery was a born gambler; I had often seen him bet all he had on any reckless chance, apparently for the fun of the thing. And so, I think, in his own strange way he rather enjoyed this theatrical situation.

"With a little wriggle of his hind quarters he made ready for the leap—the most daring leap of his life.

"Then, *zip!*—He was gone!

"Instantly we heard a scuffle as the two cats wrenched around and started off in pursuit.

"Then for a whole hour Leery played the most dangerous game a rat can play, hide-and-seek with two angry cats, touch-and-go with double death. First he led them down the street at full speed. He had his whole program mapped out in his own mind, with every stop, trick and turnabout. There was a little yard behind a house he

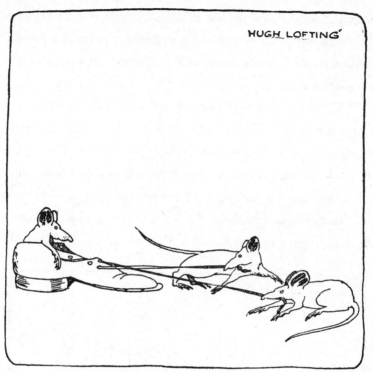

"They drew my shoe-ambulance up."

knew of. In that yard there was a small duck-pond; and in the pond a cardboard box was floating. Leery led the chase into the yard, leapt the pond, using the box as a sort of stepping-stone. The cat who was farthest ahead followed him, but found out too late that the floating box would take a rat's weight but not a cat's. With a gurgle she went down out of sight and was kept busy for the rest of the night getting herself dry. She, for one, had had enough of hunting.

"But the other, realizing that she had a clever quarry to deal with, took no chances. She stuck to Leery like a leech—which was exactly what Leery wanted, so long as he could keep out of her clutches. He would slip into a hole just an inch ahead of her pounce. Then he'd get his breath while she waited, swearing, outside. And just as she was thinking of giving him up as a bad job and coming back to our hole after me, he'd pop out again and give her another run.

"All around the town he went: down into cellars; up onto roofs; along the tops of breakneck walls. He even led her up a tree, where she thought she'd surely get him in the upper branches. But right at the top he took a flying leap across onto a clothesline—from which he actually jeered at her and dared her to follow.

"In the meantime Snip and Snop were trundling me along the road in my shoe-ambulance. I never had such a dreadful ride.

"He took a flying leap across onto a clothesline."

Twice they spilled me into the gutter. At last they reached the inn yard and somehow got me up into the wagon and stowed me away among the cabbages. As daylight appeared the wagon started on its way. Oh dear, how ill I felt! Luckily that load of cabbages came into Puddleby by the Oxenthorpe Road. They dropped me off the tail of the cart right at the Doctor's door—only just in time to save my life. But without Leery the outcast it could never have been done. One of my brothers, Snip, hustled back at once to the hole and hung around for hours waiting for Leery, worried to death that he might have paid the price of his life to save mine. For both of them realized now that even if Leery was an outcast from Rat Society, he was a hero just the same. About eight o'clock in the morning he strolled in chewing a straw as though he had spent a pleasant day in the country. . . .

"Well, after all, I suppose he was right: in the end you have to rely on your wits, on yourself."

The Volcano Rat

THE ADVENTURE RELATED BY THE HOTEL RAT reminded various members of things of interest in their own lives—as is often the case with stories told to a large audience. And as soon as it was ended a buzz of general conversation and comment began.

"You know," said the Doctor to the white mouse, "you rats and mice really lead much more thrilling and exciting lives than we humans do."

"Yes, I suppose that's true," said the white mouse. "Almost every one of the members here has had adventures of his own. The Volcano Rat, for instance, has a very unusual story, which he told me a week or so ago."

"I'd like to hear some more of these anecdotes of rat and mouse life," said the Doctor. "But I suppose we ought to be getting home now. It's pretty late."

"Why don't you drop in again some other night—soon?" said the white mouse. "There's always quite a crowd here in the evenings. I've been thinking it would be nice if you or Tommy would write out a few of these life stories of the members and make them into a book for us, a collection. We'd call it, say, 'Tales of The Rat and Mouse Club.'"

At this suggestion quite a number of rats and mice who had been listening to our conversation joined in with remarks. They were all anxious for the honor of having their own stories included in the club's book of adventures. And before we left that night it was agreed that we should return the following evening to hear the tale of the Volcano Rat. I knew it would be no easy matter for me to take down the stories word for word. But the white mouse said

HUGH LOFTING

"'Why don't you drop in again soon?' said the white mouse."

he would see that they were told slowly and distinctly; and with the Doctor's assistance (his knowledge of rat and mouse language was of course greatly superior to mine) I thought I might be able to manage it. I was most anxious to, for we both realized that by this means we would add a book of great distinction to animal literature.

Considerable excitement and rejoicing were shown when it became known that we had consented to the plan. It was at once arranged that a notice should be put up on the club bulletin-board, in the room called the Lounge, showing which member was slated to tell his story for each night in the week. And as we carefully rose from our seats and made our difficult way down the tunnel into the open air, we heard rats and mice all around us assuring one another they would be sure to come tomorrow night.

When he arose amid a storm of applause the following evening to address the large audience gathered to hear his story, the Volcano Rat struck me at once by his distinctly foreign appearance. He was the same color as most rats, neither larger nor smaller; but there was something Continental about him—almost Italian, one might say. He had sparkling eyes and very smooth movements, yet clearly he was no longer young. His manner was a rather curious mixture of cheerfulness and extreme worldliness.

"Our president," he began with a graceful bow toward the white mouse, "was speaking last night of the high state of civilization to which, through Doctor John Dolittle and our club, this community has reached. Tonight I would like to tell you of another occasion—perhaps the only other occasion in history—when our race rose to great heights of culture and refinement.

"Many years ago I lived on the side of a volcano. For all

we knew, it was a dead volcano. On its slopes there were two or three villages and one town. I knew every inch of the whole mountain well. Once or twice I had explored the crater at the top—a great mysterious basin of spongelike rock, with enormous cracks in it running way down into the heart of the earth. In these, if you listened carefully, you could hear strange rumbling noises deep, deep down.

"The third occasion when I went up to the crater, I was trying to get away from some farm dogs who had been following my scent through the vineyards and olive groves of the lower slopes. I stayed up there a whole night. The funny noises sort of worried me;

"On its slopes there were two or three villages."

they sounded so exactly like people groaning and crying. But in the morning I met an old, old rat who, it seemed, lived there regularly. He was a nice old chap and we got to chatting. He took me all round the crater and showed me the sights—grottoes, steaming underground lakes, and lots of odd things. He lived in these cracks in the mountain.

"'How do you manage for food?' I asked.

"'Acorns,' he replied. 'There are oak trees a little way down the slope. And I lay in a good big store each autumn. And then for water there's a brook or two. I manage all right.'

"'Why, you live the same as a squirrel,' I said, 'storing up your nuts over the winter! What made you choose this place for a home?'

"'Well, you see,' said he, 'truth is, I'm getting old and feeble. Can't run the way I used to. Any cat or dog could catch me in the towns. But they never come up here to the crater. Superstitious. They're afraid of the rumbling voices. They believe there are demons here.'

"Well, I lived with the old Hermit Rat for two days. It was a nice change after the noisy bustling life of the town. It was a great place just to sit and think, that crater. In the evenings we would squat on the edge of it, looking down at the twinkling lights of the town way, way below—and the sea, a misty horizon in blue-black, far out beyond.

"I asked the old rat if he didn't often get lonely, living up there all alone.

"'Oh, sometimes,' said he. 'But to make up for the loneliness, I have peace. I could never get that down there.'

"Every once in a while, when the rumbling voices coming out of the heart of the mountain got louder, he'd go down a crack and

"We would squat on the edge."

listen. And I asked him what it was he expected to hear. At first he wouldn't tell me and seemed afraid that I might laugh at him or something. But at last he told me.

"'I'm listening for an eruption,' says he.

"'What on earth is that?' I asked.

"'That's when a volcano blows up,' says he. 'This one has been quiet a long time, many years. But I've listened to those voices so long, I've got so I can understand 'em. Yes, you needn't laugh,' he added, noticing I was beginning to grin. 'I tell you I've an idea I shall know—for sure—when this mountain is going to blow up. The voices will tell me.'

"Well, of course I thought he was crazy. And after I had grown tired of the lonely life myself, I bade him good-bye and came back to live in the town.

"It was not long after that that the citizens imported a whole lot of cats of a new kind. Us rats had got sort of plentiful and the townsfolk had made up their minds to drive us out. Well, they did. These cats were awful hunters. They never let up; went after us day and night. And as there were thousands of them, life for us became pretty nearly impossible.

"After a good many of our people had been killed, some of the leaders of the colonies got together in an old cellar one night to discuss what we should do about it. And after several had made suggestions that weren't worth much, I got to thinking of my old friend the hermit and the peaceful life of his crater home. And I suggested to the meeting that I lead them all up there where we could live undisturbed by cats or dogs. Some didn't like the idea much. But beggars can't be choosers. And it was finally decided that word should be passed round to all the rats in the town that at dawn the next day I would lead them forth beyond the walls and guide them to a new home."

The Voices in
the Earth

S O," THE VOLCANO RAT CONTINUED, "THE following day a great departure of rats took place from that town. And the old hermit of the mountaintop had the surprise of his life when from his crow's nest lookout he saw several thousand of us trailing up the slope to share his loneliness.

"Fortunately the autumn was not yet over and there were still great quantities of acorns lying beneath the oak trees. These we harvested into the many funny little underground chambers with which the walls of the crater were riddled.

"Because I had led them out of danger into this land of safety, I came to be looked upon as a sort of leader. Of course, after the first excitement of the migration was over, a good deal of grumbling began. It seems people always have to grumble. Many young fellows who thought themselves clever made speeches to those willing to listen. They told the crowd that I had led them into as bad a plight as they were in before. Rat and mouse civilization had gone backward, they said, instead of forward. Now they were no better than

"A great departure of rats took place."

squirrels living on stored-up acorns. Whereas in the towns, though they may have had the constant dangers that always had to be faced in cities, life at least had some color and variety; they didn't have to eat the same food *every* day; and if they wanted to line their nests with silk or felt they knew where to find it, etc., etc., etc., and a whole lot more.

"These discontented orators got the common people so worked up against me that for a time my life was actually in danger from the mob. Finally—though I am a rat of few words—I had to make a speech on my own account in self-defense. I pointed out to the people that the life we were now leading was nothing more nor less than the original life of our forefathers. 'After the Flood,' I told them, 'this was how you lived, the simple outdoor life of the fields. Then when the cities of men arose with their abominable crowding, you were tempted by the merry life of cellars and larders. We rats,' I said proudly, 'were at the first a hardy race of agriculturists, living by corn and the fruits of the earth. Lured by idleness and ease, we became a miserable lot of crumb-snatchers and cheese-stealers. I gave you the chance to return to your healthy, independent, outdoor life. Now, after you have listened to these wretched cellar-loungers, you long to go back to the sneaking servitude of the dwellings of men. Go then, you fleas, you parasites!' (I was dreadfully mad.) 'But never,' I said, 'never ask me to lead you again!'

"And yet Fate seemed to plot and conspire to make me a leader of rats. I didn't want to be. I never had any taste or ambition for politics. But no sooner had I ended my speech, even while the cheers and yells of the audience were still ringing in my ears (for I had completely won them over to my side), when the old hermit came up behind me and croaked into my ear, 'The eruption! The voices in the earth have spoken. Beware! We must fly!'

"Something prompted me to believe him—though even to this day I don't see how he could have known, and I thought I had better act, and act quickly, while I had the crowd on my side.

"'Hark!' I shouted, springing to my feet once more. 'This mountain is no longer safe. Its inner fires are about to burst forth. All must leave. Do not wait to take your acorns with you. For there is no time to lose.'

"Then like one rat they rose up and shouted, 'Lead us and we will follow. We believe in you. You are the leader whom we trust!'

"After that came a scene of the wildest kind. In a few minutes I had to organize a train of thousands of rats and mice and get it down that mountainside the quickest possible way. Somehow or other I managed it—even though darkness came on before I started them off and the route was precipitous and dangerous. In addition to everything else, I had to make arrangements for six rats to carry the old hermit, who couldn't walk fast enough to keep up with the rest.

"So, through the night, past the walls of the town—the town that had turned us out—we hurried on and on and on, down, down into the valley. Even there, tired though we all were, I would not let them halt for long, but hurried the train on after a few moments' rest across the valley, over the wide river by a stone bridge and up the slopes of another range of hills twenty miles away from the spot we had started from. And even as I wearily shouted the command to halt, the volcano opened with a roar and sent a funnel of red fire and flying rocks hurtling into the black night sky.

"Never have I seen anything so terrifying as the anger of that death-spitting mountain. A sea of red-hot stones and molten mud flowed down the slopes, destroying all in its path. Even where we stood and watched, twenty miles away across the valley, a light shower of ashes and dust fell around us.

"The next day the fire had ceased and only a feather of smoke rising from the summit remained. But the villages were no more; the town, the town that had turned us out, could not be seen.

"Well, we settled down to country life and for some years lived in peace. My position as leader, whether I willed it or no, seemed more than ever confirmed now that I had led the people out of further dangers.

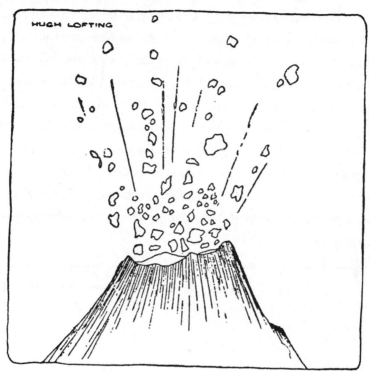

HUGH LOFTING

"The volcano opened with a roar."

"And so time passed and the second migration was declared a great success. But presently, as always seemed to be the way, I foresaw that before long we would have to move again. Our trouble this time was weasels. Suddenly in great numbers they cropped up all over the countryside and made war on rats, mice, rabbits, and every living thing. I began to wonder where I would lead the people this time. Often I had looked across the valley at our old mountain, our old home. The hermit had told me that he was sure that the volcano would not speak again for fifty years. He had been right once: he probably would be again. One day I made up my mind to go back across the valley and take a look around. Alone I set off.

"Dear me, how desolate! The beautiful slopes that had been covered with vineyards, olive groves, and fig trees were now gray wastes of ashes, shadeless and hot in the glaring sun. Wearily I walked up the mountain till I came to about the place where I reckoned the town had stood. I began wondering what the buildings looked like underneath. I hunted around and finally found a hole in the lava; through it I made my way downward. Everything of course after all these years was quite cold; and to get out of the sun into the shade beneath the surface of the ground was in itself quite gratifying. I started off to do some subterranean exploring.

"Our trouble this time was weasels."

"Down and down I burrowed. In some places it was easy and in some places it was hard. But finally I got through all that covering of ashes and lava crust and came into the town beneath.

"I almost wept as I ran all over it. I knew every inch of the streets, every stone in the buildings. Nothing had changed. The dead city stood beneath the ground, silent and at peace, but in all else just as it had been when the rain of fire had blotted it out from the living world.

"'So!' I said aloud, 'here I will bring the people—back to the town that turned us out. At last we have a city of our own!'"

The United Rat States Republic

THE WHITE MOUSE, SEEING THAT THE VOLCANO Rat seemed a little hoarse, motioned to a club waiter to fetch water—which was promptly done.

With a nod of thanks to the chairman, the Volcano Rat took a sip from the acorn cup and then proceeded.

"On my return I called the people together and told them that the time had come for our third migration. Many, when they found out whither I meant to lead them, grumbled as usual—this time that I was taking them back to the place from which we had already once taken flight.

"'Wait,' I said. 'You complained years ago that I had set your civilization back, that I had reduced you to the level of squirrels. Well, now I'm going to give you a chance to advance your civilization to a point it never dreamed of before. Have patience.'

"So, once more under the protection of darkness, I led the people across the valley and up the slopes of the sleeping mountain. When I had shown them where to dig, holes were made by the hundred; and through them we entered into possession of our subterranean town.

"It took us about a month to get the place in working order. Tons of ashes had to be removed from doorways, a great deal of cleaning up was needed and many other things required attention. But it would take me more than a month to tell you in detail of the wonderful Rat City we made of it in the end. All the things that men had used were now ours. We slept in feather beds. We had a marble swimming pool, built originally by the Romans, to bathe in. We had barbers' shops furnished with every imaginable perfume, pomade, and hair oil. Fashionable rat ladies went to the manicure establishments and beauty parlors at least twice a week. And well-groomed dandies promenaded of an evening up and down the main street. We had athletic clubs where wrestling, swimming, boxing, and jumping contests were held. All the best homes were filled with costly works of art. And an atmosphere of education and culture was everywhere noticeable.

"Of course much of the food that was in the town when the catastrophe happened had since decayed and become worthless. But there were great quantities of things that were not perishable, like corn, raisins, dried beans, and whatnot. These at the beginning were taken over by me and the town council as city property; and for the first month every rat who wanted an ounce of corn had to work for it. In that way we got a tremendous lot of things done for the public good, such as cleaning up the streets, repairing the houses, carrying away rotting refuse, etc.

"But perhaps the most interesting part of our new city life was the development of professions and government. In our snug town beneath the earth we were never disturbed by enemies of any kind

"Fashionable rat ladies went to the manicure establishments."

except occasional sickness; and we grew and flourished. At the end of our first year of occupation a census was taken; and it showed our population as ten and three quarter million. So you see we were one of the largest cities in history. For such an enormous colony a proper system of government became very necessary. Quite early we decided to give up the municipal plan and formed ourselves into a city republic with departments and a chamber of deputies. Still later, when we outgrew that arrangement, we reorganized and called ourselves the United Rat States Republic. I had the honor of being elected the first premier of the Union Parliament.

"After a while of course, rats from outside colonies got to hear of our wonderful city and tourists were to be seen on our streets almost any day in the week looking at the sights. But we were very particular about whom we took in as citizens. If you wanted citizenship you had to pass quite serious examinations both for education and for health. We were especially exacting on health. Our medical college—which turned out exceptionally good rat doctors—had decided that most of our catching diseases had been brought in first by foreigners. So after a while a law was passed that not even tourists and sight-seers could be admitted to the town without going through a careful medical examination. This, with the exceptionally good feeding conditions, the freedom of the life and the popular interest in sports and athletics, made the standard of physical development very high. I don't suppose that at any time in the whole history of our race have there been bigger or finer rats than the stalwart sons of the United Rat States Republic. Why, I've seen young fellows on our high-school athletic teams as big as rabbits and twice as strong.

"Building and architecture were brought to a very fine level too. In order to keep the lava and ashes from falling in on us we constructed in many places regular roofs over the streets and squares. Some rats will always love a hole, even if you give them a palace to live in. And many of us clung to this form of dwelling still.

"One morning I was being measured for a new hole by a well-known digging contractor when my second valet rushed in excitedly waving the curling irons with which he used to curl my whiskers.

"'Sir,' he cried, 'the chief of the Street Cleaning Department is downstairs and wants to be admitted at once. Some men have come. They are digging into the mountainside above our heads. The roof over the market square is falling in and the people are in a panic!'

"I hurried at once with the chief of the Street Cleaning

Department to the market square. There I found all in the greatest confusion. Men with pickaxes and shovels were knocking in the roof of lava and ashes that hid our city from the world. The moment I saw them I knew it was the end. Man had returned to reclaim the lost town and restore it to its former glory.

"Some of our people thought at first that the newcomers might only dig for a little while and then go away again. But not I. And sure enough, the following day still more men came and put up temporary houses and tents and went on digging and digging. Many of our hot-headed young fellows were for declaring war. A volunteer army, calling itself The Sons of Rat Freedom, three million strong, raised itself at the street corners overnight. A committee of officers from this army came to me the third day and pointed out that with such vast numbers they could easily drive these few men off. But I said to them:

"'No. The town, before it was ours, belonged to man. You might drive them off for a while; but they would come back stronger than ever, with cats and dogs and ferrets and poison; and in the end we would be vanquished and destroyed. No. Once more we must migrate, my people, and find ourselves new homes.'

"I felt terribly sad, as you can easily imagine. While I was making my way back through the wrecked streets to my home, I saw some of the men preparing to take away a statue of myself carved by one of our most famous rat sculptors. It had been set up over a fountain by the grateful townsfolk to commemorate what I had done for them. On the base was written: 'The Savior of His People—The Greatest of All Leaders.' The men were peering at the writing, trying to decipher it. I suppose that later they put the statue into one of their museums as a Roman relic or something. It was a good work of art—even if the rat sculptor did make my stomach too large. Anyhow, as I watched them I determined that I would be a leader of rats no more. I had, as it were, reached the top rung of the ladder; I had brought the people to a higher pitch of civilization than they had ever seen before. And now I would let someone else lead them. The Fourth Migration would be made without me.

"Sneaking quietly into my home I gathered a few things together in a cambric handkerchief. Then I slipped out and by unfrequented back streets made my way down the mountainside—suddenly transformed from a prime minister of the biggest government, the greatest empire our race had ever seen, into a tramp rat, a lonely vagabond."

"The men were peering at the writing."

The Museum Mouse

S THE VOLCANO RAT ENDED HIS STORY, there followed a little silence. That final picture of the great leader leaving the wonderful civilization he had built up and journeying forth alone rather saddened the audience. John Dolittle was the first to speak.

"But what became of the rest of your people?" he asked.

"I did not hear until much later," the Volcano Rat replied. "I took to the sea. I boarded a ship in the first harbor I came to and sailed away for foreign shores. A year or more afterward I learned from some rats I met—when I was changing ships to come here—that several of the young, wild volunteers had succeeded in getting the people to go to war. The results had been just about what I had prophesied. In the first battle between men and rats, the rats had easily won and driven the enemy from the mountainside. But a week later the men came back armed with shotguns, smoke-pots, and other engines of war; and in their train came cats and dogs and ferrets. The slaughter of rats was apparently just horrible. Millions were wiped out. Panic seized the rest and a general mad flight followed. The slopes were simply gray with rats as the whole population left the underground city and ran for the valley. There were entirely too many for the dogs and cats to kill, and so quite a few reached safety; but they were widely scattered. And no attempt was made to reorganize the remnant of a great race under another government. The United Rat States Republic was no more."

The white mouse now arose from the presidential chair and, after thanking the Volcano Rat for his story, reminded the members that tomorrow night, Tuesday the fifteenth, the museum Mouse had promised to entertain them. The meeting was then declared adjourned and everyone went home.

The next evening, in spite of the fact that both the Doctor and I were very busy, we were in our places in the Assembly Room by eight o'clock because we did not want to miss the adventures of the Museum Mouse. We knew him to be quite a personality. He had already interested us considerably by his observations on natural history. He looked something like a little old professor himself. He had tiny beady black eyes and a funny screwed-up look to his sharp-nosed face. His manner was cut-and-dried.

"I've lived all my life in natural history museums," he began. "Main reason why I like them is because when they're closed to the public you have the place to yourself—from six in the evening to ten o'clock the next morning, and till two in the afternoon on Sundays. This story is mainly concerned with the nest of the Three-Ringed Yah-Yah, a strange East Indian bird that builds a peculiar home; and with Professor Jeremiah Foozlebugg, one of the silliest animal-stuffers I ever knew.

"Why, just to show you how stupid that professor was: one day

"Professor Jeremiah Foozlebugg"

he was putting together the skeleton of a prehistoric beast, the Five-toed Pinkidoodle—"

"The *what?*" cried the Doctor, sitting up.

"Well, I was never good on names," said the Museum Mouse. "It was a five-toed something. Anyway, while he was out of the room a moment his dog dragged in an old ham bone and left it among the parts of the skeleton. And would you believe it? Jeremiah Foozlebugg spent days and nights trying to fit that ham bone into the skeleton of the five-toed—er—thimajigg and wondering why there was one bone left over.

"Now, when I was first married I took my wife for a wedding trip to the natural history museum. And after I had shown her all over it, she thought she'd like to settle down there. And we began to look around to decide where in the building we would make our home.

"'It must be a snug, warm place, Nutmeg,' says she, 'on the children's account. It's a pesky business raising young mice where there are drafts and cold winds.'

"'All right, Sarsparilla,' I said. 'I know the very spot. Come with me.'

"Now, what we called the Stuffing Room was a long work-shop downstairs where Foozlebugg and his assistants stuffed birds and animals and prepared specimens of plants and butterflies and things to be brought up later and put in the glass cases for the public to look at. All natural history museums have more collections and specimens presented to them than they can possibly use. And our Stuffing Room was always cluttered up with everything from elephants' tusks to fleas in bottles. Among all this junk there was a collection of birds' nests—many of them with the limb of the tree in which they had been built. For months and months this collection had lain upon a dusty shelf—nests of all sizes, shapes, and sorts. One was quite peculiar. It was the nest of the Three-Ringed Yah-Yah. In form it was quite round, like a ball, and had for entrance one little hole—just big enough for a mouse to slip through. When you were inside, no one would know you were there.

"I showed it to Sarsparilla and she was delighted. Without further delay we got some extra scraps of silk, which Foozlebugg had been using for some of his stuffing business, and lined it soft and snug—although it was already well padded with horsehair and this-tledown by the Three-Ringed Yah-Yah who had built it. Then for several days we led a peaceful, happy life in our new home. During regular hours in the workshop we lay low and often had hard work stopping our giggles as we watched Professor Foozlebugg stuffing animals all out of shape and calling on his assistants to admire them.

"Well, the children came and then we were very glad about our selection of a home. For no place could have been more ideal for baby mice than was that old bird's nest with its round walls and draft-proof ceiling and floor. Now there is one disadvantage in living in museums: you have to go out for all your meals. There's practically nothing to eat in the building, and what there is, like waxes and things of that sort, you soon learn to leave strictly alone; because those old professors use strong poisons on all their stuffing materials to keep the bugs from getting into them. Of course, even with all the doors locked any mouse can find his way in and out of a building somewhere. But occasionally when the weather is bad it is very inconvenient to have to go out for every single thing you eat. And now with a family of youngsters to feed, this problem became more serious than usual.

"So Sarsparilla and I used to take it in turns to look after the youngsters while the other went out foraging for food. Sometimes we had to go a long way and to bring crumbs from various places to the lobby of the building before we hauled them down to the Stuffing Room. Well, one night I had been up very late foraging for food and didn't get in until nearly daylight. I was dog-tired, but even then I didn't get any sleep because the children were querulous and fretful and they kept me awake. As soon as evening came, Sarsparilla left me in charge and started out on her food hunt. Shortly after she had gone the children settled down quietly, and right away, worn out with fatigue, I fell into a deep sleep.

"When I awoke the sunlight was streaming in through the entrance hole of our nest. I supposed I must have long overslept.

But I never remembered the direct rays of the sun to have shone in at our door like this before. I got up and peeped out cautiously.

"I could hardly believe my eyes. *Our nest was no longer in the Stuffing Room!* Instead we were in a glass case in one of the main halls of the museum. Around us, on various twigs and stands and things, were the other nests of the old collection that had lain so long on the dusty shelf. Our house had been put on show for the public, shut up tight in a glass case; and that stupid old duffer Foozlebugg who had put it there was still standing outside, displaying his hand-iwork with great pride to a fat woman and two children who were visiting the museum!"

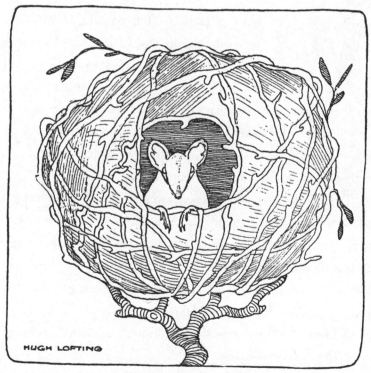

"I peeped out cautiously."

Professor Foozlebugg's Masterpiece

"WELL," SIGHED THE MUSEUM MOUSE, "you can imagine how I felt. There I was with a whole family of youngsters, shut up in a glass case. I dare not show myself outside the nest, hardly, because even when that ridiculous Professor Foozlebugg had moved away with the fat woman, odd visitors in ones and twos were always browsing by and looking in. It would be difficult to think of a more uncomfortable, unprivate home than ours had become.

"However, there were moments when that end of the hall was free from visitors and attendants. And during one of these I suddenly saw Sarsparilla with a wild look in her eye frantically hunting around outside for her lost family. Standing at the door of the nest, I waved and made signs to her and finally caught her attention. She rushed up to the glass and called through it:

"'Get the children out of there, Nutmeg. Get them out at once!'

"That was the last straw.

"'Sarsparilla,' I called back, 'don't be a fool. Do you think I

"Visitors were always browsing by."

brought the nest and the children here myself? How am I to get them out? I can't bite through glass.'

"'But they must be fed!' she wailed. 'It is long past their morning mealtime.'

"'Bother their morning mealtime!' said I. 'What about my morning mealtime? They'll have to wait. We can't do anything till the museum closes to the public—at five o'clock. You had better get away from there before you get seen.'

"But Sarsparilla was quite unreasonable. She just kept running up and down outside the glass, moaning and wringing her hands.

"'Can't you give them some of that stuffed duck there, on the shelf above your head?' she moaned.

"'I could *not*,' I said. 'Stuffed museum duck is full of arsenic. Don't worry. They can manage until five—the same as me.'

"Sarsparilla would have gone on arguing all day, I believe, if an attendant hadn't come strolling down to that end of the wing and made it necessary for her to hide.

"The rest of the day I had my hands full. For the children, having missed two meals, suddenly got as lively as crickets. They were all for climbing out of the nest—though they hadn't had their eyes open more than a few days. I could have slapped them.

"'Where's Ma?' they kept on saying. 'What's happened to Ma? I'm hungry. Where's Ma?—Let's go and find her.'

"I tell you they had me busy, yanking them down from the hole one after another. *They* didn't care how many people were looking in the glass case. All that they cared about was that they were hungry and wanted Ma—the stupid little things!

"Never was I so glad in all my experience of museum routine to see the attendants clearing the people out of the halls and locking up the doors. I knew all those old fellows in uniform well. It was a funny life they led—generally pleasant enough. One of the things they had to do was to look out for bomb-throwers. Why people should want to throw bombs or set infernal machines in museums, of all places, I don't know. But they do—or, at all events, it is always expected that they will. That's why the attendants won't allow visitors to bring in parcels: they are afraid they may contain dynamite.

"One of these old men regularly brought his lunch with him and ate it behind the stuffed elephant when nobody was looking— he wasn't supposed to, you see. And the few crumbs he left upon

"I knew the old fellow well."

the floor were the only food that I ever managed to get *in*side the museum. As he changed his coat this evening, some crusts fell out of the paper in which his bread and cheese had been wrapped. I knew that if I didn't get them that night, the charwoman would sweep them up in the morning. But while I was still gazing at them hungrily out of my glass prison, Sarsparilla came and collected them and brought them over to the case.

"'Nutmeg, I want to get these into the children,' she said.

"'Oh, for heaven's sake, have some sense!' I snapped back. 'The first thing we've got to do is to find a way in—or rather a way out.'

"'Gnaw a hole through the floor,' said she, 'quite simple. You needn't be afraid of anyone seeing you now. The night watchman won't be stirring for another hour yet.'

"'Don't you know,' I said wearily, 'that all these cases are zinc-lined? I can't bite through zinc any more than I can through glass.'

"That started her off again. She threw up her hands.

"'Why, the children will starve to death!' she cried. And she recommenced her running backward and forward like a crazy thing.

"I saw I wasn't going to get any helpful ideas from her so I began to look over the situation myself with an eye to working something out. First, I climbed all around the whole case, carefully inspecting the joints in the walls, the floor and the roof, to see if I could find a weak spot anywhere. Then I examined each shelf in turn to see if by chance I might come upon anything that could help me. And finally on the top shelf I discovered something that suggested a plan of escape.

"It was this: among the collection of birds' nests there were some of seabirds. These were set among stones, the way certain gulls and such build—just a rough hollow of twigs and seaweed laid on the shingle of the beach. Here Professor Foozlebugg had quite surpassed himself in the art of tastefully displaying specimens. He had the whole top shelf set out like a scene on a lonely island where seabirds would build. At the back there was a picture of the ocean painted, with lighthouses and sailboats and everything. And in front of this there were several stuffed birds and nests set among the stones of the beach: The stones were mostly round, of all sizes. And it occurred to me that I might very easily roll some of the larger ones off the top shelf. Then, if they struck something slanting when they reached the bottom of the case, they would fly against the glass wall and break it.

"There were nests of seabirds."

"I wasted no time in getting to work. It was necessary to pre-pare a bouncing place where the stone would fall if my plan was to be a success. I slid down to the bottom of the case and gathered together a large pile of stiff twigs that I took from the other nests. It was hard work, because most birds put their nests together pretty firmly. I made a frightful mess of the collection before I was done.

"In the meantime, not being able to keep the children in order while I was at work, I had let them follow their own sweet wills. Every one of the little beggars had got out of the nest; and now having seen 'Ma' outside the case, they too were running up and down alongside the glass and careering all over the place trying to find a way out. If Professor Foozlebugg had come in at that moment to inspect his latest work of art he would have had a great shock.

"Well, when all was ready I went down below and chased all the children up onto the upper shelves so they wouldn't get hurt by falling stones or flying glass. Then I explained to Sarsparilla, in shouts, what I was going to do.

"'Stand by,' I yelled, 'to get the youngsters to a place of safety. They're not easy to handle.'

"'All right,' she called back. 'I'll take three and you take three. And for pity's sake, be careful how you get them through the hole in the broken glass.'

"Then, just as I was about to put my shoulder under the round stone and topple it down, there came another shout from my wife:

"'Look out! Night watchman coming! Hide the children quick!'

"It was all very well for Sarsparilla to say, 'Hide the children, quick!' They had no intention of being hidden. They had seen 'Ma' and they meant to get to her as soon as possible. And as soon as she disappeared again they went entirely crazy, rushing all over the place crying, 'Where's Ma gone? We're hungry. What's become of Ma?'

"Oh dear! I never had such a time. I had no sooner caught a couple of them and hidden them behind a stuffed bird or something, before they would pop out again while I was running after the next pair.

"Luckily the night watchman was not a very wide-awake old man at the best of times, and as it happened tonight he did not swing his lantern near our case.

"When he had gone, Sarsparilla showed up again outside the glass and I got ready to try my plan once more.

"I got ready to try my plan once more."

"*Crash!*

"It worked all right and no mistake. The stone knocked a hole in the front of the case big enough for a bulldog to get through. In fact, everything would have gone splendidly if it hadn't been for those half-witted children of mine. With the crashing of the glass they just ran around like lunatics and we couldn't catch a single one of them. We had time to get away easily. But while we were still falling all over the place trying to get the family together, alarm bells in every corridor of the museum started ringing violently. The next thing, the night watchman came running through the hall shouting:

"'A bomb, a bomb!—Hey! Help!—Fire! Police!—A bomb's gone off somewhere! HELP!'

"'It's no use, Sarsparilla,' I said. 'We can't manage it now. Bring in one of those crusts of bread with you and come inside until the excitement dies down. Was anyone ever blessed with such children? Help me get them into the nest quick. With you here, they'll be quieter and more manageable. Later, if luck is still with us, we may get away.'

"And we only just got those little nuisances stowed out of sight in time. In less than five minutes from the crash of the glass people began arriving on the run. First, a constable with a notebook, from the beat outside the museum's main entrance. Then six firemen came rushing in dragging a hose. Next, the watchman's wife carrying bandages and a bottle of brandy.

"And all of them stood around the broken glass case asking about the 'bomb'—Yes, the watchman was quite sure it was a bomb—Look how it had wrecked all the nests inside!

"Then they gave their opinions, one after another: 'Russian nihilists'; 'suffragettes'; 'East End anarchists,' etc., etc. While all the time we who were responsible for the whole thing sat inside the home of the Three-Ringed Yah-Yah and listened to their silly chatter.

"Finally the great Professor Foozlebugg arrived on the scene, summoned from his bed—for it was now nearly midnight—by a messenger from the watchman. He nearly wept when he saw his latest work of art—his masterpiece—knocked all skiddle-daddle. He was much more upset about his beautiful scene on the sea-shore than he was over the museum's narrow escape from being blown up by an infernal machine. He was about to wade into the

"The great Professor Foozlebugg arrived."

wreckage then and there and put it to rights but—fortunately for us—one of the policemen warned him off.

"'Don't touch it, sir, please. With these infernal machines one never knows. A second, and more serious, explosion, sir, is liable to follow the moment you lay a finger on it. We will get the bomb experts from police headquarters. They know how to handle these things, sir.'

"Well, just that saved us from a pretty serious situation. After a little more discussion between the firemen and the constable it was decided to let well enough alone until the morning—when the bomb experts from police headquarters would take charge of affairs.

Meanwhile the policeman, the firemen, and the professor felt they might as well go back to bed. As for the old watchman, he was so scared of that second explosion that the policeman had spoken of, that the moment the rest of them had departed he locked up the doors and left that hall severely to itself.

"Which of course was exactly what we wanted. We had seven peaceful hours before us—before the charwoman would come to sweep—in which to do our moving. The first thing we did, after we had all the children safely lifted out through the broken glass, was to sit down in the middle of the hall and eat a hearty meal off the crusts that the old attendant had left behind. Then we herded the children down below by easy stages to the Stuffing Room. And there Sarsparilla kept them together while I hunted up a new home among the lumber and stuff with which the shelves were cluttered.

"But this time, you may be sure, I did *not* pick a bird's nest nor anything else that was likely to get put on exhibition while we slept."

The Prison Rat

I WOULD LIKE VERY MUCH TO KNOW," SAID JOHN Dolittle the following night when the Prison Rat was about to begin his story, "what made you take to living in prisons. I've been in prison myself. And while I always found the life very quiet and restful, I would not recommend a jail as exactly a cheerful place to make one's permanent home."

"Well," the Prison Rat began, "as a matter of fact, the story I am going to tell you explains how I took to prison life."

"Good!" said the Doctor. And everyone settled down to listen.

"To begin with then," said the Prison Rat, "you must know that I began life as a studio rat. I patronized artists' studios. They're not bad places to live. For one thing, artists, as a rule, are not very particular people; and a rat more or less doesn't bother them. And secondly, they always cook their own meals and very seldom wash the dishes—after the meals; when they do, they do it before meals. Consequently there is always lots to eat. In almost any artist's studio you can be sure of finding a fish head, or a chop bone, or a plate with gravy stuck to the bottom, if you only hunt long enough.

"Well then, after I had lived in several artists' studios and got sort of fond of the Bohemian life, I came to reside in one where the artist was kind of peculiar. He lived all alone and didn't seem to have many friends nor to put himself out to make any. This was unusual. At my other studios they had parties—often—with lots of laughter and good company. But this man hardly ever saw anyone. I think, maybe, he had been disappointed in love. But of that I am not sure. One old philosopher used to come and see him occasionally and they'd sit and talk and argue over politics far into the night.

"They'd argue over politics far into the night."

"I never bothered about listening to them much; but one evening I overheard a word that made me stop behind the coal scuttle with ears cocked. With practice I had become pretty good at understanding Man Talk—especially certain words that were repeated quite often.

"'Michael'—that was the artist's name—'why don't you get a cat?' asked the philosopher.

"'How absurd! What on earth would I get a cat for?' answered the other.

"You can be sure I was glad to hear him say that.

"'Well, a dog, then—or something,' the philosopher went on. 'You're too lonely here altogether. It isn't good for you.'

"'Oh no,' said the artist with a sort of faraway look in his eyes. 'I don't need company. I can manage . . . alone.'

"And then followed a very interesting discussion. It seemed that the artist was more of a philosopher than was the philosopher himself.

"'Why should I get a cat?' he repeated—'or a dog, or a gold-fish, or a canary—or a wife? I tell you'—he leaned over and tapped the philosopher on the knee—'if you have attachments you are not free. I am alone. If I want to go away, I can go. If I had a family or a house full of pets, I could not.'

"The philosopher finally was bound to agree with him. But just the same, I knew he was lonely, all by himself in that studio, in spite of his arguments. And the way I found it out was this: one day I slipped while I was hunting round the dishes and things for food and fell into a pail alongside the sink. The pail had no water in it; and ordinarily I could have leapt out again easily. But somehow I caught my leg as I fell and sprained it badly; and I couldn't jump an inch. And of course climbing out up the slippery sides was also quite impossible. I was trapped.

"Some time later the artist comes along, wanting the pail to carry water in. He looks into it and sees me. Of course I thought the end had come. You know how most people are: they all seem to think there is something virtuous about killing rats. And I'm pretty sure that even into his mind that was the first thought that came. Because he went off to the stove and came back with the poker. He looked determined and terrible enough. But suddenly his expression changed.

"'Oh well,' he muttered. 'I suppose your life means something

HUGH LOFTING

"He came back with the poker."

to you. Why should I kill you after all? . . . Get out of my pail. I want to wash.'

"And he deliberately rolled the pail over onto its side so I could escape. I limped off, thanking my lucky stars. I made kind of slow progress with my sprained leg; and he watched me thoughtfully as I scrambled for a hole under the sink.

"'Humph! Had an accident?' he murmured. 'Here, take this with you for supper.'

"And he threw me a bacon rind off the draining-board. I took it and tried to look gratefully at him before I disappeared into the hole.

"Then for several days after that he used to watch for me. And when I appeared, instead of firing a boot at me, as most people do to rats, he used to throw crumbs of bread and meat. He was trying to make my acquaintance.

"That's how I knew that he was lonely.

"Another thing by which I was made still surer of it was that he used to talk to me a good deal—for want of someone else to chat with—also that he talked to himself a good deal. After a while I got quite tame; and as soon as I realized he didn't mind me knocking around the place quite freely, I used to sit up on a stool beside him and watch him paint. And I took my meals with him too. He gave me an upturned bucket to sit on and seemed really interested in what I liked to eat. He always called me Machiavelli. I never understood why. Perhaps that was a friend of his.

"'Machiavelli,' he would say, 'you're the right kind of a friend to have. You don't affect my liberty. If I leave the studio I don't have to bother about you. You'll look after yourself. Here's to your good health, Machiavelli—my friend who leaves me free.'

"I used to sit up on a stool and watch him paint."

"And he would drink to me, with a bow, out of his shaving mug filled with beer.

"Now, there were two or three other rats who lived under the floor of that studio. And one day in spring three of us went off together for a day's jaunt—just for a sort of exploring trip, the way folks do in springtime. As luck would have it, a terrier picked up our trail and we got separated. The dog stuck to me finally, leaving the others alone. And he chased me a long way from home before I shook him.

"I didn't get back to the studio until three days later. To my astonishment, I found that the artist was gone. The other rats had never been as tame with him as I was. They didn't trust humans, they said, considering them a low-down, cruel and deceitful race, not in any way to be compared with rats for frankness and honesty. I asked them when and where the artist had gone. All that they could tell me was that some policeman had come and taken him away. They didn't understand Man Talk—at least, not as well as I did. But they had got the impression that it was something to do with a revolution in which the artist had taken part.

"Well, I cannot tell you how I felt. He had said that I was the right kind of a friend to have; that if he went away—it almost seemed as though he had foreseen it—it wouldn't make any difference to me. But it did. I positively wept as I went through the empty studio looking at his paintings. They were good pictures, too. And I made up my mind that I would find him if I had to seek through all the prisons in the land.

"And that was how I began my career as a prison rat."

A Rat's Pilgrimage

WELL, MY SEARCH INDEED TOOK ME to strange places and brought me into touch with strange folk. I suppose I must have visited a good two dozen jails in all. I got to know a lot of prisoners, all kinds: political prisoners, as they were called, that is, people who had quarreled with the government; pickpockets; coiners, makers of bad money; dog thieves; card sharps; men who had killed their fellow men. It was quite interesting in a way—though most of it was pretty sad.

"They were all—or nearly all—anxious to make my acquaintance. And that was the first time that I discovered that, generally speaking, it is only in prison men want to make friends of rats. Rather strange. I suppose it is because they are lonely and miserable in prison. All other places those same men would throw a brick at a rat, make a wry face and say, 'Ooh! The brute!' But in prison they would make a friend of him—yes, in prison, where they have no friends. My artist, on the other hand, had been kind to me when he was free. That was the difference, to my way of thinking, between him and other people. And I made up my mind harder than ever to keep on hunting till I found him.

"Of course in my wanderings I also made the acquaintance of many other regular prison rats. And them I questioned always, hoping they might be able to give me some clue as to where my man had been taken. Some of them thought I was a fool to keep on searching for him.

"'Oh,' they said, 'he has forgotten about you long ago. Like as not, he won't know you when he sees you. If he wanted to make pets of rats there are always lots of them in every prison. And anyway, never trust a man. Men are the sworn enemies of rats.'

"But all I answered was, 'He is in trouble and I want to find him. He was kind to me once—when *I* was in difficulties. Such things I don't forget.'

"One of the prison rats I met suggested I go back to the studio and wait till someone came who might be connected with the man I was seeking. Then by tracking him when he left, I might be led to the prison where the artist had been taken. I thought the idea was a good one and I acted on it. I went back to my old home and waited. About a week later the philosopher called. I watched him like a cat. He gathered some things together— clothes and books—wrapped them in a bundle and started away on foot.

"I followed. Luckily it was evening and the darkness gave me some chance of keeping in touch without being seen. It isn't so hard for a dog to follow a man through a town; but it is a very different matter for a rat.

"He suggested I go back to the studio."

"Well, in spite of several cats who tried to chase me off the trail, I stuck to the old philosopher for a full half hour.

"And then good luck deserted me—and him, too, poor fellow. He was run over at a street corner—a frightened horse. It was all done and finished so quickly there was hardly any telling how it happened. At first I thought the old man was killed. But he wasn't. Nevertheless, he was badly enough hurt to make it necessary to call an ambulance and take him off to a hospital.

"So there went that hope. As I crouched in the shadow of a doorway and watched them taking him away, I realized with a sinking heart that not only was I losing my one clue, but my friend, the

"Cats tried to chase me off the trail."

artist, was also losing the only other being in the world who would be likely to help him.

"Just the same, I set off on my hunt once more, more determined on this account than ever that I would find him—if I spent the rest of my life in doing it.

"Then for many weeks my pilgrimage continued without anything of importance happening. I went patiently from jail to jail, only staying in each one long enough to make sure that he wasn't there. After a while I got to do it more quickly than I had at the beginning. But it wasn't easy. You see, in most jails there were a great number of cells; and the first thing I did when I came to a new prison was to find out how many cells there were and how many of them were occupied. Then I had to discover some way of getting into each one in turn. If I couldn't get in—some of the newer jails were pretty hard even for a rat to get in or out of—I had to hang around somewhere till the prisoner was brought out for exercise so I could get a look at his face. And, because in some cases the prisoners were brought out very seldom, this took a long time.

"Well, after two or three months I began to get somewhat discouraged, I must admit. However, I did not give up hope. Something told me, in spite of what the rats had said, that I was going to find him and that I was going to be of help to him.

"Now there was a certain tune he had been in the habit of whistling around the studio when at work. And one day I had come to a new jail and looked at the prisoners in all the cells—all but one. This I couldn't find a way into; and the prisoner never seemed to get brought out. For nearly a week I had hung around that jail for the sake of that one cell alone, hoping a chance would come for me to see who was in there.

"At the end of the week I began seriously thinking of moving on to the next jail. After all, it did not seem worthwhile for me to stay so long in one prison just on account of a single cell, when there were so many other jails yet to be visited. Still, I didn't quite like to go until I had made sure.

"And I'm glad I didn't. For that same night, as I hung around on watch outside the door, I heard—at last—the familiar whistle, his favorite tune. After nearly three months' search I had run him down! My, didn't I feel pleased and proud!

"I set to work now with a lighter heart to the business of getting into that cell. So anxious was I to see him, that I took a fearful big chance. I decided to try and slip in with the warder who brought him his breakfast in the morning. This was pretty risky, because, as some of you may know, prison cells have precious little furniture that a rat can hide behind.

"Nevertheless I managed it. I stood ready in the shadow outside the door; and when the warder came along with the breakfast, I slid in close behind his heels without being noticed. Then choosing the right moment, just as he was laying down the food, I nipped across under the prison cot and waited till he went out again, locking the door behind him. Then I came boldly forth from my hiding place and showed myself.

"I stood ready in the shadow."

"'Hulloa!' said the artist. 'Why, you look cheeky and brazen enough to be my friend Machiavelli.'

"And then:

"'By George!' he added in a curious whisper. 'It *is* Machiavelli! I know him by that limp!'

"He looked thin and pale. But he seemed just as philosophical and just as ready to say funny, crazy, unexpected things as ever. He was really overjoyed to see me. He picked me up and patted me like a pet poodle.

"'My first visitor!' he kept saying—'My only visitor, in fact. Machiavelli!—Good old Mack!'

"He invited me to share his breakfast with him, making apologies for the poorness of the fare.

"But the first thing I wanted to do, now that I knew where he was, was to find a way by which I could come in and go out of that cell with more or less safety. I looked around the walls and the floor, but there was no trace of a hole anywhere—and no chance of making any in the new, well-cemented stonework. Then I looked up at the little window, high in the wall. And that gave me an idea.

"I felt pretty sure that I could gain the sill of this window by scrambling up the rough stonework inside. I tried it. He stood below watching me climb, really terrified that I might fall and break my neck. From the sill I found that the window could also be reached from the outside by means of a rainwater pipe that ran down the building near it.

"As soon as I got out I hunted up one of the rats who lived in the jail and questioned him. Also—I have told you that I was pretty good at understanding Man Talk—I listened at every opportunity I got to the conversations of the warders and attendants. And from

"I found I could gain the sill."

what I could gather I came to the conclusion that my friend was soon to be transported, that is, sent away to serve a long term of imprisonment and labor in foreign parts. Exactly when he was to be taken I could not find out for certain. But I had a feeling that it was to be soon and that there was no time to lose.

"The next thing was to find out what my friend needed for escape. I consulted a very old rat who had lived in prisons all his life and seen several men escape. And he told me that the most important thing was a file to saw window bars with. So a file, I determined, my man should have without delay. Now, the jail had a workshop in it where some of the prisoners were put to making things. But the men were always examined before they left the workshop to make sure they took no tools away to their cells. It didn't take me long to find my way into that workshop and pick out a nice sharp file—a small one that I could easily carry.

"In the middle of the night I revisited my friend—entering by way of the rainwater pipe and the window—and found him asleep. I woke him up by laying the file on his nose. At first he didn't know what to make of it. But when he realized what the piece of cold metal was that I had laid on his face, he got up and set quietly to work at once.

"Well, that's about the end of my story. It took him two nights to cut through the bar; and I had to bring him a fresh file to replace the old one, which was worn smooth. He got out of the window about midnight on the second night. No one saw him leave. Luck was with him, and the sentry at the outside wall was kind of drowsy. He got clean away and left the country before they found him. I never saw him again. My assistance had only just got there in time though. For when they came in on the third morning and found his cell empty, the prison van was already drawn up outside the gates of the jail, waiting to take him to the ship."

The Stable Mouse

MY BOOK ENTITLED *TALES OF THE RAT AND Mouse Club* was by now beginning to look pretty thick and bulky. Of course rewritten, or rather printed, the way it would be in the bound volume itself, it would not take up as much space as it did in my rough copy. Nevertheless I could see by the end of the fourth story (that of the Prison Rat) that only about one more could be included in the book. I told this to the white mouse.

"Well," said he, "of course I see that you can't make the book too thick, otherwise it would be too heavy for the mouse readers to handle—and the rats have most of the volumes in the club library as it is. But there will be a terrible lot of disappointment. There are no less than nine members still hoping that their stories will be included—and I thought myself that you'd be able to get in another two anyway."

"Who are the members whose stories are still to be heard?" asked the Doctor.

HUGH LOFTING

"'There's hundreds!' said the white mouse."

"Oh, heavens, there's hundreds!" said the white mouse. "But there are nine whom I had sort of half promised they would stand a chance. Out of that nine we will now have to pick one—and of course there will be hard feelings. Let me see: there's the Railway Rat. His is a story of travel. Then—another voyager—the Ship's Rat, our old friend of the Canary Islands, Doctor. And there's the Icebox Mouse and the Theater Mouse. I don't know much about them—newcomers to the club. Then there's the Zoo Rat, the chap who is always boasting of his acquaintance with the lion—and Cheapside says he does really go in and out of his den. Next? Let me think. . . . Oh, the Teahouse Mouse. He is a sort of a tittering nincompoop. A regular gossip, giggles all the time. It is easy to see how and why he chose teahouses to live in. I don't suppose his story is much. Scandal, most likely. I'll be glad to cross him off the list. The Church Mouse, too, we can count him out. His story will be a sort of a lecture, full of quotations and advice to young mice. And I'm *so* tired of hearing how poor he is. That leaves the Hansom Cab Mouse—his yarn will be good, I suspect. . . . And the Hospital Mouse. I tell you what I'll do: I'll get them all to give me a rough outline of their stories and I'll pick the one that I think is the best and relate it at the club tomorrow night, eh?"

"All right," said the Doctor. "And you can tell the others that maybe there will be a second volume of *The Tales of the Rat and Mouse Club*—later—which they can all be in."

To our surprise, when the Doctor and I took our places in the Assembly Room of the Rat and Mouse Club the following evening, we found that none of the members whom the President had spoken of last night had been selected to tell the fifth story for the book. Instead a mouse whom neither of us had seen or heard of before got up and was introduced as the Stable Mouse.

"Her story was sort of different, I thought," the white mouse whispered in my ear. "We want variety in the book. And those others were all jealous of one another anyway. So I decided I'd take a new member altogether."

The Stable Mouse was a quiet, ladylike little individual—rather shy. And at the beginning she had to be asked several times to speak louder, because some of the members at the back of the hall (a few of the old-age pensioners who lived in the club) could not hear her.

"This story is mostly about my first husband, Corky," she began, "a good-natured mouse, but the most frivolous-minded mate that anybody was ever asked to live with. It was largely on Corky's account that I became a stable mouse—thinking it was a safer place for him, one where he would be less likely to get into mischief and hot water. Stables are generally very good places for mice to live. There are always oats, which after all form the most nourishing and digestible food that can be found anywhere. And it is pleasant in the evenings when the horses come home from their work to sit up in the rafters and listen to them gossip about the day's doings.

"But even in a stable that husband of mine could find plenty of occasions to get himself into trouble and to keep me worried to death. One day he found a large watering hose in a corner of the stable. And he thought it would be great fun to get into it and run up and down inside, as though it were a tunnel—sort of switchback idea. He was a regular child—I see that now: he never really grew up. Well, while he was playing this game, sliding and whooping round the loops of the hose, one of the stable-boys came and turned the water on to wash the stable floor. And of course with the terrific force of the water my husband was shot out of the hose like a bullet from a gun. His switchback gave him a much bigger ride than he expected. As it happened, the stable-boy had the hose pointed out into the yard when the water first rushed forth. And I suddenly saw Corky, gasping and half-drowned, flying over the pig-house roof. He landed in the pigs' trough on the other side—and very nearly got eaten by a large hog who mistook him for a floating turnip before he scrambled out to safety.

"Often I used to think that that light-headed husband of mine used to deliberately get himself into hot water—just for sheer dev-ilment. And no amount of hard lessons seemed to teach him any

"He was shot out of the hose like a bullet from a gun."

sense. How it was that he wasn't killed in the first year of his life I don't know.

"Would you believe it? Time after time he used to get into the horses' nose-bags to steal their oats while they were actually eating! I told him often that one of these days he would get chewed up. What usually happened was that his moving around in the bags would tickle the horses' noses until they sneezed and blew him out onto the floor like a piece of chaff.

"One day this happened when the farmer who owned the place was standing in the stable with his wife. But this time the horse sneezed so hard that Corky was shot right up, nearly to the rafters. And when he came down he landed on the farmer's hat. The farmer thought it was just a drop of water leaking from the roof—it was raining at the time—and didn't take any notice. But presently while his wife was talking to him she suddenly saw Corky's nose peering over the brim of her husband's hat—wondering how he was going to get down to solid ground. Being terrified of mice, she just lost her head, screamed and struck at Corky with her umbrella. She didn't hit him, but she nearly brained her husband—who of course thought that she had suddenly gone crazy. And in the general excitement that followed, Corky, as usual, got away.

"But one day he had a very narrow escape; and if I hadn't been there to come to his assistance, it would have surely been the end of his adventurous career. Now, there was an old jackdaw who used to hang around that stable yard. Corky took a dislike to him from the start. And I am bound to say that he certainly was a churlish, grouchy curmudgeon of a bird. He used to watch from the stable roof, and if the farmer's wife threw out any nice tit-bits of food he would be down on them before we ever got a chance to start out for them. If we did get there first he would drive us off savagely with that great scissors-like bill of his. It didn't matter how much food there was, he wouldn't let us get any. The largest rats were scared of him, for he was worse than a rooster to fight with. Even the cat wouldn't face him. She would try to pounce on him when his back was turned, but she would never face a duel with that terrible bill.

"The result was that Mr. Jackdaw—Lucifer, we called him—got to be pretty much the boss of the roost round that stable yard. He knew it, too. And everybody hated him.

"He would drive us off savagely."

"Well, one day Corky came to me just brimming over with news and excitement.

"'What *do* you think?' says he. 'You know that new stable lad, the cross-eyed one with red hair? Well, he's making a trap to catch Lucifer. I saw him myself.'

"'Oh,' I said, 'don't get excited over that. He'll never catch him. That bird knows every kind of trap that was ever invented.'

"Nevertheless Corky was very hopeful. And he used to spend hours and days watching that redheaded lad trying to bag Mr. Jackdaw. First the boy used a sieve and a string, baiting the arrangement with raw meat. But Lucifer gave that clumsy

"He used a sieve and a string."

contrivance one glance and never even looked at it again. Next the lad rigged up various sorts of nets into which he hoped the bird would fly or could be driven. Corky kept running to me with reports, two or three times a day, to keep me posted on how things were going. Then horse-hair nooses were tried—and paper bags with raisins and treacle inside.

"But as I had told Corky, Lucifer was a wily bird and he seemed to know just as much about traps as the boy did. What was more, he soon got on to the fact that Corky was watching the proceedings with great interest. Because one morning he chased him away from some soup-meat on the garbage heap, saying:

"'Hoping to see me get trapped, eh? You little imp! Get out of that before I nip the tail off you!'

"'You may get caught yet, you big black bully,' Corky threw back at him as he ran for a hole. 'And I hope you do!'

"'Oh, hah, hah!' croaked the jackdaw as he set to on the meat. 'That red-haired bumpkin couldn't catch me if he tried for a lifetime.'

"But the red-haired bumpkin was a persevering lad and not so stupid as he looked. He had made up his mind that he was going to have that jackdaw in a cage for a pet. And after a good many failures, instead of giving up, he set to work observing the quarry and his habits and trying to find just why it was that he hadn't caught him. And among other things he noticed that the jackdaw had one favorite drinking place, a little pool under a tap in a corner of the stable yard. Also he noticed that the bird never flew down to settle where anything new had been set up or anything old taken away.

"In other words, the stable lad had stumbled upon the truth that birds, like mice, are afraid of anything unfamiliar. That's their great protection. They've a keen sense of observation; and whenever a yard or a corner of a garden has anything new or changed about it, they are at once suspicious and on their guard.

"So, having learned this, the bumpkin went about his job differently. He saw that whatever was changed, whatever he put out to catch the jackdaw, must be changed or put out gradually. He began by laying a twig down near the watering place—just one. Lucifer, when he came, eyed it suspiciously. But finally he decided it was innocent, walked around it and took his drink. The next morning the boy had two twigs there. Lucifer behaved in the same way. Three mornings later there were four or five twigs there. And so on, until a regular little bank of twigs surrounded the tiny pool beneath the tap; and the jackdaw couldn't get at the water without stepping on them.

"But at this point Mr. Lucifer became very wary. He walked all around the twigs several times and finally flew away. He had gone to find another drinking place.

"Corky came to me in despair.

"'You are right,' he said dolefully. 'That bird is related to the Devil, I do believe. I'm afraid he'll never be caught.'

"But suddenly the weather came to the assistance of our redheaded trapper. It was late November; and one morning we woke up to find the ground and everything covered with a white

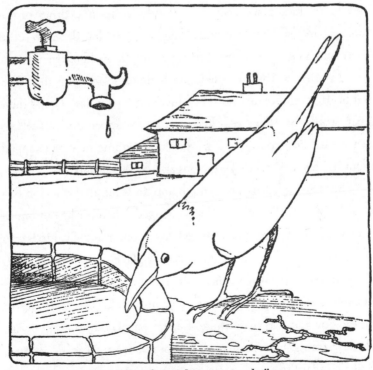

"Lucifer eyed it suspiciously."

mantle of snow and every puddle, pool, and stream topped with ice. Mr. Jackdaw came into the stable yard looking for breakfast—as usual. There wasn't any. Everything was covered, cold and silent. He looked in at the stable door. There he saw us, nibbling oats on the top of the bin. He would have come in, only he was afraid.

"'You vermin,' he sneered from the door, 'are well off, guzzling in shelter, dry and warm, while honest folk can starve outdoors, with every blade of grass buried in the snow. A pest on the weather!'

"'We would throw you some oats,' said I, 'if you hadn't always been such a mean, selfish grouch to us, driving us from every titbit even when there was enough for all. Yes, you're right: it *is* bad weather—for folks who've gone through life making no friends.'"

The Cunning of Lucifer, the Jackdaw

AT THIS POINT SOME OF THE OLD PENSION-ers at the back of the hall made another request that the Stable Mouse speak a little louder. John Dolittle suggested that she be given a tea canister or something to stand on, so that her voice would carry to the rear of the Assembly Room. After a short delay an empty mustard tin was found, which served the purpose very well. And as soon as she had climbed up onto it and overcome her embarrassment, the speaker continued:

"The jackdaw made some vulgar remark in answer to what I had said and hopped away from the door. We got onto the windowsill and watched him flopping across the yard through the deep, fluffy snow. I felt sort of sorry for him. I could see he was hungry; and in that weather he might not find a scrap to eat in a whole day. I was about to call him back and give him some oats, but Corky wouldn't let me.

"'Don't worry,' said he. 'He'll take care of himself. Serve him right, the mean bully!'

"Flopping through the deep, fluffy snow"

"As he passed his old drinking place the jackdaw just glanced at it expecting to find it frozen like all the other water out of doors. But behold! It wasn't. As a matter of fact, the red-haired lad had specially come and broken the ice even before Mr. Jackdaw was abroad.

"Lucifer was just as thirsty as he was hungry. He floundered, half flying through the snow, toward the tap. Corky got dreadfully excited as he watched him. We both guessed that those twigs were some sort of trap—though how they worked neither of us knew as yet. This morning they were half covered with snow and looked like a regular innocent part of the landscape. The water was very tempting. Lucifer hopped nearer. And Corky got even more worked up.

"Finally Mr. Jackdaw jumped up onto the mound of twigs and took a long, long drink. Corky was disappointed. Nothing seemed to happen. It looked as though whatever machinery the twigs contained had failed to go off. And it was only when the bird started to leave the drinking place that we realized what the trap was. The mound he was standing on stuck to his feet. The twigs had been covered with birdlime.

"Dear me, how he floundered and flopped and fluttered. And the more he fought and pulled and worked, the more the sticky twigs got gummed up with his feathers. We could see now that there were a whole lot of them beneath the snow; and by the time the jackdaw had them all stuck to him it was quite clear that for the present he stood no chance whatever of flying or getting away.

"Then suddenly a door opened across the yard and the red-haired lad triumphantly came forth and took possession of the helpless Mr. Lucifer. Whereupon Corky proceeded to do somersaults of joy all over the stable.

"Well, you can be sure there was general rejoicing throughout the stables and the farmyard. For not only had Lucifer made himself objectionable to us, but he was thoroughly unpopular with every living thing in the whole neighborhood.

"The lad put him in a wicker cage whose bars were reinforced with wire; and he hung the cage—of all places—in our stable. I am bound to say that once more I felt sorry for the bird. It was bad enough to be caught and imprisoned; but then to be put where other creatures, of whom he had made enemies, could look at him all day while they rejoiced in their freedom, did seem to me a bit too much.

"And, oh, what a state he was in, poor wretch! The birdlime had made all his sleek plumage messy, so that he looked like some old silk hat brought in off the dustheap. And for the first day he did nothing but bang his head against the bars, trying to get out, so that he rubbed all the feathers off the top of his head and looked worse than ever.

"Corky, the heartless little imp, had a grand time sitting outside his cage and laughing at him. He had had to run away from Lucifer so often when he was free, he was determined to make up for it now that he had a chance. I thought this was mean and I told Corky so.

"'Besides,' I said, 'I'm still scared of him—even now.'

"'Oh,' said Corky, laughing, 'what can he do, the big bully? He's fixed now for good.'

"Corky sat outside the cage and laughed at him."

"'Just the same,' I said, 'watch out. He's clever, don't forget.'

"All day long the jackdaw never said a word, not even in answer to Corky's most spiteful remarks. There was something dignified, as well as pathetic, in his downfall. He had now given up beating himself against the bars and just sat there, all huddled up at the bottom of his cage, the picture of despair. The only thing about him that seemed alive at all was his gleaming eyes full of bitter hatred. They looked like coals of fire as they followed every movement of Corky and the other mice who were taunting him outside the cage.

"It is curious how heartless some creatures can be. After Lucifer had sort of subsided that way, Corky and his friends got up on top of the cage and started dropping bits of mortar and putty down on the jackdaw's head. I tried my best to stop them, but there were too many of them and they wouldn't listen to me. Before long there must have been a good dozen gathered on top of the cage laughing and throwing things at their old enemy, the one-time bully of the stable yard. Truly Lucifer was paying a terrible price for a selfish life.

"And, alas! My fears proved right. That terrible bird was still dangerous, even when he was shut up in a cage. While those little fools were playing their heartless game one afternoon I was cleaning up our home under the hayloft floor. Suddenly I heard a dreadful shriek. I rushed out of the hole and bounded down through a trap door into the stable below.

"Corky's friends were all standing around the jackdaw's cage on the windowsill, their eyes popping out of their heads with horror. I looked for Corky among them. He wasn't there. On coming nearer I found that he was *inside* the cage, firmly held in the jackdaw's right claw! As usual, he had been more daring than the rest.

And as he had crawled over the cage he had come just a fraction of an inch too near the bird he was teasing. Like a flash—he told me this afterward—Lucifer had thrust his long beak between the bars, caught him by the tail, and pulled him inside. When I came up, Corky was still bawling blue murder at the top of his voice.

"'Be quiet!' said the jackdaw. 'Stop struggling or I'll kill you right away. Where's his wife?' he asked, turning to the others.

"'Here I am,' said I, stepping up to the cage.

"'Good!' said he. 'You are just in time to save your husband's life. I want a hole gnawed through the bottom of this cage right away—one big enough for me to get out of. Mice can eat through

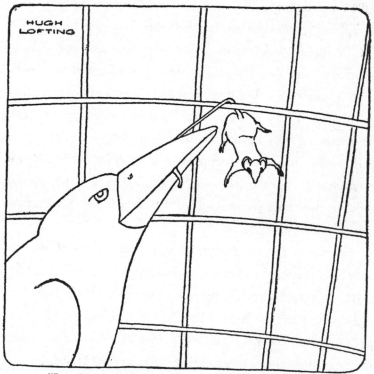

"Lucifer caught him by the tail and pulled him inside."

wood. I can't. There is room for you to get under—the legs of the cage are high enough. But please waste no time. That lad is likely to come back any moment.'

"'But,' I began, 'it would take—'

"'Don't argue!' said he shortly. 'If a hole isn't made in the bottom of this cage large enough for me to escape through before nightfall, I'll bite your husband's head off.'

"Well, I could see he meant it. And the only thing for me to do was to obey—unless I wanted to be left a widow. Lucky for me it was that the other mice were standing around. I knew I could never nibble a hole alone, in so short a time, big enough for that great hulk to pass through. And, scared to death as Corky's brave friends were, I finally persuaded them to help me.

"With the jackdaw still firmly clutching his vitals, Corky watched us as we slipped under the floor of the cage and set to work.

"It wasn't easy. And if my husband's life hadn't depended on it, I doubt very much whether it would have been done in time. The main difficulty was in getting started. As you all know—but perhaps the Doctor and Tommy do not—to begin biting a hole in the middle of a flat board is, even for a mouse, an almost impossible task. To chew off a corner, or to widen an old hole that has been already begun, that's different.

"However, I was desperate; and somehow—my teeth were sore for weeks afterward—I got four holes started in the bottom of that cage, one in each corner, in the first quarter of an hour. Then I got eight other mice, two to each hole, to continue the work. As soon as one mouse's jaws got tired I took him off the job and put a fresh mouse on. I even went down into the foundations of the stables and gathered together all the mice I could find. Corky had always been popular with the neighborhood; and as soon as they heard that his life was in danger they were willing enough to assist. In this way I had continuous relays of fresh help at work.

"Before very long we had those four holes pretty nearly joined up. There was only a little strip of wood scarcely wider than a pencil keeping the bottom of that cage from falling right out, whole.

"The old jackdaw, still clutching his wretched victim, watched the work with an eagle eye. His plan was, as soon as the bottom fell, to pry the cage over on its side. This he could easily do as soon as he got his feet on the windowsill, because the cage wasn't very heavy.

"The jackdaw still clutched his wretched victim."

"Well, we only just finished in time—in time for Corky, that is. Because I'm certain that if we had been interrupted before we had it done, the jackdaw would have surely killed him. As the bottom of the cage clattered out Lucifer let go his victim at last, and with one twist of his powerful bill, not only threw the cage on its side, but hurled it right down to the stable floor—with Corky inside it.

"At that moment the lad came in and saw his precious pet standing, free, on the windowsill. He leapt to grab him. But Lucifer, with one curving swoop, skimmed neatly over his head and out through the stable door into the wide world; while all around the bewildered lad the mice, who had freed the bird whom they hated worse than poison, scuttled and scattered to safety."

Moorsden Manor

T THIS POINT, BEFORE ANYONE WAS QUITE certain whether the Stable Mouse had finished her story or not, some sort of a commotion started at the back of the hall. There was a great deal of excited whispering and we could see that some new arrival had just turned up in a very breathless state. He seemed to be demanding to speak with the Doctor at once.

The white mouse, as president and chairman of the meeting, started for the back of the hall to see what all the excitement was about. But the newcomer was apparently in much too great a hurry to stand on ceremony; and before the white mouse had more than got out of his seat, he could be seen elbowing his way through the crowd making for John Dolittle.

"Doctor," he cried, "there's a fire over at Moorsden Manor. It's in the cellar. And everybody's asleep and no one knows anything about it."

"Good gracious!" cried the Doctor, rising and looking at his

"The chairman started for the back of the hall."

watch. "Asleep! Is it as late as that? Why, so it is. Nearly an hour past midnight! What's in the cellar—wood, coal?"

"It's chock full of wood," said the mouse. "But the fire hasn't got to it yet—thank goodness! My nest, with five babies in it, is right in the middle of the woodpile. The wife thought the best thing I could do would be to come and tell you. Nobody else understands our language, anyway. She's staying with the children. The fire started in a heap of old sacks lying in a corner of the cellar. The place is full of smoke already. There is no chance of our carrying the babies out because there are too many cats around. Once the fire reaches the wood it's all up with us. Won't you come—quick, Doctor?"

"Of course I will," said John Dolittle. He was already scrabbling his way out through the tunnel, nearly wrecking the Rat and Mouse Club on the way. "Stubbins," he called as he reached the top, "go and wake Bumpo—and send Jip along to Matthew's house. We'd better get all the help we can. If the blaze hasn't gone too far we can probably get it under control all right. Here's a note that Jip can give to Matthew, for the fire brigade—but it always takes them an eternity to get on the scene."

He hastily scribbled a few words on an old envelope with which I dashed off in one direction while he disappeared in another.

For the next fifteen minutes I was occupied in getting first Jip and then Bumpo aroused and informed of the situation. Bumpo was always the slowest man in the world to wake up. But after a good deal of hard work I managed to get him interested in clothes—and fires. Jip I had already sent trotting down the Oxenthorpe Road with his note to fetch Matthew to the scene.

Then I clutched Bumpo (still only half dressed and half awake) firmly by the hand and hurried off after the Doctor in the direction of the fire.

Now Moorsden Manor was the largest and most pretentious private residence in Puddleby. Like the Doctor's home, it was on the outskirts of the town and was surrounded by a large tract of its own land. Its present owner, Mr. Sidney Throgmorton, was a middle-aged man who had only recently come into the property. His millionaire father had died the year before, leaving him this and several other handsome estates in different parts of England and Scotland. And many people had expressed surprise that he remained at the manor all the year round when he had so many other castles and fine properties to go to.

The main gates to the estate were guarded by a lodge. And when I arrived I found the Doctor hammering on the door trying to wake the lodge-keeper up. The gates of course were locked; and the whole of the grounds were enclosed by a high wall that was much too high to climb over.

Almost at the same moment that Bumpo and I got there, Matthew Mugg, led by Jip, also arrived.

"Good gracious!" the Doctor was saying as he thumped the door with his fist. "What sleepers! The whole place could burn down while we're standing here. Can it be that the lodge is empty?"

"No," said Matthew. "The keeper's here—or his wife. One of them is always on duty. That I know. I'll throw a stone against the window."

It was only a small pebble that he threw; but the Cat's-Meat-Man put such force behind it that it went right through the pane with a crash.

Indignant shouts from inside told us that at last we had succeeded in arousing someone. And a few moments later a man in a nightshirt, with a shotgun in one hand and a candle in the other, appeared at the door. As the Doctor stepped forward the man quickly set the candle down and raised the gun as if to shoot.

"It's all right," said John Dolittle. "I've only come to warn you. There's a fire up at the manor—in the cellar. The people must be roused at once. Let me through, please."

"I will not let you through," said the man stubbornly. "I heard tell of hold-up gangs playing that game afore. The nerve of you, breaking into my windows this time of night! And how do you come to know what's going on up at the manor?"

"A man in a nightshirt appeared at the door."

"A mouse told me about it," said the Doctor. Then seeing the look of disbelief coming over the man's face, he added,

"Oh, don't argue with me! I *know* there's a fire there. Won't you please let us in?"

But the man had apparently no intention whatever of doing so. And I cannot say that he should be altogether blamed for that. For with Bumpo and Matthew we certainly must have seemed an odd delegation to call in the middle of the night.

Goodness only knows how long we would have stood there while the fire in the manor cellar went on growing, if Matthew hadn't decided to deal with the situation in his own peculiar way.

With a whispered word to Bumpo he suddenly ducked forward and wrenched the shotgun out of the lodge-keeper's hands. Bumpo grabbed the candle that stood beside the door. And the fort was in our possession.

"Come on, Doctor," said the Cat's-Meat-Man. "There's another door through here that leads into the grounds. We can't wait to talk things over with him. Maybe when the brigade comes along in an hour or so he will believe there really is a fire."

Bumpo had already found and opened the second door. And before the astonished keeper had had time to get his breath, we were all through it and running up the drive that led to the big house.

"I suppose it will take us another age to get anyone awake here," gasped the Doctor, as we arrived breathless before the imposing portico and gazed up at the high double doors.

"No it won't," said Matthew. And he let off the lodge-keeper's shotgun at the stars and started yelling, "Fire!" at the top of his voice. This din the Doctor, Bumpo, and I added to by hammering on the panels and calling loudly for admittance.

But we did not have long to wait this time. The shotgun was a good alarm. Almost immediately lights appeared in various parts of the house. Next, several windows were thrown open and heads popped out demanding to know what was the matter.

"There's a fire," the Doctor kept shouting. "A fire in your house. Open the doors and let us in."

A few minutes later the heavy bolts were shot back and an old manservant with a candle opened the door.

"I can't find the master," he said to the Doctor. "He isn't in his room. He must have fallen asleep in some other part of the house. All the rest have been woken up. But I can't find the master."

"Where's the cellar?" asked the Doctor, taking the candle and hurrying by him. "Show me the way to the cellar."

"But the master wouldn't be in the cellar, sir," said the old man. "What do you want in the cellar?"

"A family of mice," said the Doctor. "Young ones. They're in great danger. Their nest is in the woodpile. Show me the way, quick!"

The Fire

I THINK THAT, FOR BOTH THE DOCTOR AND myself, that was one of the most extraordinary nights we ever experienced. John Dolittle, as everyone knows, had for a long time now taken no part whatever in the neighborhood's human affairs. Ever since he had given up his practice as an ordinary doctor and come to be looked upon as a crank naturalist, he had accepted the reputation and retired from all social life. While he was pleasant and kind to everyone, he avoided his neighbors even more than they avoided him.

And now suddenly, through this alarm of fire brought by the mouse from the manor cellar, he found himself pitchforked by Fate, as it were, into a whole chain of happenings and concerns that he would have given a great deal to stay out of.

When Matthew, Bumpo, and I followed him into the hall of the great house we found things in a pretty wild state of confusion. In various stages of dress and undress people were running up and down stairs, dragging trunks, throwing valuables over the banisters, and generally behaving like a hen-roost in a panic. The smell of smoke was strong and pungent; and when more candles had been lit I could see that the hall was partly filled with it.

There was no need for the Doctor now to ask the way to the cellar. Over to the left of the hall there was a door leading downward by an old-fashioned winding stair. And through it the smoke was pouring upward at a terrible rate.

To my horror, the Doctor tied a handkerchief about his face, dashed through this doorway and disappeared into the screen of smoke before anyone had time to stop him. Seeing that Bumpo and I had it in our minds to follow, Matthew held out his hand.

"People were throwing valuables over the banisters."

"Don't. You'd be more trouble than help to him," he said. "If you keeled over, the Doctor would have to fetch you up too. Let's get outside and break the cellar windows. It must be full of smoke down there—more smoke than fire, most likely. If we can let some of it out, maybe the Doctor can see what he's doing."

With that all three of us ran for the front door. On the way we bumped into the old manservant who was still wandering aimlessly around, wringing his hands and wailing that he couldn't find "the master." Matthew grabbed him and shoved him along ahead of us into the front garden.

"Now," said he, "where are the cellar windows? Quick, lead us to 'em!"

Well, finally we got the poor old doddering butler to take us to the back of the house where, on either side of the kitchen door, there were two areaways with cellar windows in them. To his great astonishment and horror we promptly proceeded to kick the glass out of them. Heavy choking smoke immediately belched forth into our faces.

"Hulloa there! Doctor!" gasped Matthew. "Are you all right?"

The Cat's-Meat-Man had brought a bull's-eye lantern with him. He shone it down into the reeking blackness of the cellar. For a few moments, which seemed eternally long, I was in an agony of suspense waiting for the answering shout that didn't come. Matthew glanced upward over his shoulder.

"Humph!" he grunted with a frown. "Looks as though we'll have to organize a rescue party by the stair anyway."

But just as he was about to step up out of the area I clutched him by the arm.

"Look!" I said, pointing downward.

And there in the beam of his lantern a hand could be seen coming through the reeking hole in the broken window. It was the Doctor's hand. And in the hollow of the half-open palm, five pink and hairless baby mice were nestling.

"Well, for the love of Methuselah!" muttered Matthew, taking the family and passing it up to me.

The Doctor's hand withdrew and almost immediately reappeared again, this time with the thoroughly frightened mother mouse—whom I also pocketed.

But Matthew didn't wait for the Doctor's hand to go back for anything else. He grabbed it by the wrist and with a mighty heave pulled John Dolittle, with the window-sash and all, up into the areaway. We saw at once that he was staggering and in pretty bad condition; and we half dragged, half lifted him out of the area, away from the choking smoke, to a lawn nearby. Here we stretched him out flat and undid his collar.

But before we had time to do anything else for him he began to struggle to his feet.

"I'm all right," he gasped. "It was only the smoke. We must get a bucket chain started. The fire has just reached the woodpile. If it's allowed to get a good hold the whole place will burn down."

There is not the least doubt that that mouse who brought the news of the fire to the Doctor saved Moorsden Manor from total destruction—and possibly several lives as well. Certainly if it had not been for our efforts the place would never have been saved by those living there, even if they had been awakened in time. I never saw such an hysterical crew in my life. Everybody gave advice and nobody did anything. And the head of the servants, the old white-haired butler, continued to dodder around getting

"We stretched him out flat and undid his collar."

in everyone's way, still asking if the master had been seen yet.

However, without waiting for assistance from anyone else, the Doctor, Matthew, Bumpo, and I formed a bucket line on our own; and by it we conveyed from the kitchen sink a continuous supply of water to those burning sacks and firewood. And before very long nothing remained but a charred and hissing mass of what had promised to be a very serious conflagration.

In addition to this, Matthew discovered a tap in the garden; and with the help of a hose we got out of the stable, we brought another stream into the cellar through the broken window, which could be kept in constant readiness if the fire should break out again.

While we were attaching the hose in the garden a man suddenly appeared out of a shrubbery and accosted the Doctor in a distinctly unfriendly manner.

"Who are you?"

"I?" said the Doctor, a little taken aback. "I'm John Dolittle. Er—and you?"

"My name is Sidney Throgmorton," said the man. "And I would like to know what you mean by breaking into my lodge at this hour of night, smashing windows, and assaulting the keeper."

"Why, good gracious!" said the Doctor. "We wanted to warn you about the fire. We hadn't time to stand on ceremony. The

HUGH LOFTING

"He accosted the Doctor in a distinctly unfriendly manner."

keeper wouldn't let us in. As it was, we only just got here in time. I think I can assure you that if we *hadn't* got here, the house would have been burned to the ground."

I now saw in the gloom behind the man's shoulder that the lodge-keeper was with him.

"You have acted in a very high-handed manner, sir," said Sidney Throgmorton. "My lodge-keeper has his orders as to whom he shall, and whom he shall not, admit. And there is a fire department in the town whose business it is to look after conflagrations. For you to thrust your way into my home in this violent and unwarrantable manner, in the middle of the night, is nothing short of a scandal, sir—for which I have a good mind to have you arrested. I will ask you and your friends to leave my premises at once."

The Leather Boxes

OR A MOMENT OR TWO THE DOCTOR WAS clearly about to reply. I could see by the dim light of Matthew's lantern the anger and mortification struggling in his face. But finally he seemed to feel that to a man of this nature no words of explanation or justice would mean anything.

And certainly this Throgmorton person was an extraordinary individual. From his speech he seemed fairly well educated. But the whole of his bloated, red-faced appearance was as vulgar and as unprepossessing as it could be.

"My coat is in your cellar," said the Doctor quietly at last. "I will get it. Then we will go."

To add insult to injury, the man actually followed us down into the cellar, as though we might steal something if we were not watched. Here lamps were still burning, which we had lit to help us in making sure that there were no sparks of fire left that might smolder up again. The man muttered some expression of annoyance beneath his breath when he saw the water which flooded the floor.

At this last show of ingratitude for what we had done, Bumpo could contain his indignation no longer.

"Why, you discourteous and worm-like boot!" he began, advancing upon Throgmorton with battle in his eye.

"*Please!* Bumpo!" the Doctor interrupted. "No further words are necessary. We will go."

By the brighter light of the lamps I now saw that Throgmorton carried beneath his arm several small leather boxes. In climbing up over the woodpile, in order to see what damage we might have done on the other side, he laid these down for a moment on top of a wine cask. I was close to Matthew. In the fraction of a second while Throgmorton's back was turned, I saw the Cat's-Meat-Man open the upper one of the boxes, glance into it, and shut it again.

The box contained four enormous diamond shirt-studs.

As soon as he had his coat the Doctor wasted no further time, but made his way, with us following him, up the stairs and out of the house that he had saved from destruction.

The keeper accompanied us to the lodge and let us out. Matthew, like Bumpo, was just burning up to speak his mind even to this representative of the establishment that had shown us such discourtesy. But the Doctor seemed determined there should be no further controversy and checked him every time he tried to open his mouth.

However, at the gate we met the fire brigade coming to the rescue. This was too much for Matthew's self-control and he called to them as we stepped out onto the road:

"Oh, turn around and go back to bed! We put that fire out before you'd got your boots on."

Outside the boundaries of the Moorsden Manor estate not

HUGH LOFTING

"The box contained four enormous diamond shirt-studs."

even the Doctor could stay the tide of Matthew's and Bumpo's indignant eloquence.

"Well, of all the good-for-nothing, mangy, low-down ingrates," the Cat's-Meat-Man began, "that stuffed pillow of a millionaire takes the prize! After all we done for him! Getting up out of our beds, working like hosses—all to keep his bloomin' mansion from burning down. And then he tells us we've ruined his cellar by pouring water into it!"

"Such a creature," said Bumpo, "would make anyone feel positively rebellious. In Oxford he would not be allowed, under any circumstances, to proceed further with his obnoxious existence. It was only with the greatest difficulty that I restrained myself from hitting him on the bono publico."

"Enough," said the Doctor. "Please don't say any more. I am trying to forget it. The whole affair is just one of those incidents that it is no use thinking about or getting yourself worked up over afterward. I'm often very grateful that life has made it possible for me to keep away from my neighbors and mind my own business. This occasion couldn't be helped—but it has made me more grateful still. Thank goodness, anyway, that we got the mice out all right before the fire reached them. You have them safely in your pocket, Stubbins, have you not?"

"Yes," said I, putting my hand in to make sure. "Oh, but, Doctor, your hat? Where is it? You've left it behind."

John Dolittle raised his hand to his bare head.

"Dear me!" said he. "What a nuisance! Well, I'll have to go back, that's all."

I knew how he hated to. But the well-beloved headgear was too precious. In silence all four of us turned about.

The gate was still open from the arrival of the fire brigade. Unchallenged, we walked in and down the drive toward the house.

Halfway along the avenue the Doctor paused.

"Perhaps it would be as well," said he, "if you waited for me here. After all, there is no need for four of us to come to fetch a hat."

He went on alone while we stood in the shadow of the trees. The moon had now risen and we could see more plainly.

I noticed that Matthew was restless and fidgety. He kept muttering to himself and peering after the Doctor down the drive. Presently in a determined whisper he blurted out:

"No. I'm blessed if I let him go alone! I don't trust that Mr.

"He kept muttering to himself."

Throgmorton. Come on, you chaps. Let's follow the Doctor. Keep low, behind the trees. Don't let yourselves be seen. But I've a notion he may need us."

I had no idea what was in Matthew's mind. But from experience I knew that usually when he acted on impulse, without rhyme or reason like this, he acted rightly. I always put it down to some mysterious quality he inherited.

So, like a band of scouts, scuttling from tree to tree, we shadowed the Doctor up the avenue drive till he came to the clearing before the house. Here the fire brigade, with a great deal of bother and fuss, was in the act of departing—after its captain had made sure that the fire was really out. The big door lamps, either side of the portico, had been lighted and the courtyard was fairly well illumined. Mr. Throgmorton could be seen dismissing the firemen and their worthy captain. We saw John Dolittle go up to him, but he pretended to be too busy to attend to anything but the business of the fire brigade.

And it was only after the engine and ladder wagon had clattered noisily away, leaving the courtyard empty save for him and the Doctor, that he deigned to notice John Dolittle's presence. This time he did not wait for the Doctor to speak.

"You here again!" he shouted. "Didn't I tell you to get off the premises? Clear out of here, or I'll set the dogs on you."

"I've come back for my hat," said the Doctor, controlling himself with truly wonderful restraint. "It's in the hall."

"Get out of here!" the other repeated threateningly. "I'll have no more of you suspicious characters messing round my place tonight. I noticed you smashed the windows in the cellar as well as the lodge. Clear out, unless you want the dogs after you."

"I will not go," said the Doctor firmly, "until I have my hat."

"My goodness! But I'd love to give that fellow a crack on the jaw!" whispered Matthew, who was standing behind the same tree as myself.

The Doctor's answer seemed to infuriate Throgmorton beyond all bounds. He drew a whistle from his pocket and blew upon it loudly. An answering shout came from somewhere in the darkness of the gardens.

"Let go Dina and Wolf!" called Throgmorton.

"That's his two man-killing mastiffs," chuckled Matthew in my ear. "I know 'em—regular savages. He keeps 'em to defend the place. Now we'll see some fun."

THE TWENTY-SEVENTH CHAPTER

The Watchdogs

NEXT MOMENT WE HEARD A SCRAPING RUSH of paws upon the gravel and two gigantic dogs bounded out of the gloom into the lighted courtyard.

"Grab 'im! Go get 'im!" shouted Throgmorton.

Together the two dogs hurled themselves toward the figure of the stranger. Then Mr. Throgmorton got a great surprise. The stranger did not run or indeed show any panic whatever. But as he turned his face in the direction of the oncoming dogs he made some curious sounds, almost like another kind of growl answering theirs.

At this the two hounds behaved in a most curious manner. Instead of grasping their prey by the throat, they wagged their tails, licked his hand, and generally carried on as though he were no stranger at all but a very old and dear friend of theirs. Then, in response to an order he gave them, they disappeared into the darkness from which they had come.

Beside me, behind the tree, Matthew covered his face with his hand to keep from laughing.

"Two gigantic dogs bounded out."

"I will now get my hat," said the Doctor. And he walked calmly into the house.

As for Throgmorton, he was just speechless with rage. It had been his proud boast that these two mastiffs, Dina and Wolf, had, between them, killed a burglar who had once attempted to rob the manor. To be made ridiculous like this by such a quiet, small person was more than he could bear.

Within the hall the Doctor could now be seen on his way out—with the precious hat. Throgmorton withdrew into the shadow of a door column and waited.

"Yes, I thought so!" muttered Matthew. And he slid like a

shadow out from behind the tree and crept toward the figure of the waiting Throgmorton.

John Dolittle, unaware of anything beyond the fact that he was anxious to get away from this disagreeable establishment as soon as possible, stepped briskly forth onto the gravel. An enormous weight landed on his shoulders and bore him to the ground.

"I'll teach you," growled Throgmorton, "to walk in and out of my house as though you—"

He got no further, for Matthew had landed on top of him just as he had landed on the Doctor.

But Sidney Throgmorton, in spite of his bloated, unwholesome appearance, was a heavy, powerful man. He rose and threw Matthew off as though he were a fly. And he was just about to aim a kick at the Doctor lying on the ground when he suddenly found himself gripped from behind and lifted off his feet like a doll.

Indeed Bumpo, softly crooning his favorite African battle-song, not only lifted him, but was now proceeding to carry his portly victim bodily away toward the building.

"Well!" said the Doctor, rising and brushing off his clothes, "what an offensive person! Who would ever have thought he'd do that? The man must be out of his senses. Oh, Bumpo! Stop, stop, for heaven's sake!"

John Dolittle leapt forward—and only just in time. For the Crown Prince of the Jollinginki was apparently just on the point of knocking Mr. Throgmorton's brains out on his own doorstep.

"Well, but," said he as the Doctor grabbed him, "is he not a useless and unsightly encumbrance to the earth? Permit me, Doctor. A little tap on the geranium and all will be well."

"No, no," said the Doctor quickly. "Put him down and let us be going."

"I'll have you all in jail for this," grunted Throgmorton, as Bumpo let him fall heavily, like a large sack of potatoes, to the ground.

"If you take my tip," grinned Matthew, "you'll keep your silly mouth shut. There's three witnesses here saw you make that attack on the Doctor—slinkin' up and waitin' for him behind the doorpost. And don't forget, his honesty is as well known as yours, you know—maybe better—even if folks do call him a crank. Your money can't do everything."

"And I have witnesses too," spluttered the other, "who saw you all breaking into my lodge and using violence on the keeper."

"Yes, to save your hide and your house from burning," added Matthew. "Go on and do your worst. I dare you to take it to any court."

"Come, come!" said the Doctor, herding us away like children. "Let us be going. No more, Matthew—please! Come, Bumpo!"

And leaving the fuming, spluttering master of the manor to pick himself up from the gravel, we walked down the drive.

On the return walk all four of us were silent—also a little tired for, as Matthew had said, we had worked hard at our thankless task. And we must have been more than halfway to the house before anyone spoke. It was the Cat's-Meat-Man.

"You know," he said, breaking out suddenly, "there's something fishy about the whole thing. That's my opinion."

"How do you mean?" said the Doctor sleepily, trying to show polite interest.

"About his ingratitude," said Matthew, "his wanting to get us

"There's something fishy about the whole thing."

off the place in such a hurry and—and, well, his general manner. I don't believe he ever thought we were suspicious characters at all—maybe the lodge-keeper might have, but not the owner. Why, everyone in Puddleby knows you, Doctor—even if you don't mix in with the society tea parties and the afternoon muffin-worries. . . . And then the way things was run, up at the house, there: nobody in charge unless the 'master' is on the job. And the master wasn't. . . . Why wasn't he? What was he doing all that time while old Moses was runnin' round hollerin' for him? . . . And why—"

"Oh, Matthew," the Doctor broke in, "what's the use of guessing and speculating about it? Personally, I must confess I don't care what he was doing—or what he ever will do. Thank goodness, the whole stupid affair is over!"

But Matthew was much too wrapped up in his subject to dismiss it like that. And though he kept his voice low, as if he were talking to himself, he continued a quite audible one-man conversation for the rest of the way home.

"Yes, there's a mystery there, all right. And if anybody was to get to the bottom of it I'll bet they'd get a shock. . . . Why, even the lodge-keeper—there's another unusual thing: supposing he *was* scared by the way we woke him up, just the same, no man in his senses—orders or no orders—is going to take no notice of a fire alarm. If he didn't want to let us in, he could anyway call to his wife and send her up to the manor to find out. And then when he does follow us up to the house, and sees that there really is a fire, does he do anything to help us put it out? No, he does not. He goes and tells the precious 'master' how badly we treated him getting in to save 'em all from burning to death. And, by the way, that's still another strange thing: How did he know where to find the master? The old butler didn't know—no, nor nobody else."

The Doctor sighed gratefully as we finally reached the little gate. After this hard and trying night, the thought of a good bed was very pleasant—as was also the prospect of getting a respite from Matthew's thinking aloud.

The Scrap of Parchment

HE RESCUED MOUSE FAMILY THAT I HAD brought home in my pocket were given quarters in the club. The white mouse personally saw to it that the very best furnished suite was given to them. And, of course, they immediately became public heroes in Mouse Town. The thrilling story they had to tell of the fire; the father mouse's midnight gallop for help; their perilous rescue by John Dolittle himself; and finally the Doctor's treatment at the hands of the churlish owner of the manor, was undoubtedly the sensation of the season.

Many of the members were so infuriated over the discourtesy shown to the Doctor that they wanted to organize a campaign of revenge—which would, I believe, have utterly ruined the manor if they had been allowed to carry it out. For they planned to chew up the curtains, drill the paneling, eat holes in the tapestries, break the wine glasses, and a whole lot of other mischief that rats and mice can easily accomplish if they want to. But to their indignation, as to Matthew's, the Doctor turned a deaf ear. He wanted to forget it.

Nevertheless, in the Rat and Mouse Club Throgmorton's ingratitude and his scandalous behavior continued for a long time to be the principal topic of conversation. And any mice from the manor who dropped in of an evening were always the center of attention while they stayed, so great was the public interest in gossip from that quarter.

And it was through this that the poor Doctor, despite his earnest desire to stay out of the affairs of Sidney Throgmorton or any other neighbors, found himself finally forced by circumstances to take further part in matters that he insisted were "none of his business."

It began by the white mouse coming to me one night and saying:

"There's a mouse just run over from the manor who has lived up there for quite a while. He has something he wants to show the Doctor. But the poor man is always so busy I thought I'd speak to you first. Will you come down to the club and see him?"

"All right," I said. And I left what I was doing and went down right away.

When I got into the Assembly Room I found a whole crowd of members gathered around a mouse who seemed quite pleased with the sensation he was creating. They were all staring at a torn scrap of paper about the size of a visiting card.

"I thought this might be of importance," said the mouse to me. "Of course I can't read what it says on it. But it is made of a very unusual kind of paper. That's a subject I do know something about, paper. I wondered whether the Doctor ought to see it. Perhaps you can tell us."

I examined the slip. It was nibbled irregularly all round the edges like any piece of paper would be that had been part of a mouse's nest. But it was true: the paper itself was of a special kind.

"He seemed quite pleased with the sensation he was creating."

It was real parchment. Then I read the few words that were written in four lines across the scrap of parchment.

Well, after that I decided that the Doctor ought to see it. And without further ado I took it to him and told him so.

Matthew happened to be with him in the study at the time. And in spite of the fact that he couldn't read, he became quite interested as soon as he heard where the paper had come from.

"But what made the mouse think it would be of importance?" asked the Doctor, as he took it from me and put on his spectacles.

"On account of the nature of the paper," I said. "It's real parchment, the kind they use for special legal documents."

HUGH LOFTING

"I examined the slip."

While the Doctor was reading the few words written on the torn scrap, I watched his face carefully. And I felt sure from his expression that he guessed what I had guessed. But he evidently wasn't going to admit it. Rather hurriedly he handed it back to me.

"Yes, er—quite interesting, Stubbins," said he, turning to his work at the table. "I'm rather busy just now. You'll excuse me, won't you?"

This was his polite way of telling me to go away and not bother him. And under the circumstances I felt there wasn't anything else for me to do but go.

Matthew's interest, on the other hand, was growing rather than diminishing. And as I left the room he followed me out. "What do you make of that, Tommy?" he asked as soon as we had closed the door behind us.

"Why, between ourselves, Matthew," said I, "I think it's a will—or rather a piece of one. What's more, I believe the Doctor thinks so too. But it is quite clear that he doesn't want to have anything to do with it. And nobody can blame him, after all he had to put up with from that horrible Throgmorton."

"A will?" said Matthew. "Whose will?"

"We don't know," I said. "This is all we have, just a corner of it."

"A will, eh?" he muttered again. "I wonder where that would fit in. . . . Humph!"

"What do you mean, fit in?" I asked.

"Into the puzzle," he said, staring at the floor rapt in thought.

"I don't understand you, Matthew," said I rather impatiently. "What puzzle?"

"I'll tell you later," said he, "after I've found out a little more. But I knew I was right. There *was* a mystery in that house. Keep that piece of paper carefully."

And at that he left me, with the scrap of parchment in my hand, pondering over his words.

The Coming of Kling

FOR SEVERAL DAYS AFTER THAT I SAW NOTH-
ing of Matthew. Moreover, while I was deeply interested
in what he had said, I had very little time to think further
of his "mystery." For I was kept exceptionally busy with
my ordinary duties as assistant manager of the Dolittle Zoo, in
general—and in particular with the arrival of Kling.

Kling, who later came to be known among us as "The
Detective Dog," was such an unusual animal that I feel I ought
to devote a little space to telling how he came to join the zoo.

One day while Jip was wandering around the streets on his
own, as he often did, he came upon a mongrel terrier who was
evidently very sick. He was lying in a corner by a wall, groaning
pitifully.

"What's the matter?" said Jip, going up to him.

"I've just eaten a rat," said the dog. "And I have a dreadful
stomachache."

"My gracious!" said Jip. "Eating rats at this season! Don't you

HUGH LOFTING

"Kling"

know any better than that? You should never eat rats when there isn't an R in the month. Why, they're rank poison!"

"What's the R mean?" asked the mongrel, groaning again.

"Why, *Rats* of course," said Jip. "Come along to the Doctor at once. He'll soon give you something that will put your stomach right. What's your name?"

"Kling," said the mongrel. "Thanks, but I'm afraid I'm too ill to walk."

"All right, Kling," said Jip. "You wait here and I'll go and get the Doctor."

Jip dashed away at top speed, muttering to himself that he must speak to John Dolittle about instituting a dog ambulance for urgent cases of this kind.

When he got to the house he found that the Doctor was out. So he came to me instead. Together we hurried off at once to the rescue of the sick mongrel.

I saw right away that the patient was pretty far gone and that it would need very prompt treatment to save him. I gathered him up in my arms, sent Jip off to scour the town for the Doctor, and hurried back as fast as I could to the house.

There I found that John Dolittle had returned during my absence. I rushed the patient into the surgery, where the Doctor immediately examined him.

"It's a case of poisoning," he said. "Very likely the rat you ate had been poisoned. But we can fix you up all right. You had better stay here for a few days. You can sleep in the parlor—where I'll be able to keep an eye on you. Here, drink this. Now, Stubbins, carry him in to the sofa and put some blankets over him. He has a temperature and mustn't get chilled. Tell me, Kling, how did you come to eat a rat, anyway?"

"I was starving," said the mongrel rather shamefacedly. "Hadn't had a meal in two days."

"Well, next time," said the Doctor, "come round to our zoo— The Home for Crossbred Dogs, you know. You can always get a meal there. But please, *don't* eat rats."

Quite early the following morning I heard a most extraordinary noise in the Doctor's bedroom. It sounded as though he were moving every piece of furniture from its usual position and generally turning the place upside down. I was about to go up to see what was the matter, when he opened his door and called to me.

"Oh, Stubbins, have you seen anything of a boot of mine? I can't find it anywhere—the left one."

"No, Doctor," I said, "I haven't."

"It's most peculiar," said he. "I could have sworn I left it—both of them—beside the bed last night, just where I always take them off."

My own first duty that morning was of course to see how the new patient, Kling, was getting on. And as soon as I got downstairs I went straight to the parlor. Imagine my astonishment to find the sofa empty and the patient gone!

Utterly puzzled, I wandered out through the French window into the garden. And there, in the middle of the lawn, I found not only Kling, but the Doctor's boot as well—which the new patient was thoughtfully chewing. As I ran to him, the Doctor also arrived, with his remaining boot on one foot and a bright red slipper on the other.

"Good gracious!" said John Dolittle. "You made a quick recovery, Kling. I didn't give you permission to get up yet. What are you doing with my boot?"

There was really no need to ask. Even before the Doctor stooped and picked it up, anyone could see that the dog had chewed a large hole in the side.

"Dear me!" said John Dolittle. "Just look at that! Now what will I do?"

"Oh, did you want those boots?" said Kling apologetically. "I'm dreadfully sorry, Doctor. I thought they were an old pair you had thrown away."

"Oh no," said the Doctor. "They're my best boots—my only boots, in fact. Listen, Stubbins: after breakfast would you mind running down with this to your father? Give him my compliments and ask him if he would be good enough to patch it while you wait. I've got to go up to town tonight to address a meeting of the Zoological Society, and I can't very well go in red slippers. . . . But tell me, Kling: How comes it that you still chew boots? You're no longer a puppy, you know."

"No," said Kling, "that's true. But I've never got out of the habit since my childhood days. It is strange, I know. My mother always said it meant I was a genius; but my father said it was clearly a sign I was just a plain fool and would never grow up."

"Well, Kling," said the Doctor, "I suppose I'll have to get you a pair of shoes of your own to chew. I can't let you have mine, you know. Er—would you prefer brown or black?"

"Brown, please," said Kling. "They usually taste better. And would you mind if I had them buttoned instead of laced. I find chewing the buttons off almost the best part—very soothing."

"Certainly," said the Doctor. "But we may find it hard to get brown buttoned boots in Puddleby. It's not a very up-to-date shopping center, you understand. Perhaps you had better come with me. It's no use my buying you a pair of shoes that doesn't suit you. And I doubt if they will change them after you've tried them on—on your teeth, I mean."

So that was how John Dolittle added yet another story to his reputation in the neighborhood for eccentricity and craziness. After breakfast, while I took his damaged boot to my father's to be repaired, he took the mongrel Kling to the largest shoe shop in the town to buy him a pair of boots. The salesman was somewhat slow in getting it through his head that the customer (who was wearing slippers) wanted the shoes for the dog and not for himself. And for a whole week afterward he entertained the neighboring shopkeepers by telling them how the Doctor had requested that all the brown buttoned boots in the shop be set out in a row on the floor; and how this ill-conditioned, half-bred dog had then, at the Doctor's invitation, gone down the line and made his selection.

Kling himself insisted that his rapid recovery from the severe attack of ptomaine poisoning was largely aided by the soothing effect of chewing brown shoe leather. And certainly by that evening he seemed entirely himself and was frisking round the garden as lively as a puppy.

"Chewing a new pair of boots always makes me feel young again," said he, leaping over the flower beds.

The whole of the Doctor's household as well as all the members of the Home for Crossbred Dogs and the Dolittle Zoo took to Kling at once. And both the Doctor and I agreed that we had never met a more interesting personality in a dog—in spite of his juvenile fondness for boots. He was a good example of that rule which John Dolittle had more than once maintained: that the mongrels often have more character than the purebreds. And it was, I think, greatly to the credit of our whole establishment that none of the other animals (not even Toby, the privileged) showed the least jealousy over the great popularity that Kling enjoyed from the first day of his joining the zoo.

The Mystery of Moorsden Manor

O F COURSE IT WAS NOT LONG AFTER I HAD taken the scrap of torn parchment to John Dolittle that the white mouse came to me demanding to know what the Doctor had said about it. I had to disappoint him terribly by telling him that he had refused to show any interest in it whatever.

Jip was in my room at the time that the white mouse called. He had never quite forgiven me for having him sent back home the night of the fire—especially after he had learned later that there had been a fight and that his beloved Doctor had been treated discourteously by Throgmorton.

It was after supper, about half past eight. And while the white mouse and I were talking, the Cat's-Meat-Man also dropped in. I had not seen him in several days.

"Well, Matthew," I said, "how are you getting on with your mystery?"

"Humph!" he muttered, sinking into an armchair. "It's still a mystery, all right."

Jip cocked up his ears at that and wanted to know what we were talking about. I explained to him, in dog language, that Matthew Mugg was sure from certain things he had observed that night at the manor that there was some mystery connected with the house and its owner.

"Tommy," said Matthew, "I can't get much further until we find the rest of that will."

"I'm afraid that may be hard," said I, "from what enquiries I've made."

"Listen," the white mouse whispered to me, "I can get that mouse from the manor for you any time you want."

"All right," I said. "Send for him, will you, please? There's always a chance that he may have found out something since."

Thereupon the white mouse disappeared and Matthew and I went on with our conversation.

But it could not have been more than a quarter of an hour before the white mouse was back at my elbow again. And with him he had the mouse who had brought us the scrap of parchment.

"Tell me," I said to the Manor Mouse, "did you ever find out anything more about the rest of that paper?"

"As it happens," said he, "I did—tonight. The scrap, as I told you, had been in a mouse nest—an old one that I had discovered by accident and taken to pieces. You see, I was going to rebuild it into a new one for myself. Well, this evening I met the owner of that old nest."

"Ah!" I said. "That sounds like news. And what did he tell you?"

"Well," said the Manor Mouse, "the reason I hadn't met him before—as you know, I had made enquiries of all the rats and mice in the mansion—was that he had moved out of the house to a sort of potting-shed place in the garden. I happened to go out there looking for last year's chestnuts, and that's how I ran into him. He's very, very old—quite feeble, in fact. But he had lived longer in the manor than any of us."

"Yes," I said, "but get on to the business of the parchment. What did he tell you about that?"

"It seems that it was in the days of this Mr. Throgmorton's father when, he told me, he had lived in the old man's study on the first floor. He was building a nest for himself and his wife, and he made it behind the paneling—between the paneling and the wall. Nesting materials were hard to find. And he got into old Mr. Throgmorton's desk—by drilling a hole through the back—and went through all the drawers looking for stuff he could use to make a nest of. Papers and red tape were about all he could find. And among the papers he chewed corners off, there was this large sheet that the old man kept locked up in the top drawer. My friend used it for a foundation for his nest because he saw it was nice and thick and would keep the drafts out. It seems the old man considered the paper important; because when, a few days later, he opened the drawer and found the corner chewed off, he swore and carried on something dreadful. This mouse was watching from behind the clock on the mantelpiece and he says he never saw anyone get so angry. The old man saw right away that it was the work of mice, from the way in which the paper was nibbled. He hunted high and low for that missing corner—turned all the furniture in the whole room inside out. But of course he didn't find it because it was behind the paneling in my friend's nest. At last he gave it up and took the larger piece of the parchment away and hid it somewhere else."

"Where?" I asked, rising half out of my chair.

"The old mouse said he didn't know. But wherever it was, it wasn't in the study."

I sank back disappointed.

"Do you think," I asked, "that if all the mice in the house went to work on it they could find it for us?"

The Manor Mouse shook his head.

"As a matter of fact," said he, "we have tried. As soon as we learned from the gossip at the club that you were interested in the paper, we began a search on our own. But no trace of it could we find."

I translated for Matthew's benefit what the Manor Mouse had said, and his disappointment was even greater than mine.

"But tell me, Matthew," I said, "didn't you succeed in finding anything out yourself? When last I saw you, you were going to do some investigating on your own account."

"It wasn't so easy," said he, "for this reason: when the old man died and this Mr. Throgmorton came into the property, all the servants were changed. That's suspicious in itself of course. So trying to find out much about the family from gossip and hearsay was kind of hard. I learned some things, but nothing that seemed to help solve the problem."

At this point Jip came up to my chair and nudged my knee beneath the table.

"Tommy," said he, "for solving problems, the best hands I know are Cheapside and Kling."

"Humph!" I muttered. "Cheapside I could understand, because he is in touch with the gossip of the street sparrows. But why Kling? Why should he be good at solving problems?"

"Why, my gracious!" said Jip. "He knows an awful lot about

crime and the—er—underworld and all that. He belonged to a thief once."

"To a thief!" I cried.

"Yes. You ought to get him some time to tell you the story of his life. You never heard anything so thrilling. When he was quite a puppy he was stolen by a sort of tramp person who specially trained him in all sorts of strange dodges. This tramp used to walk through the streets with Kling on a string. And to anybody passing who looked well-off, he'd say, 'Do you want to buy a dog?' And they would usually say yes in the end, because Kling had been taught all manner of cunning tricks to fascinate them with. Then Kling, after he'd been sold, would run away from the new owner and come back to the tramp. He was trained to do that too, you see. And then the tramp would take him away to a new town and sell him all over again. Kling says that man once sold him twelve times in one month. But later the tramp invented another way to make money even faster. He trained Kling to learn the geography of the new houses he went to, and especially where the silver and valuables were kept. And the tramp would come later and rob the house, Kling acting as guide for him and showing him over the place. Then together they would go off again to a new town."

"Goodness me!" I said. "What an awful record!"

"Yes," said Jip. "But Kling had no idea he was doing wrong until one day he got talking about his adventures to a parson's dog who was highly scandalized and persuaded him to give up the life of crime. So Kling, in spite of the fact that the tramp had always treated him kindly, ran away the first chance he got and never went back to him again.

"Oh my, yes, Kling's awfully well up on crime. You see, in his life with the tramp he fell in with many odd birds, regular gangs of crooks, you know. And in that way he learned a lot about the tricks and dodges of different kinds of criminals. And then later he got a job as a police dog in Belgium and he was used to hunt down lawbreakers. Why, in Brussels, I understand, he was known as 'The Dog Detective.' Had no end of a reputation. But he didn't care for that work and after a year or so he ran away again. Then for a while he was a tramp himself—a dog tramp—said he wanted to see the world. He's had a wonderful career. And you'd never think it—unassuming and quiet, the way he is. On first meeting him one might almost think he was stupid, dragging that chewed-up shoe of his around. But I feel sure that if you and Matthew have a problem you want to solve, you couldn't do better than consult Kling."

"Yes, I believe you're right, Jip," I said. "Go and ask him if he'll come and talk to us, will you? Don't say anything about it to the other members of the Home for Crossbred Dogs. You know how enthusiastic they get. But if you happen to see Cheapside in the garden, ask him to drop in too, will you?"

While Jip was gone I explained to Matthew roughly what it was we proposed to do. Kling hadn't met Matthew yet, having arrived during the few days while the Cat's-Meat-Man had been off "investigating," as he called it.

But when, followed by Jip, the Detective Dog strolled into the room carrying one of his new chewing-boots, I thought I saw Matthew start almost uneasily. Kling, too, behaved in a rather odd manner. He stared hard at Matthew a moment through half-closed lids, as though he were trying to remember something. Then with a shake of his shoulders he settled down on the floor and began turning his boot over between his paws to find a good place to chew. Jip shot a glance at me that spoke volumes.

Knowing that Matthew didn't understand dog talk, I began by asking Kling if he had ever seen him before.

The mongrel thoughtfully pulled a button off his boot before answering.

"Oh well," he said, "what does it matter? He's a friend of yours—and the Doctor's. I've met an awful lot of people, you know. After all, a man's past is his own. I believe in letting bygones be bygones. . . . Jip tells me you have something you wanted to see me about."

"Yes," I said. "We have a problem—a sort of a mystery. Ah! Here's Cheapside too. Good! We'll be glad to have his opinion as well."

The Dog Detective

THEN FROM BEGINNING TO END, LEAVING out nothing that I thought might be helpful, I told Kling the story of our midnight summons to the fire at Moorsden Manor and all that followed it.

Jip was right when he said that anyone might at first sight think that Kling was stupid. While I talked he went on chewing his boot as though his whole attention was absorbed in that and not in what I was saying. But I soon found out that he had not only heard what I had said but that he remembered it, every word.

"Well," he began when I was done, "in a case like this the first thing I would do is to build up a story. By that I mean you lay the mystery out—you solve it before you begin, by guesswork, in other words. Then you go to work and see if you are right or not. Tell me: When you finally found Mr. Throgmorton—or rather when he found you—had he anything with him?"

"Yes," I said, "some small leather boxes."

"Did you by any chance find out what they contained?"

"Yes," I said again. "Matthew opened one when Throgmorton wasn't looking. It had four large diamond studs in it."

Kling nodded thoughtfully.

"And these two ferocious watchdogs," he went on presently, "weren't they usually kept *in*side the house? Perhaps Matthew knows."

I questioned the Cat's-Meat-Man.

"Yes," said he. "And that's still another thing I hadn't thought of before. The dogs were always brought into the house after dark and left loose to roam where they would. When they killed that burglar, they caught him just as he was opening the silver drawer in the butler's pantry. I heard that from one of the gardeners. Yes, it was strange that that night Dina and Wolf were not inside the house at all. They were being kept by someone. It seemed as though they came from the stable."

I interpreted to Kling. And he nodded again as though it all fitted in with his picture.

"Well then," he said after a moment's thought, "let us begin and build. Perhaps for the benefit of Matthew you had better explain to him once in a while what I am saying, so we can see whether he agrees with it or not. We will start off by supposing that since Mr. Throgmorton was so annoyed with you—you who came to put the fire out—*that he lighted it himself.*"

I jumped slightly. It was such a startling idea.

"Just a minute, Kling," I said. "I'll put that to Matthew."

The Cat's-Meat-Man, when I told him, also jumped.

"Why, that's a notion!" said he. "A notion and a half, by Jiminy. And yet it fits in with some things, all right. I'd been think-ing all the time that he was trying to get us off the place because he was doing something up there he hadn't oughter. I never thought of his setting fire to his own mansion—must be worth thousands and thousands of pounds, that place, with all the stuff in it. And then he kicked because we'd broken the windows. That don't sound as though he didn't care about the house.... Just the same, it's an idea worth followin' up. Tell the dog to go on."

"You see," Kling continued, "the fact that Sidney Throgmorton had his jewelry with him, also that this was the only night that the dogs were not kept in the house, makes it look as though he expected the fire anyway."

"Yes," I said, "that's so. But his loss would have been enormous just the same."

"Wait," said Kling. "Maybe we'll find that his loss would have been still more enormous if he didn't have the fire.... Well, to proceed: Now having supposed that Throgmorton set fire to his own house—it has been done before—I've known cases myself—the next question is: What did he want to burn it down for? He wanted to get rid of something, we'll say. What did he want to get rid of? Had he any people in it he wanted to kill?"

I questioned Matthew. The answer was: None that he knew of.

"Any brothers or sisters?" asked Kling.

"None," said Matthew. "That I know for sure."

"Very well," Kling went on, "then he wanted to destroy some *thing*, since people are out of the question. Why didn't he find the thing and get rid of it, instead of burning down a valuable house? Because he had tried and couldn't find it? Possibly. And almost certainly, if it was—"

"A will?" I broke in.

"Exactly," said Kling, nodding. "Yet why destroy a will? Because in it he knew, or guessed, that his father had left the property, not to him, the son, but to some other parties. If there was no will, he would get all the property because he was the only child. So, guessing there had been a will made; almost certain it was in that house; unable to find it himself but terrified that someone else might— don't forget that he got rid of all the old servants and bought two ferocious watchdogs to keep people out—finally he determines to burn the whole place up and the will with it. What does that loss matter when he had a dozen other houses and estates—which he never visited, fearing to leave the manor lest someone find the will while he is gone?"

THE THIRTY-SECOND CHAPTER

Old Mr. Throgmorton

I

T FITS, IT FITS!" CRIED MATTHEW, JUMPING UP IN his excitement when I had explained what Kling had said. "The gardener told me the father and son could never get along together. And that's why Sidney Throgmorton stayed abroad most of the time till after the old man died. And the father didn't want it known that they couldn't agree, see? So of course he would keep the will dark. It all fits like a glove. The dog's a wizard. But listen: we ought to do something quick. That man is liable to try and burn the house down again any minute."

One would have thought to hear the Cat's-Meat-Man talk that it was he who would lose most by the will's destruction. And I must confess that the fascination of the mystery and the desire to frustrate the iniquitous Sidney Throgmorton had me too in its grip by this time.

"Oh, I don't think he'll make another attempt in a hurry," I said. "It would look fishy. After all, he has got to be careful, you see. If he knows there was a will, then what he tried to do was a criminal offense—goodness, I don't wonder he was mad with us!"

"The next step for you, I should say," Kling went on, "is to try and find out to whom the old Throgmorton would have been most likely to leave his money."

At that, Cheapside, whom in our interest we had forgotten all about, hopped onto the table and started talking.

"Folks," said he, "I think I can help you there, maybe. I saw a good deal of the old Mr. Throgmorton, and a mighty fine gentleman he was. It wasn't at Moorsden Manor that I saw him, because he only spent a week or two out of every year here. But to one of his other places, Bencote Castle, down in Sussex, I used to go regular, at one time, in the early autumn. The old man, as maybe you know, retired from business when he was getting on in years. And 'e spent 'is old age, pleasant like, raisin' prize stock, cows, sheep, and horses—specially heavy draft horses. He was good to animals all round, was old Jonathan T. Throgmorton. He had bird fountains put out in all his gardens, nesting boxes in the trees and everything. And he gave one of his footmen the special job of throwing out crumbs every morning for the sparrows and wild birds. Some days, when the old man was well enough, he used to do it himself. That's how I came to know him. Besides all that, he did a whole lot toward making life easier for work animals—paid to have drinking troughs put up for horses, and kept extra help-teams, at his own expense, on all the bad hills in more than one town where he had homes. He was a friend to animals and a fine old gent, if ever there was one. I wouldn't wonder, Tommy, if he left part of this fortune to the same cause, the happiness of animals."

Before Cheapside had quite finished speaking, I got out my

pocket-book in which I had carefully preserved the scrap of parchment. I spread the fragment out and reread the few words that had been nibbled from the will. They were in four lines. The first line ran: *"trustees who shall have—."* The second line, beginning a new paragraph, was: *"I bequeath—."* The third: *"by said party or parties—."* And the last: *"an Association for pre—"*

To everyone's astonishment I suddenly sprang up and said:

"Let's all go and see the Doctor—just as quickly as we possibly can."

The Manor Mouse excused himself, saying that he ought to be getting back home as it was late and his wife might be anxious. As we left the room the white mouse told me he would accompany his friend as far as the gate and would rejoin me in a minute or two. Together the rest of us—Matthew, Jip, Kling, Cheapside, and I— proceeded at once to the study, where we found John Dolittle, as usual, at work on his books.

"Doctor," I cried, bursting in, "I'm dreadfully sorry to interrupt you, but I really feel you ought to hear this."

With a patient sigh he laid down his pen as I poured forth my tale.

"Now don't you see, Doctor," I ended, showing him the scrap of parchment again, "it is practically certain that when this piece is joined to the rest that last line will read, *'an Association for the Prevention of Cruelty to Animals,'* or some such title. For that is the cause in which this man had already spent great sums of money while he was alive. And that is the cause which the wretched son Sidney Throgmorton has robbed of probably a large fortune. Doctor, it is the *animals* who have been cheated."

We all watched the Doctor's face eagerly as he pondered

for a silent moment over my somewhat dramatic harangue. At length I thought I saw from his expression signs of sympathy, if not agreement.

"But, Stubbins," said he quietly, "aren't you basing most of this on guesswork, conjecture—though I admit it sounds plausible enough. Tell me: What do you want me to do?"

"Doctor," I said, "we've got to get that will."

"Yes, yes, I quite see that," said he. "But how? Even if we got into the house—risking arrest for burglary and all that—what chance would we stand of finding it, if Sidney Throgmorton, living there all the time and hunting for it ever since his father's death, couldn't find it?"

I saw at once that he was right. The difficulties of the task I proposed were enormous. But while I stood there silent, discouraged and perplexed, I suddenly heard the white mouse out in the passage squeaking at the top of his voice:

"Tommy, Tommy! They've found it. They've found it! The mice have found the will."

The Secret Cupboard

THE WHITE MOUSE WAS SO BREATHLESS WITH running when he appeared at the study door that he could hardly talk. I lifted him to the table, where between puffs he finally managed to give us his message.

Apparently, just as he was seeing the Manor Mouse off at the gate, a rat had run up and said that they had at last located the document. The old man had hidden it, it seemed, in a secret cupboard on the top floor of the house. They couldn't get the will out because it was a large, heavy roll of parchment; and the hole that they had made into the cupboard (through the brickwork at the back) was very, very small. Indeed, it was so tiny that the two rats who had made it couldn't get through it. But they could see that there were papers of some sort inside. So they had gotten the very smallest mouse in the manor and sent him in to make an examination and give them a report. And they were now quite certain that the document was the will, because it was made of the same kind of parchment and had a corner missing corresponding with the one in my possession.

Well, as you can imagine, the excitement among us was tremendous. And when, a moment later, the rat in question himself appeared, confirmed the story, and offered to lead the Doctor at once to the secret cupboard, I could see that the thrill of the Moorsden Manor Mystery was beginning at last to take hold of John Dolittle himself. Matthew was all for starting right away.

"No, now wait a minute," said the Doctor. "Not so fast. This is a serious thing. If we should be wrong and get caught we will have hard work to explain our actions—especially with Sidney Throgmorton anxious to put us all in jail anyway. We must proceed carefully and make as few mistakes as possible. Let me see: What time is it? Eleven forty-five. We couldn't attempt it before two o'clock in the morning anyhow. We must be sure everyone's abed first. Listen, Jip: You run over there to the manor and tell—by the way, could you get into the grounds, do you think?"

"Oh yes," said Jip. "I can slip through the bars of that big gate easily."

"Well," said the Doctor, "don't be seen, for heaven's sake. They might shoot you. Then just nose quietly round the house till you get a chance to speak to those two watchdogs, Dina and Wolf. Tell them to expect me about two o'clock. Goodness knows how I'm going to get into the house. That I'll have to find out when I get there. Anyway, tell them not to be worried or give any alarm if they hear latches being forced or anything like that. Do you understand?"

"All right," said Jip. And he hopped through the open window into the darkness of the garden and was gone.

"Now the next thing," said the Doctor, "we'll need a rope. See if you can find my alpine rope up in the attic, Stubbins, will you, please?"

"Shall we be taking Bumpo along, Doctor?" asked Matthew. "Better, don't you think? He's a handy man in a tight place."

"Er—yes, I suppose so," said John Dolittle. "Though the trouble with Bumpo is that he is sometimes a trifle too handy."

"Then I'll go and start getting him woke up," said the Cat's-Meat-Man. "It's a long job as a rule."

Well, although we had two and a quarter hours in which to make our preparations, it did not seem any too long. One after another the Doctor, Matthew, Kling, Cheapside, the white mouse, and I would keep thinking of things we ought to take, or do, to insure success to the expedition. And when John Dolittle finally looked at his watch and said that we ought to be starting, it did not seem as though more than a few minutes had elapsed since he had made up his mind to embark upon the venture.

Fortunately there would be no moon till somewhere about three o'clock in the morning. So, to begin with anyhow, we had the protection of pretty complete darkness.

In spite of the fact that I shared Polynesia's confidence in the Doctor's luck and success, I must confess I felt quite thrilled by the risks ahead of us as we quietly opened the gate and trailed down to the road.

The Doctor and Matthew had worked out most of the details of our campaign before we left and had assigned to each of us what parts we were to play. So there was no talking as we plodded silently along the road toward the manor.

At a point where the limb of a large ash tree overhung the high wall of the estate we halted and the Doctor uncoiled his rope. With the aid of a stone tied to a long length of twine, we got the rope's end hauled up over the branch and down to the road again. Up this we all swarmed in turn. Meanwhile Cheapside kept watch in the branches above to see that no one surprised us on the manor side, and Kling below kept an eye open for late wayfarers that might pass along the road.

When all of us were inside the grounds and the rope hauled over after us, Kling went off to enter, like Jip, through the bars of the gate.

When I got down out of the tree the first thing I noticed was Jip's white shadow flitting across the sward to meet us.

"It's all right," he whispered to the Doctor. "I've told Dina and Wolf. They say they will be on the lookout for you and will show you round the place when you get in."

"Yes, but it is the getting in that is going to be the job, I'm afraid," muttered John Dolittle. "Listen, Jip: from here I've no idea of even where the house lies—through all this shrubbery and park land. Lead us to it, will you? And bring us up on the wooded side. We don't want to cross any open spaces."

"Very good," said Jip. "I'll take you to the kitchen-garden side. You'll have cover all the way up. But if you should get spotted and have to run for it, tell everyone to follow me. I know the easiest and shortest way out."

Then in single file we trailed after Jip, who kept us behind bushes and hedges for what seemed like a good ten minutes' walk. Suddenly we found ourselves against the wall of the house itself. Here I noticed for the first time that Kling had rejoined us.

"Listen," I heard him whisper to the Doctor, "you've got that rat in your pocket still, haven't you?—the one who lives here."

"Yes," said John Dolittle. "And the white mouse too."

"Well, that rat is your best chance for getting in," said Kling.

"If you let Matthew force a lock you're liable to have complications with the police afterward. Send the rat into the house through a hole—he'll know lots of them leading down into the cellar. And tell him to get you the master's latch key. It'll be in his bedroom, on the dressing table, you may be sure."

"Splendid!" whispered the Doctor. And he at once took the rat from his pocket and explained to him what Kling had said. Then he let him go upon the ground and we waited.

It was about five minutes later, I should say, when I felt something small and sharp hit me on the head. Even through my cap it stung. From my head it bounced to the ground. And by the dim starlight I could see it shining dully where it lay. I picked it up. It was a small key. Apparently the master's bedroom window was directly above our heads; and the rat, to save time, had thrown the key out to us.

I slipped it into the Doctor's hand and in silence we moved round toward the front of the house.

The Wild Ride of the White Mouse

I T HAD BEEN AGREED THAT ONLY MATTHEW should accompany the Doctor to the top floor. I was to remain downstairs in the hall; and Bumpo was to stay outside the house. His and my parts in the plot were mostly those of watching and standing on guard. In case of emergency we had signals arranged and were to assemble at a certain point.

As the Doctor very, very quietly opened the front door with the latch key, I got my first real scare of the evening. With uncanny suddenness, both together, the two great ferocious heads of the watchdogs popped out to greet him.

Within the hall where the darkness was quite intense, I confess that I was quite glad that my duties carried me no further. As we had arranged, I sat down on the floor by the front door and began my watch. Jip, thank goodness, stayed with me. Matthew and the Doctor, each with a hand on the collar of one of the guiding watchdogs, were led away swiftly and silently through the inky blackness, up the carpeted stairs, to the rooms above.

It seemed a perfect eternity that they were gone. Before the evening was over I decided that I didn't care for the profession of burglary a bit. It was a little too thrilling. Every time the breeze rattled a window or swung a curtain whispering across the floor, I was certain that we had been discovered and someone was coming after us with a pistol or a club. It was a great temptation to open the front door and let in the little light of the starry sky without. But I had been told to keep it closed lest the draft be detected by any of the household.

At last Jip whispered:

"Don't get scared now if someone bumps into you. They're coming down the stairs again. I can smell 'em."

A moment later the wet muzzle of Dina, leading the Doctor across the hall, dabbed me in the ear. It was a good thing Jip had warned me—I would probably have started hitting out in all directions if he hadn't. I rose and carefully swung open the front door. The dim forms of the Doctor and Matthew passed out. I followed. With a pat of thanks, John Dolittle turned and shut the two dogs in behind us, letting the tongue of the night-latch gently into its socket with the key. Then he took the rat from his pocket, gave him the key, and set him on the ground. From somewhere out of the general gloom of the garden Bumpo's huge figure emerged and joined us.

Once more under Jip's guidance we began the journey across the park toward the walls. I was simply burning up to ask the Doctor if he had succeeded, but I managed to restrain my curiosity till we stood again beneath the ash tree. Then at last I felt it was safe to whisper:

"Did you get it?"

"Yes," he said. "It's in my pocket. Everything went all right.

We were able to open the cupboard and close it again too, leaving it so no one would know we were there. But of course I haven't had a chance to read the will yet. Come along now, where's that rope?"

Again, one by one, we swarmed to the top of the wall, transferred the dangling rope to the other side, and slid quietly down onto the roadway.

With a general sigh we set off toward home. As we passed the gate we noticed the gray of the dawn showing in the east. Like silent ghosts Kling and Jip slipped out through the bars and dropped in behind the procession.

On reaching the house we all hurried to the study. I got some candles lighted while the Doctor spread the will out on the table. It was a tense moment for all of us as we leaned over his shoulder.

Sure enough, a piece had been bitten out of the document at the corner. And when I added the fragment I had in my pocket it fitted perfectly. Then, without going through the preliminary preamble of the document, the Doctor traced that paragraph with his finger. This is what he read out: "I bequeath the sum of One Hundred Thousand Pounds for the endowment of an Association for the Prevention of Cruelty to Animals. The Trustees will select—"

But he was not permitted to get any further. Matthew, Bumpo, and I suddenly started cheering and dancing round the table. And it was quite some minutes before our enthusiasm had let off enough steam to allow us to listen to any more.

As we settled down into our chairs again I noticed the Doctor staring fixedly at something Matthew was turning over in his fingers. I started as I saw what it was—one of the diamond shirt-studs from Sidney Throgmorton's little leather box.

"Er—where—did you get that, Matthew?" asked the Doctor in a low, somewhat fearful, voice.

"Oh, this?" said the Cat's-Meat-Man, trying hard not to look guilty. "This is a little souvenir I brought along from the manor."

For a moment the Doctor seemed too horrified to speak.

"Well," Matthew went on, "it wasn't his, you know, after all, with him robbin' the animals of that whole fortune what was coming to them accordin' to the will."

"But when, how, did you take it, Matthew?" asked the Doctor. "I thought you were with me all the time."

"Oh, I just dropped into his bedroom to take a look around, as we passed his door going up the stairs," said Matthew. "These pretty playthings was in a box on the dressin' table, and I couldn't resist the temptation of bringin' one along as a souvenir."

With his hand to his head the Doctor sank into a chair as if stunned.

"Oh, Matthew, Matthew!" he murmured. "I thought you had promised me to give up that—that sort of thing for good."

For a moment we were all silent. Finally the Doctor said:

"Well, I don't know what we are to do now, really I don't."

The white mouse crawled up my sleeve from the table and whispered in my ear:

"What's the matter with the Doctor? What has happened?"

I explained to him as quickly and as briefly as I could.

"Give me that stud, Doctor," said he, suddenly darting across the table to John Dolittle. "I'll get it back into its box before you can say Jack Robinson."

"Goodness! Do you think you could?" cried the Doctor, immediately all cheered up. "Oh, but look: the daylight is here now.

The disappearance of the diamond is most likely already discovered. And think of the time it would take you to travel there—at your pace!"

"Doctor, it wouldn't take long if he rode on my back," Jip put in. "If I carry him as far as the house, he can soon pop in through a hole and slip upstairs. It's worth trying."

"All right," said the Doctor. "Any port in a storm."

And to Matthew's great disappointment, he leaned across the table, took the valuable jewel out of his hands, and gave it to the white mouse.

"You'll save us from a terrible mess," he said, "if you can get it there in time. Good luck to you!"

The white mouse took the stud in his paws, jumped onto Jip's back, and disappeared through the garden window at a gallop.

After he had gone there was an embarrassed, uncomfortable pause. Finally the Doctor said:

"Er—Stubbins and Bumpo: you will not of course—supposing that this matter ends satisfactorily—mention it, ever, to a living soul."

Ill at ease, but very much in earnest, we nodded our promise of silence.

"As for you, Matthew," the Doctor went on, "I must warn you now, once and for all, that if any other occurrence of, er—this sort takes place we shall have to sever relations permanently. I know I can trust you where my own property is concerned, but I must feel secure that you will regard the property of others in the same way. If not, we can have nothing further to do with one another. Do you understand?"

"Yes, I understand, Doctor," said Matthew in a low voice. "I ought to have known I might be putting you in an awkward situation. But—well, no more need be said."

The Doctor turned as though to go into the garden. He looked about him for his hat. And suddenly a look of horror came slowly into his face.

"Stubbins!" he gasped. "Where is it?"

"Don't tell me," I cried, "that you left it again—*in the manor!*"

Our Arrest

IT WAS TRUE. IN THE THRILL AND EXCITEMENT OF our nocturnal adventure none of us had noticed whether the Doctor had come away from the manor bareheaded or with his hat on. But now that we came to think of it we could all recall that he had worn it on the way there. Next, he himself remembered clearly that in getting into the secret cupboard he had laid it aside on a chair because it was in the way.

"Dear me!" he sighed, shaking his head. "That's the kind of a burglar *I* am—leave my hat behind me, the one thing that everybody in the neighborhood would recognize as mine. . . . Hah! It would be funny if it wasn't so serious. Well, more than ever depends on the white mouse now. Dear, dear! Anyhow," he added as Dab-Dab appeared at the door, "let's not meet our troubles halfway. Breakfast ready, Dab-Dab?"

"No," said the housekeeper, coming forward into the room and lowering her voice. "But there are three men walking up the garden path. One is carrying your hat. And one is a policeman."

At that Matthew sprang up and in a twinkling was half out of the garden window. Then, apparently changing his mind, he stopped.

"No, Doctor," said he, coming back into the room, "I ain't goin' to skedaddle and leave you to face the music. I bin in jail before. I'll tell 'em I done it."

"Look here, Matthew," said John Dolittle firmly. "I want you to do one thing only throughout the rest of this business, and that is keep your mouth closed tight—unless I ask you to talk. Stubbins, will you please let them in?"

I went and opened the door. I knew all three men by sight. One was Sidney Throgmorton; the other his lodge-keeper; and the third our local police sergeant. The sergeant's manner was distinctly apologetic. He knew John Dolittle, and this duty was distasteful to him. Throgmorton's behavior, on the other hand, was offensive from the start. He brushed by me before I had invited him to come in and walked straight to the Doctor's study.

"Ah!" he cried. "We have the whole lot here, sergeant—the same party exactly that came pretending to put the fire out when they wanted to learn their way around the house they meant later to rob. Put them all under arrest and bring them at once to the manor."

The sergeant, while he was somewhat impressed by Throgmorton's position in the community, knew what his duties were without being told. He addressed himself to John Dolittle.

"This gentleman has brought a charge, Doctor," he said. "A valuable diamond was stolen from his house last night and your hat was found on the premises this morning. I shall have to ask you to come up to the manor, please."

We were all glad that the early hour gave us practically empty streets to walk through. For certainly our party with the sergeant for escort would have set gossip running all over Puddleby if there had been many abroad to see us.

Hardly a word was said the whole way by anyone except Throgmorton, to whose indignant fumings no one seemed to want to make any reply.

At the house the old manservant let us in and we went straight upstairs to the master's bedroom. Here Throgmorton at once plunged into a dramatic recital, for the sergeant's benefit, of how he had arisen at his usual hour of six and had at once noticed that his stud box had been moved from the place where he had left it the night before. He opened it, he said, and found one stud missing. After the servants had been summoned and a search made of the house, the Doctor's hat had been found in a room on the top floor. This, and the fact that we had all behaved in a suspicious manner the night of the fire, at once convicted us in his minds as the culprits.

"Just a minute," said the Doctor. "Is the box now in the exact place where you found it when you got up?"

"Yes," said Throgmorton.

"Well, would you show us, please, just how you went to the dressing table and opened it?"

"Certainly," said Throgmorton. "I walked from the bed, like this, and first threw back the curtains of the window, so. Then one glance at the dressing table told me something was wrong. I stepped up to it—so—lifted the box and opened it. Like this. . . . What the—!"

At that last exclamation of astonishment we all three breathed a secret sigh of relief. For it told us that the white mouse had done his work. I shall never forget Throgmorton's face as he stood there, staring into the box he had taken up to demonstrate with. In it there were not three studs as he had expected, but the complete set of four.

The sergeant looked over his shoulder.

"There's been some mistake, sir, hasn't there?" he said quietly.

"There's b-b-b-been some trickery," cried Throgmorton, spluttering. Indeed, his discomfited indignation was understandable enough in the circumstances. He would much sooner have gotten John Dolittle into jail than have recovered his stud. And this small, quiet man seemed to have a knack for making a fool of him at the most dramatic moments.

"If you didn't do it," he snarled, swinging round on the Doctor and pointing a fat, accusing finger at him, "how did your hat come to be in my house?"

"I think," said the Doctor, "it would be best if I gave you an answer to that question in private."

"No," snapped Throgmorton. "If it's the truth, there's no harm in the police sergeant hearing it."

"As you wish," said the Doctor. "But I thought you would prefer it that way. It has to do with a will whose existence we discovered by accident."

Astonishment, fear, hatred flitted across Throgmorton's face in quick succession during the short moment that passed before he answered.

"All right," he said sullenly at last. "We will go down to the library."

In a silent, very thoughtful procession we returned down the several flights of stairs. At the tail of it came Matthew and myself.

"Thank goodness for the white mouse, Tommy!" he whispered

in my ear. "But I don't like trusting that fellow alone with the Doctor."

"Don't worry," I answered. "We'll be outside the door. He'll hardly dare to start any violence with the sergeant here as a witness. His game's up."

I heard the big grandfather clock in the hall strike as the Doctor and Throgmorton went into the library and closed the door behind them. And it was exactly three quarters of an hour before they came out.

Throgmorton was very white, but quite quiet. He immediately addressed himself to the policeman.

"The charge is withdrawn, sergeant," he said. "A mistake—for which I tender my apologies to—er—all concerned. I'm sorry I got you up here so early when there was no need."

Again in silence we trailed across the wide carpeted hall and out into the gravel court.

At the gate we bade farewell to the sergeant, whose direction was a different one from ours. I noticed that the Doctor made no comment upon the matter to him.

When he was well out of earshot Matthew asked eagerly:

"But, Doctor, how did you explain your hat's being there?"

"I didn't," said John Dolittle. "But I told him that all four of us were convinced he lit that fire himself. And after that he was much more anxious that I should keep my mouth shut than that I should do any explaining. He has got sort of scared of me now, I imagine. And he probably thinks that I can prove he lit the fire. Which I can't. But it is just as well that he should think so, because I feel sure he did. He is going back to Australia now."

"To Australia!" cried Matthew. "Why?"

"Well, he has to earn a living, you see," said the Doctor. "The will left not only the hundred thousand pounds to the prevention of cruelty to animals, but when I came to read it through I found it left the rest to other charities."

When the outcome of the Moorsden Manor mystery became generally known in the Dolittle Zoo, jubilation and rejoicing broke forth and lasted two whole days. Accustomed as it was to celebration, Animal Town admitted it had never seen the like before. The white mouse's genius for parade organization surpassed itself; and he was elected to a second term of office as mayor on the strength of it.

He felt since animals in general had by the Doctor's victory come into such a considerable fortune, that this occasion should be made a larger and more important one than any in the history of the zoo. So for the second day's celebrations he got the Doctor's permission to send out an invitation to all the creatures of the neighborhood who wished to come. An enormous amount of preparation was made in expectation of a large attendance. The whole zoo was most gaily decorated, with ribbons and bunting by day and with lanterns and fireworks by night. Great quantities of all sorts of things to eat and drink were bought and set out at several buffets in the enclosure.

But the crowd that actually did come was even much, much vaster than had been anticipated. All the regular members of the Rat and Mouse Club, the Rabbits' Apartment House, the Home for Crossbred Dogs, the Badgers' Tavern, the Squirrels' Hotel, and the Foxes' Meeting House had to set to and do duty as hosts. So did Gub-Gub, the Pushmi-Pullyu, Chee-Chee, Too-Too, Dab-Dab, and Polynesia. And even with this extra help it was only by working like bees that they managed to feed and entertain that enormous crowd of visitors.

As for the Doctor, Matthew, Bumpo and me, we were kept busy running between the house and the town for more, and still more, refreshments, as the ever-increasing attendance did away with what we had already. Too-Too the accountant told me afterward that according to his books we had bought more than a wagonload of lettuce, three hundredweights of corn and bird seed, close to a ton of bones and meat, four large cheeses, and two dozen loaves—besides a great lot of delicacies in smaller quantity.

Within the old bowling green it was almost impossible to move along the lawns, so thronged were they with hedgehogs, moles, squirrels, stoats, rats, badgers, mice, voles, otters, hares, and whatnot. At frequent intervals cheers for the Doctor, old Mr. Throgmorton or his association for the prevention of cruelty to animals would break out in some corner and be rapidly taken up all over the vast assembly. Every tree and shrub in the zoo enclosure—and throughout the whole of the Doctor's garden, too—was just packed and laden with perching birds of all kinds and sizes, from wrens to herons. The din of their chatter was constant and terrific.

Before the day was over the grass of the bowling green was all worn away by the continuous passing of those millions of feet. And after the guests had departed it took the members of the Dolittle Zoo another whole day to clear away the scraps and put the place in order.

The End

DOCTOR DOLITTLE'S PUDDLEBY ADVENTURES

WRITTEN & ILLUSTRATED BY HUGH LOFTING

Contents

Introduction *Doctor Dolittle and His Family*   253

THE SEA DOG

1   *The* Sea Swallow   259
2   *The Dog Hero*   266
3   *The End of the* Sea Swallow   274
4   *Rover Disappears*   283
5   *The Remains of the* Sea Swallow   291
6   *Ship Ahoy!*   298

DAPPLE

1   *The Champion*   307
2   *A Wild Breakfast Party*   316
3   *Mad Dog!*   323
4   *The Doctor Gives a Lecture*   327

THE DOG AMBULANCE

1   *The First Patient*   333
2   *The Mishap at Kingsbridge*   338
3   *The Reception at the Surgery*   343

THE STUNNED MAN

1   *The Robbery*   347
2   *The Footprint in the Copse*   353
3   *The Shoe that Fit the Footprint*   358
4   *The Dog Detective Contemplates*   363
5   *Tiger Lily's Trail*   370

6   Toggle's Silence   376
7   How the Mare Got Away   381
8   News from Toby   387
9   Tiger Lily's Return   392

THE CRESTED SCREAMERS
1   Regent's Park   401
2   Cheapside Tells a Story   406
3   Currants for the Screamers   411
4   Cheapside Has a Narrow Escape   415

THE GREEN-BREASTED MARTINS
1   The Land of the Gambians   421
2   The Doctor's Plan   425
3   Speedy-the-Skimmer   429
4   The Martins Are Saved   433

THE STORY OF THE MAGGOT
1   Experiment No. 179   441
2   Danger Ahead!   449
3   The Maggot Goes on a Journey   454
4   The Ship's Rat   460
5   Trip to the Galley   465
6   Garbage-Can Canoe   472
7   A Ride on a Canal Barge   477

THE LOST BOY
1   London Zoo   489
2   John Dolittle Brings Home a Guest   494
3   Trouble at the Circus   500
4   The Guest Departs   508

Doctor Dolittle
and His Family

I N THE BEGINNING DOCTOR DOLITTLE WAS A
people's doctor. He prescribed pills and tonics and mended
broken bones the way regular doctors do. Besides working
at the profession of doctoring sick people, he also doc-
tored animals. In the course of caring for his animal friends he
acquired so many regular animal boarders in his house that there
was barely room for a human patient to get in the front door. He
had white mice in the piano, rabbits in the pantry, and a pig who
slept in the vegetable bin. Even the linen closet was occupied by
a family of squirrels.

When his human patients complained of the crowding and
refused to come to him unless he got rid of the animals, Doctor
Dolittle stopped doctoring humans entirely; he became an animal doctor only. Polynesia, the parrot who became a member
of the Doctor's household, helped him change from a people's
doctor to an animal doctor. She taught him to speak the language of the animals. Being a parrot, Polynesia could talk in

two languages—people's language and animal language. She was able to explain to the Doctor the meanings of the nose-twitching, ear-scratching, and tail-wagging signals that make up the language of animals.

"But, Polynesia," said John Dolittle, "birds don't have noses to twitch and ears to wag and—a—er—it's all too confusing."

"Not at all, Doctor," replied Polynesia. "Birds speak a language all their own. Just listen to those nut hatches on the window ledge. Hear how they chatter and whistle and make clucking noises. The little fellow—the one with the dark markings on his wings—he's showing his friend the sights around Puddleby. He just told the other one that this is Doctor Dolittle's house."

"My goodness! You don't say so!" said John Dolittle. "Do let me write it down." He rushed to his desk and brought out a notebook. "Now tell it slowly," he said as he scribbled away. "I must get it all down so that I won't forget."

It wasn't long before Doctor Dolittle was able, not only to understand what the animals were saying but to speak their language as well. At first it was difficult because he had to learn to twitch his nose and scratch his ears as they did. The hardest part was the tail; he had to use his coattails for that. The animals were amazed at the strange way the Doctor's coattails flew around when he spoke to them. But very soon they became accustomed to it and understood him as well as they did their own animal friends.

Dab-Dab, the duck, was the Doctor's housekeeper. She cooked and scrubbed, dusted and cleaned, and went to market twice a week to keep the larder filled with assorted foods for the Doctor's strange family.

Gub-Gub, the pig, who also lived with the Doctor, fancied

himself an authority on foods. He had a great curiosity that was always getting him into trouble.

The household accounts and the Doctor's business dealings were taken care of by Too-Too, the owl, who was a famous mathematician—among animals, of course.

Jip, the dog, had many duties. He organized and helped build and manage the Home for Crossbred Dogs, which occupied a large part of the Doctor's garden. Whenever there was a job of scenting to be done, Jip had no equal. He could follow the trail of a man who was miles away simply by identifying the tobacco the man smoked.

When small objects—some as small as a pin—had to be found, Whitey, the white mouse, went to work. He had microscopic eyes and could see even the colors of a grain of dust.

Another member of the family was Chee-Chee, the monkey, who spent part of the time with the Doctor at Puddleby-on-the-Marsh and the other part in Africa where the climate was more to his liking. Whenever the Doctor went on a voyage he always sent for Chee-Chee to act as guide in following hidden trails and paths through jungles and foreign lands. He would climb the highest trees and swing along from limb to limb through the tangle of branches, calling out to the Doctor and his party the way the paths led.

Among the Doctor's animal friends who lived at Puddleby a good deal of the time, was a two-headed animal called a Pushmi-Pullyu. He had a head at each end of his body and could eat with one while talking with the other. The Pushmi-Pullyu said this enabled him to avoid talking with his mouth full.

Cheapside, the London sparrow who made his home in the ear of a statue on St. Paul's Cathedral in London where he could see everything and know everyone who passed through the great city, was perhaps the most versatile of the Doctor's friends. John Dolittle often called on him for information about the movements of ships and people, and Cheapside never failed to find the answers.

Early in his career as an animal doctor, John Dolittle took into his home a young boy by the name of Tommy Stubbins. Tommy, as the Doctor's chief assistant, learned to speak the language of animals and helped Doctor Dolittle with their care. Because the Doctor was a busy man, it was Tommy Stubbins who wrote down the adventures of the great doctor and his animal friends.

In the little town of Puddleby-on-the-Marsh, where the Doctor and his family lived, Matthew Mugg, the Cat's-Meat-Man, sold food for animals. Naturally he came to be a great friend of the Doctor and Tommy and often assisted them in their problems with the animals.

There were others who lived with the Doctor for short periods: Kling, the Dog Detective; Dapple, the prize Dalmatian; Toby and Swizzle, the circus dogs; and Bumpo, the African Prince—son of the king of Jolliginki.

The stories which follow in this book were written by Tommy Stubbins about the Doctor and his animal friends.

Olga Michael

THE SEA DOG

The Sea Swallow

THE HOME FOR CROSSBRED DOGS WAS ONE of the most popular clubs in Doctor Dolittle's zoo. This was an institution which Jip, the Doctor's dog, had persuaded John Dolittle to establish for mongrel dogs who were left to wander the countryside without proper places to sleep or sufficient food to keep their ribs from showing.

Very soon after the Doctor's return to Puddleby-on-the-Marsh, kennels were built at the lower end of the garden for dogs who preferred private quarters. And one large house was added for those who liked to spend their time with company. The large house was also used as a sort of club room.

It was to this club that the Doctor and I, Tommy Stubbins, went one evening on our regular tour of inspection. As we entered the building we were astonished at the quiet, for usually, even during meals, the Home for Crossbred Dogs was a pretty noisy place. Proceeding to the dining room we found the explanation for the stillness: an after-dinner story was being told by one of the members.

The entire company was paying rapt attention, and but for the voice of the speaker, not a sound could be heard.

The Doctor did not like to interrupt. He was always most particular not to interfere with the liberties of the various clubs in his zoo. He quietly sat down to wait till the story should be over, and I followed his example. Very soon we were both as deeply interested in the story as any of the audience.

The speaker was a rugged, thick-set sort of collie mongrel. Neither the Doctor nor I knew very much about him beyond the fact that he was one of the earliest applicants for membership when the club was first opened. His most important reason then for joining was that he could never settle down under private ownership. There wasn't liberty enough, he said. Now it appeared that he had spent a good deal of his life at sea. We learned afterward from Jip that he was known among the members as the Sea Dog, and was one of the best storytellers they had.

"This ship," he was saying, "was a nice enough ship—so was the crew, for that matter. But the captain, well, the captain was peculiar. Full of discipline, you know. And the trouble was that he felt that everything on his ship had got to come under his old rules and regulations—not only the crew, but dogs as well. I do believe that skipper would have made the very rats in the hold toe the line and keep a watch if he could. And of course that didn't suit me. I had always been as free as the air and on most ships I'd sailed with I had been given all the liberty I wanted. You might wonder why I stayed on this one—the *Sea Swallow* she was called. Well, I often wondered myself. At many a port I'd go ashore saying, 'Now that's the end. I'll not go back. Finish.' But sure enough, when the hour for sailing came, I'd find myself dawdling down to the wharf just in

"The speaker was a collie mongrel."

time to catch her before she let go her moorings. Why, I couldn't tell you. But in spite of old Captain Burton and his strictness, I stuck with the *Sea Swallow* for over two years. And if she hadn't got wrecked, maybe I'd be with her still. And the curious thing is that I was the one who caused her wrecking—though I didn't mean to. And how it came about is the yarn I'm going to tell you tonight."

At this a slight rustle of movement ran through the audience as the dogs settled down or sought new places where they could listen more comfortably. A few of the smaller dogs in the front rows looked round and, seeing John Dolittle at the back of the room, whispered to one another proudly that he had joined the audience.

"Captain Burton," the Sea Dog went on, "didn't believe in

having anything loose around his ship. Everything had to be fastened up—dogs included. And whenever he saw me about the decks he'd always call for one of the men and tell him to lock me up in the carpenter's shop. The carpenter's shop was right up for'ard in the fo'castle. It was one of the dullest, most uninteresting places in the whole ship. And after I had spent an awful lot of time imprisoned there I began trying to think out some way of escape. It had two portholes, and I found I could reach one of them by jumping up onto the carpenter's bench. Outside there was nothing visible but the sea rushing aft and a gull or two sailing around. It occurred to me as I peered through, why shouldn't I just hop into the sea and get back onto the open decks of the ship further aft?

"Well, I wasn't a very experienced sea dog then or, of course, I would never have even dreamed of such a thing. But I was that bored with the stuffy old carpenter's shop, I imagine I wasn't thinking of anything beyond getting out. Presently I heard four bells ring. That told me it was two in the afternoon. I calculated that if I waited till half past two the captain would then be taking his after-lunch nap, and maybe I could enjoy two or three hours' liberty before he spotted me and had me locked up again. So I sat on the carpenter's bench looking at the sea flying past, till I heard five bells. Then I just leapt through the porthole as though it had been no more than a hole in a fence.

"It's a wonder I'm alive to tell the tale. I was always a good swimmer, and plunging down into the rushing sea didn't bother me at all. But when I came up, shaking the water out of my eyes, and began to look at the side of the ship slipping by me at nine knots an hour, I saw not a thing that I could cling on to—let alone climb up. I've often wondered since just how I expected to be able to climb back onto the ship. I suppose I had some notion there would be a rope ladder

HUGH LOFTING

*"I could reach one of the portholes by jumping up
onto the carpenter's bench."*

hanging down, or something of the sort. But even if there were, it is very doubtful if it would have saved me. Anyway, as the tail end of the ship slipped up to me and then past I thought, 'Well, that's the end of you, you blockhead! You're free, all right. But now, unless you can find yourself an island to get onto, it's going to be a short life and a wet one.'

"But I wasn't destined for a watery grave. On the stern rail of the ship as it went gliding by, one of the cabin boys was leaning. Luckily he was looking down into the water—dreaming of home, I suppose, or something. And presently he sees my head go bobbing by in the foam of the wake.

"'Jiminy!' says he. 'There's old Rover fallen overboard.'

"And quick as a flash he grabs up a coil of light rope and heaves it out astern with a mighty nice aim. The tail end of it fell right across my face, which by this time was a good thirty yards behind the ship.

"'Good dog!' he calls. 'Grab it, Rover, grab it!'

"And grab it I did—in my teeth. The salt water gurgled into my throat, but I managed to blow it out again, like a whale, without letting go. Then very gently Snooky—that was the cabin boy's name—began hauling in the rope. The drag of the rushing sea was fierce. But he kept an upward lift on the line so as to prevent the water from filling me up. And presently he had me alongside the ship, where the pull of the water was stronger than ever.

"He began lifting me, like a fish on the end of a line."

"'Now,' says he, 'hold on like death!'

"I took an extra grim bite on the rope and he began lifting me, like a fish on the end of a line, bodily out of the water. In midair I spun till I was dizzy, but I didn't let go. And soon he had me over the rail and standing beside him on the deck.

"I tried to show him I was grateful. At first he had no idea of how I came to be floating in the sea. He supposed I had been kicked off the ship by the captain or the bo'sun. But when he came to look into the matter he found that I had been locked in the carpenter's shop. And that the only way I could have got out, since the door was still locked, was through the porthole—also, because there was no one in the shop beside myself, I must have jumped out. That set him thinking.

"Snooky, the cabin boy, had had to put up with a good deal of kicking and cuffing himself from the 'Old Man,' as we called the captain. And this made him extra sympathetic with me. He thought that any dog who would just jump into the sea to gain his liberty must be a pretty brave animal. He didn't know I was just a plain fool, but that's neither here nor there.

"'All right, Rover,' says he. 'I'll keep your secret—anyway as long as I can. You've been drowned, you understand—jumped into the sea and went right down to Davy Jones's locker, bless you! Ship's carpenter will unlock the shop around seven bells, and he'll find you gone and the port open. So, of course, you must be drowned. In the meantime, I'll stow you away in the hold or a locker or something, and when no one's around I'll give you a run. And I'll see you get three square meals a day. They don't know how to treat a dog aboard this ship—nor a cabin boy, neither. But use your sense now, Rover, if you want to stay free. Lie low—like a drowned dog should. You're dead and buried, remember that.'"

The Dog Hero

I T WAS A CURIOUS THING," THE SEA DOG WENT on, "to find myself far freer in many ways after I was dead than I had been before. The cabin boy, Snooky, was as good as his word. How he managed it without taking any of the ship's company into his confidence, I've no idea. But somehow he kept me hidden on that craft and not a soul knew. One day he would stow me in the hold where I'd lie on a sack among barrels and packing cases; another, he'd shift me in a great hurry, secretly, to one of the store lockers where ropes and spare gear were kept. You see, on big ships there are many places that only get visited once in a long while in the course of a voyage. And the cabin boy made it his business to find out as far as possible ahead of time when these places were likely to be opened.

"But the most wonderful part of all was how he took me out for runs—mostly after dark, of course. There wasn't a day passed that he didn't somehow give me a bit of exercise. There's no doubt that he knew the habits of all of the crew by heart, hour for hour. Just the same, it is quite a feat; not only to keep a dog's presence on a ship a secret, but to give him exercise into the bargain. And he managed to bring me food as well. It wasn't always enough—I strongly suspect that he often went without, himself, in order to feed me—but I was able to survive on it all right.

"And then I found that besides winning a new kind of freedom I had suddenly became a hero, too. I fancy that often happens to folks after they are dead. The captain remarked one day:

"'What has happened to that dog? I haven't seen him around lately.'

"'He has been drowned, sir,' said the first mate.

"'Drowned!' cried the captain. 'How was that?'

"'You had him shut in the carpenter's shop, sir,' replied the mate. 'When the carpenter went in there the door was locked as usual, the port open, and the dog gone. Must have jumped into the sea, sir. Hasn't been seen since.'

"This upset the captain quite a little—and it upset the crew a good deal more. They had been fond of me and, in their rough way, kind. Sailors, you know, are a very superstitious lot. My death, when it became known, was taken as a most unlucky sign. Often when I was in hiding I'd overhear them talking about me. All my faults had been forgotten: only my good qualities were remembered—after my death. I decided I was a pretty fine dog. I even wept a little over my own sad end as I listened to them.

"'After all,' said one, 'a ship's dog is a mascot. The Old Man didn't treat him right. That's why he jumped into the sea. Poor old Rover! I remember well the first voyage he sailed with us.'

"'Aye,' said another. 'It's a bad sign, the worst possible sign of ill luck, when a ship's dog dies at sea. I wish I hadn't signed on this voyage.'

"About three days after my disappearance everybody aboard was talking about me. My sad and untimely death had cast a gloom over the whole ship. And the Old Man, although he was captain and boss of the roost, was in high disgrace. The crew didn't openly mutiny or show disrespect, of course. But in many little ways they managed to make him feel that it was his harsh treatment of me that had caused me to jump through the porthole, and that whatever bad luck followed would be his fault.

"And then—quite unintentionally—I made matters much worse myself. This way: One evening I was dreadfully hungry. I knew food wouldn't be served till four bells—in the dog watch. I peeped out of the deckhouse cupboard where Snooky had hidden me. Oh, I was so hungry! There was no one about and darkness was coming on. The fo'castle bell wasn't more than ten feet away. I nipped out, took the rope of the bell in my teeth and rang it: *Dong, dong—Dong, dong,* four bells! Probably the first time that the dog-watch bells were ever rung by a dog.

"Well, all I had meant to do was to hurry up the cook with grub. But what I actually did was to throw the whole ship into something like a panic. I dashed back to my hiding place and pulled the door shut behind me. But through the crack I could see what happened. First, men came running up on deck from below, down from the bridge, from every corner of the ship.

"'Who rang that bell?' bawled the officer of the watch.

"The bo'sun promptly set to work to find out. He questioned every man and boy of the crew. All denied it. Finally they dispersed. Well, I was still hungry. I slipped out and rang the bell again. This

"I took the rope of the bell in my teeth."

time the bo'sun had the whole crew with him below—except the quartermaster at the wheel—and he knew none of his men *could* have rung it. When he came rushing back on deck he looked strangely pale and scared. So did many of the men. They examined the bell in silence. There was no means in evidence by which it could have been rung accidentally. Finally one old salt grunted out in a hoarse, frightened sort of whisper:

"'It's old Cruikshank all right. Gee! I wish I hadn't sailed in this craft!'

"'What does he mean—*old Cruikshank?*' I heard a cabin boy ask of one of the deckhands.

"'Why, John Cruikshank, the pirate,' said the deckhand. 'We are passing over where he was drowned right now. And on any vessel that is doomed to go down, old Cruikshank's ghost rings the ship's bell as it goes over his grave. Every sailor knows that. I reckon this is this boat's last voyage, all right. Keep your life preserver handy when you climb into your bunk tonight. That's all.'

"From that moment," the Sea Dog continued, "things aboard the *Sea Swallow* began to go wrong. Sailors are strange folk. Of course they were more superstitious in those days than they are now. Many of the little happenings were nothing more than the natural mishaps of everyday life aboard ship. But the crew couldn't see that. My disappearance had been a bad enough sign; but when the ship's bell began ringing itself as we passed the latitude of Cruikshank's grave, then everything that happened after that was, for them, merely part of the chapter of accidents through which the *Sea Swallow* was sailing to her watery doom.

"I never saw men get so irritable and jumpy in my life. To make matters worse, one or two serious things happened as well. Sickness broke out on board. Several men had to keep to their bunks. Next, a seaman who had gone aloft to attend to the rigging fell and hurt his leg so badly that he had to join the sick list, too. Then bad weather came along just as the skipper was shorthanded. Quite a storm blew up and shoved the ship away off her course. Following that came a long spell of fog, when they couldn't see the sun to take their bearings by and find out where they were.

"All of this the crew blamed on the captain for his ill-treatment of me, which had caused my disappearance and brought on the bad luck. Very soon the men, with overwork and general jumpiness, reached a state bordering on mutiny. Then one night when I was going for a little quiet stroll I was seen by one of the deckhands, who let out a howl and ran up onto the bridge.

"'I seen the ghost of the dog, Captain,' he stuttered through chattering teeth. 'Old Rover, sure as I'm alive I met 'im walking on the deck.'

"As there was a fog on, the captain was taking the wheel himself. At first he wouldn't believe it. But the man swore it was true and offered to take him and show him. The skipper called to the quartermaster near him on the bridge to take the wheel. Then he followed the scared deckhand down the companion ladder. In the dark he didn't notice that the quartermaster, worn out with doing double duty, had fallen fast asleep standing bolt upright.

"Hearing the captain and the deckhand coming down to look for me, I sped along up for'ard as far as I could go. I thought I would have the peak to myself. I had forgotten all about the lookout. I nearly scared him to death. At the first glimpse of me he left his post and ran yelling toward the bridge. It seemed I had roused the whole ship now and must be caught for certain. But just at that moment there was a dull thud and the ship came to a complete standstill, listing to starboard. Everything that wasn't fastened down slid along the decks for yards—including me.

"In the fog, with no lookout and no one in charge of the bridge, we had run aground.

"For the first time since I had been fished out of the water by Snooky I began to get scared myself. The lurch of the ship as she keeled over to starboard swung my door closed with a bang. And there I was, shut in a closet with the ship going down maybe, and no way of getting out or of telling what was happening.

"Then I thought to myself, 'Well, Snooky knows where I am. He won't get off the ship without me.

"'But what if Snooky should be killed—or kept so busy by the bo'sun that he couldn't come for me? In any case, of course he would get in an awful row when he let on that he had been hiding me. Might he be afraid to own up and just go off and leave me?'

"All these thoughts flitted through my mind as I sat there in the darkness of the closet and listened to the men shouting and running about on the decks outside. Presently, to my great joy, Snooky dashed in, just to comfort me, not to take me out yet. It seemed the skipper had hopes of saving the ship. We had run onto a sandbar or something. And with the sea calm the way it was, this might be possible.

"Almost immediately Snooky dashed away again, trying to close the door after him lest the bo'sun should see me. But I shoved my nose out so he couldn't close it. And he saw what I meant.

"'All right, Rover,' said he. 'I'll leave it ajar. Then if I can't come for you you'll be able to swim for it anyway.'

"And it was lucky for me—and him—that he did. The captain's efforts to get the ship off not only did not accomplish anything, but they wasted much valuable time that should have been spent in preparing to abandon the ship. The bank we had run onto turned out to be part sand and part rock. I am not sure that the skipper suspected the ship had torn a hole in herself, but certainly he had no idea how large a one. Presently, with the filling of the hold with water, the ship gave a terrific lurch from starboard to port. She lay over so far, the decks were half underwater and too steep for anything but a fly to walk on.

"I heard yells and cries all over the ship. Many of the men I

"I shoved my nose out."

imagined had been hurled into the sea by the sudden lurch. And I knew from the list on her that all the lifeboats on one side must be useless.

"Something told me that the serious moment had come and that I had better get out into the open without delay. I flung the door open with all my weight and scrambled out onto the crazily sloping decks."

The End of the Sea Swallow

AND I WAS ONLY JUST IN TIME.

"'Look out!' yelled a voice from the darkness nearby. 'She's going down!'

"Suddenly I felt the ship sliding back off the bar. She righted herself as she slid. But she went on settling fast and then began to tip, stern down, bow up. In the darkness I couldn't see much, but I knew it was the end. Soon the decks were rearing up skyward like the side of a house. I didn't want to slide down onto the top of the tangled gear. The sea was rushing and gurgling into the aft portholes with a terrible noise. I hopped up onto a pile of rope and leapt clear over the rail into the sea.

"My one idea at first was to get off, away from her, far enough to be clear of the wash when she disappeared. I had no notion then what we had struck, whether there was land near or not. As I said, with the stillness of the night, the sea was pretty calm—luckily. I struck out away from her, but also somewhat toward the direction she had been traveling in. It

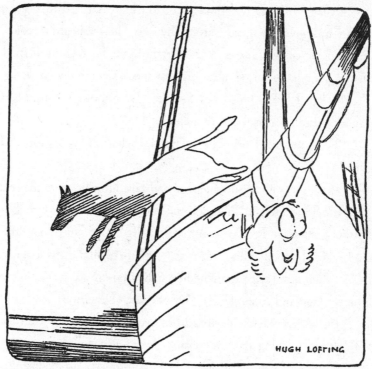

"And leapt clear over the rail into the sea"

was here, I thought, if there was land at all, that I would find it.

"On the way I heard and saw several of the crew swimming near me. It looked as though none of the lifeboats had got away at all. I wondered what had happened to poor Snooky. After swimming another ten minutes I stopped and listened. Away off to my right I thought I heard through the fog the sound of breakers. If it was, that meant land of some kind. I was in good form and I reckoned I could go on swimming like this for another half hour yet. Turning my nose in that direction, I plowed ahead.

"I hadn't gone very far before I heard a great splashing near me. At first I was scared—of sharks. But on second thought I told myself that no shark ever made a racket like that and they were almost unknown in these waters anyway. Then I heard a voice, Snooky's voice, gasping and calling through the fog for help. I turned again and spurted off at my best speed toward the voice.

"When I found him I saw at once that Snooky was in a bad way, exhausted and as feeble as a child.

"'I'm done for, Rover,' he groaned. 'Wind . . . My wind's all gone.'

"Well, I was just distracted. He had saved my life from the sea. Never had I wanted anything so much as I wanted to help him. But I saw instantly that I could do nothing till I had made sure about this land, which I hoped to find off to my left there behind the veil of fog. Before I left him I tried to make him understand I was just going to look for land and coming back. But of course I couldn't.

"I was glad that the darkness hid his face from me as I turned and left him gasping and floundering alone.

"I knew of course," the Sea Dog continued, after pausing a moment to take a lap or two from a water bowl that stood near, "that if I didn't get back to Snooky soon, he wouldn't be there anymore. I never swam so hard in my life.

"Presently I thought I could catch the whiff of land through the dampness of the fog. It was a great night for smelling. I put on still more speed. The murmur of breakers—or whatever it was—sounded clearer. Now I felt pretty certain there was land ahead. How far? That was the question. Soon the water began to grow frothy and foamy around me. . . . And then—oh, it was a wonderful moment, I can tell you! My feet touched bottom! I scampered up a flatly sloping beach. It was very little I could see through the darkness and the mist. But it *was* land: that was the important thing. I

turned, and making as sure of my bearing as I could, plunged back
into the water in the direction I had come from.

"I hoped Snooky would still be splashing or calling. If he
wasn't, I would have hard work finding him. After I had swum
what I calculated was about the distance I had come, I stopped
and listened again. All was still. My heart grew cold. Was I too
late, then? . . . But what was that? I held my breath. The night was
as still as a church. . . . Yes, it was a groan—a little way ahead.
Frantically I plowed on. And presently I ran right into him. He
seemed more dead than alive, but his chin was still above water.
I wondered if he would have sense enough to do what I wanted

HUGH LOFTING

"He seemed more dead than alive."

him to do. I took his coat sleeve in my teeth and shook him. He opened his eyes and seeing me seemed to give him courage. He grabbed hold of my coat between the shoulders and I started off. All I wanted him to do now was to float. So long as he didn't throw his arms about me I could do the rest.

"It was heavy work and I had to go slow. With a freight like him in tow, I had to nurse my wind. But the calm weather was in my favor and, luckily, Snooky had sense enough to see what I was trying to do and to help me. He could still just keep his chin up, lying flat, but he hadn't wind or strength enough to swim another stroke. Yard by yard, as I towed him along, I heard that surf-roar coming nearer through the fog. Presently he heard it too and managed to gasp out:

"'Good dog, Rover! You'll do it yet. Good old dog! Land ahead!'

"When at last he felt the sand bumping his feet beneath the water, new life seemed to come into his exhausted body. And with me beside him he staggered up the beach through the darkness— then fell among the stones of the shingle in a dead faint. As he fell a little wind came whispering off the land. I lay down beside him breathing and blowing like a grampus. . . ."

Much earlier in the course of the Sea Dog's story I had noticed Jip come into the hall. With a nod of approval he had settled down near us to listen. I could well understand that the speaker was popular with the club members as a spinner of yarns. The Home for Crossbred Dogs was by no means an easy audience to address— as I knew from experience. Yet this evening the large gathering, from the beginning of the story to the end, never stirred, not even when the Sea Dog paused to moisten his throat at the water bowl.

Every listener, silent, wide-eyed, with ears cocked, waited for him to go on.

"The next day," he continued after a moment, "I awoke to find the sun shining brightly down upon a pleasant island. Poor Snooky was still fast, fast asleep. Without waking him, I rose and trotted along the beach to explore a bit.

"The first thing I noticed was the masts of our stranded ship sticking up out of the sea. The shelf or bar, or whatever it was she had come to grief on, was apparently wide enough to keep part of her above water still. But she was ruined—anyone could see that. And the next rough sea that came along would certainly beat her to

HUGH LOFTING

"The first thing I noticed was the masts of our stranded ship."

pieces in no time. She lay out from the land about three-quarters of a mile. I found various members of the crew, all fast asleep, scattered along the beach. From the slant of the sun I reckoned it was about five o'clock in the morning.

"Then I wandered inland into the hills of the island. It wasn't tropical exactly—sort of half tropical. The climate was good. I smelled deer and rabbits everywhere. I decided we might have fared much worse. Next, I smelled the scent of a man. I followed it and came upon the captain—also fast asleep.

"The sight of him made me think that maybe I had better go and wake Snooky before I did any more. So I went back to the beach and pulled him gently by the sleeve.

"He woke with a start and I managed to convey to him that I wanted him to follow me. I took him to where the captain lay. And, as I had expected, he was not at all anxious to awaken him. He was still scared of what might happen if it became known that he had hidden me. Then I led him away into the higher parts of the island. And I started to look for water. I followed a deer track and it led me, as I hoped it would, to a drinking hole—a beautiful rocky hollow in the hills where a sparkling stream leapt in at one end and trickled out at the other. At sight of it poor Snooky gave a cry of joy, flopped down and took a drink. So did I—for I was as thirsty as a red herring.

"After we had had a drink and a wash I caught a rabbit. We hadn't any matches to light a fire, so we had to eat it raw. Then we both felt better. Snooky took off his clothes and hung them on a bush to dry. After that we set about making some sort of a shelter in which to live.

"Later in the day we heard sounds from the beach where the

rest of the crew had woken up and were stirring about. I thought maybe we had better keep an eye on them. So I led Snooky quietly down the hillside, where we presently found a flat rock jutting out through the foliage, from which we got an elegant view of the beach and all that was going on.

"The men, under the direction of the captain and bo-sun, were trying to save things off the old ship before the sea broke her up. Some of the best swimmers had swum out to her and had got one of the lifeboats free from the tangled gear. In this they were now plying backward and forward between the beach and the ship, bringing stores ashore.

"About noon Snooky and I saw smoke rising from down below. So we knew that the crew had succeeded in finding some matches still dry. And a little later smells of food cooking made both our mouths water as the wind swept the odor upward toward our hillside lookout. By the time the second night had come on, I knew that poor Snooky was pretty lonely for human company—and human food. Of course he had me. But that's the way humans are: one man is company enough for a dog, but one dog isn't company enough for a man—at least not for long.

"The cabin boy was still afraid of the anger of the captain if he should find out that he had been hiding me on the ship when everyone thought that I was drowned. And, though he often sneaked down within earshot of the crowd on the beach, he never showed himself. And, of course, they, no doubt, supposed that he'd been drowned.

"After a while I decided that there was no reason why we shouldn't share some of the luxuries that the crew were enjoying. And while Snooky was asleep one night I slipped down to the beach and did a little reconnoitering. I waited in hiding till the conversation round the beach fire had died away and I was sure that all the men were asleep. Then I sneaked up to where I knew the stores were kept—under a shelter of boughs and tarpaulins.

"I have to smile every time I think of that night, for before day broke I had made several trips up and down the mountain. And when Snooky awoke the next day, he found beside his bed of leaves an elegant piece of corned beef, a loaf of bread, a tin of sugar, and half a Gloucester cheese—the first real food besides raw rabbit he had seen in four days. Also—a very important item—I had brought a box of dry matches."

Rover Disappears

LAS! POOR OLD SNOOKY GOT LONESOMER and lonesomer. He was just dying to go down and join that crowd on the beach. And still he hadn't quite the courage to face the captain. If I had known how to, I believe I would have told him to go without me and let me stay in the wilds of the island. I felt sure I could pick up a living all right, for a while anyhow, with the rabbits and the freshwater brook and the rest. It would have been lonesome for me, of course, I knew that. But dogs can stand lonesomeness better than men can. And, anyway, I would have willingly done it for him who had saved my life and done so much for me.

"But the trouble was, of course, I *couldn't* tell him. I could make him understand simple things—by signs and so forth—but that was too hard. Then I said to myself, I said:

"'Now, Rover, my boy, you're standing in this lad's way. If you weren't here he would have no cause to fear the skipper, and he could go right down and join the crew and be happy. Suppose they sail away without him some time and he perishes on this island alone. It will be your fault—Rover, my boy, *you've got to disappear.*'

"This idea of the crew sailing away without him had bothered Snooky, too, I knew. All day and every day—pretty near—he'd lie hidden in the bushes watching the crowd on the beach below. They had rigged up a flag mast, hoping passing ships might see it and come to the rescue. As I watched him watching them, it became quite clear to me that he was terrified that any day they might grow tired of waiting to be rescued and would put to sea in the lifeboats and leave him behind.

"That evening he says to me, he says—he liked to talk, you know, even though he supposed that I couldn't understand—'Rover,' says he, 'I'll go down tonight. The worst the skipper can do is give me a licking. I'm sick of being alone. I'll go and face him tonight.'

"And when darkness had come he made his way down toward the bright fire on the beach. He sneaked up quietly—to see how the land lay. As it happened, the captain was just haranguing one of the crew for something he'd done wrong. Sparks seemed to be flashing from the skipper's eyes. He surely could look terrible, could Captain Burton, when he was mad. And tonight he was madder than we had ever seen him. . . . Well, poor Snooky lost his nerve once more and crept back again up the hill.

"'I'll do it tomorrow, Rover,' says he, as he lay down to sleep. 'I'll really do it tomorrow—if I don't, maybe they'll sail without me and then I *will* be in the soup. As sure as I'm alive, I'll go down and face the captain tomorrow. And you'll come with me, Rover. We may get it hot. But it will be better than this. I'm sick of being alone.'

"Well, I was afraid that when the morning came he would lose

"He was haranguing one of the crew."

his nerve again. So that night I determined I would just disappear, in order that he need have no further cause to fear the skipper.

"About midnight, when he was snoring away like a bear, I gave him one last look and hit the trail. It was a biggish island, a good ten miles long and two or three wide. I wandered off toward the other end of it, away from the beach and the crew. I must confess I felt very miserable at leaving him, but at all events I had the satisfaction of knowing that I was doing the right thing.

"When morning came I heard him running through the woods, calling and searching for me.

"'Rover, Rover, where are you?'

"But I just lay low, knowing that after a while he'd give up and go down to join the crew. He didn't give up in a hurry, though. Plucky boy, he didn't want me to be left behind. All that day I heard him, off and on, at different parts of the island, trying to find me. But when evening started to come on I heard him no more and I knew he had gone to the beach.

"That night was a very wretched night for me. I kept telling myself that sooner or later a ship would come to get water or something and would take me off the island. But I didn't succeed in cheering myself up much. We dogs miss human company pretty badly when we have grown up with it, and I had become very, very fond of Snooky, the cabin boy.

"When the dawn came, the island seemed strangely silent. I thought I'd go down to the other end and spy around a little to see if he had really joined the crew. So very quietly I made my way along through the underbrush. I came to Snooky's old camp. He wasn't there. 'Well,' I thought, 'he has gone, then. Good luck to him!'

"I went on down to the lookout rock and scanned the beach. The boats were gone too—and the crew. Of course it was what I had expected, planned, to be left alone on the island thus for his sake. But when I looked down at the empty beach and realized that they were *all* gone, that the thing was done, never to be undone, it was a great shock. I was sort of stunned by it. It was all very well to tell myself that a ship would come, but the captain evidently didn't expect any, or he wouldn't have taken to the wide ocean in a cockleshell lifeboat.

"I lay down on the rock and stared out over the flat, empty sea. I felt more miserable, lost, and scared than I have ever been in all my life.

"'Alone!' I muttered. 'Alone on an uninhabited island!'"

The Sea Dog paused a second or two with an odd stare in his eyes as if he saw again that vision of his own loneliness on the uninhabited island. The audience, eager as it was for him to go on, waited with its usual patient respect till he should come out of his reverie. At length he shook himself a little, as though to throw off the gloom of his thoughts, and jerking up his head he continued.

"How long I sat on there I don't know. But finally I decided I had got to make the best of a bad job. To begin with, I thought I would explore the island thoroughly from end to end. There was much of it I had not yet seen. This bit of land was likely to be my

HUGH LOFTING

"The audience waited with its usual patient respect."

home for some time to come. I had better know all there was to
be known about it. I set out and in one day I traveled all round it.
I found many interesting places: caves, bays, streams, cliffs, and
whatnot. I even came upon signs of human habitation, a long time
disused; but whether they were relics of shipwrecked sailors or of
native inhabitants of an earlier age, I could not tell. At various
points I established homes for myself—just shelters, you know,
where I could take refuge any time when night overtook me in
that part of the island. I marked these places and took careful
note of their whereabouts so I'd remember how to get to them in
case of need.

"I found there was lots of game on the island. Rabbits were
plentiful. I noticed a kind of grouse, partridges, plovers, some geese,
and a great variety of seabirds. Many of these, as you know, build
their nests on the ground among the stones of beaches or on rock
ledges. And I made a note that their eggs would form a good article
of diet at certain seasons of the year. There was also plenty of deer
and larger game, but that I didn't bother with. I found the tracks of
a few dangerous animals as well, what might be a puma or mountain
cat of some sort. But I decided that with all the rabbits and birds to
eat, these would not bother me.

"Next I began to plan out my day's work. With no company at
all, I had to have something regular to do, of course. I decided that
since I couldn't signal to any passing boat, like a man could, the next
best thing was to make sure that I didn't miss any that might come
for water or fresh fruit. Such a thing was possible. The island was
big enough. So in order to make sure that no vessels called without
my knowing it, I established lookout stations on the summits of the
hills that commanded a view of the sea all round the horizon. Also

I planned to take note of the direction of the prevailing winds in order that scent might help me in detecting the approach of ships. I was going to make it a part of the daily program to visit these lookout stations regularly.

"The next day it rained—miserably, steadily. This brought up another problem in my new wild life. I realized now fully for the first time what we dogs had done to ourselves by becoming part of human life instead of wild life—to which we at one time belonged. What about the weather? I had got to expect all sorts. It was autumn now. I had no idea what the winter in these parts might be like—certainly the nights were nippy enough already. And then food? That was another thing that must be thought of in connection with the changing seasons. There was plenty now. But would the supplies be procurable later in the year? Maybe the birds left for other lands. Well, I calculated, there should always be rabbits. And though I was by this time heartily sick of the taste of rabbit—to this day the smell of 'em will make me run the other way for miles—I felt I should be easily able to manage till the season changed.

"But what I did do in preparation for colder weather was to line all my caves with thick beds of dry leaves and wild hay. Also I laid up a goodly store of wild corn in the husk. This I had found was good, nutritious chewing and grew in abundance in the swamp-flats on the southern side of the island.

"A week passed. I told myself that I could manage this kind of life as well as any wild dog—there are still some in Australia, you know. But was I lonely? Oh dear! Don't speak of it. At the end of the week there came another rainy day. I slopped through the long round of my lookout posts. The sea was dark with rain and you couldn't see more than a mile or so, but I went the rounds anyway. Finally real darkness came on and I was glad to see it. I was wet, weary, and wretched. Miserably I was toiling my way up the hills toward one of my higher caves. In the damp evening air all scents were very keen, and this made me remember that there were other beasts who had noses as keen as mine. For the present I wasn't going to trust these meat-eating animals till I knew their habits better. I was making for a certain deep hole in a rock wall where I knew no night-prowling enemy could take me by surprise.

"Suddenly, on my way up the hillside, I smelled *smoke!* From where could it come? No underbrush fire could start naturally on a day as wet as this had been. Maybe the island was inhabited after all. Natives, perhaps. If there were any, they would of course stay hidden till the crew had left. Anyhow, I must find out. Forewarned is forearmed. Through the dank twilight and the dripping wet underbrush I took up the trail of smoke, determined to see without being seen. It led me over the ridge in the middle of the island and down the other slope. On this coast broad sands spread themselves out at low tide a good mile in depth. From a shoulder I saw, away down below, the glimmer of a fire on the beach. One solitary figure, with his back to me, was squatting before the blaze motionless. Like a stalking wolf, yard by yard, I crept downward, nearer. Finally in the still, wet darkness sounds came to me. The man was weeping. No, it wasn't a man: it was a boy. And what was this new scent coming with the smoke? . . . Yes . . . Yes, it was—*It was Snooky.* He must have missed the boats. He had delayed too long in facing the anger of the captain and they had gone without him.

"I let out one tremendous bark of joy—like a pistol shot in the damp, silent night—and raced for the beach. I was alone no more!"

THE FIFTH CHAPTER

The Remains of the
Sea Swallow

WORDS CANNOT DESCRIBE," THE SEA Dog continued, "poor Snooky's joy at the sight of me. At first my bark nearly scared him to death, bursting as it did on the solemn silence of the sea and the rain-soaked island. But when he peered through the twilight and realized that it was I racing toward him across the sands of the beach, he flung his arms wide open with welcome.

"'Rover!' he cried. 'Rover! I thought you had gone with the crew.'

"Then he clutched me to his heart and wept and laughed over me, pouring forth the story of his search for me, of how he had missed the boats and decided when I did not answer his call that I had gone with them. Of course I could not make him understand why I had not answered, but he could tell anyway that I was tremendously glad to see him again.

"He looked starved. I knew that he had not the skill to catch rabbits himself. A few shells scattered round the fire showed me that a small ration of oysters and such fish was probably all that he had

"He flung his arms wide open with welcome."

had to eat in several days. I had a fine pair of fat rabbits stored away in a cave. These I went and got for him and we roasted them at the fire and ate them. Then I conducted him up the slope a little way to where I had one of my sleeping places, well lined with dry leaves and hay. There we made another fire with the matches that he had been careful to keep dry. Soon before a cheerful blaze he spread his wet clothes, and from the shelter of the cave we watched them as they steamed. He had evidently lost heart at finding himself entirely deserted. But my reappearance seemed to put new life into him, and right away he became cheerfully busy doing all the little things that help to make life pleasant under conditions of hardship.

"As it was a little early to go to bed yet, I presently left him and went down to the beach to see what had been left by the crew.

"I had suspected that it wouldn't be much. And it was indeed precious little: a few old packing cases, empty tins, bottles, and such rubbish. The tarpaulin was gone and all the food stuffs. Away out in the gloom of the sea the masts of our stranded vessel were still visible. I hoped, as I turned back to go to bed, that the fair weather would hold long enough for Snooky and me to get to her before she was broken up by the waves.

"On my way back toward the cave I suddenly realized with a sort of guilty feeling that after all I had been responsible for Snooky's getting left behind. Firstly, if it hadn't been for me, he would of course have stayed with the crew from the beginning. And secondly, if he hadn't wasted the whole day hunting over the island for me he would have rejoined them in time to catch the boats. But then, I reminded myself, if it hadn't been for my assistance, he would most certainly have been drowned the night the ship was wrecked. And, as a matter of fact, as things turned out, my delaying his departure saved him a great deal of hardship and was the best thing that could have happened in the end.

"The next morning I was up bright and early and was greatly pleased to find that the weather was still fair. After our breakfast of cold roast rabbit I took Snooky down to the beach. The water was calm and smooth. I plunged in and started swimming out to the ship. A little puzzled, Snooky waited for me on the shore.

"I reached the *Sea Swallow* and scrambled on board. In the waist of the vessel I saw that there were still lifeboats left in good condition, but so hopelessly tangled up with the gear that it would take a deal of work to launch them.

"I began barking to Snooky on the shore."

"Then I began barking to Snooky on the shore. He saw at once what I wanted, and taking off some of his clothes, he set out to swim to me. I went halfway to join him and give him courage, and he made the trip all right, even if a bit winded.

"When he had got his breath back somewhat I showed him the lifeboats. And he promptly went to work to cut them loose from the tangle of ropes. He knew a good bit about seamanship, Snooky did, even if he was only an apprentice. Of course the boats were far too heavy for a man to lift them over the side single-handed. But by means of a block and tackle, which he lashed to the masthead, he finally hoisted one boat's bow high in the air, and making it fast like that, he swung its stern over the side and lowered it into the water.

"All the oars had been taken away by the crew or washed overboard. But with the water calm, it was no great matter to paddle it as far as the land with such flat pieces of wood as we could tear loose from the broken ship. As soon as we had her beached, we dragged her well up out of reach of the surf and set about making better oars from the pieces of packing cases that the crew had left upon the shore.

"And now, with a boat of his own, Snooky cheered up no end. Life was indeed made much easier and we felt that if the worst came to the worst we had something to put to sea in—though such a plan would of course be highly dangerous. The trip to and from the ship became a simple matter. We ransacked the old wreck from stem to stern and brought ashore hammers and axes and other tools with which to make things. We also found some foodstuffs the crew had overlooked that had not yet been ruined by the sea: a sack of dried beans, a bag of flour—the inside part of which was still good—and a tin of ship's biscuit.

"In addition, we got several pieces of sailcloth, part of which we used to make a sail for our boat and part for a signal flag to attract passing ships.

"On one of the summits of the island there was an old dead pine tree. This Snooky stripped of its branches with a hatchet. And to its top he fastened an enormous flag. It was a distress signal that on a clear day could be seen for miles and miles.

"Then with pieces of plank we built ourselves a beach hut and furnished it with table and chair, and even with a few plates and dishes that we saved from the wreck. Altogether, after two days'

"Snooky stripped it of its branches."

work—which kept us occupied and cheerful—we felt we had a pretty decent home on our island and were prepared for almost anything. And when at last bad weather came along and a storm pounded the poor *Sea Swallow* to a litter of driftwood, we congratulated ourselves that we had got everything out of her that was of any use to us before it was too late.

"A week after that I noticed that Snooky was beginning to get miserable and downcast again. I tried to cheer him up by being as lively as possible myself. But I saw he was thinking of home and pining for human company. And it was evidently in his mind to put to sea in the boat—a foolhardy undertaking, which I had hoped he would put off till all hope of rescue had been abandoned. It seemed to me that for the present we were very well off where we were. With our new equipment, I felt we could carry on for months, if necessary, during which time some vessel would be sure to call and take us off.

"But almost every day Snooky would mess about with the boat, touching her up with tar, making masts for her and other things to fit her up for a voyage. I was against it. I was certain that to put to sea in such a little bit of a craft, with a crew of one, could only lead to disaster."

THE SIXTH CHAPTER

Ship Ahoy!

T HE MORE SNOOKY THOUGHT ABOUT PUTTING to sea, the surer I became that it was the wrong plan for us to follow. I used to lie awake nights trying to think out things I could do to keep him from embarking on a voyage that I felt would mean certain destruction for both of us. I took several of the more important parts of the boat's furnishings—ropes, rowlocks, and the like—and hid them. He was kept busy renewing or providing makeshifts for these. And in that way I managed to delay him for several days.

"But I could not do this sort of thing too often without arousing his suspicions. And the day came when especially fine weather tempted him to make a start. So it seemed that the only course left was for me to disappear again. This I did. And poor Snooky, just as he was about to put to sea, had to go hunting and whistling all over the island for his dog.

"Neither could that device be repeated too often lest he decide one day that I had met with some accident and that it was useless for

"I saw a vessel off to the northeast."

him to wait. Under cover of the bushes and woods I kept watch on him, and when I thought that he was about to give me up for lost I'd reappear again, trying to look as though I had just returned from a rabbit-hunting expedition.

"I did this twice, and on the second occasion I thought I had lost him for good. I had gone off just at the moment when he seemed on the point of departure, and I calculated that I could give him at least two days to hunt for me before he'd decide to go alone. Well, while I was wandering around the far end of the island I saw a vessel off to the northeast and headed for our shores. I watched her for a minute till I was certain that she meant to visit us. Then, fairly bursting with the good news, I sped away to tell Snooky.

"When I got to the beach, imagine my horror to find that he had gone! I sped at once up to one of my lookout stations, and from there I saw his boat, a mere chip in the wide ocean, far out to sea, making away with sail set. I barked and yelped for all I was worth. But even while I did it I knew that it was impossible for my voice to reach him at that range.

"Then I hustled back to meet the incoming ship. I knew Snooky could not have seen it yet, because the island lay between the vessel and him. My hope was that I could somehow make the crew understand that he had put to sea without seeing them and that he must be picked up at all cost.

"I was, of course, tremendously excited and anxious. First of all, I was worried that the ship, seeing no sign of human life, might leave again right away, without perhaps even putting a boat ashore. Our flag after all might have been set up and left there by castaways years ago. And my other great fear was that Snooky might just go sailing on over the horizon and miss this one great chance of rescue.

"I watched the ship as she cautiously approached the island. Presently I could make out the man swinging the lead for soundings. And a little later, to my great delight, I saw them drop anchor and lower a boat.

"'Well,' I thought to myself, 'now they're here, they can't go away again in such a hurry. I'll have time to take another look at Snooky.' And back I hurried once more to the lookout and scanned the sea to the sou'westward.

"To my horror, not a sign of the boat was anywhere visible! I could hardly believe he had had time to sail beyond the horizon. But there it was: he was gone. Maybe some accident had happened to him. Or perhaps a sudden stiff breeze had sprung up out there and carried him swiftly out of sight.

"Dismally at last I turned away from looking at the empty sea and made my way down toward that part of the shore where the ship's boat would most likely land. All my joy at the sight of her and the prospect of rescue was gone now. Yet, of course, it would have been madness to remain behind just because he was not to accompany me. I would make friends with the boat's crew, I told myself, and they would, no doubt, take me off onto their ship.

"This I did. They were a nice lot of men. They took me into the little boat and then proceeded to row around the island to see if there was anyone else to be picked up. When they came in sight of our beach hut they went ashore again, taking me along in the hope that I'd guide them. But I just sat down on the sands to show them that any hope of human rescue was past.

"'He's the last of them,' the men muttered, shaking their heads as they watched me. 'Must be he's the only survivor, a dog!'

"Presently as we were getting back into the boat to go to the ship I suddenly startled them all by barking at the top of my voice. Round a little headland to the westward a small sailboat was tacking into the wind. It was Snooky! He hadn't gone at all. I imagine he had just wanted to scare me so I wouldn't delay him again. And coming back, keeping close inshore within the shelter of the land, his boat had been invisible from my lookout.

"That," said the Sea Dog, "is practically all of my story. When we reached the ship we were given a wonderful welcome

"He's the only survivor, a dog!"

and treated like heroes. Snooky soon forgave me for the various tricks I had played on him to delay his sailing. For had I not been the means of his getting a comfortable passage home after all? And as a matter of fact, he learned later that though the rest of the *Sea Swallow*'s crew had reached port, they only did so after weeks of terrible suffering and hardship. And from that, by a combination of luck and management, he had been spared.

"For a good many voyages more we stuck together as ship-mates. But at last I grew weary of the sea and gave up the life altogether."

As the Sea Dog left the little platform at the end of the

room, the noise of the applause was truly deafening. The deep barks of the big dogs mingled with the shrill yelps of the little ones, and the general chorus could be heard a mile away. The speaker had to come back onto the platform seven times to receive the appreciation of the audience before the noise finally subsided.

Then suddenly a new cry was taken up and repeated all about the hall:

"The Doctor! Speech, speech! The Doctor! Speech!"

John Dolittle had, in his interest in the story, long since forgotten the mission that had brought him tonight to the Home

HUGH LOFTING

"'Members,' said he, 'you must excuse me.'"

for Crossbred Dogs. Now that his presence in the hall had been thus publicly announced, the eyes of all were turned on him and it became quite evident that he stood no chance whatever of escaping without first addressing the enthusiastic gathering. Bowing cheerily right and left, he made his way through a forest of wagging tails and flapping ears and stepped up onto the platform.

"Members," said he, "you must excuse me from any speech making this evening. And after listening to the Sea Dog's yarn I do not feel that you are in any need of outside entertainment. At the Rat and Mouse Club we had a series of life stories told by the members. These were taken down by Manager Stubbins and later printed in rat and mouse language to become part of the club library. I think it would be a good idea if you did the same here. Your house committee can assist President Jip in making a selection. When the stories are told here I should very much like to be invited to attend. For the present, after thanking you for a pleasant evening, I must wish you good night."

DAPPLE

The Champion

I THINK THAT OF ALL MY EXPERIENCES AS MANAGER of the Dolittle Zoo, I enjoyed those connected with the Home for Crossbred Dogs the most. Of course I had always known that there was a great variety in the characters and personalities of dogs; but I certainly never realized *how* great a variety till I began to take part in the daily life of this mongrels' club.

There was one member of the home who was purebred. This was Dapple the Dalmatian. Not only was he purebred, he was a prizewinner with a pedigree ever so long and gold medals and ribbons and honorable mentions to his credit from nearly all the big dog shows. For these reasons he was not, strictly speaking, eligible as a member of the home. And when he first arrived there were certain members who objected because he wasn't a mongrel. But Dapple explained to the committee that it wasn't after all his fault that he was born purebred, and as he was already very popular with almost every dog in the club, he was finally accepted in spite of his aristocratic breeding.

He was one of those dogs whose coming to the Dolittle Zoo had caused the Doctor a good deal of trouble with their owners. Dapple belonged to a most extraordinary lady. She was very stout and used to make herself look still larger by the ruffles and frills she wore. Jip always said that she reminded him of an enormous, highly-scented cream puff. When Dapple first ran away to join the club she came after him (in a carriage and pair with two footmen) and took him away again. She blamed the Doctor for his coming. But Dapple ran away so many times that finally she saw it was no use. It was clear that the dog himself preferred the simple joys of the mongrels' club to the extravagant luxury of her elaborate household. So, saying that the dog couldn't after all really be purebred to desert *her* home for a mere zoo, she turned up her nose and bade her pet good-bye for the last time—to Dapple's great delight—and departed.

I don't just know how it came about, but this dog was selected to tell the second of the after-dinner stories (or autobiographies, as I called them in my book). And when John Dolittle and I came into the dining room the following evening, we found Dapple already installed on the speaker's platform and the rest of the club sitting around waiting. The committee did not want the story to begin till the Doctor and I arrived.

Our appearance was welcomed with yelps of greeting and sighs of relief. I found myself a comfortable corner where I could spread out my papers for taking down the record. The Doctor was at once surrounded and carried off to another corner by all his adoring friends, who wanted to sit beside him. Silence gradually settled down over the dining room and Dapple began.

"I fancy," Dapple said, "that my story's chief interest for

"An enormous cream puff"

you will lie in the fact that it is the story of a purebred's life. How often have I envied you happy mongrels! For my existence from the beginning was a monotonously purebred existence. With my entrance into your club this week, I have, almost for the first time, obtained that liberty which you have enjoyed all your days.

"I will begin from the time when I and two of my brothers and two sisters found ourselves in a dog shop on sale. We were put into a little pen with straw on the bottom and 'PEDIGREED PUPPIES' written across the front. To begin with, we didn't like it at all. But you know the way puppies are: it didn't take us long to forget our troubles and we soon began to play and wrestle together and had a pretty good time. The boy who looked after us and gave us our meals was a very nice lad; and whenever he wasn't busy he would join in our games.

"Customers would come into the shop and look at us. And one by one my brothers and sisters were all sold and I was the last to be left. I felt very sad about this at first. But the shop-boy did his best to console me and took me out for walks after his work was done.

"'Dapple,' he used to say, 'you're the best-looking pup of the whole family. Those customers don't know anything about dogs—for all their knowing airs they put on—or they would never have left you to the last. But I'm glad they have. I wish I had the money to buy you myself. But you're so expensive. That's on account of your pedigree, you see. Five pounds. Think of it! For a little round dumpling like you! You should feel proud. And me only earning five shillings a week!'

"I used to watch the customers that came in. I grew to like the shop-boy more and more. And as time went on I became less and less anxious to be sold. I used to pretend to be very ill-natured so the customers wouldn't buy me. When they'd put their hands into the pen to stroke me I'd growl and show my teeth.

"'Oh!' they'd say. 'Snappish, eh? No, I don't want that dog. Couldn't trust him with the children.'

"And to my great relief they'd leave my cage and go on to look at the collie pups who lived next door to me. But one day a man came in whose cheerful smiling face I rather liked from the very beginning. As usual I growled to show that I wasn't to be trusted with children, as soon as he tried to pet me. But, to my great surprise, he took not the slightest notice. Maybe he didn't have any children. Anyway, he seemed to know that I was just putting it all on, because instead of starting back and going away, he just laughed and went right on stroking me. And soon I gave up trying to scare him off and started to play. He seemed such a jolly, honest, nice man that I didn't mind even if he did buy me.

"Well, in the end the man bought me and took me away to his country home. It was a very nice home and I felt sure right from the start that I had been very lucky and was going to enjoy my life there. My owner seemed to be a sort of country gentleman—not terribly rich, but quite well off. He didn't work. His time was occupied fishing and hunting and looking after his very large and lovely country estate.

HUGH LOFTING

"I started to play."

"It appeared that the shop-boy had been right and that I was destined to turn out a very specially fine specimen of the Dalmatian breed. As soon as I began to grow up a little, all of my owner's friends who came to stay with him made flattering remarks about me and prophesied that I was surely going to be a prizewinner. In time my owner began entering me for dog shows. Oh dear, how I hated those shows! For weeks beforehand I used to get dieted and scrubbed and brushed and trimmed and fixed so I would look my very best. I wasn't allowed to go out in muddy weather lest I mess up my immaculate coat or get my nails dirty. And when the show came off I had to sit for hours on a bench waiting for the silly judges to come around and examine me—when all I wanted was to be out in the nice wet fields chasing hares or digging for rats.

"I took many prizes—ever so many. I suppose, as such things go, I really had a wonderful career. For three years I carried off the highest honors in the Dalmatian class from every show I was entered for. My picture was in all the sporting papers. And I even had my portrait painted in oil colors by a famous artist. I got a stiff neck standing still while it was being done.

"But I didn't care for my show career a bit. My owner seemed to realize this and as soon as the shows were over he would always let me out in the fields to get as dirty as I liked and have a good time till the next show came along. It amused him. He even used to get dirty himself, helping me to dig for rats.

"This very nice man was fond of betting on the racehorses. That was his ruin. He was just as unsuccessful on the racetrack as he was successful at the dog shows. He lost and lost and lost. Soon he began to have to sell things to make good his losses. Part of his fine country estate was put on the market. Then some of his horses; beauties, they were. One thing after another went, but still he wouldn't stop betting. He was always hoping that he'd make a big win and get back all he had lost.

"I began to wonder when I would get sold. I knew that at the shows he had been offered tremendous sums for me by millionaire dog fanciers. And much as he liked me—we were tremendous friends—it would only be natural, with all this need for money pressing on him, that some day he'd be tempted to part with me.

"After a few more months things got so bad that my owner was actually in want. There were many days when he didn't get enough to eat. And I created quite a sensation by bringing him home chickens that I took from the poulterer's shop in the village as I passed. It never occurred to me, I'm afraid, that there was anything wrong in my taking them. But the poulterer seemed to think there was. And I realized, after I had been caught and taken to the police station a second time, that I was giving my owner a good deal more trouble than profit.

"Of course as things went from bad to worse it began to look quite unavoidable that I must be sold. For even some of his household servants had not been paid their wages in a very long time.

"The day came. A woman who had often admired me at the shows offered a particularly high price when the poor man was at his wits' end for money. He made the farewell short—for which I was glad. Neither of us cared for emotion or a show of sentiment, and if I had to go I wanted to do so quickly and as quietly as possible.

"'I'm sorry, Dap,' said he, giving me a final pat on the head. 'I feel horribly guilty, selling you. But—well, good-bye and good luck to you, old boy.'

"I felt dreadfully sad—and resentful, too. Not against him, for

"Bringing home chickens from the poulterer's shop as I passed"

I saw that as the situation was it couldn't be helped now, but against my pedigree. If I hadn't been so beastly well bred, my value would have been only a few shillings. And it would have hardly been worth anyone's while to sell me.

"As I was led away by my new fat mistress I muttered to myself, 'Oh, why, *why* wasn't I born a mongrel?'

"Then my life entered upon an entirely new chapter. The woman who bought me was fabulously rich. She had enough servants and carriages and silver dishes and porcelain bathtubs for six people. I shall never forget my disgust the first evening when I was brought to her home. Tea was being served and her drawing room was full of women guests, all jabbering and munching cakes. She had me led in to show me off to them.

"'My dears,' she cackled, 'isn't he a beauty? I paid a terrible price for him. But I just *had* to have him—to go with my new gown, you know. The spots on his coat match the polka-dot silk perfectly—just perfectly!'"

A Wild Breakfast Party

"CAN YOU IMAGINE MY DISGUST?"

Dapple's elegant, well-bred nose seemed to curl upward with scorn as he appealed to his audience. He was surely a beautiful creature to look at. Dalmatians were a more popular breed then than they are now. As a boy I had always called them "plum-pudding dogs," on account of their black spots. But I don't know that I had ever seen a purebred champion before. And certainly such a homely title did not seem at all fitting for as fine a dog as this.

"That was what I had come to," he went on. "That was all my wellbredness and pedigree were to mean in the end: to be bought by an hysterical, cackling, empty-headed woman *because I matched her new polka-dot gown!* The shame of it—for a sporting dog like me! I was now to be part of a boudoir's furnishings. I ground my teeth with rage. And that very night of my arrival was the first time I ran away—the first time out of a dozen.

"'So I'm to match a polka-dot dress, am I?' I muttered furiously. 'All right. Then I'll get rid of my spots.'

"I knew John Dolittle well, of course, and I came straight to his home as soon as I got away.

"'Doctor,' I said, 'I want you to paint out my spots, or dye me a new color, or something. I just will not be part of that woman's wardrobe. She wants to take me out on a string so people will stare at us and say how smart she is. You must do something. I simply can't bear the thought—the fat nincompoop!'

"Well, the Doctor sympathized with me and I do believe he might have done it if he hadn't had so many rows already about dogs running off from their owners to come and join his club in the zoo here. I hung around still trying to persuade him, and while I was at it the wretched woman herself turned up to claim me. She had had me traced by droves of detectives. She is so horribly rich.

"So back I had to go to my doom as a boudoir ornament. She hugged me and kissed me with joy at getting me back. Then she put some perfume on me. She said I ought to use the same perfume as she wore. Think of it: me—*perfumed!*

"Oh, I forgot to mention that this woman had a husband. It isn't any wonder that I forgot to mention him, because he really wasn't of any account anyway. He was just a husband to her—and a nuisance to me. He used to get bossed and henpecked to death by his wife, and I suppose he felt *he* had to boss someone, so he tried to boss me. She used to send him to take me out for runs in the evening, and he was always trying to teach me silly tricks that I didn't want to know, shouting orders at me in a loud voice so the passersby could see what a masterful character he was. He would send me

"Then she put some perfume on me."

on errands to fetch his walking stick, which he would deliberately leave behind against a tree or a wall. So silly! I usually brought back a dead rat, if I could find one, or a banana skin instead. I already knew a whole lot of good tricks. But the only fun I got out of these was trying to spoil his show and appearing as stupid as I could possibly be. Then he used to make me carry his newspaper in my mouth, but I always dropped it in the first puddle I passed.

"What a life! And how I longed to get away from it! One of the most terrible things about it was that I began to find my own character changing. My old owner had been a healthy, outdoor man of a calm, sensible disposition. With him I had grown into a sensible, sporting country dog. Now, being constantly with this hysterical woman who was always weeping over me—she insisted on telling me all her troubles, which were wholly imaginary and quite tiresome—I found to my horror that I was becoming a snappy, irritable, spoiled lapdog. Like her, in fact. It was a dreadful discovery. I was always running away, but I always got brought back again. My one ambition was to get into the Doctor's club here and become once more a calm, sensible, worthwhile dog. Then I thought that maybe I'd have better luck if I went back to my old owner next time I escaped. I hoped, somehow, he'd keep me. Well, I got to his place after a long and strenuous journey only to find that his home had now been sold to someone else and he had gone abroad.

"Then, after I had been brought back to the scented boudoir for about the tenth time, I thought up a new plan. I had seen a mad dog on the streets one day and noticed that everyone was in great terror lest he bite someone. His eyes flashed and his mouth frothed. I practiced in front of one of the boudoir mirrors, making my eyes flash—terrible. Then I stole a piece of shaving soap from the husband's dressing room and practiced making my mouth foam with lather. It wasn't pleasant, but it looked wonderful.

"'Good!' I said to myself as I went to bed that night after my secret rehearsal. 'Tomorrow I'll be a mad dog. Then they'll *have* to get rid of me.'

"I have done a few crazy things in my life," the Dalmatian continued, "but never, I think, anything quite so crazy as pretending I was a real crazy dog. It is a wonder I'm alive. You see, with the case I had seen on the streets—when the mad dog went running round with staring eyes and frothing mouth—things happened differently.

HUGH LOFTING

"I practiced in front of one of the mirrors."

The people just fled away from him, scared blue. I didn't know that it is the custom to shoot mad dogs. I suppose nobody had a gun handy that time. But this time they had—several.

"Well, to begin from the beginning: I had timed my outbreak of madness to take place while my mistress was having breakfast. I had kept my piece of shaving soap handy from the night before, and while she was drinking her first cup of coffee I got it all frothy in my mouth. It was her habit to give me a lamb cutlet at breakfast time. She had no idea of feeding dogs. I was already losing my figure from being continually fed between meals. That's how she lost her figure too—if she ever had one—by eating tidbits at odd times. So my lamb cutlet, specially cooked, was brought in by the footman on a silver tray in the usual manner, and my mistress took it by the paper frill and called to me:

"'Come along, Dappy darling,' said she. 'Mama give little Dapsy his breakfast.'

"That's the way she used to talk. It almost spoiled my appetite many a time. I came up to her, but instead of taking the cutlet, I took her hand in my teeth—not to bite her, really, you understand. Poor old thing, she certainly meant to be kind enough. But I had to play the part of a mad dog properly. She started back with a scream. Then I snarled and big gobs of white soapsuds slobbered from my

"*The footman jumped through the window.*"

mouth. I rolled my eyes. Then I threw a somersault and bit the carpet. Next I bit the footman in the leg—I owed him one anyway. Then I bit the table in the leg and the breakfast dishes capsized with a crash onto the floor. After that I leapt onto the sofa and let out a bloodcurdling howl like a lost wolf.

"My mistress sprang up and ran for the door. The footman had already jumped through the window—into a bed of geraniums.

"'Oswald!' the woman shrieked—that was her husband's name—'Oswald! Come quick! The dog's gone mad!'"

THE THIRD CHAPTER

Mad Dog!

ELL, OSWALD CAME. BUT HE DIDN'T stay very long. I made one snarling rush at him and he, too, dived through the window into the geraniums.

"Then the butler arrived on the run. Bells were ringing, doors slamming, and people yelling all over the house by this time. The butler was a fat and pompous booby. He was armed with a golf club. I tore his pants for him as soon as he appeared, and all he succeeded in doing with the golf club was to smash a couple of valuable vases on the mantelpiece. He, too, beat a hasty retreat— to get more help, he said. Meantime I rushed round the breakfast room in circles, tossing cushions in the air, tearing down the curtains, upsetting furniture, howling, blowing soap bubbles all over the place. Oh, I was the grandest thing in mad dogs you ever saw.

"The trouble was I was too good. After I had thoroughly wrecked the breakfast room I dashed out into the hall, pulling down a hatrack playfully as I passed, and from there I rushed on into the garden. In the garden, for the first time, I realized what I had done. All over the place, behind bushes and trees and things, I saw men lurking with guns. *Bang! Bang! . . . Bang! Bang!* I was fired on from all sides. The noise was like a war. How I escaped goodness only knows. She had about twenty gardeners, but I suppose that they were all, luckily, bad shots. They didn't hit me. The only one that got hit was the butler—in the pants, the same pants that I had already torn. He got over it all right. But, poor man, it was his unlucky day.

"I sped right down to the end of the garden, making for a gate whose bars I knew I could get through. I reached it in safety, gained the road, and raced away in the direction of the

"Behind bushes men were lurking with guns."

Doctor's house. Behind, the yells and shots of the enemy followed hot on my heels.

"'Mad dog!' they bawled. 'Look out! His bite's poisonous! Shoot him! Mad dog!'

"Everyone ahead of me ran for their gates, climbed lampposts, popped behind doors, leapt over walls, anything to get away from poor me, the enemy of society. It began to look as though I had been a bit too clever and that my grand plan might cost me my life.

"'The Doctor,' I kept muttering to myself as I stretched out at full speed. 'He's my one chance. He can explain to these idiots. The Doctor! I'll be all right if I can only reach John Dolittle's house before they fill my hide full of lead.'

"As I raced down the road I began to wonder not only whether I was really crazy myself, but also whether the whole world had gone crazy, too. I'm sure, at all events, that that's what anyone coming suddenly upon the scene would have thought. The cry of 'Mad dog!' was taken up and passed from house to house, so that the news of my coming actually got ahead of me, and soon I found myself beset behind and before. People leaned out of second-story windows and threw flowerpots at me off the sills as I passed; policemen shot at me with pistols; one fellow tried to lasso me with a rope; another drove a big van across the road to head me off. Every man's hand was against me.

"But somehow, through the whole gauntlet, I wriggled and darted and jumped and squirmed. In my excitement I swallowed my shaving soap, which made me feel deathly ill, but of course I couldn't stop.

"Luckily for me, the noise and hubbub had brought the Doctor to his gate before I got there. And as soon as he saw it was me that was being chased he opened the gate, let me slip in, and closed it behind me. Bullets and buckshot spattered against the stone coping of the wall as I sped up the steps, across the garden, and into the house. The Doctor—I wonder he wasn't killed himself—raised his hands in truce and walked halfway down the steps to meet my pursuers.

"'That dog is mad!' yelled one of the gardeners rushing up with a gun. 'What did you let him into your house for? He might bite someone!'

"Of course in less than five minutes there was a crowd around the foot of the steps like a theater crush. Everybody talked at once. Some demanded that I be brought out and shot at once. And just as it began to look as though the crowd might thrust John Dolittle aside and take the law into its own hands, my mistress arrived with her husband and a whole army of menservants.

"Of course the Doctor had guessed right away that I was pretending—even before I gasped it out as I sped by him up the steps. He planted himself firmly in front of the closed gate and faced Oswald the husband, who had now, with a dozen flunkeys at his back, become very brave.

"'You have my dog, sir!' said he, shaking his fist in the Doctor's face. 'The dog is mad. It bit my wife and several of the servants. It must be destroyed at once. Let us in, please.'

"'Pardon me,' said the Doctor very politely—I was listening in great anxiety just below the study window—'the dog may be yours, but these premises are mine. You cannot come in. Now just calm down a moment and let us talk this over.'

"'I will not listen to you,' cried the valiant Oswald. 'The dog is a danger to public health. It must be destroyed. It bit my wife who, in spite of her injury, has come here to see that no one else is harmed. The dog must be destroyed at once—immediately.'"

The Doctor Gives a Lecture

B Y THIS TIME THE CROWD HAD GROWN STILL larger, all the stragglers having come up to be in at the kill. And things began to look really serious for the Doctor. A couple of old farmers in the rear began to harangue the mob, encouraging them to rush the gate. From my hiding place behind the study window I saw the crowd surge forward suddenly. I was still panting, breathless, from my long run. And the prospect of having to break out at the back of the house and be chased some more was not at all pleasant.

"But the Doctor wasn't to be easily brushed aside. He suddenly snatched a gun from the hands of one of the gardeners, and, bringing it to his shoulder, he faced the mob.

"'Stand back—everybody!' he commanded shortly. 'This is my home and no one can enter it without a search warrant signed by a magistrate.'

"At that, greatly impressed, the mob fell back instantly. I wondered what was going to happen next. But before the Doctor could say any more, my mistress suddenly fainted into her husband's arms. I suppose she had just remembered how seriously she'd been wounded. Anyway, she nearly squashed poor Oswald, who was a small, frail man, with her enormous weight.

"That took the general attention off the 'mad dog' for the moment. The Doctor, calling to Dab-Dab to bring some water from the house, personally attended to the lady and she was soon brought round.

"Then he gave her a lecture. He assured her as a doctor and a veterinary surgeon that I wasn't mad at all. He told her kindly but firmly that she didn't know anything whatever about bringing up

"My mistress suddenly fainted."

dogs—that he was well acquainted with me and was sure that she had ruined my disposition by turning me from a sporting outdoor dog into a silly boudoir pet.

"'So you see, Madam,' he concluded, 'instead of being mad or having rabies, Dapple has merely started the habit of—er—hysterics—which, in fact, he has caught from you. Hysterics, Madam, you should know, while a very minor disorder, is highly contagious.'

"Some of the policemen had now arrived. And the farmers had been urging them to go in and get me. But when it became known that the little man defending his home with such firmness was a doctor of medicine, a veterinary surgeon and a naturalist of great renown, the attitude of the whole crowd became entirely different. With such an authority maintaining that I was *not* mad, who would dare to invade his home and shoot me?

"'I am quite willing,' said the Doctor, turning to the policemen, 'to assume entire responsibility for the dog—provided this lady will leave him in my care. And I think, Madam,' he added, addressing my mistress, 'that you have had abundant proof that the dog does not like the home you have given him. This, as you know, is the fourth or fifth time that he has run away and come to me for refuge. Don't you think that it would be more humane and best from all points of view if you left him here?'

"'For my part,' Oswald began, suddenly recovering from his squashing, 'I wouldn't have the wretched cur in the house again for anything. I would sooner . . .'

"His enormous wife turned and glowered at him, and the poor little man shriveled and subsided.

"'Oswald,' said she, 'this is my affair.' She turned to the Doctor.

'I am very disappointed in the dog,' she said. 'He was sold to me as a purebred. He couldn't have been that to prefer such a place as this'—with a magnificent gesture she waved a fat arm toward the Doctor's small and modest house—'to my home. I never wish to set eyes on the ungrateful creature again. I couldn't have treated a child of my own with greater kindness.'

"She began to weep.

"'But don't you see?' said the Doctor, advancing toward her full of sympathy. That was just the trouble. You were too kind to him. He didn't want to be spoiled. He wished to be himself. He—'

"The woman waved him aside.

"'Enough!' she cried. "You may keep him. I never wish to see the ungrateful creature again—Oswald, lead me to my carriage.'

"And thereupon, behind the curtain of the study window, I threw a somersault for sheer joy as the portly lady got into her victoria and drove away—for good—leaving me in John Dolittle's home. I am quite myself again now. But I believe I'd have become a real mad dog if I had stayed with her much longer . . . truly the Doctor is a great man."

THE DOG
AMBULANCE

The First Patient

I T WAS ABOUT THIS TIME THAT THE DOG AMBU-
lance was started. This institution (the idea, you may
remember, was originally Jip's) belonged to and was organized entirely by the club. It was the first thing of its kind
in history. And I felt that a description of it and the events that
accompanied its inauguration could quite fittingly be included in
my book, *Tales of the Home for Crossbred Dogs*. On consulting Jip I
found that he agreed with me and we decided to put it in following
the Dalmatian's story.

For several days in succession we had had serious cases of dog
casualties on the streets: dogs run over; dogs kicked by horses; sick
and homeless strays, etc. Many of these cases when brought to the
surgery were so far gone that the Doctor had a hard time pulling
them through.

"Tommy," said Jip, coming to me at breakfast one morning,
"we've got to have a dog ambulance. I'm sure we can get the Doctor
to agree to it because I've already spoken to him about it—the time

we brought Kling here when he was poisoned—and he thought it was a good idea. In the home we have a couple of mongrel greyhounds. They're kind of funny to look at, but they're awful speedy. They have already volunteered to take it in turns doing duty. So we will have no difficulty with that part of it. What we need is the ambulance carriage itself and some harness for the greyhounds. Do you think you could build us a carriage and get your father to make us a set of harnesses?"

"Well, Jip," I said, "I don't know. But I am quite willing to try."

So that same evening I went over to the Stubbins' cobbler shop where I found that my father, though he was pretty busy, would make us the harness in his spare time. Then I set to work with Bumpo, the African Prince, who prided himself on being something of a mechanic, and out of a pair of rubber-tired perambulator wheels, a few springs out of an old bed, and some pieces of packing case, we constructed a very decent-looking runabout, light enough to be drawn by a dog. We painted it white, put a Red Cross flag on it and a bell. It was quite an elegant turnout.

When the harness was ready we hitched up one of the mongrel greyhounds, and Jip, as assistant casualty surgeon, drove around the zoo enclosure at a speed of thirty miles an hour—greatly to the astonishment of the inhabitants of Animal Town.

All concerned were very proud of the new dog ambulance. Night and day, from then on, one of the greyhounds was kept harnessed up in readiness to answer an emergency call.

"That's fine, Tommy," said Jip. "Something that was really needed. Those serious cases can be brought to the surgery now with the least possible delay."

Well, as such things often happen, now that we had a brand-

HUGH LOFTING

"It was quite an elegant turnout."

new dog ambulance ready for all emergencies, we got no cases to try it out on. Suddenly all dog casualties seemed to cease. The gallant greyhound steeds stood in the harness from dawn to dark and never a call came for their services.

Jip, Kling and Toby, the chief organizers of the Animal Town First Aid, were dreadfully disappointed. Finally Jip became so anxious to try out the new ambulance that he and Toby decided secretly between them that if no case came along soon they would have to make one.

After many days of idle waiting they had (without telling either the Doctor or me) proudly led their ambulance out through the streets of Puddleby on their own. This they did partly because they wanted the townsfolk to see the elegant equipage in all its glory, and partly because they might find a "case" by chance to try it on.

While they were parading through the town they came upon Gub-Gub, the Doctor's pet pig, in a back street sitting on a garbage heap. He was a great garbage-heap explorer, was Gub-Gub. The poor pig had eaten some bad turnips and was looking rather green in the face from a slight stomachache.

"Ah! A serious case!" cried Jip, rushing the ambulance up alongside the garbage heap in grand style. Then, with great dispatch, Orderlies Kling and Toby, under the direction of Surgeon

HUGH LOFTING

"He was a great garbage-heap explorer."

Jip, pounced upon the wretched Gub-Gub and began hauling him onto the ambulance. They would have sooner had a dog patient to try their new equipment on, but a pig was better than nothing.

"Leave me alone!" bawled Gub-Gub, kicking out in all directions. "I've only got a stomachache. I don't want to go on your ambulance!"

"Don't listen to him," ordered Jip. "He's delirious. Appendicitis, most likely. It's a rush case, men. Get him on quick!"

The three of them rolled Gub-Gub's portly carcass onto the ambulance. Jip sprang into the driver's seat while Toby and Kling sat on the "delirious" patient to hold him down.

Like a shot the mongrel greyhound bounded away at full speed for the Doctor's home. Meanwhile Jip clanged the bell for all he was worth to clear the road ahead and drown the bellowings of the first case to be brought to the Dolittle surgery by the dog ambulance.

THE SECOND CHAPTER

The Mishap at Kingsbridge

I T WAS A THRILLING RIDE—THRILLING FOR THE staff of the ambulance, for the townsfolk who looked on and, most of all, for the patient. Certainly all records established up to that date were easily broken so far as sheer speed was concerned. But as to time—from picking up a case to delivery at hospital—that was another matter. Indeed, the original case never reached the surgery at all—in the ambulance. But I must tell the story in the proper order.

Streaking up High Street with clanging bell, the strange vehicle shot under horses' noses, past traffic policemen who ordered it to stop, round corners on two wheels, scattering scared pedestrians right and left. At Kingsbridge it met with its first accident. Here the road narrowed as it crossed the river. In trying to avoid a peddler's barrow, the greyhound steed went a shade too near a lamppost. With Gub-Gub's extra heavy weight added to that of the two orderlies and the surgeon, the springs of the ambulance were being taxed to their utmost anyway. The hub of the right rear wheel only just touched the base of the lamppost. But it was enough to throw the overloaded, careening carriage off its balance. On one wheel it shot across the road and dumped its entire contents— surgeon, orderlies, and patient—over the parapet of the bridge.

As it happened, the river was at low tide. At such time, wide stretches of black mud margined the narrow, swiftly running stream. This in a way was providential—for the patient, but not for the staff. Gub-Gub's rating as a swimmer was very low, and had the river been at high tide he would have had a hard time reaching the bank. Jip, Kling and Toby, on the other hand, would have much preferred a clean bath to the fate that awaited them below the bridge. All four

HUGH LOFTING

"Dumped its entire contents over the parapet"

landed with an oozy splash into the tidal mud. It broke the fall nicely, but it didn't improve their appearance. Entirely black from head to foot, the gallant staff still remembered its duty to the injured and proceeded to dig the struggling, squealing patient out of his mud bath.

Fortunately, the distance to firmer ground was not more than a few yards. Somehow the patient, who on account of his weight had sunk deeper in than the others, was hauled and dragged to solid territory. He may not have been a proper case for the ambulance when they had forcibly carried him off from the garbage heap, but by the time they had got him out of the mud of the river he was in considerably greater need of attention.

Regaining the bridge, the staff, now completely garbed in a new uniform of black mud, rolled the patient back onto the ambulance, jumped in after him, and went away as fast as ever. In fact, they went even faster, for their mishap at the river had caused quite a crowd to collect and they were afraid they might be stopped at any minute.

For about a mile all went well. But as they turned into the Oxenthorpe Road at full gallop, they met with still another accident. A sleek, overfed Pomeranian was crossing the road with great dignity. Suddenly, seeing the extraordinary carriage bearing down upon him at thirty-five miles an hour, he lost what little wits he had, ran first this way and then that and finally wound up under the front wheels of the ambulance. The carriage did not entirely capsize, but it tipped up sufficiently as it went over him to shoot the patient out again—this time into the gutter. The fiery greyhound steed was brought to a standstill and that keen—perhaps too keen—medical student, Jip, ran back to take charge of the situation.

The patient was lying on his back in the gutter, his four trotters waving in the air, yelling blue murder. Up the middle of the road the fat Pomeranian was also lying on his back and howling—mostly with indignation and fright. Surgeon Jip and Orderlies Toby and Kling held a hasty professional consultation. The ambulance could hardly take both casualties. Their first duty was to their original patient. On the other hand, the dog ambulance was originally intended for dogs, and here was a fine case ready at hand.

However, while the discussion was still going on, Gub-Gub, fearing he might have to continue his hazardous ride in the ambulance, suddenly sprang up and took to his heels. Sore as he was from his fall and his stomachache, he had had enough of Jip's first aid.

This solved the problem for the staff of the dog ambulance very

HUGH LOFTING

"Jip grabbed the Pomeranian, carrying him like a puppy."

nicely. Jip grabbed the Pomeranian by the scruff of the neck and, carrying him like a puppy, dumped him into the ambulance, sprang in once more, and gave the word to go.

It wasn't until after the flying carriage had done another mile that he suddenly realized that he had left his two orderlies behind. But Kling and Toby, by putting on their best speed, came in on foot a very good second and third in the race for the surgery.

The Reception at the Surgery

J IP, KLING, AND TOBY WERE ALL SADLY disappointed at the Doctor's reception of the dog ambulance the first time it returned from active service. I am bound to say that the equipage had lost much of its original smartness. The wheels were bent and wobbly, the bell post was twisted up like a corkscrew and the bell gone, the first aid box beneath the driver's seat had burst open and bandages were trailing from it in the dust of the road behind. As for the staff, caked with mud and dust from head to foot, well, you could just tell that they were dogs and that was all.

The patient, as soon as the ambulance came to a halt, got out of the stretcher without waiting for assistance and at once began a long and indignant speech to the Doctor. He accused Jip and his assistants of first knocking him down by reckless driving, and then kidnaping him right in front of his own gate.

No sooner had he finished his tirade than his mistress, who had followed in a cab, appeared upon the scene and began another long accusation. She assured the Doctor that she had heard a good deal about him and his crazy wild animals and she meant to appeal to the police. Things had come to a pretty pass, she said, when a man trained a gang of dogs to kidnap and steal other dogs.

The Doctor was just getting ready to answer her when Gub-Gub arrived, howling like a lost child who had been punished for something he never did. He began the third discourse upon the wicked deeds of the Red Cross Brigade who had carried him off against his will, thrown him over a bridge into the river, then rushed him over bumpy streets a few more miles and finally pitched him out into the gutter.

By the end of the last of these speeches the staff of the dog ambulance was beginning to feel that its services in the public good had been somewhat misdirected and not wholly understood. The greyhound steed slunk away to the zoo enclosure, where Bumpo undid his harness and separated him from the dilapidated carriage. As for Jip, Kling and Toby, they made no attempt to explain to the Doctor, but went miserably down to the fish pond and washed the mud from themselves. Not a word was said till they were on their way back to supper. Then Jip broke the silence with, "We shouldn't have started with that ridiculous pig. He always puts a hoodoo on everything."

THE STUNNED MAN

THE FIRST CHAPTER

The Robbery

KLING, WHO CAME TO BE KNOWN AS THE Detective Dog, lived at Doctor Dolittle's Home for Crossbred Dogs.

Gub-Gub, who dearly loved a mystery, tried to get Kling started on some new plot, because he was anxious to see a real detective at work. And by chance his wish was presently granted in a rather peculiar way.

Jip, who had been nosing about the neighborhood in search of a bone he'd buried and lost, came upon a man lying in the middle of the road, unconscious. He immediately routed us out of bed and led us to the stranger.

Once more Fate had pushed John Dolittle, willy-nilly, into the affairs of his neighbors. For, of course, even if he had not been a doctor, he would not have refused first aid to the injured at his door. Bumpo, who was living with us at the time, and I, helped him carry the man in and lay him on the table in the surgery.

The man was not seriously injured, though from the tremendous

HUGH LOFTING

"A man was lying in the middle of the road, unconscious."

bump on the back of his head I had at first thought he might be. The Doctor brought him round after a few moments. And the first thing he said when he opened his eyes was: "I've been robbed. A lot of money has been stolen from me."

"Ah!" said Gub-Gub, who was listening at the surgery door, "the Mystery of the Stunned Man. Good! I'll get Kling."

The man seemed from his appearance to be a groom or stable-man of some kind. As soon as he had gathered his wits together a little he began pouring out the story of his troubles without waiting for any questioning or encouragement from the Doctor.

"I had forty pounds with me," he said, "what the boss had given me to take to the bank at Oxenthorpe. I had just stopped a minute to tie my bootlace outside your gate here when someone hit me a terrible blow on the head from behind. Then all was darkness till I woke up here. There will be an awful row when the boss finds out the money's gone. You'll stand by me, sir, won't you? You'll bear witness to what I say? Be you a doctor, sir?" he ended, looking round the surgery at the bandages and bottles.

"Er-yes, I'm a doctor," said John Dolittle. "But why be anxious? Your story will, no doubt, be believed—so long as you state it exactly as it happened. All we know is that we found you unconscious in the road. We can't bear witness to anything further than that. If you were robbed it is quite possible that the police may be able to get the money back for your employer."

Gub-Gub, the pig, emerged from under the surgery table and nudged the Doctor's leg.

"I've brought Kling," said he. "He'll soon solve this."

"No," whispered the Doctor quickly. "This is the police's affair, not ours. We will stay out of it."

"Well, you see," the man went on, "you never can tell. The boss might even say that I stole the money. But you'll stand by me, won't you, Doctor?"

"I'll do what I said," the Doctor answered, apparently somewhat annoyed. "I can't do any more. But don't be worried. Tell your employer the truth and I'm sure that everything will come out all right. Do you feel steady enough to walk now?"

The man got down from the table and tried a few paces.

"Yes," he said, "I reckon I can manage now. Thank you, Doctor. I'll be going. But maybe I'll have to call on you as a witness later."

"That's all right," said John Dolittle. "I'm very busy, but I'll be willing to state what little I know of the case. Do you want me to send a message to have them come fetch you?"

"No, thank you," said the man. "I can walk."

As we followed the man out into the garden and watched him descend the steps, I noticed that Kling and Jip were examining the road opposite the gate with great care. Gub-Gub, deeply interested in the proceedings, was looking on. But the two dogs made him keep his distance; they were evidently anxious that no meddling pig's trotters should spoil the tracks in the dust.

As soon as the man had disappeared, the Doctor hurried away to his study to get in a few minutes' work at his books before breakfast; while I, to kill time till Dab-Dab, the duck housekeeper, should summon us to the kitchen, strolled down onto the road to watch the Detective Dog's investigations. Jip came up to me as I reached the foot of the steps and spoke in whispers, looking backward over his shoulder with respectful awe at Kling, the great expert.

"He's marvelous, Tommy," he said, "simply marvelous. He has already found out that half what that fellow told us wasn't true and that there were a whole lot of other things he didn't tell us at all. For one, he had a horse with him."

"Goodness! Perhaps he was a highwayman," put in Gub-Gub, who had sneaked up and joined us. Jip ignored the remark with contempt.

"I thought I was pretty good at tracks myself," he went on. "But compared with Kling, I'm just a beginner. On this case he hasn't said very much so far. But it's my opinion that he already has the whole thing straightened out in his mind."

As a matter of fact, Kling, since he had left the police service in Belgium, had not, he admitted, had any desire to return to that kind of work. It was now quite clear to me that the flattering admiration of Gub-Gub and Jip had been too much for the famous dog detective and had gotten him started on his old profession again. After breakfast the two dogs disappeared (no doubt on business connected with "the case"); and it did not seem to me that any harm could be done so long as they didn't drag the Doctor into it.

But the next morning Dab-Dab woke me up in a great state of indignation.

"Tommy," said she, "you must make those wretched dogs stop this detective rubbish. What do you think they've done now?"

"I've no idea, Dab-Dab," I said, sitting up and rubbing my eyes sleepily. "No idea at all."

"Well, come down to the porch and look," said she.

Still only partly awake, I threw on some clothes and followed her downstairs.

"Open the front door," said she.

I did so. And an enormous pile of old, disreputable-looking shoes, which had evidently been stacked up against the door, spilled into the hall. While up the path from the gate Jip and Kling were just arriving, each with another old shoe in his mouth, to add to the pile they had collected.

"Good gracious, Kling!" I cried. "What's this? Anyone would think that the Doctor had gone into the secondhand clothes business from the mess you've made of the porch."

"Sh! Tommy," whispered Jip. "Close the door and come outside a minute. Kling will explain."

"Explain! Rubbish!" squawked Dab-Dab angrily. "Kling just brought those shoes here to chew. He's as bad as Gub-Gub and his vegetable mysteries. If you dogs don't clear that mess off my porch before breakfast you won't get any—no, nor any lunch either," she added as I closed the door on her wrath and followed the dogs down the path.

The Footprint in the Copse

ITHOUT FURTHER WORD THE TWO OF them led me out onto the road, turned to the right and took me about a quarter of a mile in the direction of Oxenthorpe. Then, through a farm gate, they jumped into a meadow and struck out across it toward a copse in the middle. Looking around to make sure that no one should see us enter, they finally led me into this through a hole in the surrounding hedge. Inside there was a clear open space beneath the trees where the earth was damp, mossy, and practically grassless.

"This," said Kling, leading me across to the foot of an oak tree, "is where the money was buried. In fact, there is the money itself—in that bag."

The earth here was all dug up where the dogs had evidently rooted down following a scent. Among the loose earth there was a small linen bag. I picked it up and shook it. It jingled with the sound of gold.

"Now, Tommy," said Kling, "come over here."

"It jingled with the sound of gold."

I followed him a few yards away from the tree to where a mossy hollow spread its green freshness beneath tall overhanging hawthorns. It was a place which in wetter weather would have been a pond or bog.

"You see that?" asked Kling, pointing with his nose.

"Yes," said I, "a footprint."

"Well, that's what we collected the shoes for," said he. "We want a shoe to fit that print."

"But how on earth," I asked, "do you expect to find it—out of all the shoes in the world?"

"We don't," said Kling with the patient air of a professor

arguing with an obstinate, stupid child. "We don't expect to find it among all the shoes in the world, but only among the shoes that were thrown away last night in this immediate neighborhood. Which is a very different matter. We know that the man who made this print threw his shoes away, because when we followed up the tracks and scent we found that he had done part of his journey in stockinged feet. That's why we've gone round collecting all the shoes we could find under hedges and everywhere. And now we want you to pick out from the pile we've gathered a shoe that fits that print."

"But why, Kling," I asked, "would not the scent you followed have led you to the man, even more surely than your knowing who it was that made this footprint?"

"Scents are freakish things," said Kling, frowning. "It was clear and distinct this far and led us, as easy as pie, to where the money was buried—and even beyond it for a way. But we lost it about a half mile from here. We lost the stocking-feet tracks, too. The man, whoever he was, knew something about covering his own trail— probably an old criminal."

"Then you don't think that the fellow that Jip found in the road could have hidden the money himself?" I asked.

"Certainly not," said Kling quickly. "We made a note of his scent when he was in the surgery. Whether he was in part- nership with the man who took the money away and buried it, I have yet to find out. I suspect he was. Because the story he told the Doctor was *not* a frank statement at all. But he was not the one who brought the money here and buried it. That was done by the party who made that footprint. And then, I imagine, real- izing that he had left tracks behind him, he got scared, took his shoes off, and threw them away."

"But how do you know that he threw them away?" said I. "Why couldn't he have carried them in his hand?"

"Of that," said Kling, "we are not as yet absolutely sure. But we are pretty certain. For one thing, if he was afraid of the tracks giving him away to the police—he had made a whole lot of footprints in a field close to where the man was struck down—he would be afraid to have the shoes in his home. For another, he was already burdened with a spade, and perhaps other tools to do his digging with. It is certain that he was not far from home or he would never have attempted to make the return journey in his stockinged feet."

"Do you think," I asked, "that he himself might have struck the man Jip found, while quarreling over the gold or something?"

"Perhaps, but I don't think so," said Kling. "It is more likely, in my opinion, that he found the man lying in the road before Jip got there; that he at once became terrified, thinking him dead or dying, that he would be blamed for it—since his tracks were in the road leading to the man's body.

"And of course it is most likely," Kling went on, "that the next thing he'd think of, after covering his own tracks, would be the hiding of the money, either because that also would throw suspicion on him or because he hoped to come later and dig it up after the row had blown over. So one of the first things we have to do before we go away from here is to cover our own tracks, leave everything as we found it, and set someone on guard in case the man returns. That, however, I fear there isn't much chance of his doing for a longish time. Still, good detectives leave no loopholes. We'll get Toby or Swizzle to hide in the bushes here and watch."

"Then you think we had better leave the money where it is?" I asked.

"Oh, certainly," said Kling. "It will be quite safe so long as we have one of the dogs watching. And we will be much more likely to find out things if we don't let on to what we already know. The best detectives always pretend to be as ignorant and as stupid as possible."

So, thereupon we proceeded to set the stage in the copse just as we found it. Kling, realizing that he probably had an experienced criminal to deal with, took the greatest pains to make sure that we left no trace to show that we had been there. After the earth had been put back into the hole on top of the money bag, he went over all the ground inside the copse slowly and carefully. Wherever the moss or the little under-shrubs had been beaten down by our feet, he straightened everything up to wipe out all traces. He even examined the encircling hawthorns lest we might have broken any leaves or left limbs drawn back showing where we had come through.

"I'll bring Swizzle and Toby up here as soon as we get back," said he, as we struck off across the fields for the gate. "They can take it in turns to keep watch."

Before leaving I had taken a rough tracing of the footprint with a pencil and paper, so as to be able to get an idea of which shoes might fit. Of course it wasn't very accurate, but I calculated that with its aid I could cut down the number of shoes I must bring up here to try—even if I did not succeed in making sure at the house.

The Shoe that Fit the Footprint

O N OUR WAY BACK, AS WE APPROACHED THE Doctor's house, we saw three men descending the steps. The Doctor was standing at the gate at the top watching them. He looked worried and puzzled.

Kling at once shot off and overtook the men. He pretended to be doing nothing in particular; but I noticed by the way he stopped and sniffed in passing them that he was looking for a scent he knew.

"Who are those men, Doctor?" I asked as I joined him and walked up the garden path toward the front door.

"Oh, bother it, Stubbins!" said he rather irritably, "I don't know and I don't want to know. It is something in connection with this man we found stunned in the roadway—and the money that was missing. Those two big fellows are plainclothes men, or private detectives or something of the sort. They wanted to know if I could identify the little man they have with them. He is under arrest, it seems, on suspicion of having done the deed. They asked me when I had seen him last. I never saw him before—thank goodness! I've no idea who he is."

"But I have, Doctor," said a voice behind us. And turning we found Matthew Mugg, who had mysteriously appeared from somewhere in the garden and joined us.

"That little bloke was Tobias Wilkes," he went on. "I know him well."

"But I don't," the Doctor put in hurriedly. "What on earth are all those shoes on the front steps for?"

"Oh, Kling is doing some investigating on his own account," said I. "He thinks he can find out who struck the man."

"Good gracious!" cried the Doctor. "For pity's sake, don't let us have any more mysteries or detective work around here! Haven't we had enough already?"

And leaving us abruptly he fairly ran round the house to the side door to return to his work at which he had been interrupted.

"It'll go hard with poor Tobias," said Matthew thoughtfully as he watched the Doctor's figure disappear, "if he can't prove that he was somewhere else that night. His reputation's none too good anyhow. The Doctor's fibbing when he says he never saw him before—unless he has forgotten, convenient-like maybe. Why, he caught Tobias poaching pheasants not over a month ago. That I know, because I was helping Tobias myself at the time—only the Doctor never saw me."

As I climbed over the pile of old shoes and opened the front door, Kling ran up to me.

"Tommy," said he, "I'd like to see you alone a moment."

"Well, Kling," I said when we were within the hall with the door closed behind us, "what is it? Was that little fellow the man who hid the money? I saw you sniffing at him as you passed."

"No, of course he isn't," said Kling impatiently. "Those lanky detectives are just plainclothes fools. This man smells entirely different. The fellow who made that footprint in the copse was the one who hid the money. What I want you to do now, Tommy, is to find the right shoe, if you can, among that pile. I've got to take Toby and Swizzle up to the copse and put them on guard. Blackie and Grab are keen to do it, but I'm afraid of fighting dogs for a job of this kind. They'd go for the man if he came, I know. All we want is small, clever dogs who will follow the fellow and see where he takes the money. So hurry up, will you? Now they've got the wrong man under arrest, we've got to get busy."

Immediately after he had gone I set to work with my tracing. Most of the pile of shoes were far too large or too small to leave any doubt. But one pair fitted suspiciously well. Jip was watching me with great interest.

"I remember where we found that pair," he said. "It was in a ditch at the bottom of the field where the copse is. Let's follow Kling up there right away and try it in the footprint itself."

So away we went without further delay.

We found the Dog Detective giving final instructions to his able lieutenants, Toby and Swizzle. He was very carefully repeating to them for the second time the exact place and manner they were to lie hidden and how they were to change guard at intervals. Swizzle, the clown dog, was taking it all as a joke; but Toby, the self-important, was treating it very seriously.

It was a thrilling moment when we laid the shoes over the footprint. It couldn't have fitted better.

"Good!" muttered the Dog Detective. "That is a big step in the chain of evidence."

"But, Kling," I said, "I don't see how you're going to find the man even now that you are sure that you've got his shoe."

"No," said Kling with some condescension, "having no experience as a criminal investigator, you wouldn't. But you see, I already have my suspicions—and an idea of where to look for my man. In fact, I am pretty certain—by guesswork it is true—of where the man lives. But several men live in the same place. With this shoe I can now tell which of the men it was who hid the money."

"Good gracious!" I said. "I had no idea that you had got that far. And where does the man live, might I ask?"

"He lives," said the Detective Dog, "at least I strongly suspect he does—in the same place as the stunned man lives; in the stable hands' quarters up at Squire Jenkins's place. If you will come with me we will now proceed there and continue our investigations."

I knew Squire Jenkins's place quite well. It was about two miles down the Oxenthorpe Road from the Doctor's house. Here in a fine old Georgian mansion the squire (who many years ago had been one of the Doctor's patients) kept a large establishment with hunting stables, foxhound kennels, and all the other things that in those days went with a big country house.

Around the wide yard behind the main building were the quarters for the grooms and stable hands—of which the squire kept at least a dozen. This yard was reached by a private road whose gate was always open.

"It is my idea," said Kling as we reached the gate, "to drop the shoe in the middle of the yard and then retire to see what happens. We may have luck; we may not. We shall see."

I hardly expected that anyone would object to my going down the private road. But I thought it best to make myself as little noticeable as possible in any case. I knew that no one would be likely to interfere with Kling.

Unchallenged, we got into the yard, where I lounged behind a hay cart and watched Kling take his shoe out into the middle and drop it. Then he went smelling around just like any stray dog looking for rats.

From time to time various grooms and boys crossed the yard engaged on stable business of one kind or another. All passed the shoe with barely a glance.

But finally a lanky sort of a man with a very disagreeable face came out of a stable door carrying a saddle under his arm. The shoe lay right in his path as he crossed from that corner of the yard to the opposite. As his eye fell on it he gave quite a start. Then, glancing round nervously to make sure no one saw him, he hastily snatched it up from the ground, hid it under the saddle, and hurried on. Kling, who had appeared to be examining a gutter on the other side of the yard trotted carelessly across his path, sniffing, before the man disappeared into what seemed to be the harness room.

Then he dawdled around to my side of the hay cart.

"Did you get a good look at his face, Tommy?" he whispered.

"Yes," I said, "I'd know him again anywhere."

"Good!" whispered the Dog Detective, pretending to scent another rat. "Then let's be going, shall we?"

THE FOURTH CHAPTER

The Dog Detective
Contemplates

ITHOUT FURTHER WORDS WE LEFT the yard together and made our way down the private road. At the outer gate Jip joined us.

"Well, Kling," I said, after we had tramped about half a mile in silence, "what is the next move?"

The Dog Detective, deep in contemplation, made no response.

"Sh!" said Jip. "Don't disturb him. He's thinking. Sometimes over his knottiest cases he goes into these moods for hours—and days—at a time. He'll speak when he's ready."

And Jip was quite right. Kling did not speak for another two and half hours. As soon as he got home he took out one of his old chewing shoes onto the lawn. There the reverie of the great investigator continued, while Jip and I sat around with our mouths open, wondering when he would have done enough thinking—and chewing—to say a little something. In this Gub-Gub came and joined us—though Jip was quite firm in making him keep his distance from the meditating detective.

"You've no idea, Tommy," he whispered to me, "what a time we've had with that ridiculous hog. He is just determined to follow this case inch by inch. There were moments when we simply had to run to get away from him. You can imagine how much chance two Secret Service dogs like us would stand of finding out anything with a large grunting pig lumbering along behind us everywhere we went. I managed to shut him into the tool shed once, but he bellowed so loud that the Doctor thought someone was being killed and came running out from his study to see what was the matter—Goodness! Look at Kling. I believe he has found it."

The Dog Detective had ceased his thoughtful chewing. He was staring, motionless, at the lawn between his feet.

"I wonder," we heard him mutter to himself at last, "I wonder. It's possible—quite probable, in fact . . . Humph!"

Then suddenly he threw the boot aside, sprang up, and disappeared out of the gate leading down the steps onto the road. Jip and I followed him, running. So did Gub-Gub—greatly to Jip's annoyance.

In the road outside the gate the great investigator proceeded to run back and forth over the scene of the crime.

"Yes," he hissed at last, "it was—I'll bet my last boot it was . . . Tommy, our next job is to find a horse . . . a horse . . . a horse whose off hind-shoe has a bent nail in it."

"Why?" I asked. "What do you want him for?"

"Because he is the one who stunned the man," said Kling.

"Goodness me!" I cried. "You don't say! Kicked him senseless, do you mean?"

"No, that's the confusing point," said Kling. "He *didn't* kick

"Suddenly he threw the boot aside."

him—of that I'm certain. And yet I'm positive that he is the only one who could have stunned the man. But how the dickens he did it I've yet to find out."

After a few moments of thought Kling turned back to me.

"Tommy," said he, "I think I'll get you to go down to those stables and do a little inquiring among the hands. If you get them chatting they will, maybe, tell you things which I, of course, couldn't learn—that way—unless I talked their language. Meantime I've got some other business in connection with the case to attend to alone. Oh, and Jip, listen! You might go up to the copse and see if Toby or Swizzle have anything to report."

Having thus given his assistants their orders, Chief Kling trotted away on his own affairs.

I proceeded at once to the squire's place, where I strolled leisurely into the stable yard and tried to engage some of the hands in friendly conversation. It wasn't very difficult. I soon found a lad polishing a snaffle bit who seemed glad to have someone to talk to while he worked. I began by making a few remarks about horses—on which subject he was anxious to show how much he knew. Then I steered the conversation onto the topic of the robbery. The affair had apparently upset the whole establishment quite a little. The man who had been stunned had been the squire's second head groom. I gathered that he wasn't at all popular with the rest of the stable hands, who were almost pleased that he had been knocked on the head. But the fact that the roads around peaceful Puddleby were evidently not safe for a man to travel alone, was a very different matter and had caused considerable indignation.

"Still," the boy ended. "I reckon they got the right party in handcuffs now, sure enough. That fellow Tobias Wilkes will have hard work proving it wasn't him. Squire got two smart detectives down from London, private detectives. He don't trust the police of these parts, squire don't—thinks they be all fools. But them London fellows didn't take long over making an arrest. And they say they can prove that Wilkes came along that road just about the time that Fred Langley got knocked on the head. And I'll warrant that before long they'll prove he struck the blow and took the money. But he's an artful dodger, that Wilkes. What beats me is how he hid the horse he stole. It's easy to hide a bag of sovereigns, but 'tain't so easy to hide a horse."

HUGH LOFTING

"Squire got two smart detectives down from London."

"Oh, was there a horse stolen too?" I asked, trying hard not to show too much interest.

"Surely, there was," said the lad. "One of squire's best hacks; a chestnut mare. She wasn't very young, but she was as fine a mare as you could find in these parts. And she just disappeared after that night as though the earth had swallowed her up. Squire was more upset about her than he was about the money. She wasn't no hunter, but she was his favorite road hack and the cleverest horse, the prettiest pacer, I ever saw. Her name was Tiger Lily."

Before I left I learned that Langley, the man who had been stunned, was very friendly with the groom who had picked up the shoe. This fellow's name was Smedley. They happened to cross the yard together while I was still talking to the lad. Also I found out that Tiger Lily, the mare, was to have been shod at the Puddleby farriers the morning that she disappeared.

I felt quite proud, as I walked homeward, of my success. I found Kling waiting for me—also Matthew Mugg, who told me he had been making inquiries down in the town and had learned that the general opinion was that Tobias Wilkes would go to jail for a long term.

In a quiet corner of the garden, Kling, Jip, and I held a little conference.

"We've got to hurry this thing along more than ever now, Kling," said I, "if we are to save Tobias from an unjust sentence."

"All right, all right," said Kling, "I know. The next thing is to find this mare, Tiger Lily. With her story—if we can get it from her, and I fancy the Doctor will be able to—the whole case will be complete. The Doctor doesn't want to be mixed in it, I know, but he will hardly refuse when we show him that it will save an innocent man from jail. I found a shoe that I am certain is Tiger Lily's about a mile along the road from where the man was struck down. I know it is hers because it had the bent nail in it which showed in the hoof marks not far from the Doctor's gate. Tracking her might have been possible if we had followed this clue the morning the man was found. But by this time, of course, with all the cart wheels and hooves going over the road dust in the meantime, that is out of the question. What we need now is a dog with a peculiar gift in scent."

"How do you mean?" I asked.

"He means," said Jip, "a dog with a special nose for horses. Almost any dog is good on man scents. But one who can tell one horse from another by scent is pretty rare. Still, there are such dogs. Listen, Kling! Let's go down to the home and see what we can do there."

Together the three of us crossed the big garden to the zoo enclosure. The Home for Crossbred Dogs happened to be just setting to on the evening meal. Jip at once went to the head of the center table and beat upon it for silence with a ham bone. The chatter and rattling of dishes ceased instantly.

"Members," said Jip, addressing the dining room in general, "we have particular and urgent need of a dog with a good nose for horses—one who can follow a single horse scent across the whole length of England, if need be. Is there any member present who thinks he could do that?"

Tiger Lily's Trail

LMOST IMMEDIATELY AFTER JIP CEASED speaking, a dog left the sideboard buffet where he had been helping himself to sausages and shambled forward through the crowd toward the speaker. He was indeed a sorry-looking animal. He had only one eye; he walked with a limp and seemed quite, quite old. I remembered him at once. He was a mongrel foxhound whom Jip had got into the club long after it was full, by using a lot of influence with the committee and the Doctor.

"Well, Mike," said Jip, as the veteran came to a halt at the center table, "do you think you could do it?"

"I don't think," said the old dog, swallowing half a sausage that he had brought with him from the sideboard, "I know I could. I was born in a hunting kennel. But because I wasn't purebred they would never let me run with the pack. Still, I thought my nose was as good as any of 'em—even if I hadn't the speed and the looks. It was a dull life. There was hardly anything for me to do except hang around the stables, where the men used to laugh at me because I was crossbred.

The hounds used to make fun of me too. One day I followed the pack anyway, even though the whips tried to beat me off. Of course I couldn't keep up the whole run, but I stuck with 'em for a good six or seven miles. Then I was blown. While I was resting, one of the huntsmen got thrown as he tried to jump a hedge. He was a parson, a nice old fellow who had often been kind to me. His horse took fright and bolted immediately, over the hills and far away. The idea came to me to try and follow this horse and find him for my friend the parson. And after I had got my wind back, I up and went after him. The whole countryside was, of course, full of the scents of horses. Just the same, I succeeded in singling this one out and trailing him down. I found him grazing fifteen miles away from the place he had spilled his rider. Then I knew I had an extraordinary and special scent for horses. And when I began to experiment and train it, I discovered that I could pick one horse out of a hundred with my eyes shut. It is a real gift, but, of course, no use in a foxhound kennel. To them hunting folk I was just a poor scrub mongrel, good for nothing. Have you got something I can take the scent from for this mare you have lost?"

"Yes," said Kling, "we've got a shoe. It hasn't been handled. I left it just where she dropped it."

"Good!" grunted Mike. "I'll find her all right. Just wait till I've eaten my sausages. I'll be with you in a minute."

And turning, the old veteran shambled back to the sideboard to finish his evening meal.

"Listen, Tommy," said Jip, "this is likely to be a long run. If we set out on it tonight, you had better bring a supply of food and a blanket to sleep in. Goodness only knows how far old Mike may take us."

"All right," I said. "I'll go and get ready. When Mike has finished come and tell me."

Not wanting to worry the Doctor, I merely told him that Jip, Kling, and I were going out for a moonlight tramp and might not be home till late the next day. But I borrowed a little money from him in case we should need it. Then, by the time I had made up my bundle of the blanket and sandwiches, the three dogs were already waiting for me in the hall. Poor Gub-Gub tried very hard to join the party, but of course we couldn't take him.

The daylight was just starting to wane as we set out. Kling at once took us to the place where he had found the shoe. Old Mike sniffed at it, grunted, and trotted off.

It was a strange journey, and a strenuous one. Very soon I saw that with the coming darkness I stood a good chance of getting left behind. For the dogs, eager and long-winded, set a terrible pace at the start—in spite of old Mike's limp. Jip, after I had had to call to them more than once to wait for me, suggested that I tie a string to his collar so that I could keep in touch.

It seemed as though Tiger Lily had been pretty sure of her direction; for the scent hardly every halted or dawdled around. She had just hit across country, regardless almost of anything. There were places where she had evidently leapt high hedges, forded streams, swum lakes, and waded bogs. More than a dozen times I was on the point of telling the dogs that they would have to go on alone to find the trail's end. But the thrill of the chase fascinated me and kept me going through it all.

About midnight I told them that I thought it was time we all took a rest, for I saw that they, too, were pretty well winded. The four of us, therefore, ate a sandwich apiece, rolled ourselves in the blanket under a tree, and went fast asleep.

Next morning, after another sandwich all round, we were up

and going again through the dewy fields almost before the sun had arisen. Till now I had very little idea of where we were, beyond the guess that we had come in a northeasterly direction away from Puddleby, and had made about twenty miles. And even with the daylight I wasn't much the wiser. The dogs, from their conversation, seemed better acquainted with the neighborhood than I was. One village that we skirted looked, however, vaguely familiar to me. I asked Jip if he knew the name of it.

"Yes," said he, "that's Digby Royal."

"Digby Royal," I muttered. "Curious! The name sounds familiar, too. Could I have been here before?"

"Yes, that's Digby Royal."

And then it dawned on me that I had once on a journey with the Doctor changed coaches at a town of that name. I tried to remember what place we were going to on the journey. But that year the Doctor and I had done a good deal of traveling together about the country in pursuit of ferns, the study of which greatly interested him just then. Still, I thought, I ought to be able to remember.

For some hours, as we trudged along behind Mike, I cudgeled my brain, annoyed with my poor memory.

At last it came to me.

"Jip," I cried, "I have an idea of where this trail may lead us."

"Where?" he called back.

"To the Retired Cab and Wagon Horses' Association," I said. "I've just remembered where we were going when we last passed through Digby Royal."

"By Jingo!" muttered Jip. "That's so. I've gone there many times with the Doctor myself. And this is the way we always came. We're now approaching Bentlake. That's where the Doctor and I stopped for lunch last time. Humph! I wonder if you're right."

"Well," I said, "it is certain that the mare would have heard of the Doctor's home for retired horses, living as she does almost next door to John Dolittle's house. And it would be natural enough if she went off by herself, meaning to run away for good, that she would make for that as the best hiding place—in fact the only place where she would be safe from the interference of people."

Jip said no more but trotted on after Kling and Mike, wrapped in thought.

The trail artfully went around all the towns as though the mare (I remembered the stable lad's speaking of her extraordinary cleverness) had realized that she would be in danger of being stopped if she passed through streets with no one leading or riding her. On the way we found places where she had evidently lain down to hide from passersby behind high hedges or in the sheltering refuge of a copse of wood.

I became quite interested in the prospect of meeting this highly intelligent horse. And I began thinking about what Kling had said: that he was sure she had stunned the man—but not by kicking him. Could she have known something about him, disliked him perhaps, and stunned him on purpose to escape. And, above all, how in the world had she done it?

HUGH LOFTING

"We found places where she had lain down."

THE SIXTH CHAPTER

Toggle's Silence

A S WE DREW NEARER TO THE DISTRICT where John Dolittle had established his now well-known Retired Cab and Wagon Horses' Association, Jip and I became surer than ever that my guess had been right. The hills and the farms round about were more familiar territory to me than much of the country nearer home. For I had spent many pleasant days here with the Doctor talking to Beppo and Toggle, the famous old plow horse with green spectacles.

At the main gate to the Rest Farm these two were standing, when we at last came in sight of it, almost as though they had been expecting someone's arrival. They were delighted to see Jip and myself. Of the other dogs, Kling and Mike, they seemed suspicious until we introduced them as part of our party.

Inside the lovely meadows we stretched ourselves beneath the giant elms and ate the last of our sandwiches. We were all weary and dead beat after our long journey.

When I came to question Toggle about the chestnut mare,

"Beppo and Toggle were at the main gate."

to my great astonishment he first remained entirely silent. Then, evidently ill at ease, he assured me that no such horse had joined the association. He turned to old Beppo, who also gravely shook his head. Then Kling came up behind me and whispered in my ear:

"They've promised to say nothing. You can see that. Tiger Lily must be here. Old Mike says her scent is all over the place. She's hiding behind a hedge or something."

"Well, couldn't Mike nose her out?" I whispered back.

"Better not," said Kling. "The chances are she would just jump a fence and bolt. And then we'd have another fifty-mile chase to catch up with her again. Let me talk to these old fellows. If the mare is scared it will be best to get them to make her listen to reason."

Thereupon Kling explained to Beppo and Toggle (who were the president and vice-president of the association) that, first of all, we were quite certain that the mare was here. Secondly, that it was wrong of her to try and stay hidden, because an innocent man was in danger of being sentenced for something he hadn't done; and to clear up the matter, it was necessary to tell the police how Langley had been stunned. Also that the squire, who valued the mare highly, would want to claim her, and the Doctor would get into trouble with him when it became known that she had taken refuge at the Dolittle Rest Farm.

"So you see," Kling ended, "it would be far better if you two went to Tiger Lily and persuaded her to come and have a talk with us. Tell her that Tommy will promise to make no attempt to capture her against her will. But we must see her."

Finally the two old horses seemed to see the sense and fairness of what Kling had proposed. They told us to stay where we were while they drew off a short distance and conferred together in whispers. A little later we saw them disappear behind some hedges and for a while we saw nothing more of them.

"I wouldn't wonder," Kling whispered, "if Tiger Lily has been listening all the time somewhere quite near. We've got to be careful how we handle this mare, Tommy. I've a notion she's full of what Bumpo calls temperamentality—skittish and wayward, you know. Lookout! Here she comes."

I don't think I shall ever forget my first sight of Tiger Lily. For never had I seen a more beautiful, enchanting animal. She suddenly appeared in a gap in the hedge between the two old veterans. It

HUGH LOFTING

"'I wouldn't wonder if she has been listening,' Kling whispered."

may have been that their aged, broken-down look served to set off her clean, well-groomed, dainty grace. But as she stood there she seemed to me to have something of the almost supernatural about her. From her alert, clever eyes to her neat, slender fetlocks, she was a picture to warm the heart of any man.

It was very evident that though she had consented to come to the parley, she was not placing any great confidence in the promise that she would not be captured. At an easy supple walk she picked her way down the slope in our direction, but paused a good thirty paces from us and would come no nearer. I noticed those intelligent eyes taking in not only every detail of ourselves, but glancing around and beyond to make sure that the way of escape would be easy if any attempt should be made upon her liberty.

As I got up to address her I felt a new and peculiar pride in my knowledge of horse language, since it enabled me to converse with a creature such as this.

"How do you do, Tiger Lily?" I said, smiling to reassure her. "I am glad that you consented to come and talk with us. Please have no fear. You are not among enemies. We come, as Toggle has no doubt told you, from John Dolittle's house. It is necessary, for the sake of a man who has been wrongly arrested for striking down Fred Langley, that we hear your story of the night and early morning when the thing happened. Won't you please tell us?"

The mare thought for a moment. Then she threw back her shapely head and blew gently through her silky nostrils. The white of her muzzle and a star between her eyes were the only spots that broke the even, glossy chestnut of her coat.

"Yes," she said at length. "I'll tell you the whole thing as far as I know it. But I will not come with you. So you can put that out of your minds right away."

How the Mare
Got Away

I WAS DISAPPOINTED AT THE MARE'S WORDS. BUT before I had a chance to make any comment, Kling whispered: "Don't try to persuade her now. Wait till she has told us her story. Let her get more confidence in us first. Take her easy."

"This thing goes back," Tiger Lily began, "quite a long way— to the time when the road hacks were a much more important part of the squire's stables than they are now, when people used the roads more and these diabolical railway things that are doing their best to ruin the countryside, hadn't been invented. In those days most of the journeys that the squire and his guests made were done on horseback. But later, when the hunters took over most of the stables, I and a few hacks that were still kept were put into the stalls at the north end of the yard, and Langley, the second groom, was put in charge of us. Up to that time old George Gibbons, the head groom, had had the management of us, and things were different. The squire is an easygoing man and a great deal went on in his stables that he never knew of. That fellow Langley is a low-down, cruel, thieving rat. You must excuse my language, but he deserves it, every bit. As soon as he was given sole charge of the hack stables, with the buying of the fodder and everything, he started to cheat the squire right and left. He cheated us, too. He got the corn chandler to serve us with cheap moldy oats, maize with worms in it, and bad hay. And all the time he was charging the squire for the best quality, which was what old Gibbons had always got for the stables.

"More than that, he was cruel. He never let the squire see him, but when no one was around he was always beating us, kicking us, and treating us abominably. There was another fellow almost as mean and low as himself, called Smedley."

(Kling here glanced at me and nodded significantly.)

"Langley made Smedley sort of second-in-command of the hack stables, and when one wasn't knocking us about and swearing at us the other was. Well, one day I noticed these two doing a good deal of whispering and confabbing together and I guessed that they were hatching some plot. All I hoped was that I wasn't going to be in it. But when Langley came and saddled me and took me out of my stall about two o'clock the next morning, I saw that I was going to be in it. It was evident that he meant to steal me—or that's what I feared at the time, anyway—and it turned out later I was right. The prospect of being owned and ridden by that horrible man for the rest of my life was too awful for anything. And right away I began to look for a chance to escape from him."

Kling at this point moved restlessly in the grass as though impatient to hear whether the outcome of Tiger Lily's story fitted in with his own guesswork version of the case.

"Well," the mare went on after a moment, "Langley led me out through the yard, taking care to walk me always on the soft places so

HUGH LOFTING

"I guessed they were hatching some plot."

my hooves would make no noise. Even after he reached the highway he seemed afraid to get up on my back, lest, I suppose, I should go away at a trot and wake someone in the stables. When he had come opposite the Doctor's house he stopped. He had already been looking back a good deal. It seemed to me as though he were expecting someone to join him, for he kept muttering words of annoyance. After standing there a little while he started to go back along the road a short way, so that he could see around the bend. He didn't take me with him, fearing again, no doubt, the noise I might make in turning. But he had a long leading rein in his hand. It permitted him to get about five or six yards away from me. I thought of suddenly giving a tug, wrenching the rein out of his hand and bolting. But I saw he had it wound around his wrist and I was afraid to try it.

"He remained standing there a moment with his back to me. It seemed somehow the right time to make an attempt to get away. And while I was wondering how I'd go about it I felt one of my hind shoes, as I shifted my weight from one leg to the other, slip off my hoof into the dust of the road. This at once gave me an idea. From where I stood I could not reach to kick him. But if I could only throw that shoe accurately enough to hit him on the head with it, the trick would be done. As it happened, when I was once in pasture with some other horses I had had a shoe come off and had amused them and myself by slipping it on again and throwing it quite long distances. It can be done, if you are only patient enough and a few of the old nails remain standing up in the shoe to get a hold by.

"It was a slim chance, but it was worth trying. I looked back over my shoulder and took careful aim. Langley was standing quite motionless, still looking down the road for his friend who didn't come. I pressed my hoof firmly down onto the shoe so I could pick it up. Then I drew up my right hind foot slowly and shot it out in the direction of Langley's head with all my force. The shoe skimmed through the air whistling and hit him on the head with a thud. He had his cap tilted well back, otherwise it would certainly have killed him. He dropped like a stone and lay still."

"Then what happened to the shoe?" asked Kling.

"It bounced off his head," said Tiger Lily, "and fell a good twenty feet distant. At first I was afraid of being tracked if I ran away with only three shoes, and I turned and went back for it. I pressed the nails well home into the old holes and managed to keep it on for a few hundred yards. Then, as I was jumping a

HUGH LOFTING

"The shoe hit him on the head with a thud."

hedge to get into a field, it came off again, and I saw it was hope-less to try and keep it any longer. So I just hit across country to come here."

"You never went up close to the man again after he fell?" asked Kling.

"No," the mare answered. "I only went around him to get the shoe, which lay off to the side of the road."

"That's how I knew you hadn't kicked him," said Kling. "Your standing backward tracks were all too far away to reach him with a kick. But you dragged the man a little before you got clear, did you not?"

Tiger Lily's bright eyes opened wide as she looked at this mysterious dog who seemed to know everything.

"Yes," she said. "The leading rein was wound so tight about his wrist I couldn't get free. But I only dragged him a couple of feet before it slipped away. How on earth did you know?"

"Pshaw!" said Kling, tossing his head. "The track where he had been drawn along in the dust was as plain as a pikestaff. Now tell us, did you see anything of the man Smedley that night—or rather morning?"

"Yes," said Tiger Lily. "I can just say that I saw him. When I went back for the shoe I got a glimpse of him hurrying down the road. I'm pretty certain it was he. But, of course, I didn't wait till he came up. In fact, that's why I jumped the hedge. I didn't want anyone to see me and follow me. . . . That is all of my story. Now I think I'll be going."

"Oh, but just a minute, Tiger Lily," said I. "Don't you see that your staying here is likely to make things very awkward for Doctor Dolittle? If you came back with us, it—"

"I am *not* coming back with you," the mare quickly interrupted, getting ready to bolt. "Nothing in the world would induce me to."

"Don't get her scared," whispered Kling. "All right," he said aloud, turning to the mare again. "We are not going to force you. But listen: If John Dolittle comes here, will you speak with him?"

"Oh, certainly," said Tiger Lily. "Of course."

"Very good, then," said Kling. "Thank you very much for your information. Let us be going, Tommy."

And as soon as we had said good-bye to Toggle and Beppo we made our way out through the main gate.

THE EIGHTH CHAPTER

News from Toby

UMPH!" SAID I AS WE STARTED OFF ALONG the road. "Just the same, we didn't do a bad night's work. We found the mare and we got her story. Poor old Doctor! It looks as though we shall have to drag him into it after all. Do you think she will come—even with him, Kling?"

"Oh, of course," said the Detective Dog. "All her panic is over those two low fellows, Langley and Smedley. I don't blame her myself. But, after all, she doesn't know us, and she is in a sort of hysterical state. Once the Doctor guarantees her that she won't have to have anything to do with those two, she'll come all right. I learned from some of the dogs around the stable yard that the squire himself is very kind to his animals. And you heard her tell us that she was happy there until that horrible Langley got put in charge."

"I wonder what is the quickest way we can get back," said Jip. "Old Tobias Wilkes is the one that I'm thinking of. I wish we had something faster than our legs to carry us."

"Look here," I said. "I got a little money from the Doctor before I left. Let's hurry on to Digby Royal and see if we can't catch a coach from there. I think I have enough for the fare."

So, putting our best foot forward, we reached Digby Royal before noon. Luckily a coach was leaving at half past one. After asking the cost of the journey, I found that I had enough to buy us all a light lunch in addition—of which we were all more than glad.

We got back to Puddleby about teatime. Dab-Dab was very angry with us for not letting her know we would be away so long; and Gub-Gub was consumed with interest to know where we had been, what we had done, and how much we had found out.

I waited till tea was over before I tackled John Dolittle on the subject of his going to interview Tiger Lily.

"You're the only one who can bring her back, Doctor," I said, after I had outlined the situation to him. "There's no doubt about that. And I'm really afraid that if the squire's detectives get combing over the country they will find out where she's hiding and then they'll be after you. It would be best, I think, if you went and saw her right away and tried to make her listen to reason."

The poor Doctor, who was in the midst of a very important treatise on the subject of moths, looked up at me wearily, but said nothing.

"And besides," I added, "we need you to get Wilkes out of this. He's in a very serious situation."

Well, the Doctor finally saw, of course, that if he didn't take a hand in it, it was going to be a very complicated business for all concerned, and a decidedly grave one for Tobias Wilkes. When I had finished he sent me for Kling, and asked the Detective Dog to tell him his version of the story from beginning to end. After which he sat silent for a little, thinking.

While we were still waiting for him to speak we heard a pattering of paws on the gravel outside the study window and suddenly Toby sprang up onto the sill.

"Kling!" he cried. "Someone came back after the money while I was on the watch. That fellow Smedley—from Squire Jenkins's place."

"Well, did you trail him?" asked the Detective Dog.

"Yes," said Toby. "And he came down the Oxenthorpe Road. I think he's going into Puddleby on foot. He has only just gone by our gate. But you'll have to hurry if you want to catch him."

In a moment the Doctor and I were out in the front garden

"Toby sprang up on the sill."

and leaping down the steps. After us came not only Kling, Toby, and Jip, but Blackie the retriever and Grab the bulldog as well. At a distance of not more than a couple of hundred yards from the gate we saw the figure of a man hurrying along toward the town as fast as he could go. He looked over his shoulder, and seeing us, put on even more speed—indeed, he seemed about to break into a run.

"Go after him, Blackie," said the Doctor quietly. "Don't hurt him, but just get ahead of him and keep him where he is till we can catch up."

Blackie, followed by Grab and Jip, shot after the hurrying figure, which they promptly surrounded and brought to a standstill.

At first when the Doctor came up and spoke to him, Smedley's manner was a mixture of fear and brazenness. But after it had been explained to him that his partnership with Langley and all the other details of the case were well known to us, he was just terrified and nothing more. He started to excuse himself for his part of it, trying to throw the entire blame upon Langley. But the Doctor cut him short.

"There is only one thing that can save you from a heavy sentence," said he. "And that is that you do exactly as I tell you. To begin with, give me the money."

Smedley was evidently for a moment going to deny that he had it. But something about the Doctor's determined look and the fact that he already seemed to know everything, made him realize that that would be useless. Shamefacedly he brought the linen bag out of his pocket and handed it to the Doctor.

"The next thing," said John Dolittle, "go and get Langley and bring him to my house—that one there, with the steps leading up to it. If your friend should be unwilling to come, just explain to him that it will cost him his liberty as well as yours. We have both your descriptions. You could not get far. If the two of you are not at my house within half an hour I will inform the police of all that I know."

THE NINTH CHAPTER

Tiger Lily's Return

S A PRECAUTION, KLING DISPATCHED HIS
able lieutenant Toby to shadow Smedley when he left
the Doctor's house. But this turned out to be unnecessary. Apparently Langley was quickly persuaded
that it was wiser to fall in with the Doctor's orders than to try to
get away, for less than twenty minutes later we saw the two men
coming up the garden path. I opened the front door myself and
took them at once to the Doctor's study.

Kling and I were the only others present at the interview. John
Dolittle did not take long over it. In as few words as possible he
showed them that the whole truth of the case was in his possession
and what he now proposed to do.

"Much will depend," he ended, "on whether the squire decides
to drop the case or not. I am hoping for your sakes—though you
richly deserve punishment—that I can persuade him to go no further with the matter if the money and the horse are restored to him.
What I should recommend you to do is to go away from this district

altogether and make a new start. And remember, if at any time you are tempted to go in for this sort of crooked game again, that your faces are well known to me and several witnesses here."

The two men, who had been very plainly terrified of what the Doctor might do, were quite overjoyed at this permission to escape. As a matter of fact, they wasted no time over it, but got out that same evening and were never seen again in the neighborhood of Puddleby.

The Doctor's interview with the squire was somewhat more difficult. Indeed, if the old squire had not known John Dolittle so well, it is doubtful if it would have been successful at all. But finally, after the Doctor had talked to him for quite a while, he agreed to withdraw his detectives from the case. And as it was they who had accused Tobias Wilkes, that was the end of that charge, and Wilkes was released.

"And if, Squire," said the Doctor as he was leaving, "you should find that one, or perhaps two, of your stable hands suddenly depart from your employ, you will not make any attempt to trace them up, eh?"

At this the squire looked sharply at his old friend and pondered a moment before answering. Finally he laughed.

"All right, Doctor," said he. "You know more than you're letting on to, I reckon. No, I'll go no further with the business. I've come out of it pretty well thanks to you. I've got the money back, and if you can find Tiger Lily for me I'll be glad enough to call quits. Seems to me you've been to a peck of trouble on my account. Maybe the day will come when I can do something for you."

"The job now, Stubbins," said the Doctor as we came away from the squire's house, "is to tackle Tiger Lily. I hope she will not be unreasonable. If she is, there will be nothing left but to buy her from the squire and leave her at the Rest Farm. And goodness only knows how much that will cost. . . . Well, we shall see."

The Doctor set out for the Rest Farm the following day, and Kling and I accompanied him.

As a matter of fact, I was half hoping that the mare would refuse to return, because then there might be a possibility, when she had been bought by the Doctor, that I would sometime get a ride on her. I felt it must be great fun to ride a horse as clever as Tiger Lily.

As usual, a tremendous fuss was made over John Dolittle by all the members of the association when he arrived at the gate. And he was kept busy answering questions for a good half hour before he had a chance to bring forward the matter of his own business.

One of the horses went off and brought Tiger Lily, who was still keeping to the secluded parts of the farm for fear any people passing on the road might recognize her. The difference between her manner with John Dolittle and that in which she had received me and Kling the other day was very noticeable. She seemed genuinely glad to see him and came right up to where he stood with all the confidence in the world.

Then very gently, just as though he were chatting about the weather or anything, he told her she need have no fear about going back because the two men she disliked had already left the squire's employment, never to return. He promised her, moreover, that if the groom that took Langley's place wasn't to her liking, he himself would speak of it to the squire, who would surely see that her complaints were attended to.

She listened thoughtfully, and at the end she said:

"She listened thoughtfully."

"All right, Doctor, I'll come. But I want you to promise me as well that when my riding days are over you will buy me from the squire and let me come back here."

"Certainly," said the Doctor. "I feel pretty sure that the squire will consent to that. Now, did you bring a saddle with you?"

"Yes," said she. "But I rubbed it off against the scratching post. I had to bite through the girths to do it. But I dare say you can patch it up for one journey."

To my great delight, the Doctor, who knew that I was crazy to ride the beautiful mare, suggested that I take her back while he and the dogs went by coach. Tiger Lily very graciously consented to this also—though she told me before the journey was over that I was about the worst horseman she had ever traveled under. Just the same, it was the grandest ride I ever had; and I learned more from her remarks on the way about "good hands" and a firm seat than I had ever known before.

When we were seated at supper that night (Dab-Dab had, among other things for us, a late crop of very wonderful green peas), Gub-Gub as usual demanded that we give an account of our day's doings. We told him that Tiger Lily had been brought back and restored to the squire.

"But what about Tobias Wilkes?" he asked.

"Oh, I went down to the police station," said the Doctor, "with the squire himself. Wilkes is already released from custody."

"Custardy!" grunted Gub-Gub, bringing his nose up out of a plate of peas. "Who's custardy?"

"No, it's nothing to do with custard," said Jip contemptuously. "The Doctor means that he is already released from jail. Your mind is just a food mind—as has been remarked before."

"Well, there are worse kinds of minds than food minds," said Gub-Gub. "Goodness! I wish I had brought my food spectacles to supper with me. These peas are so small I can hardly see them. Hump! So Wilkes is released and the mare returned. Then I suppose that's the end of the Mystery of the Stunned Man. Kling is a fine detective and it was an elegant mystery. I wonder what the next one will be?"

"There are not going to be any more," said the Doctor quickly.

"I should think not indeed!" snorted Dab-Dab, glowering indignantly upon Gub-Gub.

"After all, a little mystery goes a long way," put in Chee-Chee the monkey.

"In Africa," said Polynesia, "there was a good deal too much mystery. On the other hand, it was a wonderful climate. I don't like the way that wind is wailing in the chimney. Heigh-ho! I suppose the summer's over already and the blithery, shivery time is beginning. I think I'll borrow one of the Doctor's socks and make a sweater out of it."

"But if we're not allowed to have any more mysteries and detective cases," said Gub-Gub, "what are we going to do for amusement the long winter nights. The Doctor is always too busy now to tell us stories round the fire."

"Listen, Stubbins," said the Doctor, "I think we had better go over to the Home for Crossbred Dogs right away and speak to Kling before he gets started on a new problem of some kind. I really can't have any more interruptions. I am dreadfully behind-hand with my book on moths."

"So am I—on my book," said Gub-Gub, pushing his plate forward for more peas.

"Your book!" screeched Too-Too. "What book are you writing, for pity's sake?"

"*The History of Food*," said Gub-Gub quietly. "A most important work. It's nearly done. I only have seven more volumes."

THE CRESTED SCREAMERS

THE FIRST CHAPTER

Regent's Park

WHEN DOCTOR DOLITTLE WAS PRE-
paring his *Canary Opera* to be shown in
London, he went to the zoo in search of
bird-singers and bird-dancers for the choruses.
Cheapside, the London sparrow, and Becky, his wife, went along
to help. Gub-Gub the pig, who assisted the Doctor in the produc-
tion of the show was eager to be in on the casting.

"Can I go to the zoo?" he asked.

"You can *not*," snapped Cheapside. "Do you want to get us
arrested? 'Ow far do you think the Doc would get with a full-sized
porker afollowin' 'im through the crowd?"

So, much to poor Gub-Gub's disappointment at again being left
behind, the Doctor finally set out with only the sparrows for company.

"'Ow long is it since you was at the zoo, Doctor?" asked
Cheapside when, after forty-minutes' walk, they were beginning to
approach the neighborhood of Regent's Park.

"Oh my!" said John Dolittle, "it must be—let me see—it must

be more than two years now, Cheapside, since I was there."

"Humph!" said the sparrow with a knowing air. "I reckon you'll find it changed considerable. Much bigger. But you'll 'ave a better chance to see the kind of thing you want. The collection of birds 'ere is the best in Europe now."

"How do you know?" asked the Doctor.

"Oh, I've been around all the zoological gardens on the Continent," said Cheapside very grandly. "You know we used to live in Regent's Park, as I told you. And Becky, 'ere, has been pestering me ever since we left to go back there. But I always told 'er you can't beat St. Paul's. It's more central. One time she was at me so hard that I told 'er I'd take 'er on a trip around the zoos of Europe—just to pacify 'er like. But when she come back she was more in love with Regent's Park than ever."

"What countries did you visit?" asked the Doctor.

"Pretty near all of 'em," sighed Cheapside. "We did a grand tour. But we was both glad to get back to London. Still, some of them furrin' cities wasn't so bad. They've got an awful big zoo in 'Amburg and another in Hantwerp. But I didn't think much of them. I liked Paris. They've got a nice place there they call the Jardong day Plonks—fine lot of parrots and macaws. Noisy things. But the park I liked best in Paris was the Twiddle-didee Gardens, near the Lufer Palace. There's an old feller there—nobody knows 'ow old 'e is—who makes a specialty of feedin' the sparrers. 'E's done it for years. 'As 'is picture took regular, 'oldin' up 'is 'and with crumbs, and sparrers settling all over 'im. 'Course, while me and Becky was in Paris, *we* got most of the crumbs. Them French sparrers ain't much good at fightin'. Some of them is so polite with their 'After you, sirs,' that I wonder they don't starve to death. I liked Paris pretty good. Becky 'ere said she thought it was a kind of frivolous place. From there we went on to Geneva, Switzerland— you know, where the cuckoo-clocks come from. There they've got a park, about the size of a backyard, what they calls the Jardong Onglays—that's the parley-voo for the English Garden. The cheek of 'im! There's nothing English about it. Ain't even got dandelions in it. From there we went on to Rome, Barcelona, Madrid, and all the rest. We did a regular tour. But we was both glad to get back to dear old London."

"Yes," said Becky, "and you made straight for St. Paul's and settled down in the noisiest part of the city. That's all that travel did for you. Instead of broadening your mind, it made you narrower than ever. Who would want to make his home in the most crowded corner of the city—right on top of the Royal Exchange—when there's Regent's Park and all that fine open country to live in?"

"Oh well," said Cheapside, "don't let's 'ave that old argument all over again. 'Ere we are, comin' to the park now. Most of the leaves is fallen. But it's nice any time of year."

As John Dolittle entered at the gates of Regent's Park he had to admit that this was indeed, as Mrs. Cheapside had said, an ideal place for a city sparrow to make his home. Big elms, horse chestnuts, and all manner of other trees rose from the wide greenswards. Fine, well-kept flower beds bordered the walks. Snug, secluded shrubberies, fenced off from the public, offered safe and quiet nesting thickets. Nor was it by any means too countrified for a city-bred bird. Human company, from which the house sparrow seldom stays far away, was here in plenty. Nursemaids, pushing perambulators and leading children, were everywhere. And through this park all the visitors to the Zoological Gardens had to pass. There were open-air restaurants, where families out for the day could take their meals at little tables beneath the big elms. The plump, well-fed sparrows gobbling up the crumbs showed that no bird need starve in this part of London.

"Yes, Doctor," said Cheapside, when John Dolittle called his attention to this, "but for grub I'm still better off in the city proper. For good kitchen service the Café de Gutter 'as got this beaten easy."

"The Café de *what?*" asked the Doctor.

"The Café de Gutter," Cheapside repeated. "You know—the all-night coffee stall—lunch wagons. 'Ere in the park folks only 'old picnics in the summer. Cold, perishin' winter days, when a sparrer is really 'ard up for a bite, you can't get anything 'ere. Oh, when it's warm, yes, you could choke a helephant to death on all the 'ard-boiled heggs and sandwich scraps a' blossimin' on the lawns. But not in winter—hoh, no indeed! Folks don't come out lookin' at the pretty polar bears when there's an east wind blowin'. But the coffee stall, that's open all night. Cabbies, bobbies, street washers, market gardeners coming up to the counter regular every five minutes, dribblin' their crumbs down onto the pavement. I know this bloomin' city back to front, I do. And I says, to keep the wolf from the door—in all weathers, mind you—roost me next to the Café de Gutter."

"Well, you could live here in summer," said his wife, "and go back to the cathedral for the winter, couldn't you? That's what I've been asking you to do for the last three years and more. It's better for the children, too—to be brought up in this quiet, restful park, instead of goin' to sleep every night to the racket of the cab wheels and the yelling of the newspaper boys."

"That's all right, Becky," said Cheapside. "But, just the same, our youngsters 'ave all thriven on it. When some of 'em was peevish and wanted special dainty foods, there wasn't nothing you'd mention that I couldn't get you at a moment's notice. You remember them hasparagus tips I pinched from the Covent Garden Market at four o'clock in the mornin', when Bertie was 'avin' spasms in 'is stummick? Huh! Like to know where you'd get such dainties anywhere else in a hemergency. No, take it all round, Becky, you can't beat St. Paul's. It's so central."

Cheapside Tells a Story

EVEN BEFORE THEY REACHED THE ENTRANCE to the zoo enclosure John Dolittle was greeted by several animals that inhabited the park in a free, wild state. Portly wood pigeons flew down from the great elms, cooed good day and told him they were glad to see him in the city. Squirrels, full of cheeky energy, came bounding out from under rhododendron bushes and bade him welcome. For these creatures Cheapside, proud as Punch to be the great man's guide, showed the most utter contempt.

"All squirrels are thieves—natural pickpockets," he said. "And all wood pigeons are gluttons. When Becky and me lived here regular it took us all our time to get a decent meal when them fellers were around."

At the entrance to the zoo the Doctor paid his admission at a little window.

"You don't 'ave to pay for us, Doc," chuckled Cheapside. "We fly in over the top. And, anyway, we're entitled to season tickets because we used to be residents 'ere."

"Squirrels came bounding out from under the bushes."

"You ought to be members of the Royal Zoological Society," laughed the Doctor.

"Well, I reckon we know as much natural 'istory as some members I could mention," said Cheapside.

Inside, the first thing the Doctor noticed was that some of the pens were being painted and many evidently just done.

"Oh, it's a good zoo, this," said Cheapside, gazing round with pride. "They always keep it spic and span. The paint smells awful while it's drying. But this zoo is the cleanest, best kept in the world."

In a big space near the bandstand there was a restaurant. And the Doctor thought that before starting on his tour of inspection he would like a cup of tea. So he sat down at one of the small tables and was presently served by a waitress. Becky and Cheapside shared the Doctor's meal (much to the envy of the other zoo sparrows who gathered around) by standing beside his teacup and gobbling the cake crumbs that fell from the great man's plate.

"Over there," said Cheapside, "on t'other side of the bandstand you 'ave our prize exhibit."

"It looks to me like another tea garden," said the Doctor, gazing across the clearing.

"That's what it is," said the sparrow. "It's the members' enclosure. See the sign: 'For members only.' It's for members of the Royal Zoological Society. That's for fear you might think it was for members of the monkey 'ouse. That old scarecrow in the 'igh black 'at, that's Sir William Gigglebeak, F. R. Z. S. 'E knows less about natural 'istory than any man living. But 'e 's always on show 'ere, drinking 'is tea in the members' enclosure. Did you ever see such a face? I wonder the children don't throw 'im peanuts. Look at 'im a' gazin' at us through 'is monocle, super-silly-ass like. 'E's wonderin' who you are, Doc. That's a joke, isn't it? 'Im what don't know one end of an animal from another, puttin' on airs with you, the greatest naturalist the world ever saw! Yes, that's a good one, that is."

"What is that large cage next door to the enclosure?" asked the Doctor, pouring out a second cup of tea.

"Oh, that's the Crested Screamers' Aviary," said Cheapside. "Good fellows, they are, Screamers. All birds like 'em. From time beyond recollection they've protected smaller birds from harm— when they was wild, that is. That's why I used to get currants for 'em when I lived 'ere. They love 'em."

"Currants?" said the Doctor. "Where did you get them?"

"I used to pick them out of the members' buns," said Cheapside, "over at the teahouse next door. Yes, old William Gigglebeak 'ad to go without currants in 'is bun when I lived 'ere. They all went to the Screamers. It's funny, that saved my life once—doing them a good turn."

"How was that?" asked the Doctor.

"It's a long story," said Becky, gobbling a piece of bread that John Dolittle had given her.

"Well, I should like to hear it," said the Doctor. "What you tell me of the Screamers protecting all other birds interests me. Go ahead, Cheapside. We have a long walk before us to get round the whole collection. And I'll be glad of another ten minutes' rest."

"Well," Cheapside began, "it was about a month after I came to live 'ere that the Crested Screamers were first brought to the zoo. I remember their arrival well. There was considerable excitement in the bird collection all around, because, of course, we knew their reputation. And me, along with half a dozen other sparrows what made the zoo their home, goes to call on the newcomers. They seemed kind of mopey and down-in-the-mouth, 'cause they'd only just been captured not so long ago. So we tried our best to make 'em feel they were among friends. And the first thing I asks 'em is what they like best in the food line. They wasn't very interested, to begin with. But presently, when a few of 'em had worked up an appetite, they admits that their greatest delicacy was currants, dried currants.

"'All right,' I says, 'I'll have to see what can be done,' and off I flits on a sort of foragin' expedition. I goes to the ordinary restaurant and tea shops. Then I visits the old feller who keeps the sweetmeat stall—you know, sells chocolates and goodies for the children.

But I don't find no currants—pretty much everything else in the food line, but no currants. So then Becky says to me, she says: "Ow about the Members' Enclosure? They 'ave tea there continual. Let's go and see if we can't get some currants there.'

"So we trundles off together to inspect the members' menoo. Well, we was just disgusted. They kept nothing but seed cake. Seems old Gigglebeak was very partial to it. Then I puts on my thinking cap. And after considerin' heavy for a while I says to Becky, I says, 'We've got to fix it so they keep currant buns or currant cake in the Members' Teahouse.'

"'Yes,' she says, 'but 'ow are you goin' to manage it?'

"'The rats,' I says. 'Let's go and see the rats.'"

Currants for the
Screamers

HEN WE GOES TO THE BACK DOOR OF THE house kitchen and 'angs around there till an old rat comes chasing 'isself out of a hole next the cellar winder.

"'Look 'ere,' I says, grabbin' 'im by the tail. 'I would 'ave words with you. Them Crested Screamers what came in last night is a special kind of bird what always protects smaller birds in the wild state. It's up to us to see that they're kept comfortable when they're down on their luck and in captivity, see? Now, they only keep seed cake 'ere for the members. What we want you to do is to pinch the seed cake or spoil it in some way—you have the run of the larder and you know where it's kept, and all that—and continue pinchin' it or spoilin' it till they give up keeping seed cake and take currant buns, see?'

"'Oh no,' 'e says, wiggling 'is whiskers virtuous-like, 'I don't see 'ow I can do that.'

"'Well,' I says, 'you jolly well find out a way—and quick. It's up to all us fellers that makes our home in the zoo 'ere to see that the Screamers are treated right in return for what they've done for the smaller fellers when they was free. And if you don't fall in with my ideas, I'll tell every bloomin' animal in the zoo to treat you as a foreign henemy. You live on the scraps fed to the exhibits, same as what we do. Well, take my word for it, you'll 'ave a very thin time if you don't do as I say. Now, get all your friends on the job and hop about it.'

"Them rats," Cheapside continued, "managed it all right. In fact, they started out by doing it too well, you might say. What do you think they did? The oldest of 'em—oh, an artful old dodger, 'e was—the one I'd spoken to, 'e goes and spills a bottle of rat poison on the seed cake. 'E'd been at the game so long, dodging traps and ferrets and all the other inventions for killin' rats, that 'e knew the smell—even with a cold in 'is 'ead—of every rat poison on the market. And in all 'is cunnin' ways 'e 'ad instructed the other rats that lived under the teahouse. Well, 'e knew where the bottle of poison was kept and after I left 'im 'e goes and spills it all over the seed cake what was set out in the pantry for tomorrow's tea."

Cheapside paused a moment, grinning thoughtfully.

"You never saw such an 'ow-d'ye-do," he chuckled presently. "That afternoon about four o'clock me and Becky 'ears a great commotion over at the Members' Enclosure. We 'ops across to see what it was all about, and there was Sir William Gigglebeak being carried off to 'ospital with a terrible pain in 'is stummick. You know, the funny part of it was that that particular rat poison was Sir William's hinvention—'is only contribution to the science of natural 'istory, in fact. And 'e was very proud of it. But 'is nose wasn't scientific enough to catch the smell of it on the seed cake. So I says to Becky, I says, "E ought to rechristen 'is mixture *Members'*

Poison and mark the poison *For Members Only* like the sign on the teahouse.'

"'But lor bless me!' she says, 'this is serious, you know. We can't 'ave the members killed off like this. You better go and see that rat again and tell 'im to think of something else.'

"'All right,' I says. 'Though I don't fancy most of the members would be any great loss to natural 'istory. Still, maybe you're right.'

"So we goes round to the teahouse kitchen and tells our friend 'is methods, while they was thorough, was a bit drastic, and 'e must find some other way to cure the members' taste for seed cake. But as a matter of fact, there wasn't no need for no further conspirin' on

"Sir William Gigglebeak carried off to hospital"

our part. Old William Gigglebeak got well again after about two weeks of colic; and when 'e showed up again at the enclosure, the first order 'e gave was that 'e didn't want to see no more seed cake in the teahouse, never no more. Then they ordered in a lot of currant buns and plum cakes for the members' tea; and we was all right. Me and Becky and a dozen of our pals used to spend two hours every afternoon picking up currants from under the chairs and even nicking them out of the buns on the tables when no one was lookin'. And we put our collection together every evening and took 'em across to the Crested Screamers and dribbled 'em in through the wire netting on the top of their cage."

Cheapside Has a Narrow Escape

ELL, EVEN THOUGH THEY WAS IN captivity, the Screamers still did one small bird a good turn. And that was me. We 'ad a family of young ones in the nest and Becky 'ere used to ask me to go and get 'er suet every once in a while to feed 'em. You know young birds need a certain amount of meat. And sometimes I would get bits of fat out of the lions' den when they was sleeping after a heavy meal; and sometimes I'd get it other places. And among these places was the Owl House. In those days the Owl House stood next to the Screamers' Aviary, on the other side of the Members' Enclosure. It was a low shed, with the usual runway at the back, covered with wire nettin'; and it was divided into six compartments. In the center was the Great Horned Owl—an ugly old sinner if ever there was one! 'Our Mr. Grouch' we used to call 'im. Never had a good word to say to nobody.

"Our Mr. Grouch, the Great Horned Owl," Cheapside went on, "didn't like me poppin' into 'is cage for bits of meat—said so more than once and warned me to keep out of 'is territory if I didn't want me bloomin' 'ead bit off. But, as 'e usually slept on 'is perch most of the day, I used to slip through a tear in the netting and help meself without askin' 'is permission.

"One day Becky sent me out to get some suet, and after huntin' around several cages and pens without success I says to meself, I says, 'I'll go and try me luck in Mr. Owl's dinin' room.' And off I goes. Well, it was a fine afternoon and our Mr. Grouch was snoozin' on 'is perch, dead to the world. So I pops in through the rent in the nettin' and starts foragin' around quiet-like. I 'adn't been there more than a minute or two before a keeper comes in. And I slips behind the door, so I won't be seen. The keeper sweeps the place up a bit, and then, as luck would 'ave it, before he goes out he stands a heavy iron plate, what was used for the owl's meat, right over the hole in the nettin' what I'd been using as a door to get in and out by.

"Mr. Grouch had hardly woke up for the keeper's coming. And as soon at the coast was clear I starts hunting not for suet, but for a way to get out. The iron plate was much too heavy for me to move, so I searches the netting all over to see if I can find another hole to get through. I knew, of course, that, once Mr. Owl wakes, when the darkness comes it was all over with me. 'E'd warned me to keep out. And in the dark, against his eyes and quick flight, I wouldn't stand a chance. 'E'd just eat me. That was all there was to it. So you can bet I searched the nettin' pretty thorough. But not one blessed place could I find where a sparrow could get through.

"'Well,' I thought, 'my only 'ope is to 'ide somewhere till daylight. Then he'll go to sleep again and I may slip out when the keeper comes in with 'is breakfast.'

"So I tucks myself away in the corner behind 'is drinking bowl, says a prayer and 'opes for the best—wonderin' what Becky's thinking when I don't come back with the suet. Darkness begins to come on and Mr. Owl stretches 'isself and wakes up. The first thing he does is sniff!

"'Oh Lord!' I thinks to meself. ''E smells me already!'

"And, sure enough, 'e starts right away 'unting around every corner of his place, just as though he knew for certain I was there. My fevvers stood straight up on the top of me 'ead with fright. At last 'e comes to the drinking bowl, peers behind it with those great eyes of 'is, glowin' like lamps in the dark, and see me!

"'Now I've got you, you little devil!' 'e says. And he jumps

"Now I've got you, you little devil!"

for me. I shoots up into the air. And then a grand chase began all around the cage.

"'It's no use,' I keeps sayin' to meself. "'E's bound to get me in the end. 'Is speed's twice as good as mine.'

"But I'd forgotten my friends, the Crested Screamers, next door. They'd seen me go into the Owl House, and they 'adn't seen me come out. And when they 'ears the two of us flutterin' around they guessed what was wrong. And suddenly the whole lot of 'em—a dozen there was—starts screaming at the top of their voices. And the watchman, thinkin' some animal has got loose, comes rushin' out with a lantern and goes all along the aviaries, to find out what the matter was. Then, seeing the Great Horned Owl a' thrashin' around the cage after something in the dark, he opens the door. And before you could say Jack Robinson I was on the outside, lookin' in, makin' faces at Mr. Grouch and thankin' my lucky stars and the Crested Screamers."

"My gracious!" said the Doctor. "You had a narrow escape. But all's well that ends well."

"That's Shaker-spear—all's well wot ends well—ain't it, Doc?" asked Cheapside.

"Yes," laughed the Doctor. "Shakespeare said it first. It's a most useful quotation—fits a lot of situations. Shall we get on with the search?"

"Righto!" said the sparrow. "Come on, Becky, let's show the Doctor the owls. They'd make a roarin' good endin' for the first act of 'is opera. Sort of a *'Oo, 'Oo, 'Oo's the Crew, Wot Sails the Bloomin' Bloo,* chorus."

THE
GREEN-BREASTED
MARTINS

The Land of
the Gambians

MANY YEARS AGO DOCTOR DOLITTLE WENT
to Africa to cure the monkeys who were sick. The part
of the country where he landed was called the Land of
the Jolliginki and the King of the Jolliginki didn't like
strangers in his lands. So he threw the Doctor and his family into jail.
Prince Bumpo, the King's son, was kindhearted and secretly let the
Doctor and his animal family escape. They made a hasty departure
from the land without carefully checking their provisions.

Poor Bumpo, who knew little about the needs of a sailing
voyage—having lived on land all his life—had gone into the King's
cellars and, in the dark, snatched any boxes that were near at hand
and popped them into the Doctor's ship.

Dab-Dab, the duck, who was chief cook on the voyage, was
horrified when she opened box after box and found nothing but
yams—a sort of sweet potato.

"Yams! Yams!" she complained. "How can I prepare a decent
meal with nothing but yams!"

"Heavens preserve us!" groaned Gub-Gub the pig. "But I know that the King ate parsnips as well because I smelt them when those horrible soldiers were dragging us through the palace jail. Oh Bumpo! Why didn't he look in the boxes? I'll starve before I eat that stuff!"

"Oh, be quiet!" snapped Dab-Dab. "You wouldn't starve if you didn't eat until you got home! There's enough fat on your ribs to feed you for a month!"

"Now, now, Dab-Dab," said the Doctor. "It's natural for pigs to be fat. How do you cook yams?"

"I wouldn't know!" said Dab-Dab in a huff.

"It's quite easy," said the Pushmi-Pullyu. "You peel the yams, cut them up and fry them in the palm oil. That's what is called palm oil chop, the commonest dish of the Africans. I'll show you how it's done."

"Thank you," said the Doctor. "It's lucky we had you with us—without somebody who knew African cooking we might have starved."

"What's this stuff?" asked Jip, the dog, who was undoing one of the other boxes. "It smells horrible!"

"Dried locusts," said the Pushmi-Pullyu. "They are a kind of large grasshopper. You fry them, too. They're quite good."

"Pooh! Insects!" snorted Jip.

Everybody was very hungry. And after the Pushmi-Pullyu had shown them in the ship's kitchen how to prepare palm oil chop they all tried it and were surprised to find that it was not half bad. The grasshoppers, however, of which there was a great quantity in the hold, they refused to touch.

But after a few days having the same dish for breakfast, lunch and supper began to get tiresome. Now, for the first part of the journey home the ship kept sailing along northward, still in sight of the coast of Africa. And one night, after supper, when they were all feeling more than usually tired of palm oil chop, the Doctor said:

"I think it would be a good idea, as soon as we have got safely past the Kingdom of Jolliginki, if we stopped and went ashore some place and got a few bananas. I have no doubt that these yams are very nourishing, but I for one, am heartily sick of them."

"I think that would be a very good plan," said Gub-Gub.

The next day about ten o'clock in the morning they passed the mouth of a beautiful river.

"That looks like a good place to get bananas," said the Doctor. "I think we'll steer the boat in there and see."

So the ship's nose was turned toward the land, and presently they entered the mouth of a very lovely, wide stream. Passing up the river a few miles, between thickly wooded banks, they finally brought the ship to anchor close to a large town of straw huts.

This town happened to be the chief town of the Gambian people whose country stretched for some miles inland from this point.

The Doctor remarked at once that it was a much pleasanter country than the one they had left, and the town bigger and better built than that of the Jolliginki.

The swallows which were flying along over the Doctor's ship turned also when they saw the boat change its course, and, entering the river, they settled down upon the banks around the ship, causing great astonishment to the local people. The townsfolk were not accustomed to have many boats visit their harbor, but to have one accompanied by a great flock of birds was, of course, something they had never seen before.

Stepping ashore, the Doctor was greeted by the Chief of the Gambians, who asked him very politely if there was anything he could do for him. The Doctor made the Chief a present of an extra pocketknife he had, and then explained that he needed provisions for his ship and that he had come into this port expecting to find at least some fruit.

The Chief asked him what foodstuffs, besides fruit, he would like. And Gub-Gub smacked his lips while the Doctor reeled off a long list of eatables.

"I am not sure," said the Chief, "that I shall be able to get you all these, but I will get you as many as I can."

He then gave orders to several servants and messengers who stood about him in attendance. And before long the Doctor and his animals saw a long line of porters going down to the ship with loads of food upon their heads.

"How wonderfully simple!" said the Doctor, watching them. "Now if I had stopped at Liverpool to have the ship provisioned it would have taken me a week to get that done."

The Doctor's Plan

J OHN DOLITTLE THEN THANKED THE CHIEF many times and asked him if there was anything he could do for him in return. But the Chief, who seemed no end pleased with his new pocketknife, told him that no return or thanks were necessary—it was a pleasure, he said, and he hoped the Doctor would call again.

Returning to the river bank, John Dolittle saw that some great commotion was going on among the swallows. They had been joined by a number of green-breasted birds with whom they were now chartering and jabbering away in a very excited and agitated manner.

Now, the martins—this particular kind was the green-breasted martin—are first cousins to the swallows. And they were now telling their troubles to those swallows who were traveling with the Doctor. Apparently their beautiful wings had become very popular as a decoration for felt hats, and the poor martins were being trapped and shot in great numbers in order to meet the demand. This was what all the commotion was about which John Dolittle saw as he came back to his ship in the river.

When the Doctor got close to his ship six of the swallows who were leaders came to him and complained of the treatment that their cousins, the green-breasted martins, had suffered from the bird hunters.

"If something isn't done about this soon," said the swallows, "the martins in this country will be wiped right out. It's a perfect shame."

"But couldn't they go somewhere else?" asked the Doctor, "to some other land where they wouldn't be hunted for hats?"

"At any other time they could," said the swallows, "but this is the nesting season for them. And the eggs and young birds cannot be left to get cold."

"Humph! What do these martins live on?" asked the Doctor.

"Flies—the same as we do," said the swallows. "Mosquitoes and small moths are their favorite food. But they will eat any kind of flying insects. Now, in this country many of the mother birds whose husbands have been killed are dying of cramps, sitting on their nests afraid to leave to get food, and with no mates to bring it to them."

"Dear me! This is a terrible thing," said the Doctor. "Terrible! I'll go back and speak to the Chief about it."

So the Doctor went and asked the Chief if he could not do something to stop the killing of these beautiful birds.

The Chief said he would do what he could and at once sent messengers throughout the whole of the country with orders that the killing of martins must stop.

Then John Dolittle came back to his ship and sent word to the martins of what he had done. The martins thanked him, but asked that he remain here a few days to see if the orders were carried out.

So for some days the Doctor's ship stayed in the river, after it had been moved a little further from the town to a better anchorage. And John Dolittle now had time to travel up the stream by canoe to explore and see the country.

When he got back, the martins came to him again, saying that the Chief's orders were not being obeyed, that two hundred more birds had been killed secretly and put on felt hats since he left.

For a moment the Doctor was silent, frowning with furious indignation. Then he asked that all the leaders of both the martins and the swallows meet him in the cabin of his ship right away to discuss the situation.

"Now, tell me," said John Dolittle as soon as they had all found comfortable places around the big table to perch on, "you martins live on flies, mosquitoes and moths, do you not?"

"Yes," said the martins, "but only on the smaller moths; the big fuzzy ones give the young birds hiccups. We like mosquitoes best—for summer diet there's nothing like a good, juicy mosquito."

"Fine!" said the Doctor. "Now, my idea is this: Mosquitoes sting people, you know—most uncomfortable. And moths eat clothes. And a lot of other insects, like flying ants and beetles, would be a fearful nuisance to people, if you birds did not keep them down by eating them. What I propose is that you should stop eating flies and insects for a while. They will then become a great pest. Then perhaps I'll be able to persuade the hunters to obey the Chief's orders and leave you alone."

"But what are we to live on in the meantime?" asked the martins. "We're not finches and starlings; you know we must have insect food."

"Ah!" said the Doctor. "I hadn't thought of that."

Then Gub-Gub, who with the other animals was listening intently (since the conversation was about food), said:

"Doctor, I have an idea."

"Splendid!" said John Dolittle. "What is it, Gub-Gub?"

"Downstairs in the hold of this ship," said the pig, "there are fifty packing case full of dried locusts. Why can't the martins live on them while you bring the hunters to their senses?"

"Excellent!" cried the Doctor. "Do you think," he asked, turning to the martins, "that you could feed your babies on dried locusts for a while?"

"Oh, certainly," said the martins, "if we had to."

"All right," said the Doctor. "Now listen: We must make a thorough job of this. I want you leaders to send out messengers to all the fly-catchers and insect-eaters in this district—martins, swallows, swifts, whippoorwills, shrikes, every kind. Tell them that dried locusts in plenty will be set out on the deck of this ship for them to come and eat and take to their young ones. But no live insect must be touched from now on till I give the word. Understand? And if we can't persuade the hunters within a very short space of time I shall be greatly surprised. The conference is over. Now, send out your messengers and keep me informed of how things are going."

By nightfall the leaders returned to the Doctor and told him that his orders had been carried out. All the insect-eating birds (of which there are a great number of different kinds in Africa, a fine hunting ground for bugs) had willingly agreed to help by leaving all moths, mosquitoes and ants strictly alone.

Speedy-the-Skimmer

AND FOR THE NEXT TWO WEEKS THE SCENE around the Doctor's boat was very festive, with myriads of brightly colored fly-catchers of all kinds coming and going to feed on the dried locusts set out for them on the deck.

At the end of twenty days the results of the Doctor's plan were quite surprising—even to John Dolittle himself. For, you see, all the insects, now being left strictly alone by the birds began to lay thousands and thousands of eggs and to have huge families, and to multiply and increase in the most alarming way.

The first sign of success that came to those on the ship was when Gub-Gub woke up in the middle of the night, crying out that he was all over mosquito bites. One by one the rest of the ship's company were awakened and kept awake by the stinging flies.

"Ah, hah!" said the Doctor, sitting up in bed and busily swatting in all directions. "This is splendid. I wonder how the hunters like this."

But the mosquito plague grew and grew—more terrible every

hour. Those on the ship really suffered a great deal for the sake of their friends, the martins. When the Doctor and the animals ventured on deck in the morning they found the air outside thick with mosquitoes and flying ants, and they were finally driven back by the pests into their cabin again. Then they slammed the doors shut and stuffed up every crack to keep out the swarming insects.

Poor Gub-Gub was a dreadful sight—he was, in fact, nothing but one large pink mosquito bite. The Doctor had to put him to soak in a bathtub of boracic acid to reduce the swelling. And as for the Pushmi-Pullyu, having no tail to use as a fly swat, he had a perfectly terrible time. But he never grumbled.

Of course, they could not very well stay shut up in the cabin without any fresh air for days on end. And soon the Doctor realized that he must get some protection from the flies for himself and his animals. So he sent for one of the swallow leaders.

In answer to his summons, it was the chief of the leaders that came, a very neat, trim little bird, with long, long wings and sharp, snappy eyes. Speedy-the-Skimmer he was called, a name truly famous throughout the whole of the feather world. He was the champion fly-catcher of Africa, Europe, and America. For years every summer he had won all the flying races, having broken his own record only last year by crossing the Atlantic in eleven and a half hours at a speed of more than two hundred miles an hour.

"Speedy," said the Doctor. "I and my party are imprisoned in our ship here. We dare not go out to take the air or stretch our legs for fear of the mosquitoes and biting flies. Can you do anything for us?"

"Why, certainly," said Speedy. "I'll get a few hundred wrens to mount guard over the ship here and keep the mosquitoes away from you and your party. They'll take care of you. Your scheme is

"Speedy-the-Skimmer he was called."

working splendidly, doctor. The hunters are having a frightful time. They're much worse off than you are, you know, because they wear fewer clothes and the flies have more room to bite. I'll send you the wrens right away."

So saying, Speedy flew off. And from that time on the Doctor's ship had a special guard of nine hundred wrens—very small birds, but marvelous fly-catchers. John Dolittle and his pets were now able to come safely out on deck and take the air and enjoy themselves.

Two days after that, in the morning before it was quite daylight, the Doctor said to Jip:

"I think I ought to go ashore into the town to see what's going on. I notice that the ants and beetles have started increasing at a great pace the last day or so. I'm a little bit uneasy. I mustn't let this thing go too far."

From the deck the animals watched the Doctor depart. For protection he had gloves on his hands, and his head, all but the eyes, was covered with a red handkerchief.

"I'm glad he didn't take any of us with him," said Gub-Gub, who was now entirely recovered from his bites. "Just look at the flies swarming around his head!"

It was not long after John Dolittle left that Too-Too, the owl, suddenly cried:

"Oh, look! Here comes the Doctor back, running. Goodness, he's all excited—waving his arms! See! I wonder what has happened in the town."

Dab-Dab, Gub-Gub, Jip, Too-Too, the Pushmi-Pullyu, and the white mouse crowded to the rail of the ship as the Doctor came bounding down to the river.

"What is it, Doctor," called the owl as soon as the Doctor was within earshot, "flies?"

"No," gasped the Doctor, as he came panting up on the deck. "Ants!—flying ants, black ants, red ants, white ants—ants in hundreds and thousands and millions. You can't see the houses any more—nothing but mounds and mounds of ants."

"What has happened to the people?" asked Dab-Dab.

"They've shut themselves inside the houses. But the ants are eating the houses up—they're only made of grass. It's what they'll do when they've eaten the houses that I'm afraid of. Heaven help the people if the ants are still hungry then! Too-Too, get the Skimmer for me as quick as you can. Hurry, or the whole of Gambia will be wiped out!"

The Martins Are Saved

S O OFF WENT TOO-TOO TO FIND SPEEDY.

"My gracious! I had no idea matters had gone so far as this," said the Doctor, sitting down and mopping his brow. "It's lucky I went today to take a look at the town. I kind of thought that something was wrong . . . I do wish Too-Too would hurry. There isn't a moment to lose. Ah, good! Here he is—and the Skimmer, too!"

"Speedy," said the Doctor as soon as the trim little bird had settled on the deck. "The town is being eaten up by ants. Tell all the fly-catchers to go back to work. Take them up yourself to the town and clear those ants away. Hurry, for pity's sake! It's the biggest job you ever had to do. You'll need every fly-catcher you can raise. And hurry, Speedy, as fast as you know how."

Then the swift and famous Skimmer rose high in the air on his curved and flashing wings of blue. And reaching to terrific height, he began letting out shriek after shriek—a high, piercing whistling cry. Those on the deck of the ship below watched him as he swept the sky in dizzy circles, calling, calling, calling: "Tee-wee-hee! Tee-wee-hee! Tee-wee-HEE!"

And very soon, in answer to the swallow leader's cry, fly-catchers of every description, color and kind left whatever they were doing and came swirling into the air in a dark and ever growing mass above the Doctor's ship.

Then suddenly, led by Speedy-the-Skimmer, the enormous army of birds made off for the town at a terrific pace. The rush of those millions of wings through the air was like the North Wind gone mad.

"Come along," said the Doctor. "We must see that the people are rescued from their plight. I started this—I've got to see it through."

The animals all jumped up and followed him as he left the ship and raced off toward the town.

As they drew near to it a curious buzzing noise reached their ears. Tremendous—like some great machine purring, whirring smoothly—it grew and grew; the noise of millions and millions of insects working busily in the sun.

When the animals got closer the sight that met their eyes was indeed a strange one. You couldn't see the houses of the town at all. Over everything in view lay a thick moving carpet of ants.

"Golly!" said Too-Too. "How on earth are they ever going to get out from under that mess?"

But even while he spoke the fly-catchers swept down upon the moving carpet in countless numbers. And then began the most terrific battle ever seen by mortal eyes.

It lasted three hours. And, although the fly-catchers won, by the time the last of the ants and beetles and moths and mosquitoes had been driven away, the birds were so exhausted that they sat and lay and squatted in panting, weary millions on the ground, hardly able to move their wings another flip

And now could be seen what work of havoc the insects had done. The straw thatching of the huts was all eaten away; only the bare poles remaining. The shade trees before the doors were stripped of their leaves, bare, as though winter had come in a night. And from within the frames of the dwellings frightened, huddled figures gazed out at the Doctor and the millions of birds who had saved them from destruction. They were covered with mosquito bites, but their lives were saved. The Doctor and Speedy-the-Skimmer had arrived only just in time.

In a little while the hunters came timidly out of the wrecks of their homes, and then John Dolittle made a speech to them.

"You have today been rescued from a great and terrible danger. And it was these little green birds you see about you here that saved you—the same birds that, in spite of your Chief's orders, you shot and trapped to make hats out of. They came to me on my arrival in your land and complained. And, seeing no other way to bring you to your senses, I told them to stop doing the useful work, which they do for you all their lives. That work is the eating of flies and insects. I hoped when you should see what happens when that work is stopped that you would realize how foolish you have been in killing them. Do you realize it now?"

Then all the hunters rose up and shouted:

"We do, we do!"

"I am glad of that," said the Doctor. "Do you promise that the green-breasted martin shall for all time be safe and unharmed in your land?"

"We do, we do!" shouted the hunters. "The green-breasted martins who saved our lives this day shall be a sacred bird forever! Woe to anyone who touches a feather of the Sacred Martin! May the Fifty-nine Curses of Hullagoozelum fall upon his head!"

Then the Chief, in a deep bass voice, began reciting the curses for the benefit of anyone who should henceforth molest a martin:

"May his hammock strings break in the dead of night, letting him fall into the deepest mud. May he, when he rests beneath the palm at noon, have hard and knobby coconuts descend upon his head. May he—"

"That will do please," the Doctor interrupted. "You can recite

"A sacred bird forever"

the rest of the Fifty-nine after I'm gone. I see that many of your community have been severely bitten by the flies. If those of you who wish for medical treatment will come down to my ship your injuries will be attended to."

And now for many hours John Dolittle, M. D., was kept more than busy attending to fly-bitten hunters. His supply of witch hazel, bay rum, boracic acid, ammonia, and bicarbonate of soda soon ran out. And he had to get herbs from the jungle and boil them down and make more lotions for his many patients.

It was halfway through the night before he was done, and he was very weary. But the hunters, after his treatment, were feeling fit as fiddles. The doctor then set to helping them rebuild their homes.

Then a feast was made ready by the Chief in honor of the Doctor, and everybody sat down, and there was much laughter and merriment.

The next morning the Gambians provisioned the Doctor's ship with proper foods for the balance of the journey. There was bacon and flour, prunes and cocoa for the Doctor, parsnips and cabbages for Gub-Gub, and plenty of tea and sugar for everyone. They even remembered to include some bones for Jip and seeds for Too-Too and the white mouse. When they finally brought aboard two bales of hay for the Pushmi-Pullyu the hold was full to the hatches.

"Goodbye, goodbye!" cried the people as the ship slowly moved away from the harbor. "Safe journey home!"

THE STORY OF
THE MAGGOT

Experiment No. 179

OCTOR DOLITTLE HAD MANY CURIOUS interests; among them a desire to discover how different small insects and worms got scattered about the earth.

During one of the periods when the Dolittle family was living quietly at Puddleby-on-the-Marsh, the Doctor and I, Tommy Stubbins, were preparing a pamphlet on the subject of bug travels. The means by which geological distributions had come about had interested the Doctor for a long time and he was working day and night to complete a particular experiment that he had begun that week.

Gub-Gub, the Doctor's pet pig, and I were discussing some minor details when the Doctor walked into the room with a tray of maggots.

"Stubbins," said he, "I want to do some experimental work with these. If you will come with me, we will begin with listening machine number seventeen."

This was a sort of amplifying and warming machine that the

Doctor had built to make the tiny sounds of bugs and worms loud enough for human ears.

"Ugh!" grunted Gub-Gub, glancing into the tray. "What gooey, messy-looking things!"

Without further delay the Doctor and I proceeded to our apparatus sheds and set to work. We had quite good results. It seemed that several of the maggots—particularly one large and lively white one—had somehow got the drift of Gub-Gub's remark and were considerably offended by it.

"He had no right whatever to call us gooey and messy," said the maggot. "Personally, to me pigs and people are much more gooey and messy than nice, clean, athletic maggots. And we would be glad if you would tell him so."

"And you know, Stubbins," said the Doctor, after I had written this down into a notebook under the heading Experiment No. 179, "I quite sympathize with their feelings in the matter. This idea of er—revulsion and dislike on the part of one member of the animal kingdom for another is quite baseless and stupid. Myself, I've never felt that way toward any living thing. I won't say that I'd choose a maggot or a snail to make a warm personal friend of. But I certainly would not regard them as being unclean or less entitled to respect than myself. I will certainly speak to Gub-Gub.

"Now we want to get some information from these maggots about their geographical distribution. I would like to know roughly over what parts of the world their species is to be found. This big fellow seems quite lively and intelligent. Just raise the temperature another five degrees, will you Stubbins? And turn on a trifle more humidity. Then we will question him."

To begin with, we had some difficulty in making him under-

"Turn on a trifle more humidity. Then we will question him."

stand the idea of geographical distributions. Finally, after we made several attempts, he said:

"Oh, I know what you mean: journeys and voyages, eh?"

As a matter of fact, it wasn't precisely what we meant, but the Doctor thought it best to let him go on. He seemed anxious to talk and it was quite likely that we might get the information we wanted more easily by this means than by trying to get a too difficult scientific idea into his head.

"We are, as you probably know," he began, "nut maggots. We never live in or feed on anything but nuts. Moreover, the nuts have to be of a certain kind—or, rather, two or three kinds. I have heard that at former times our people also lived on other things. But this was long, long ago, and we have got so used to nut life now that I doubt if any member of our species could exist in any other surroundings. Birds were our greatest enemies, a certain kind of woodpecker being our deadliest. But so long as we kept inside the nuts, of course, we were pretty safe. And as this was most of the time, the journeys and voyages we made were not very large or extensive. Sometimes we would be dissatisfied with the nut we were living in and would move out of it, walk along a branch of the tree and into another one. And then, other times, perhaps too many maggots would be occupying one nut and all the meat would be getting eaten up, and we would have to make a change for that reason. Sometimes, on those occasions, when there were, we'll say, four of us in residence there, we would draw lots to see which of us had to move out.

"And again, sometimes we made, for us, the much larger journey from one tree to another. This was done when the tree had something wrong with it and the nuts were not ripening well. And at all such times of moving we had to be most careful that we were not seen by our bird enemies because, of course, at our pace even such journeys took quite a long time.

"You have asked me," said the maggot, "to tell you something of our society and community life. Of course, I don't know exactly what kind of things you'd like to hear about. We live in colonies— almost always. Yet there isn't very much social life with us. It is nothing unusual for maggots living on the same tree not to make one another's acquaintance throughout their whole lives. And often enough even those living on the same limb would never meet. No, I can't say that we are a neighborly lot. It is only those that actually live in the same nut that know one another well—and sometimes they feel that they know one another too well. A nut, after all, is pretty close quarters.

"But news does get around, even in maggot society. In one colony where I lived some time ago there was considerably more social life than in most. This was because the nut trees were in a somewhat wild part of the country on an old tumbledown sort of ranch. The farmers very seldom bothered us, spraying and pruning the trees the way they do in most places. And for some reason or other the birds were scarce, too. So we could move around in the open, if we felt so inclined, a good deal more freely than we usually do.

"We live in colonies."

"In this colony there was a quite extraordinary character. He was a very fast traveler, for one thing, holding all the records for speed. He could hop out of one nut, travel along a limb, and drill his way into another nut in quicker time than any of us. He was very daring, too. I've never known such an adventurous maggot. Even when he knew birds were around he'd hop in and out his front door, apparently just for the daredevil fun of the thing.

"As it happened, he occupied at one time the same nut as I did myself—just the two of us. And I got to know him quite well. He was certainly an extraordinary individual. We often had long talks in the autumn evenings as we lay snugly curled up within the walls of our nut home and the wind without, whistled and lashed the boughs of the tree around in the wildest manner.

"The fall was liable to be a pretty troublesome time for us, because when the wind got really high the nuts that were getting ripe would often be blown to the ground.

"This happened to us one stormy night and I was glad I had my adventurous friend as a partner, I can assure you. Our home was blown clean off its stem and went bouncing down through the other branches and finally landed in the grass a good thirty yards away from the trunk of the tree.

"'Come along,' said he, 'we've got to get away from here—else the pigs will be around. They eat up all the windfalls—maggots and all.'

"So, in spite of the wind and the cold, we crawled out of our nut where it lay among the grass and set out on the long voyage of thirty yards to get back to the tree trunk.

"My gracious, what a journey it was, to be sure! You human animals, of course, cannot understand what difficulties, for a maggot,

"Our home was blown clean off its stem."

have to be overcome in a trip like that. You tramp through the meadows and underbrush as though they were nothing at all. But for us every blade of grass, every stick, every rootlet, every stone and leaf has to be climbed over laboriously.

"In the ordinary way, of course, when a catastrophe like that happened to a maggot home, the rest of the colony would never expect to see the occupants again. One neighbor would say to another: 'Did you hear about old So-and-So? His home was blown away last night.' And, according to whether that particular member of the colony was popular or not, the other neighbor would reply: 'Dear, dear! That's too bad.' Or he'd just shrug his shoulders and say: 'Well, it can't be helped.' We took our neighbors' misfortunes—and our own, for that matter— philosophically. Indeed, I think I can say without boasting that we maggots are distinctly a philosophical race."

Danger Ahead!

S O YOU CAN EASILY SEE WHEN, FOUR DAYS later, my friend and I were sighted halfway up the tree trunk coming back to the colony and a new home, after being blown away in a full gale a distance of thirty yards, that our reappearance caused no little commotion.

"Myself, I was too tired and worn out to move another step when we finally reached the top branches where the nuts were. But my adventurous and hardy friend at once set about hunting for a new nest to live in, one that should be in a good firm place where the wind wouldn't knock it down easily.

"In this he was assisted by other members of the colony. As I said, we are not a neighborly lot as a rule, but the story of our sad catastrophe and plucky return had soon got around and there were many willing to help us.

"A big, sound nut in a good place was soon found, and two strong maggots started to drill it for us. This, in our weary state, we were very glad to have them do, because late in the year like that, the inner shell of the nut is getting very hard and drilling is a slow and laborious business. We usually drill earlier, when the shell is softer.

"While our friends prepared a home for us, other maggots brought us food—which we needed desperately—and we rolled over on our backs and gave our feet a rest. When we were snug and safe inside, we both curled ourselves up and slept like tops.

"It was late in the evening when we awoke. Both being terribly hungry again, we set to on the walls of our house and ate large quantities of nut. We found that we had chosen well, for our new home was juicy, sweet, and ripe. To a maggot there is a tremendous lot of difference among the nuts on a single tree.

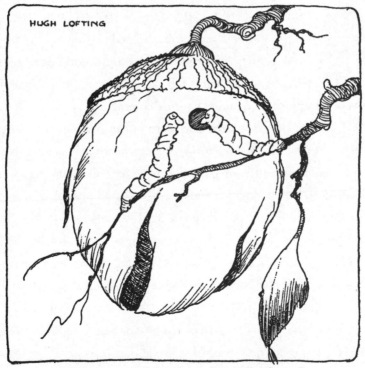

"Two strong maggots started to drill it for us."

"We started talking over our adventures, and I found my friend was very dissatisfied that he had been born a maggot. He had a great and burning ambition to travel. In making him a maggot instead of a bird or a deer, Fate could not have been more unkind.

"'Just the same,' said he, 'I have no intention of letting it make any difference to me, so far as I can. I mean to travel. I enjoyed that wild journey the other night. It was a challenge. And though I was desperately worn out, it gave me the thrill of conquest, exploration, and achievement.'

"'But how,' I asked, 'do you hope to perform big journeys? It takes us days to move over a distance that the other creatures can do in a few seconds. It seems to me that for us it is much wiser to accept the life that was given to us and stay snug in our homes. We have no means of self-protection, either. Almost any animal living can kill us if it wants to. Adventure is all very well, but I believe in safety.'

"Before replying, my friend raised his head, bit a piece of nut out of the wall, and chewed on it through a moment of solemn contemplation.

"'Well, you know,' said he at last, 'I've been studying the other creatures a good deal of late. And I've come to the conclusion that no matter what you're born—an elephant or a fly—life gives you certain handicaps. It is only by being adventurous that you can overcome those drawbacks and do what you want.'

"'Humph!' I murmured. 'I understand what you mean. Just the same, I can't see how a maggot is going to make himself into a great traveler.'

"'Well,' said he, 'perhaps not a great traveler for a bird or a

deer or a man. But I don't see why I shouldn't be a great traveler—
for a maggot.'

"'You're that already,' I replied. 'There isn't a member in the
whole colony who doesn't admit that you've got more distance and
speed—and nerve—to your credit than any of us. It seems to me
that you're sort of hard to please.'

"'Oh, pshaw!' said he, lying back luxuriously against the
curved wall of our home and brushing his two seventh feet together
to knock off some crumbs of nut. 'I haven't done anything yet—nor
been anywhere. Still, I may do—someday.'

HUGH LOFTING

"*'Bad news, neighbor,' he said.*"

"'But I don't see how you're going to go about it,' I repeated. 'Our equipment for traveling is just ridiculous.'

"'There are other means of traveling,' he answered, 'besides one's own feet. Do you suppose that if man—who is, perhaps, the greatest traveler of all—walked everywhere that he'd get—'

"At this moment our conversation was interrupted by someone scratching at the door. I arose and pulled out the husk material with which we always stopped up our holes to keep the wind out. To my surprise it was broad daylight. Having slept through the previous day, we had talked away the greater part of the night that followed. Outside, our neighbor, who lived in the next nut up the branch, was gazing in at me with alarm written all over his face.

"'Bad news, neighbor,' he said. 'The farmer is gathering the nuts. He and his helpers have begun at the lower end of the plantation. But they do not take long in stripping a tree. We are all getting out as fast as we can. I thought I would come and warn you, thinking you were asleep.'"

THE THIRD CHAPTER

The Maggot Goes
on a Journey

ELL, YOU COULD HAVE KNOCKED ME down with a feather. For many seasons, according to tradition anyway, the nut plantation had been neglected. The nuts had ripened on the trees, fallen to the ground in the autumn and either rotted or been eaten by pigs. No pruning or spraying had been done for years. And while we knew that this couldn't last forever—because the trees were gradually spoiling for want of attention—still we never expected that a nut crop would be gathered from trees that had been so long left to themselves.

"I craned my neck out of our hole and looked backward toward the south end of the plantation. And there, just as he had said, were men with ladders and poles and ground sheets stripping the trees of their fruit. In my tree, all about me, maggots were falling from the limbs above ours, hoping to drop into the soft grass and get away in time, rather than be gathered—with their homes—into the big baskets that the men carried. Panic had seized the whole colony.

Of course, many struck the limbs as they dropped and were injured more or less; and still more, never aroused from their sleep, were gathered up with the harvest and taken away.

"I thanked the neighbor who had so kindly warned us, and he at once disappeared. Then I grabbed a large piece of nut that lay on the floor and called to my friend:

"'Come on! This looks like a voyage long enough to satisfy even you!'

"To my astonishment, he didn't even stir, just lolled back against the wall and smiled at me a reckless smile.

"'I'm in no hurry,' he said quietly. 'Who knows? The farmer's

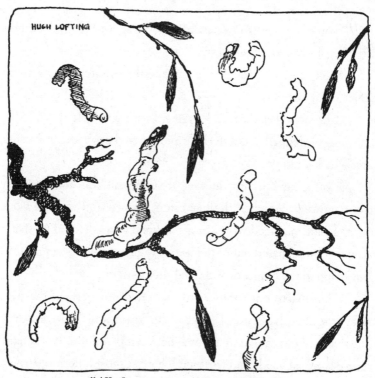

"All about me, maggots were falling."

basket may be the very thing that will take me on a voyage worthy of my dreams. If they are harvesting this old, run-down plantation, it must mean that nuts are precious this year. Why not stay and be—er—harvested, and, most likely, exported to foreign lands?'

"'But good heavens!' I cried, 'You may be eaten, squashed—anything! This is madness.'

"Again he smiled, bit off another piece of nut out of the wall, and chewed on it carelessly.

"'One has to be adventurous,' he said, 'if one would travel and see the world.'

"Aghast, I gazed at him. What could one do with such a maggot?

"'You don't have to come with me,' he said presently. 'I admit it's risky. Do as you think best.'

"Well, there had never been any question whatever in my mind about going with him.

"'I'm sorry,' I said. 'Just the same, I wish you luck.'

"And I stepped out of the hole and hurried down the tree trunk as fast as I could go.

"I got clear only just in time. I suppose I was about twenty feet from the tree when the harvesters arrived and went to work on it. I had managed to reach a blackberry tangle, and in that I remained hidden and out of the way of their trampling feet till they had stripped the branches and filled their baskets.

"There were one or two little wizened nuts left on the tree. After the men had gone I climbed up again and took refuge in one that had got caught in a crotch between two limbs. It was quite secure from all winds and weather. There, almost a hermit, I spent the winter—mostly sleeping—till the spring sun came again to warm us into life and bring a new crop to the tree."

"Very wise of you, indeed," said Doctor Dolittle to the maggot. "For of course it was impossible for your friend to survive."

"That's where you're wrong, Doctor," said the maggot. "He *did* survive. My friend eventually returned, much older and wiser, but still adventurous and reckless as of yore. And this is the story that he told me of his travels as we lolled once again in the security of a warm home while the night wind moaned through the branches:

"'After you had gone,' my friend said to me, 'our home was gathered into the big baskets, dumped into a wagon, and taken away—with me inside it, of course. The wagon lumbered off out of the plantation and followed a hard, knobby road for quite a distance. Arriving at some kind of a warehouse, the baskets were taken out and the nuts were dumped into big piles and stripped of their outer shells. I was a little afraid that my nut might be smashed in this business because it was done with heavy tools. And, watching from my open hole, I could see that many were spoiled and crushed in the process.

"'However, my home escaped injury, and with thousands of others it was put into a packing case, fastened up with nails and boards, and set on one side to await some other kind of transport.

"'Well,' I thought, 'so far so good. I wonder where we go next.'

"'I did not have so long to wait. The next day we were again loaded into wagons and set off on still another journey by road. This was somewhat longer than the first had been, taking the best part of two whole days. At the end of it I realized with a thrill that we had come to the sea coast. So we were to go abroad after all! Our packing cases were unloaded onto a wharf. My nut had fortunately been packed close to the outside of the case and right up against

"Put into a packing case and fastened up"

a crack between two of the boards. And so it was possible for me, when the case was standing right side up, to peep out from my hole and see what was going on.

"'There seemed to be great activity on the wharf. Numbers of men were running around, to and fro, loading stuff into a big ship. Such quantities of things! Sacks, bales, barrels, tin cans, kegs, boxes, everything. Our pile of cases was about the last to be put in. For this I was glad. I felt I'd stand a chance of seeing a little more of the voyage if I wasn't loaded down at the very bottom of the cargo.

"'But, as a matter of fact, it made no difference, because after we were slung up on the big derricks and dumped into the hold, heavy cover boards were put over us and fastened down with wedges, so we couldn't see anything anyway.

"'It was a long and tedious voyage, and the inside of the ship smelled terribly. I didn't get seasick because, of course, any nut maggot gets so used to being swung about on the end of a tree limb that the motion of a ship is just child's play to him. But it was awfully monotonous.

"'One thing I was glad of and that was that after a week or so it began to get warmer all the time. This, I felt, must mean that we were coming to a pleasant country. I found a few other maggots in other nuts in my packing case. And we helped one another pass the time away by chatting and guessing what the country would be like to which we were coming.'"

THE FOURTH CHAPTER

The Ship's Rat

NO, I CANNOT SAY I CARED MUCH FOR THE life of the sea as we maggots led it. Going visiting from nut to nut was about all there was to do. And before the voyage was over I knew the inside of nearly every nut there was in that packing case. One advantage it had, however, and that was freedom from the dangers with which our life was usually beset. There werc no woodpeckers or bug-hunting birds to bother us, and no farmers to spray us with chemicals. Some of my fellow travelers said that they thought this was the ideal life and that no maggot could ask for anything better. But it hadn't nearly enough variety and excitement in it for me. By this time the nuts were getting dry and oily—the way people like them for the table—and we had all got so fat eating them that we could scarcely move.

"'Well, at last one day, after it had become quite hot, we heard a great commotion going on above us—the tramping of feet, whistle blowing, bell ringing, and so forth. And soon the cover boards were lifted off the hold. We had arrived at some harbor.

Our excitement was intense. I immediately hurried back to my old nut, the one near the crack in the packing case, from which I would be able to observe things. Our case got slung up among the first loads. And while it was dangling from the end of the rope in midair I got a wonderful view.

"'Our ship was standing at anchor in the middle of a lovely wide bay. Smaller craft were moored up to us alongside to take off the freight. A couple of miles away across the blue water lay the most beautiful land I have ever seen. Purple mountains, clothed in palms and luscious jungle growth, rose against a cloudless sky. At the shoreline a pretty little town, all white, clustered and shimmered in the sun.

"'And that was all I saw. Suddenly—I don't know exactly what happened—but some new strain was thrown on the rope that held us, dangling there between the sky and the deck. The seam or crack against which my nut was leaning gaped open a little wider. I don't suppose it was more than a quarter of an inch. But it was enough to let my nut out and it bounced upon the deck, nearly shaking me out of it bodily, then rolled away. My packing case with all the other nuts—and the maggots, too—was lowered over the side to go ashore—without me!

"'Words cannot describe how I felt. After coming all that way, to have this silly little accident upset my plans! And what was going to become of me now? My solitary nut was just sitting there on the open deck, waiting for someone to step on it. A seaman kicked it out of the way with his boot. And I, with my house, was rolled into the scupper of the ship.

"'There a boy who was helping with the ropes picked it up and put it in his mouth to crack it.

"'Well,' I thought, 'this is the end of my life of adventure.

"'But fortunately it was a large nut with a good stout shell. While the boy was turning it around in his teeth, trying to break it, one of the men bawled an order at him. He at once took it out of his mouth, put it in his pocket, and went to work. If the man hadn't shouted the order at that exact moment I wouldn't be here to tell the tale. It was that that saved my life.

"'Presently, as the work at the ropes grew warmer, he took off his coat and laid it down on a windlass. There it remained for several hours till he finally took it up again and carried it down to his cabin. Here he hung it on a peg and did not put it on again all day.

"Fortunately it was a large nut."

I was afraid, of course, from moment to moment that he would put his hand in the pocket and, discovering the nut, complete the work of cracking and eating it.

"'But finally he came back to the cabin and went to bed. And after I heard him snoring sound asleep I sighed a great sigh of relief. I knew I was safe for the night, anyhow.

"'Well, there I was, for the present out of danger it was true, but with no way of telling how long my security would last. Not beyond the morning, I felt pretty certain; and then I remembered that sailors worked in shifts or watches and that I could not be sure that the boy would sleep more than four hours.

"'I wondered if I had better get out of the nut right away and leave his pocket while it was still possible. My chances of reaching another nut in which to hide were not, of course, very good. For one thing, the packing cases had most likely all gone ashore; and for another, the distance from the boy's cabin to the hold would be very considerable. There were other things I might hide in at a pinch, like apples and biscuits—even though they were not, strictly speaking, the kind of home that was proper or agreeable for a nut maggot. But the problem would be finding where the apples and biscuits were kept aboard ship—and then getting there myself.

"'I lay and pondered for quite a while over this—for me a very serious matter. Finally I decided to go. Even to get clear of the coat would take me, I calculated, going at my best speed, at least three-quarters of an hour.

"'When I was halfway out of my hole I heard a strange sound and drew back. It was a breathing noise, a sort of sniffing—and quite close. Within the safety of my nutshell I waited, listening.

"'It didn't take me long to determine what the sound was. It was a rat. I had heard them before. Nuts are a favorite food with them—and this one—a ship's rat—had smelled mine in the coat pocket and was coming after it.

"'I wasn't terribly scared, as a matter of fact, because I knew that my kind of a nut had a shell that would take a rat a day at least to gnaw into. Still, I was annoyed because it certainly meant that my plans would be upset and delayed. Snuffling and panting, the rat climbed into the pocket. He found the nut right away, of course—and at once made attempts to gnaw it open. Realizing that it was a big job to get at its meat inside, he then took a grip of it by one end and started to carry it away.

"'Good!' I thought to myself. 'He will probably live near the ship's foodstuffs. This may be a splendid way to get out of here. I'll sit tight and see what happens.'"

Trip to the Galley

ND SO, CARRIED IN THE RAT'S MOUTH, I and my home left the pocket of the ship's boy's jacket and covered in ten minutes a distance which it would have taken me on my own feet weeks to perform. It was most amusing to me to see how the rat handled the nut. It was heavy for him and, after he had carried it in his mouth for a few yards, he would set it down and roll it forward with his paws. Along beams, girders, through scupper holes, the stress of the work changing always with the roll and pitch of the ship, that rat somehow got my nut transferred from the quarters where the crew slept to the next compartment. This was a sort of storage room for sails and ropes. Here he evidently felt that he was safer than he had been in the men's cabin, because he left me and my nut a moment and went to fetch his wife. She, a large lady rat, came and inspected the situation with her husband. They conferred a long time. The nut was now on top of a big pile of canvas and the difficult job was before them of rolling

"They conferred a long time."

it, or lifting it, over an enormous crease in one of the sails.

"'Suddenly their discussion was interrupted. The door of the sail room opened and two men in a great hurry entered to take away some sails. As the rats scuttled to safety, my nut was rolled down off the pile. One of the seamen saw it go. He picked it up. And then, back I went into a pocket.

"'Dear me!' I thought. 'Here I am as badly off as I was before.'

"'The seaman went up on deck, carrying the sail with his companion. There I found that we were now well out to sea again and that darkness had come on. Wind and rain were lashing across the deck. The men had hard work getting the sail into place. I was carried in the man's pocket high up into the rigging while he tied ropes and fixed the canvas.

"'When he came down he was all wet with the rain. Even where I was, snug inside my nutshell, while the water did not actually reach me, I could feel the dampness of his coat and the wet atmosphere of his pocket. I was chilled to the marrow.'

"My friend never quite recovered from that chilling," said the maggot from inside the listening machine. "We maggots are very sensitive to dampness—especially cold dampness. Rheumatism, you know, Doctor."

"How extraordinary!" said the Doctor. "I would have thought rheumatism was foreign to maggots."

"Not at all," replied the maggot. "Our legs get quite stiff with it at times."

The Doctor turned to me. "Be sure and get that all down, Stubbins," he said. "It may prove very valuable in my experiments."

The maggot waited a moment for me to finish scribbling and went on:

"My friend told me those few hours in that wet pocket stiffened him so he could barely walk for days. He was relieved when the sailor took off his coat and proceeded to shake the rain off it. For again Fate took a freakish hand in his affairs.

"'My nut was shaken clean out of his pocket,' he said, 'and went bounding across the floor into a corner.'

"'"What was that I dropped?" said the man as my nut clattered away across the room.

"'He got down on his hands and knees and began groping about the floor. Then he struck a match. I trembled for my safety. If he found it he would certainly crack the nut open—either with his teeth or his boot. Finally he spied it away off under a bunk in a far corner. For a while he fished for it with a stick. And then, to my great relief:

"'"Oh, pshaw!" he said. "It's not worth bothering with—just a nut." And he went to bed.

"'And now, when I put my head out of the hole and looked about me, I found that I had been brought back to the same room where I was before. I imagine it was a sort of general sleeping quarters for all the sailors. They seemed to take it in turns to come down and have a rest there.

"'Once more I began to consider leaving my nut home and

HUGH LOFTING

"He spied it under a bunk."

trying to reach the place where the foodstuffs were stored. But this time I hadn't more than a few minutes for consideration before I heard the rat again. Getting my nut out of the corner may have been difficult for the sailor, but it was an easy matter for the rat. He gave one grunt as he realized he had found his lost property, then promptly picked it up in his mouth again and started off.

"'Neither was the sail room such a difficult territory for him this time, now that some of the canvas had been removed. With his wife's assistance he easily rolled my home over the far side, where they took it down a hole and pushed it out into a third room.

"'This I knew at once, from the smells around, was a sort of food store, eating place, or kitchen. I decided now that I had got to part company with my nut as soon as a chance offered. It was certain that the rat's home would not be far away, and if they once got the nut there, they would probably keep gnawing at it until they got through the shell.

"'So, when their backs were turned a moment in consultation, I crept out of the nut and got away as fast as my chilled feet would carry me. They did not see me leave. And a moment later they rolled the nut down into their own hole and I never again set eyes on my home in which I had traveled so far and had so many hairbreadth escapes.

"'Well, I suppose that was about the riskiest thing I ever did in my whole life, when I crept out of that nut aboard ship, not knowing where my next shelter, nor my next meal, was to come from. The room was, as I had thought, a sort of kitchen. I guessed that it would not be used by the cooks before daylight. That should give me at least three or four hours to look around. In a ship's kitchen anyway, it was a comfort to realize, I had no enemies but cooks.

"'From the floor I started out to find some table leg or other means of climbing upward. I knew that foodstuffs would be most likely up high, on shelves in cupboards and the like. Finally, after a tremendous amount of work, I got to the upper levels. The shelves contained nothing but jugs, bottles, cups and dishes, especially arranged so that they could not fall from the rolling of the ship. I decided the food must be in the cupboards on the other side of the kitchen.

"'So there was nothing for it but to make the long, tedious journey down again to the floor, across and up the other side. I did it, though I was badly out of breath before it was over. Next came the

"Finally I got to the upper levels."

job of getting into the cupboards. They were all locked. I hoped there might be space enough under the door to admit my small bulk. But there again I was disappointed. At length I hit upon the rather ingenious idea of getting through the keyhole.

"'Inside I met with more bad luck. There were plenty of food-stuffs there, but they were all in tins, tins with the covers on. Getting into them was absolutely hopeless. I turned away, retraced my steps through the keyhole, and began a general search around the kitchen. Perhaps I might find some odd pieces of biscuit or apple lying around that would serve as temporary shelter and food till I could establish more permanent quarters. But pretty soon I realized that that too was out of the question. And the reason was not far to seek. Any scraps or leavings were taken care of by those wretched rats. There seemed to be dozens of them about the kitchen. Several I saw actually nibbling up crumbs from the table and the floor.

"'Well, you'd never guess where I finally took refuge—in a rattrap! This contained a very old piece of ship's biscuit as bait. The rats knew it was a trap and they wouldn't go near it. And so I realized, as I crawled into it and noted the daylight showing through the porthole, that after all I was safer here than I might have been in any more regular food, from both rats and men.'"

THE SIXTH CHAPTER

Garbage-Can Canoe

WELL, IT WAS A STRANGE PLACE INDEED to travel in, the bait in a rattrap. And yet I did it. I made that whole sea voyage, back to the port I had started from, in that moldy piece of ship's biscuit, which—luckily—even the rats wouldn't eat. We went to many other ports before we got home. At some of these I was tempted to try getting ashore. But as I noticed we never stayed more than a day or so, I decided that discretion was the better part of valor and I'd better stay where I was. My chances of finding a means of getting ashore in that short time were very poor.

"'And, I suppose, when all is said and done, things could not have turned out better for me than they did. My rattrap was the safest place for a maggot on the whole ship. Our visits to all these other foreign ports served moreover to take up considerable time, so that by the date the vessel had got home again the winter was passed and spring had made outside travel possible for me once more. If I had arrived in the winter I could never have been able to go ashore without dying of the cold.

"'The problem of getting ashore bothered me a good deal. I worked out several plans while we were on our way back. But none of them seemed very hopeful. At length I determined to wait and see what chances offered themselves when I got to port. It was almost impossible to foretell what conditions I would be confronted with, anyhow. Which again, more by good luck than good management, proved itself to be the wisest thing I could have done. It is funny how throughout my whole voyage things seemed to be done for me, rather than by me, and always for the best.

"'After we moored up at our home port, a good deal of cleaning was done about the ship. Among other places, the kitchen was turned out and thoroughly scrubbed. The cook's assistant came upon the rattrap and decided that since it hadn't caught any rats on a whole voyage it ought to have something done to it. He changed the bait, replacing my piece of moldy biscuit with a hunk of yellow cheese. The biscuit, which he threw on the floor for the time being, was later swept up with some other rubbish and dumped into a wooden box.

"'Now,' I thought to myself, 'comes the serious question: Where is he going to throw the rubbish? If he shoots it overboard into the water that will be the end of me.

"'The cook's assistant lifted the box wearily and carried it up the companionway to the deck.

"'So,' I thought, 'soon now the question will be decided: Overboard or where?

"'He carried it at once to the side of the ship and then threw the whole thing, box and rubbish and all, into the river.

"'In that short moment when I was on my way through the air

toward the water I gave up all hope. To swim a little, to be eaten by a fish or be drowned, was all I could hope for in the circumstances. But my star of good luck still seemed to be following me. The box landed on the water with a loud whack! right way up. Being made of wood and containing no heavy rubbish, it did not sink. It settled in the water down to about half its own depth, and then, like a listing, waterlogged boat, it began to drift down the river with the outgoing tide.

"'A dozen gulls at once swooped upon it to pick out the tidbits they liked. Now, mark how curiously Fate protected me: If the scrap of biscuit in which I traveled had been at the very top of the rubbish, I'd have been gobbled up by the first gull that reached the box. On the other hand, if I had been too deep down, I would have been below the water line and drowned before I could have scrambled higher. A large sardine tin on top of my biscuit protected me from the fighting, squealing gulls above and the rest of the rubbish below me kept me up out of the water.

"'Meanwhile, my gallant garbage-can canoe sailed on down the stream. After a little, when the gulls decided they had got all they could out of my strange craft, they deserted it and went off in search of other fodder. The river was wide, as most are near their mouths—and the box at first floated out into midstream. This looked bad because, if we reached the sea, heavy weather would soon sink us, of course. But presently, to my great joy, I saw that a small crosscurrent near a bend was swinging our course over toward the left bank. I had now crawled out of the biscuit fragment and was perched on the edge of the box at the top, like a mariner on the lookout. The left bank of the stream had trees on it at the next bend—trees that overhung the water. Would we touch the land

"Gulls at once swooped upon it."

there? If we did, I could soon scramble ashore and all would be well.

"'Dear me! No castaway seaman ever watched more anxiously for his approach to land than I did to see where the currents would carry my box of garbage. Darkness was coming on. To go out on the bosom of the ocean meant certain destruction. My heart sank as the current that was swinging me over toward the shoulder of the land covered with alders suddenly seemed to bend back toward the center of the stream. The rest of the river was pretty straight, and ahead of me lay the darkening sea with all its threatening, gloomy expanse. My box, too, was sinking somewhat lower, but there still remained about six inches of its sides above the surface of the stream.

"'And then just when things looked worst, a strong wind sprang up, blowing from the right bank. Once more Fate had interfered to keep me alive. Across the quite powerful course of the current the breeze blew my crazy craft toward the shoulder and the alders. We touched an overhanging bough that dropped into the water and immediately we were brought to a standstill.

"'I wasted no time, you may be sure. Humping along as fast as I could go—for there was no telling how long we would remain moored in the stream, which gurgled and swirled around the curves of the bank—I scrambled up onto a twig that touched the top of the box. Goodness! No words can describe my joy at feeling I was once more back on a tree. It wasn't a nut tree of course, but to be on living wood of any kind after all those months of anxiety was something that nothing can convey to you unless you experience it.

"'Now alder trees, which are a swampy, watery sort of thing, have a kind of catkins on them. They are not edible—for us maggots, at all events—but I wasn't at all particular at that moment. I give you my word. There was a real storm blowing up of which the wind had been a kind of forerunner. In the half dark I found one of these berry things, which was partly dried, and drilled my way into it for all I was worth. The meat was bitter, but I was only looking for a shelter from the coming storm and a place to sleep. And once in, my goodness, how I did sleep! You couldn't have awakened me with a hammer.'"

A Ride on a Canal Barge

"A MOST EXTRAORDINARY STORY," SAID THE Doctor. "I'm curious to know how he got back to you."

"Well," replied the maggot, "I'm willing to go on if you are." With that he gave a huge yawn and dug his fists into his eyes.

"Dear me!" cried the Doctor. "You're tired. I must apologize for keeping you up so late. Tommy, that will be all for tonight. We can continue tomorrow—that is, if it's all right with the maggot."

"Quite all right, Doctor," said the maggot. "But I would appreciate some food and a rest right now."

John Dolittle then transferred the maggot from the listening machine to the tray where other maggots were busy eating bits of nut and apple.

"I hope the nuts I have supplied are the sort you care for," he said to the maggot.

"Yes, thank you," replied the tired worm. "They are exceptionally good."

"Well," said the maggot the next morning after Doctor Dolittle had placed him in the listening machine. "My friend's adventures were by no means ended. Of course, once he was among real vegetation again, life became almost a tame affair for him, even though he was not yet in his native country or anywhere near the kind of nut tree that we always regard as home.

"But again a kind Fate took him by the hand, as it were, and led him back to the very spot from which he had started. As he was making his way from one bush to another in a sort of general search for nut trees along the riverbank, he climbed into a flowering hawthorn. The voices of children reached his ears. And presently a party who had come a-maying stopped at the bush and began gathering the blossoming branches. Soon my friend found himself transferred from the bush to the arms of a small girl who was almost invisible behind the enormous bunches of blooms she was carrying.

"'I began by keeping very still,' my friend told me. 'Then presently, when an opportunity came, while the little girl was looking the other way, I crept along the branch till I reached a dense tangle of leaves where I could hide myself. The branches had been tied at the bottoms into bunches with string. So I felt I would be safe here, at all events for a while. Being already very hungry, I ate a few of the hawthorn leaves and found them not half bad, though somewhat bitter in flavor.

"'And then I started out on still another stage of my journey, as part of the baggage of a picnic party. These children with their aunt who accompanied them, lived, it seemed, in London. They had come out for a day in the country and were taking back the wildflowers to their city home. They went by coach, which probably made me the first maggot to travel by passenger stage. I saw

HUGH LOFTING

"Almost invisible behind the blooms she was carrying"

something of the great city, too. Because when they arrived in London they left the coach and took a cab quite a distance through the thronged, busy streets before they reached their destination. Of course I could not see very much, not daring to creep out of the bunch of leaves too far. But I felt quite a thrill at traveling in this manner and listening to all the noises of the town.

"'At the children's home the bunch of hawthorn was placed in a big vase on a sideboard in the dining room. Here I lived as long as the flowers lasted, which was about a week. There was a dish of nuts on the sideboard, and at night I would creep down out of the flowers, drill my way into a nut, have a meal, and creep back again.

"'Later, when the flowers withered and were thrown out into the garbage can, I was once more faced with the proposition of foraging for myself. But while I was still wondering what I should do, the man who emptied the garbage cans in that part of the town came along and carried me away. I was, of course, a little anxious as to where I was going to be taken.

"'It seemed a long distance. The wagon rumbled on and on until it got to the outskirts of the city. Then it stopped and the contents were dumped into an empty lot near the edge of what seemed to be another river, but it turned out to be a canal. I wasted no time, but set off right away to get to some pleasanter surroundings. By this time it was getting dark again and I could not see very well, making my way mostly by feel. After scrambling up and down the assortment of objects with which the place was littered, I came upon some more solid thing made of wood and began to scramble up it. This led me to a flat, hard surface where the going was much easier.

"'It was only after I had explored around this for several hours that I discovered I could not get off it, except by the way I had got on. For it was surrounded by water. It was, in fact, a barge moored close to the bank of the canal, and the object by which I had got aboard it was a gangplank. The barge had come there to dump rubbish the same as the wagon had done.

"'I wasn't at all anxious to go off on another voyage by water just then, so I scurried around to find the gangplank to get ashore by. But I was too late. It had been taken away. The dawn was just showing in the east and by its pale light I now saw men moving around the barge, throwing off the mooring ropes. A team of horses was harnessed to a post in the bow and presently they began, by walking along the banks of the canal, to tow the barge slowly down the stream.

"'I was in despair. The barge contained nothing in the way of food or shelter and, as far as I could see, there was no getting off it. I sat there for about an hour watching those horses plod along, dragging the barge through the canal. Suddenly, the landscape began to look familiar. First a tree, then a piece of open field, and then I recognized *our* tree upon a ridge. It was the plantation where I had left you, my friend, so long ago!

"'But the barge wasn't stopping—it was going by! How to get ashore? I couldn't swim, yet the distance to the land was short—not more than six feet. The towrope I realized, was the only connection with dry land. For one wild moment I had a notion to scale the bow-post and walk this two-hundred-foot tightrope to the horses' backs. But how to get down after I got that far stopped me. I'd never be able to jump from such a height. And as for crawling down the horse's leg—that was impossible.

"'So, desperately watching my native country slipping by at the rate of three miles an hour—a truly breakneck speed to a maggot's mind—I cudgeled my brain for some other means of getting ashore. I crept out over the counter and, standing on the vertical side of the barge, I saw that some of last year's leaves were floating on the surface of the stream. A wind had blown them off the banks. If I could only get on one, it might serve as a raft to reach the bank. Then, at great risk of being washed off by lapping wavelets, I crept lower still till I was less than a quarter of an inch from the surface of the water. There I waited for a leaf to float by near enough for me to step onto it.

"'At last one did brush past, touching the side of the barge right beneath my nose. I was only given a second to make the change. A misstep meant certain death. Yet I did it. With my rear legs still gripping the side of the barge, I took hold of the leaf with my front pair. Then I let go! I flopped into the water with nothing but nose out! But the leaf was a stout one. It didn't tip up while I slowly drew myself aboard it.

"'After the barge had gone on a few hundred yards or so and the ripples of its wake had died away, I noticed to my horror that the leaf on which my life depended was simply surrounded with fishes. They were all watching me like tigers; their eyes shining as bright as colored marbles through the water.

"'As yet there were only small fry around me. But very soon their interest began to attract the larger ones. Before a moment had passed, the water around my leaf was full of big, evil-looking shadows, cruising

HUGH LOFTING

"I flopped into the water with nothing but my nose out."

silently around, waiting for a chance to snap. I kept myself curled up in the center of the leaf—feeling somewhat safer there. But, although a favorable wind was carrying the leaf slowly toward the bank, there was no telling when the larger fish would grow bold enough to nip it down under the water and snatch me as I sank.

"'About three feet from the shore, realizing, I suppose, that their prey was escaping them, they began. One big fellow made a leap out of the water bodily, curving over as he came down, evidently calculating on striking the center of the leaf's top. But fortunately the wind freshened just at that moment and he fell harmlessly into the water with a splash, missing his mark by two inches.

"One big fellow made a leap."

"'After that they went for me hot and heavy. Fish after fish, some of them nearly a foot long, struck at the leaf—sometimes two or three together. But their wild competition came to my assistance. One large fish, pushed out of the way by a still larger one, snapped at the shore-end of the leaf—the second grabbed at the other end. And between the two of them they flicked the leaf bodily into the air off the surface of the water—rather the way you can, by bending it, snap a card out of your fingers and make it jump.

"'I had lost my hold by now and was catapulted up still higher than the leaf. I must have been thrown a good four feet into the air! I could see the fishes watching me greedily as I sailed upward. I shut

"They flicked the leaf into the air."

my eyes, expecting to slip down the throat of one of those gaping monsters. When, plop! I landed, stunned, on the bank. I was safe in the soft grass!'"

The maggot, talking from the listening machine, stopped and looked off into space. I was writing furiously, trying to get everything down word for word.

"I do hope he wasn't injured," said the Doctor.

"No," replied the maggot, "he was quite all right when he came out of his daze. You see, he was now only a few hundred yards from his home. It took him four weeks to cover those yards. And that is how he came back to me and to the home tree from which he started."

"It's strange he didn't turn up when I gathered you and your friends for this experiment," said John Dolittle.

"No, not strange," said the maggot. "He didn't stay more than a couple of months before he was off on another adventure."

"You don't say," replied the Doctor. "I should have thought he'd had enough traveling."

"Not my friend," said the maggot. "You know how it is, Doctor. Once a person starts wandering, there is no keeping him at home."

"Humph!" muttered John Dolittle, smiling. "I know what you mean."

THE LOST BOY

London Zoo

OCTOR DOLITTLE; CHEAPSIDE, THE LONDON Sparrow; and Becky, the sparrow's wife, were in the Zoological Gardens looking for birds of all sorts to sing in the Doctor's *Canary Opera*. On the way to the bird enclosure they came upon many signs which read: "Lost Children Will Be Taken to the Ladies' Cloakroom."

"Yes," said Cheapside, noticing the Doctor reading this sign for the third time. "That's so the mothers and fathers and uncles will know where to look for their nippers when they get lost. Folks is awful careless. On Saturdays and Sundays the ladies' cloakroom is just full of little lost Willies and Aggies. I always used to say they ought to learn 'em tricks and put 'em in a pen alongside the monkeys."

Shortly after this, as the Doctor was passing one of the ponds for waterfowl, he noticed a small redheaded boy trying to wade out to feed the ducks. Fearing he might tumble in, the Doctor leapt over a low railing and grabbed the child by its pinafore. Then he looked around to find the youngster's mother or guardian. But no one at all seemed to be with him. The Doctor questioned him, but all the boy would answer was:

"I want to feed the ducks."

"Take him to the ladies' cloakroom, Doctor," said Cheapside. "Don't argue with him. He's lost, all right. Come along. I'll show you the way."

So, with the Doctor leading the little fellow by the hand, they set off along a winding path through shrubberies.

At the cloakroom the woman in charge took the child and thanked the Doctor for bringing him.

"The Doctor grabbed the child by its pinafore."

"This is the second time he's been brought back today, sir," said she. "I've no idea who owns him. No one has put in a claim."

"I don't wonder at that," whispered Cheapside to Becky at the door. "'E's no beauty. I wouldn't be surprised if they lost 'im on purpose."

"Sh!" said Becky. "Maybe 'e's heir to a throne or something. I've heard tell how princes was lost deliberate by wicked uncles and things."

"Heir to a kitchen chair!" snorted Cheapside with disdain. "'E ain't no prince. Princes don't 'ave 'air that color."

The boy seemed to have taken a liking to the Doctor. For when he was left in the woman's charge, he bawled heartily at John Dolittle's departure. And about half an hour later, when the Doctor was busy conversing with the birds in the East Aviary, he suddenly found the redheaded child once more standing beside him.

"'E's escaped from the cloakroom again," said Cheapside in disgust. "Better tell the woman this time to lock 'im in the cupboard— or maybe we'll be arrested for kidnapin' before the day's over."

Once more the Doctor returned the lost one to the care of the woman in charge of the cloakroom. And this time he gave her special instructions to guard him carefully till his parents came for him.

"Dear me!" said John Dolittle, as he hurried back to the aviary. "This has wasted quite a little of our time. I wonder who he is—look, it is beginning to get dark. We had better abandon our search for today."

In spite of the lateness of the hour and the growing darkness, Mr. and Mrs. Cheapside insisted on seeing the Doctor home. And together they left the Zoological Gardens and set out for Greenheath.

"I'll probably decide on pelicans for the bassos and flamingoes for baritones," said the Doctor. "The higher voices we can do with linnets and such like, which we will get from the fields. Do you think you would be able to get me some pelicans and flamingoes, Cheapside?" the Doctor asked as they made their way through Regent's Park.

"Well, maybe," said the sparrow. "I know of one place about ten miles from the city where a rich feller has a whole lot of fancy waterfowl—pelicans among them. How many would you want?"

"About six, I should think," said the Doctor, "and six flamingoes, too. But eight or ten would make a better chorus."

"Yes, that would be enough to sing anyone to sleep—for good—I should say," murmured the sparrow. "Maybe there's that many at this feller's place. I'll take a run over there in the morning and let you know. I ain't sure about the flamingoes. Maybe I'll have to go elsewhere for them. You wouldn't want to buy them, would you?"

"Not if the gentleman will lend them to me," said the Doctor. "You see, the—what's that white, shadowy thing over there, hopping about among the trees?"

"What—where do you mean, Doctor?" asked Cheapside, peering through the trunks of the dim-lit park.

"Funny! It's gone now," said the Doctor. "I could have sworn I saw something pop behind that elm over there, the other side of the beds. Perhaps it was my imagination."

"Maybe some animal's got out from the menagerie—a deer or something." said Becky. "If it is, good luck to him, I say. I'd hate to live in captivity."

"Yes," said the Doctor. "I dislike the idea myself of animals being confined against their will. In my private zoo in Puddleby the cages all had locks on the *inside*, so the animals could get out when they wanted or shut themselves up at night, just for the sake of privacy, you know. But, oddly enough, although they were all free to go when they chose, none of them ever ran away."

"Yes," said Cheapside, "but yours was a real zoo, Doc—run on proper lines. You always had a waiting list of animals to get *in*, instead of out. Goodness, don't I remember that old sleepy black bear you had who could never wake 'isself up in time for breakfast! You ought to 'ave seen that zoo, Becky. Beat anything we saw on the Continent. Old Mr. Bear asked the Doctor for an alarm clock. And every night when he locked his own door, to keep out the tramps and the rats, you'd 'ear 'im a-windin' that old tin timepiece of 'is. O' course, 'e couldn't tell the time—used to look at the back, instead of the face, pretendin' 'e knew 'ow. But 'e knew enough to get up in time for breakfast when it went off in the mornin'! Ah, that was a real zoo, that was—bless me! What's that runnin' be'ind us? Didn't you 'ear footsteps?"

John Dolittle Brings Home a Guest

THEY WERE NOW AT THE EDGE OF GREEN-
heath. And the wide-open Common, dotted with gorse
clumps, stretched before them in the dim starlight. The
three of them paused, listening.

"Hark to me, Cheapside," whispered Becky. "I believe there's
something following us. Let the Doctor go on ahead and you and I
hang back and do a little scouting. I think I 'eard something moving
the other side of those bushes over there."

So the Doctor went on his way across the Common of Greenheath while Mr. and Mrs. Cheapside hung back. And, keeping
near the ground, where they would not be seen in the dim light, they
set to work to find out who or what it was that was following them.

John Dolittle had pretty nearly made up his mind that it must
be some animal, possibly escaped from the zoo, that was determined
to attach itself to his household. He had experienced this before
many times. So great was his reputation among animals of every
sort that he was constantly followed by lame dogs, rabbits, moles—

all sorts of beasts who wished to consult him medically or see if they could be taken into his private circle of pets. But, the Doctor argued with himself, if it was nothing more than that, why did the creature not come forward to see him, instead of slinking around like this in concealment?

As he walked forward over the springy turf of the heath, John Dolittle expected the sparrows any minute to overtake him with news. But a good quarter of an hour passed without his hearing anything. And he could see the outline of his own circus tents not more than a few hundred yards away before Cheapside alighted on his shoulder and giggled:

"He could see the outline of his own circus tents."

"What d'yer think, Doctor? It's our redheaded friend, the nipper who was lost in the zoo."

"Good heavens!" cried John Dolittle, stopping short. "The boy we left in the cloakroom?"

"The very same, Doctor," said Cheapside. "If I was you, I'd turn around and go back through the city some other way. That's about your only way of losing 'im."

"But, my gracious, Cheapside, I can't do that!" said the Doctor. "The child's lost. I can't leave him to wander around in the night like this. Where would he get supper? Where would he sleep?"

"Good lord, Doc!" said the sparrow impatiently. "That ain't your concern. What are you goin' to do, adopt 'im?"

"Well, I certainly can't leave him out here," said the Doctor. "Where is he? I'll have a talk with him."

So Cheapside guided the Doctor back a few yards to where Becky was keeping an eye on the boy behind a clump of gorse.

"Hulloa, my friend," said John Dolittle in a kindly voice. "Didn't your parents come for you at the ladies' cloakroom?"

"No," said the boy.

"But how did you come to be lost at the zoo?"

"I wasn't lost by my parents," said the boy. "It was I who lost my parents. I want to be a menagerie-keeper. So I ran away from home and came to the zoo. But they would keep taking me to the ladies' cloakroom and saying I was lost. Then when it began to get dark and I saw they were going to close up the place, I thought I'd follow you."

"Why?" asked the Doctor.

"Because I like you," said the boy.

"But what of your mother and father?" asked the Doctor.

"Oh, they're all right," said the boy. "They've got lots more children. I set out to seek my fortune—I want to be a menagerie-keeper."

The Doctor took out his watch and peered at it in the dim light of the stars.

"Humph!" he muttered. "There's nothing else for it. You had better come and spend the night with me. And tomorrow I must try to get in touch with your parents."

"Who's that?" asked Gub-Gub as the Doctor entered his wagon, leading the redheaded youngster by the hand.

HUGH LOFTING

"'Who's that?' Gub-Gub asked."

"This is a young man who followed me all the way from the zoo," said the Doctor, as the animals all gathered about him examining the small stranger. "He will spend the night with us. But I must get busy in the morning and find out who his parents are. Otherwise I may get arrested for kidnaping."

"For catnipping, did you say?" asked Gub-Gub the pig.

"No. For kidnaping," the Doctor repeated. "That is, for stealing him. Some people might not believe that he followed me so far. Have you got some extra sheets, Dab-Dab?"

"Oh, I suppose I can find him a place to sleep somewhere," said the housekeeper, wagging her tail in a harassed manner. "Tut-tut! I wonder you wouldn't have more sense, John Dolittle, than bringing him here when you know the wagon is so crowded already."

"But I didn't bring him," said the Doctor. "He followed me, I tell you. I couldn't leave him out on the heath with no blankets or anything."

"Well, anybody else would have found some other way out of the difficulty," snorted the duck. "It's bad enough to have you bringing in stray animals of every kind. But children! You don't realize what you've let yourself in for. Children make a terrible mess of a home. Gub-Gub will have to give up his bed and sleep on the floor."

"Oh, goodness!" groaned the pig. "What with dieting for the opera and sleeping on the floor, I might as well be—"

At this point Matthew Mugg entered the wagon. In a few words the Doctor told him about the boy and the necessity for putting him up.

"Why don't you let him sleep in the menagerie, Doctor?" said Matthew. "There's two or three empty stalls there, with lots of clean straw."

"Did you say a menagerie?" asked the boy, his large round eyes showing intense interest. "What is this place?"

"This is a circus," said the Doctor. "The Dolittle Circus. And I am John Dolittle, the manager."

"A circus!" cried the youngster, stepping on Gub-Gub's tail in his excitement. "But how splendid! I set out to seek my fortune and I've found it. It's just like Dick Whittington. I wanted to be a keeper in the zoo. I thought you must be something interesting when I saw you talking to the birds, like St. Francis. Of course I'll sleep in the menagerie. I'll sleep with the elephant."

The boy, in spite of his being clearly tired from his long walk, was now all agog with the interest of his new position. He asked a thousand questions at once. And when supper was brought in, he was so absorbed by the animals sitting around the table like people that he hardly ate anything. John Dolittle did his best to dissuade him from sleeping in the menagerie. But he was absolutely determined to spend the night with the elephant. And finally the Doctor had to carry him over there, almost too sleepy to keep his eyes open, and put him to bed under a pile of blankets. Alongside of the enormous animal, he looked like a grasshopper next to a horse.

"Now, for heaven's sake," said the Doctor to the elephant, "don't roll in your sleep. If necessary, stay awake. It will only be for one night. Tomorrow I hope to get this young man back to his parents."

THE THIRD CHAPTER

Trouble at the Circus

AFTER SPENDING A SLEEPLESS NIGHT HIM-
self, wondering whether the elephant had rolled on
the child, the Doctor sped across to the menagerie
almost before it was daylight. There he found the
would-be keeper busily washing the elephant's face with a flannel. The enormous creature, realizing that the young tyrant
meant well, was bearing the performance with patience while
the boy walked about over his face, scrubbing it vigorously.

"I wish you'd take him away and let me get some rest," said
the elephant miserably in answer to the Doctor's "Good morning." "I've hardly had a wink of sleep all night. I was so scared by
what you said. When I did doze off I kept dreaming that I had
squashed him out as flat as a pancake. And the first thing he did
when he awoke—before I had a chance to get up—was to find a
cake of soap and a floor rag and start cleaning my ears. I hardly
slept a wink."

"Neither did I," said the Doctor.

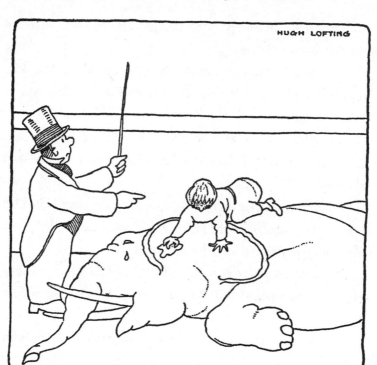

HUGH LOFTING

"The would-be keeper busily washing the elephant's face with a flannel"

The boy had now gotten hold of the menagerie broom and was busy brushing the elephant's hair with it.

"Er—pardon me," said John Dolittle, taking it from him. "But large animals don't have to have their hair brushed or their faces washed in the morning. They make their own toilet. How would it be if we went across to my wagon and had some breakfast?"

After a good deal of coaxing, the young adventurer was taken off—much to the poor elephant's relief—to the manager's van.

The first thing that Gub-Gub said when they entered the wagon was:

"Doctor, I didn't sleep a wink all night. I shall have to go to bed immediately after breakfast."

"Yes, and he kept me awake, too," growled Jip the dog, "groaning and scratching the floor with his feet to make it soft!"

"Humph!" said the Doctor. "But you were not the only ones who did not sleep. Well, let's have breakfast, then maybe we'll all feel better."

"I told you you were in for something, Doctor," said Dab-Dab as she set the porridge on the table. "Children are a handful. One child is more nuisance than a dozen animals."

"Yes, perhaps you're right, Dab-Dab," said the Doctor, sitting down. "I wonder why that is. Are you ever sorry you weren't born a man, Jip?"

"Good Lord, no, Doctor!" said Jip. "I wouldn't be a man for anything."

"Why?" asked the Doctor, reaching for the cream.

"Men—people—worry such a lot," said Jip. "Their life is so—er—so complicated, difficult. Dogs never worry unless they're hungry or cold—or when they've lost their friends. Oh no, I'm glad I wasn't born a man."

"That's rather curious, you know," said John Dolittle. "There have been philosophers who say that people are born over again—that some men have been animals and some animals men. It's called the theory of reincarnation."

"Then I bet Gub-Gub was a cook last time he was on earth," said Jip.

"Well, you can be sure I was a good cook, then, anyhow," said Gub-Gub indignantly. "I'll bet you I never served up anything as poor as this diet gruel. Gee, I'll be glad when that opera's over! This training is ruining my disposition."

The small red-haired adventurer apparently was highly pleased with his new home and had no intention of ever leaving it. All day long he insisted on helping with various parts of the show. He succeeded in getting in everybody's way to such an extent that it seemed that if something wasn't done about him soon there would be a general strike in the Dolittle Circus.

During the main performance in the big tent his determined efforts to take part in the show nearly cost him his life, when the lion stumbled during a balancing act and sat on him heavily. And the Doctor soon realized that Dab-Dab had been quite right and that one child could make more trouble than a dozen animals.

Seeing that it was urgently necessary to get him back to his home as soon as possible, the Doctor made a special trip into the city and put an advertisement in all the papers that a lost child with red hair could be claimed at his establishment on Greenheath. Meanwhile the youngster, realizing the dream of his life, continued to have a wonderful time and to make himself what he thought was useful. He went into the clown's dressing room when no one was looking and daubed grease paint all over his face and pinafore. He called on the snakes during their performance and upset the tent and brought it down on top of the audience that was gathered there. He inspected the Pushmi-Pullyu, the two-headed animal, and made that poor, patient animal give him a ride on his back. He went to the performing otters' tent and fell in their tank and nearly drowned before they fished him out.

By nightfall, when the Doctor and Matthew were reduced to

HUGH LOFTING

"He daubed grease paint all over his face."

a state of complete exhaustion, keeping him out of harm and mischief, the young adventurer announced that he intended to sleep with the elephant again that night. And in spite of that poor animal's begging to be allowed to get a good night's rest undisturbed— and the Doctor's trying for half an hour to dissuade the boy from his intention—he finally went to bed with his big friend, much to the relief of everyone except the elephant.

"I don't know what I'll do," said the Doctor to Dab-Dab after supper, "if his parents don't come for him tomorrow. Advertising in the paper is about the only hope we have. I had expected that they'd be here today."

"It's your own fault," said Dab-Dab, "for bringing him here. You should have taken him to the police station."

"That's an idea," cried the Doctor. "Why didn't I think of that? Oh, but he wouldn't like it. He is having an awfully good time here."

"And what about the time we're having?" asked Dab-Dab. "You'll have that poor elephant sick again if you don't get that little imp out of here—and you know what a handful he is when he's sick. I saw him just break down and weep when he heard that the child was going to sleep with him again tonight. Take the little nuisance to the police station. They'll be kind to him—and they'll find his parents a lot quicker than you can.

"Humph!" murmured the Doctor. "I suppose there's something in what you say. Well, if his parents don't come in the morning, I'll take him over there."

No one showed up the next day to claim the boy, and Dab-Dab kept at the Doctor till she made him do as he had said he would. And about noon John Dolittle set out with the young man and left him in the care of the local superintendent of police.

Everyone in the circus, especially the poor elephant, was greatly relieved to learn that he had gone, and the whole staff, which had been on the verge of open riot for two days, settled down once more to a peaceful life.

All that night again the Doctor hardly slept. This time his worry was not that the elephant might roll upon the boy, but how the youngster was getting on at the police station.

"You know, Dab-Dab," he said at breakfast the next morning, "it seems such an inhospitable thing to do. The lad was having such a wonderful time here. And although I know, of course, that the police will treat him nicely, children are so funny, you understand. I couldn't help admiring the youngster—such pluck and determination—following me all that way from Regent's Park. And then for me to turn him over to the police! It's been bothering me all night. I think I'll run across as soon as I've had breakfast and see how's he's getting on."

"Oh, for heaven's sake!" said Dab-Dab wearily. "I know what that means. Now, you listen to me, John Dolittle; that boy could get along and take care of himself anywhere. Don't you worry about him."

"Yes, perhaps," said the Doctor. "But just the same—hulloa! What's this?"

At that moment two policemen in uniform appeared at the wagon door. Between them stood the redheaded boy.

"Heavens preserve us!" cried Dab-Dab. "Here he is, back gain. And you were going to go after him!"

"Good morning, sir," said one of the policemen. "The superintendent presents 'is compliments and says would you mind taking this young man back into your charge? Every effort, the superintendent says, will be made to find his parents. But in the meantime, if you wouldn't object to keepin' 'im, the superintendent will be much obliged."

"Why," asked the Doctor, "wouldn't he stay with you?"

"'E didn't seem to care for the station house, sir," said the constable. "'Owled and 'ollered all night, saying 'e wanted to go back to the menagerie. And the superintendent says—beggin' your pardon, sir—'e reckons that's the proper place for 'im. 'E's broke all the windows and nobody got a wink of sleep—prisoners and neighbors and everyone complainin'. It seemed as though the only thing to pacify 'im was to fetch 'im back 'ere. So the super-intendent tells us to bring 'im and deliver 'im to you at all costs."

The small boy, now that he was back in his beloved circus, was wreathed in smiles. He greeted all the animals in turn—who didn't seem nearly as pleased to see him as he was to see them. The Doctor rose from the table a moment to put the canary cage out of his reach. And when he turned back to the door again he found that the two policemen had sneaked off without waiting for further words and left the young adventurer on his hands once more.

The Guest Departs

"W ELL," SNORTED DAB-DAB, "PERHAPS IN the future you'll believe me, Doctor."

"Oh yes, indeed, Dab-Dab. I agree that there's a lot in what you say," said John Dolittle as the young man pulled the lamp down on the floor with a crash. "Children are sometimes—er—a trial. But, you know, in some ways I'm sort of glad to see him back again—no, those geraniums don't need any more water, young man. I gave them some water before breakfast. Besides, that's hot water. You know, after all, Dab-Dab, this is a children's circus. It seems sort of proper that we should have one child on the staff."

"If you do, you won't have anybody else on it—long," snapped the duck.

"Perhaps his parents don't mean to claim him at all," said the Doctor thoughtfully.

"Heaven forbid!" said Dab-Dab devoutly.

"Maybe we can train him," murmured the Doctor thoughtfully.

"No, those geraniums don't need any more water, young man."

"Then train him to keep away from me," said Dab-Dab, as the child upset the coffeepot over the clean tablecloth.

Once more the Dolittle Circus was thrown into a state of turmoil by the return of the strange young person whose determination to be menagerie-keeper had already caused so much trouble.

One of the first things to happen that day was the appearance of the circus's regular menagerie-keeper at the door of the manager's van.

"I've come to give notice, Doctor," said he.

"Why, what's the matter?" asked John Dolittle.

"That young nipper's the matter," said the man. "I ain't 'ad no rest since 'e's been around. I warned you that I'd have to go unless he stayed away from my animals. Then when I 'eard 'e'd been took off to the police station I supposed we were going to 'ave some peace. But this morning 'e's back again and 'is interference and tricks is worse than ever. I want to give notice."

"Well," said the Doctor, "of course, if you've made up your mind. I wouldn't try to persuade you to stay. Have you got another position in view?"

"I don't need no other position," said the keeper. "Since you've been running the show on the sharing system I've saved up a tidy penny. And now we're in London, I'd like to take a small shop somewhere and settle down."

"Oh, then it isn't only on account of the boy that you want to leave?" said the Doctor. "Well, I'm glad that you and your wife are able to take to the kind of life you prefer. After all, that's the most important thing. But I'll be sorry to lose you."

"There you are!" said Dab-Dab to Jip as soon as the man had left the wagon. "Another getting rich and retiring from the Dolittle Circus. While the Doctor goes on slaving without a penny to his name! Dear old Puddleby, will we ever see it again! I often wonder! All the Doctor ever saves up is new responsibilities and cares—like this young redheaded nuisance."

With the departure of the menagerie-keeper the duties of Manager Dolittle and Matthew Mugg were increased. For until a new man was found to fill the post, they had to take turns looking after the animals. And this was not made easier by the young adventurer, who insisted that he take the keeper's place and could hardly be kept out of the menagerie at any time.

But the next morning, to Dab-Dab's great delight, the youngster's mother at last turned up. When she demanded her child, the Doctor took her over to the menagerie and, expecting her to be most delighted to find her boy safe, showed her the lad sleeping peacefully between the weary-eyed elephant's knees. With a shriek she clutched the child to her bosom and turned upon the poor Doctor in a fury.

"How dare you keep my son with your wild animals?" she screamed.

"But that was what he insisted on himself," said the Doctor. "I didn't want him to sleep here—neither did the elephant."

"I never heard of such heartless cruelty," yelled the woman.

"You—you monster!"

"I'm going straight to the police station this minute. I'll have the law on you for this, you—you monster!"

In a storm of tears—in which the red-haired one joined—the woman departed—and did actually go and report the Doctor to the police. But, as it happened to be the same station that had harbored the young man for a night, the superintendent decided that the Doctor was more to be pitied than prosecuted and gave thanks that the young man was at last restored to the bosom of his family.

The End

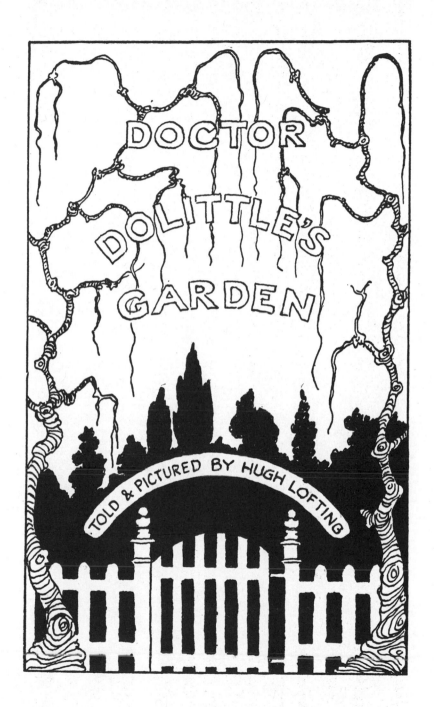

DOCTOR DOLITTLE'S GARDEN

TOLD & PICTURED BY HUGH LOFTING

Contents

PART ONE

1   The Dog Museum   519

2   Quetch   524

3   The Dick Whittington Dog   530

4   The Children's Hospitality   534

5   Gypsy Life   538

6   The Acrobat   545

7   The Monastery   551

8   The Shepherd in Distress   558

9   City Life   562

10   The Hermit Dog   566

11   The Topknot Terriers   574

12   Dogs' Jobs   586

PART TWO

1   Insect Languages   591

2   Foreign Insects   596

3   Tangerine   600

4   Domestic Insects   609

5   The Water Beetle   614

6   The End of the Journey   621

7   The Colony of Exiles   625

8   A Lifetime of Twenty-Four Hours   631

9   Dab-Dab's Views on Insect Life   636

10	The Giant Moths	641
11	Otho the Prehistoric Artist	646
12	"The Days Before There Was a Moon"	651
13	Memories of Long Arrow	655
14	Blind Travel Again	661
15	Gub-Gub Halts the Game	664

PART THREE

1	Bumpo's Concerns	671
2	The Tapping on the Window	675
3	The Giant Race	678
4	The Awakening of the Giant	683
5	Keeping a Secret	687
6	The Butterflies' Paradise	693
7	The Home of the Giant Moth	700
8	Flowers of Mystery	704
9	Smoke on the Moon	709
10	Too-Too's Warning	714
11	Our Midnight Visitors	723

PART FOUR

1	Bumpo Clears the Garden	733
2	The Mounted Police	740
3	The Errand	746
4	The Stowaway	751
5	The Doctor's Reception	757
6	Crossing "the Dead Belt"	763
7	The Two Sides of the Moon	770
8	The Tree	774

PART ONE

The Dog Museum

I SUPPOSE THERE IS NO PART OF MY LIFE WITH THE Doctor that I, Thomas Stubbins, look back on with more pleasure than that period when I was Assistant Manager of the zoo.

We had come, as I have told you elsewhere, to call that part of the Doctor's garden "Animal Town." One of my greatest difficulties was in keeping down the membership in the various clubs and institutions. Because of course a limit had to be put on them. The hardest one to keep in check was the Home for Crossbred Dogs. Jip was always trying to sneak in some waif or stray after dark; and I had to be quite stern and hard-hearted if I did not want the mongrels' club disorganized by overcrowding.

But while the Doctor and I were agreed that we must keep a fixed limit on all memberships, we encouraged development, expansion, and new ideas of every kind on the part of the animals themselves that would help to make Animal Town a more interesting and more comfortable place to live in. Many of these were extremely interesting. Among them was the Dog Museum.

For many years the Doctor had had a museum of his own. This was a large room next to the study where bones, mineral specimens, and other natural-history things were kept. There is an old saying: Imitation is the sincerest form of flattery. A natural interest in bones often led the dogs to contemplate this display and finally to start a museum of their own.

This was helped to some extent by a peculiar dog who had some months before become a member of the club. The peculiarity of his character was that he had an inborn passion for collecting. Prune-stones, umbrella handles, doorknobs—there was no end to the variety of his collections. He always maintained that his prune-stone collection was the largest and finest in the country.

This dog's name was Quetch. He was a great friend of Toby, who had first introduced him and put him up for membership at the club. He was a good second to Toby in upholding the rights of the small dogs at the clubhouse and seeing that they didn't get bullied out of any of their privileges. In fact, Blackie and Grab always said that the small dogs, with Toby and Quetch to champion them, bossed the club a good deal more than they had any business to. Well, Quetch it was (he was a cross between a West Highland terrier and an Aberdeen) who first suggested the idea that the mongrels' club should have a museum of its own. With his passion for collecting, he was probably counting on getting the job of museum curator for himself—which he eventually did.

The house committee met in solemn council to discuss the pros and cons and ways and means. The idea was finally adopted by a large majority vote and a section of the gymnasium was screened off to form the first headquarters of the museum.

Quetch (he was always called "Professor" by the other members of the club)—Professor Quetch, besides being a keen scientist, had a genius for organization almost as good as the white mouse's. And even he could not find fault with the general enthusiasm with which the Dog Museum was supported, and contributed to, by the members of the club. There was hardly a dog in the home who didn't turn to collecting and bringing in material. And Quetch the curator had his paws more than full receiving and arranging the continuous flow of specimens of every kind that poured in.

The museum was not confined to natural history. It was also an archaeological or historical museum. The bones department was

HUGH LOFTING

"*Professor Quetch*"

perhaps the largest. Personally, I don't think that any student of comparative anatomy would have found it scientifically very helpful. For the bones were mostly beef, mutton, and ham bones.

But not all. There were fish bones. In fact, there was one whole fish, which Professor Quetch proudly ordered me to label, "The Oldest Fish in the World." I could well believe it was. Blackie the retriever had dug it up—from the place where someone had carefully buried it a long time ago. Its odor was so far-reaching that the members of the Badgers' Tavern (which was at least a hundred yards away from the Home for Crossbred Dogs) sent in a request that something be done about it. They said that while they were not usually oversensitive to smells, this one kept them awake at night. Professor Quetch was very much annoyed and sent a message back to the badgers that they were a lot of lowbrow, meddlesome busybodies who didn't appreciate science. But some of the Doctor's neighbors across the street also complained; and the "oldest fish in the world" had to go—back to the garbage heap.

The archaeological side of the Dog Museum was even more varied and extensive than the natural history departments. Here could be found Quetch's own priceless collection of prune-stones, umbrella handles, and doorknobs. But these formed only a small part of the whole. The habit of digging—generally for rats—natural to all dogs, now led to the unearthing of treasures of every variety. Saucepan lids, bent spoons, top hats, horseshoes, tin cans, pieces of iron pipe, broken teapots, there was hardly anything in the way of hardware and domestic furnishings that wasn't represented. A sock that had been worn full of holes by the great Doctor himself was one of the most sacred and important exhibits.

For the first few days there was a general frenzy of digging. Jip and Kling had heard the Doctor say that the Romans had once had a military camp on the site now occupied by the town of Puddleby. They were determined that they'd find Roman jewelry if they only dug patiently enough. Among other places they tried was Colonel Bellowes's tulip bed. They had just dug up a bulb when they were seen by the colonel and chased. But they got away—and home with the bulb. And that was how the Botanical Department of the museum began. The bulb in question had a label set under it reading:

This orchid was donated by the famous naturalist and explorer, Jip. The intrepid collector was disturbed at his work and chased for miles. He eluded his pursuers, however, and succeeded in bringing back this priceless specimen to the Dog Museum.

HUGH LOFTING

"They were seen by the colonel and chased."

THE SECOND CHAPTER

Quetch

THE DOG MUSEUM CONTINUED FOR MUCH longer than I had thought it would. My private opinion had been that the dogs were only captivated by the novelty of the idea and would drop it altogether when its newness had worn off. Some weeks after its beginning, the collections had grown so fast that they filled the whole gymnasium. During the semifinal bout of a wrestling contest, a Great Dane threw Blackie the retriever through the dividing screen and landed him in the middle of the Botanical Department. It was clear that the gymnasium was getting crowded out by the museum.

So a second meeting of the house committee was called. And it was decided that since athletics were equally important as science, most of the junk should be thrown out, and only those things kept that were really genuine and of special application to dogs and dog history.

Jip's famous golden collar (which he only wore on holidays and occasions of importance) was made one of the star exhibits. There

"The semifinal bout of a wrestling contest"

were also a few bones that Professor Quetch insisted had been chewed by the great dogs of history. There was also a small keg, which he said had been carried round the necks of the St. Bernard dogs who went to the aid of lost travelers in the snow-swept passes of the Alps. How he knew the record of these relics no one could tell. On the other hand, no one could deny it when he put up a label under a veal bone saying that this object had been the earliest plaything of the Empress Josephine's pet poodle.

At all events, the enormous array of hardware and rubbish that had formed the first displays gave place to one or two glass cases where a small collection of objects of great virtue was set forth. And for many years these remained a permanent part of the institution, and all visitors, whether dogs or people, were shown them. Professor Quetch never allowed visitors into the museum, however, without personally conducting them, to see that they didn't lean on the cases—if they were people—or, if they were dogs, that they didn't take away the historic bones.

The third story in the *Tales of the Home for Crossbred Dogs* was Jip's own tale of how he had posed for the great George Morland and helped the lame man's dog earn money for his crippled master. For the fourth story Professor Quetch himself was called upon. Both Toby and Kling had often told me that they knew that he had led rather an interesting life, and I could well believe it, for he was certainly a dog of individuality and character. He was not easy to persuade, however. In spite of his being, like Toby, a self-important, plucky little animal, he wasn't boastful or given to talking about himself. He had always, when asked to tell the story of his life, made the excuse that he was too busy with his duties as curator of the museum.

However, now that the museum had been considerably reduced in size, he did not have to give so much attention to it. And one day Jip came to me highly delighted with the news that Quetch had promised tomorrow night to give us an account of his life, which was to be entitled "The Story of the Dog Who Set Out to Seek His Fortune."

Feeling it would probably be a good yarn well told, I asked the Doctor if he would come and listen. In former times he had frequently attended the dogs' after-supper storytellings. But of late he had seldom had the time to spare. However, he said he would make this a special occasion and be there without fail.

When the following night came, the dogs' dining room was jammed. For not only was every single member present, eagerly waiting to hear the yarn, but it turned out that this was Guest Night, the second Friday in the month, when members were allowed to bring friends to dinner as guests of the club.

"I was born," Professor Quetch began, "of poor but honest parents. My father was a hardworking Aberdeen terrier and my mother was a West Highland of excellent pedigree. Our owners were small farmers in Scotland. My father helped regularly with the sheep. In spite of his size, he was a mighty good sheepdog and could round up a flock or cut out a single ewe from the herd

"He was a mighty good sheepdog."

with great skill. When we children were puppies we got fed well enough, because we were easy to feed, not requiring much more than milk. But as soon as we began to grow up into regular dogs it was another story. We saw then that the farmer that owned us had hardly enough food most of the time to feed his own family and the hands who worked for him, let alone a large litter of hungry terriers.

"We lived in a stable behind the farmhouse where we had an old disused horse stall to ourselves. It was well lined with dry straw, snug and warm. One night I happened to lie awake late and I overheard my mother and father talking. Their names were Jock and Jenny.

"'You know, Jock,' said my mother, 'very soon that farmer is going to get rid of these puppies of ours. I heard him talking about it only the other day.'

"'Well,' said my father, 'I suppose that was to be expected. They'll keep one or two, I imagine. I hope they leave Quetch here. He seems a bright youngster and is already quite a help to me with those silly sheep. For the rest, I think they're rather stupid.'

"'Stupid indeed!' snapped my mother with great indignation. 'They're every bit as clever as their father, that's certain.'

"'All right, have it your own way, Jenny,' said my father, snuggling his nose down into the straw to go to sleep—he never cared for arguments anyway—'have it your own way. But you can hardly expect McPherson to keep the whole litter when he can barely support his own family.'

"With that my father fell asleep and I fell to thinking. First of all, it seemed to me very wrong that dogs should be disposed of in this haphazard, hit-and-miss fashion. If we were given away, to whom would we be given? Had dogs no rights at all? My father was a worker on the farm, doing his daily job as faithfully and as well as any of the clodhoppers who drove the plow or cut the corn. And here he was calmly talking about his own children being given away as though they were apples or turnips! It made me quite angry. I lay awake far into the night wondering why dogs were not allowed to lead their own lives and shape their own careers. It was an outrage. I got myself quite worked up over it. And before I fell asleep I made up my mind that no one was going to give *me* away as though I were no more than an old pair of shoes. I was an individual, the same as the farmer himself. And I was going to make the world acknowledge that fact or know the reason why."

The Dick
Whittington Dog

ERHAPS THE ONLY NOTABLE THING ABOUT this yarn of mine is that it is the story of a dog trying to lead his own life. I know of course that there are many of you present who have struggled to do the same. That was one reason why I wasn't keen to tell a story: I didn't feel that my life had anything particularly thrilling about it. But at all events, what small adventures I ran into may have been different from your own, and the way I attacked the problem of winning liberty and independence for myself may interest you.

"A few days after I had overheard my parents' conversation I began to see that my mother's fears were right. Almost every day McPherson the farmer would bring friends of his in to see us, hoping they'd be willing to adopt one or other of us. As luck would have it, I was selected the very first. A stupid fat man—I think he was a farmer too—chose me out of the whole litter. I wouldn't have chosen him from among a million. He had no wits at all and no—er—refinement, none whatever. He turned me over and prodded me and examined me as though I were a pig for the fatting market instead of a dog. I determined right away that whatever happened, I wouldn't become *his* property. Luckily he couldn't take me immediately and he asked McPherson to keep me for him a couple of days, at the end of which he would come and fetch me.

"I had heard of boys setting out to seek their fortunes. Never of a dog. And yet why not? The more I thought of the idea, the more it appealed to me. I had to go somewhere if I didn't want to be taken away by that stupid man. I had seen nothing of the world so far. Very well, then: I would set out to seek my fortune—yes, tomorrow!

"The next morning I was up before any of the farm was stirring. I had collected several old bones, and with these as all my earthly possessions tied up in a red handkerchief, I set out to carve a career for myself. I remember the morning so well. It was late in the fall and the daylight would not appear for an hour yet. But an old rooster was already crowing in a hoarse voice through the misty chill air as I gained the road and looked back at the farm buildings huddled in the gloom of the hollow. With a light heart I waved my tail at him and trotted off down the road.

"Dear me, how inexperienced I was! I realize that now. Literally I knew nothing—not even the geography of the immediate neighborhood around the farm. I didn't know where the road I was traveling along led to. But at that time such a thing only added to the thrill of the adventure. I would stick to this road, I told myself, and see what fortune it brought me to.

"After I had jogged along for about an hour I began to feel very much like breakfast. I therefore retired off the road into a hedge and opened my bundle of bones. I selected a ham bone that had not been quite so thoroughly chewed as the rest and set to work on it.

"I set out to carve a career for myself."

My teeth were young and good and I soon managed to gnaw off the half of it.

"After that I felt much better, though still somewhat hungry. I repacked my baggage, but just as I was about to set off I thought I heard a noise on the other side of the hedge. Very quietly I crept through, thinking I might surprise a rabbit and get a better breakfast. But I found it was only an old man waking up in the meadow where, I suppose, he had spent the night. I had a feeling of camaraderie with him. He was homeless too, and, like me, a gentleman of the road. Within the thicket I lay and watched him a moment. There was a herd of cows in the field. Presently the man went and began milking one of them into a tin that he carried. When he had the tin filled, he brought it back to the corner of the field where he had slept and set it down. Then he went away—I suppose to get something else. But while he was gone, I crept out of the hedge and drank up all the milk.

"Considerably refreshed, I set off along the road. But I hadn't gone more than a few hundred yards when I thought I'd go back and make the man's acquaintance. Maybe I felt sort of guilty about the milk. But anyway a fellow feeling for this adventurer whom I had robbed made me turn back.

"When I regained the corner of the meadow I saw him in the distance milking the cow again. I waited till he returned. Then I came out and showed myself.

"'Ah, young feller me lad!' says he. 'So it was you who pinched my milk. Well, no matter. I got some more now. Come here. What's your name?'

"Well, he seemed a decent sort of man and I was glad of his company. On both sides it seemed to be taken for granted that we would travel together along the road. He was much better at foraging food than I was—in some ways; and I was better than he was in others. At the farmhouses he used to beg meals, which he always shared with me. And I caught rabbits and pheasants for him, which he cooked over a fire by the roadside. Together we managed very well.

"We went through several towns on our way and saw many interesting things. He allowed me complete liberty. That I will always remember to his credit. Often at nights we nearly froze. But he was a good hand at finding sleeping places, burrowing into the sides of haystacks, opening up old barns and such like. And he always spread part of his coat over me when he lay down to sleep."

The Children's Hospitality

UT THE DAY SOON CAME WHEN MY NEW friend played me false. He wanted money. I fancy it was to get coach-fare to go to some other part of the country. I don't know. Anyway, one afternoon he knocked at a farmhouse door. I thought that as usual he was going to ask for food. Imagine my horror when he said to the woman who answered the door, 'Do you want to buy a dog, ma'am?'

"I just ran. I left him standing at the door there and never looked back. It was such a shock to my faith in human nature that for the present I did nothing but feel blue. Puzzled, I went on down the road, still seeking my fortune, alone. It was only later that I began to feel angry and indignant. The cheek of the man, trying to sell me when he hadn't even bought me!—Me, the free companion of the road who had been in partnership with him! Why, I had caught dozens of rabbits and pheasants for that ungrateful tramp. And that was how he repaid me!

"After jogging miserably along for a few miles I came upon

some children playing with a ball. They seemed nice youngsters. I was always fond of ball games and I just joined in this one, chased the ball whenever it rolled away and got it for them. I could see they were delighted to have me, and for quite a while we had a very good time together.

"Then the children found it was time to go home to supper. I had no idea where my own supper was coming from so I decided I'd go along with them. Maybe they would let me join them at their meal, too, I thought. They appeared more pleased than ever when I started to follow them. But when they met their mother at the gate and told her that I had played with them and

"*She promptly chased me off with a broom.*"

followed them home, she promptly chased me off with a broom. Stray dogs, she said, always had diseases. Goodness only knows where she got that from! *Stray* dogs too, if you please. To her, every animal who wasn't tagged on to some stupid human must be a stray, something to be pitied, something disgraceful. Well anyway, to go on, that night it did seem to me as though mankind were divided into two classes: those that enslaved dogs when they wanted to be free; and those that chased them away when they wanted to be friendly.

"One of the children, a little girl, began to cry when her mother drove me off, saying she was sure I was hungry—which I was. She had more sense than her mother, had that child. However, I thought I'd use a little strategy. So I just pretended to go off; but I didn't go far. When the lights were lit in the dining room, I waited till I saw the mother's shadow on a blind in another part of the house. I knew then that the children would be alone at their supper. I slipped up to the window, hopped onto the sill, and tapped gently on the pane with my paw. At first the children were a bit scared, I imagine. But presently one of them came over, raised the corner of the blind, and saw me squatting on the sill outside.

"Well, to make a long story short, the youngsters not only took me in, but they stowed me away in a closet so their mother wouldn't see me, and gave me a fine square meal into the bargain. And after they were supposed to be fast asleep, one of them crept downstairs and took me up to their nursery where I slept under a bed on a grand soft pillow that they spread for me. That was what I call hospitality. Never was a tramp dog treated better.

"In the morning I managed to slip out unseen by Mama and once more I hit the trail. Not only was one child crying this time, but the whole four of them were sniffling at the garden gate as I said goodbye. I often look back on those children's hospitality as one of the happiest episodes in my entire career. They certainly knew how to treat dogs—and such people, as we all know, are scarce. I hated to leave them. And I don't believe I would have done it if it hadn't been for their mama and her insulting remark about all stray dogs having diseases. That was too much. So, with a good plate of oatmeal porridge and gravy inside me—which the children had secretly given me for breakfast—I faced the future with a stout heart and wondered as I trotted along the highway what Fortune would bring forward next."

"One of them crept downstairs."

THE FIFTH CHAPTER

Gypsy Life

BOUT THREE MILES FARTHER ON I OVER-
took a gypsy caravan creeping along the road through
the morning mist. At the rear of the procession a
dog was scouting around in the ditches for rats. I had
never met a gypsy dog, so, rather curious, I went up to him and
offered to help him hunt for rats. He seemed a sort of a grouchy
silent fellow but I liked him for all that. He made no objection to
my joining him, and together we gave several rats a good run for
their money.

"Little by little I drew the gypsy dog out and questioned him as
to what sort of a life it was to travel with the caravans. These people
too were folk of the road like me, and I had serious thoughts of
throwing in my lot with them for a while. From what he told me,
I gathered that a dog led quite a free life with the gypsies and was
interfered with very little.

"'The grub is kind of irregular,' said my friend, who had got over
his grouchiness somewhat and seemed inclined to take to me. 'But

then the whole of the gypsy business is irregular, one might say. If you can stand that you'll probably rather like the life. It's interesting, traveling around all the time. We do see the world, after all. If we have hardships, at least it's better than being treated like a lap dog, trotted out on a leash and living on the same street all the time. Why don't you try it for a while? Just tag along with me. No one will mind. Likely as not the gypsies themselves will never even notice that you've joined the caravan—at least not for a few days, anyhow."

"I did not need very much persuasion and it turned out eventually that I did join the gypsies and on the whole had quite a good time with them. My friend had certainly been right about the food. To say it was irregular was putting it mildly. There were many days and nights when there simply wasn't any. But the gypsy dog, through long experience in this kind of life, knew all sorts of dodges for getting provender under difficult conditions. I strongly suspect that my friend was one of the cleverest larder burglars that ever lived. Often I didn't even know where he got the supplies from, and no amount of questioning would make him tell. Many a night when we were both starving, around suppertime, with the prospect of going to bed hungry beneath the caravans, Mudge would say to me—that was his name, Mudge—

"'Oh, golly! I'm not going to bed hungry. Listen, Quetch: I think I know where I may be able to raise some fodder. You wait here for me.'

"'Shall I come too?' I'd say.

"'Er—no. Better not, I think,' he'd mutter. 'Hunting is sometimes easier single-handed.'

"Then off he would go. And in half an hour he'd be back again with the most extraordinary things. One night he would bring a steak-and-kidney pudding, tied up in the muslin it was boiled in—complete, mind you, and steaming hot. Another time it would be a roast chicken, stuffed with sage and onions, with sausages skewered to its sides.

"Of course it didn't take much detective work to tell, on occasions of this kind, that Mudge had just bagged someone else's dinner. I'm afraid I was usually far too hungry to waste time moralizing over where the things came from. Still, I strongly suspect that some good housewives called down many curses on Mudge's head during the course of his career. But the marvelous thing to me was how he did it without ever being caught.

"Another time it would be a roast chicken."

"Yet the life was certainly pleasant for the most part. We visited all the fairs and saw the towns in holiday mood. It was in these days that I met Toby, who was, as you know, then a Punch-and-Judy dog. Yes, I liked the gypsy life—chiefly because we were nearly always in the country, where a dog's life has most fun in it. Along the lanes there were always rats to dig for; across the meadows there were always hares to chase; and in the roadside woods and copses there were always pheasants and partridges to catch.

"That chapter of my life lasted about three months and it ended, as did the one before it, suddenly. We had been visiting a fair in a town of considerable size. Part of our own show was a fortune-telling booth. Here an old gypsy woman, the mother of our boss, used to tell people's fortunes with cards. A party of quite well-to-do folk stopped at the booth one day to have their fortunes told. Mudge and I were hanging around outside the tent.

"'Let's get away from here,' he whispered to me. 'I don't like the looks of this mob. I lost a friend like that once before.'

"'Like what?' I asked.

"'Oh, Joe,' said Mudge. Joe was the name of our boss. 'Joe never notices any stray dogs who join the caravan till somebody else notices them. Then he tries to sell them. . . . This friend of mine was a whippet. One of the visitors to the booth took a fancy to him and Joe just sold him then and there. I'd never get sold because I'm not nifty-looking. But you, you're smart enough to catch anyone's eye—specially the women. Take my advice: fade away till this mob's gone.'

"Mudge was already moving off, but I called him back. I was interested in this fortune-telling business. I hoped to get my own fortune told by the old woman. She read people's palms. I had been looking at the lines in my paw pads and they seemed to me quite unusual. The future interested me. I was keen to know what sort of a career I had before me. I felt it ought to be a great one.

"'Just a minute, Mudge,' I said. 'Why get worried? How can Joe sell me when I don't belong to him?'

"'Don't you worry about that,' said Mudge. 'Joe would sell anything, the Houses of Parliament or the coat off the prime minister's back—if he could. A word to the wise. Fade away.'

"Mudge's advice was sound, but for me it came a bit late. I noticed as I turned to follow him that one of the women was already pointing at me and that Joe, to whom she was talking, was very interested in the interest she was showing. For about half an hour after that I saw nothing more of Mudge. I had moved round to

"I had been looking at the lines in my paw pads."

another part of the fairgrounds till the visitors should have departed from the fortune-telling booth.

"While I was looking at a strong man lifting weights, the gypsy dog suddenly came up to me from behind and whispered:

"'It's all up, Quetch. You'll have to clear out. That woman liked you so much that she said she'd buy you when Joe offered you to her. He is hunting for you everywhere now.'

"'But why,' I asked, 'can't I just keep out of the way till the woman has gone?'

"'It is no use,' said Mudge. 'Joe won't rest till he has sold you, now that he knows you're the kind of dog the ladies take a fancy to. What's more, if he misses this sale he will likely keep you on a chain right along, so as to make sure of you next time someone wants to buy you.'

"'Good gracious, Mudge!' I cried. 'Would he really do that? But tell me: Why do you yourself live with such a man? Come with me and we will go off together.'

"Mudge grinned and shook his head.

"'Joe is all right to me,' he said. 'He may not be what you'd call exactly a gentleman. But he's all right to me. You're a stranger, you see. He looks on me as one of the tribe, the Romany folk, you understand. Their hand is against every man, but not against one another. Even if I were good enough looking to bring him a ten-pound note I doubt if Joe would sell me. He is an odd one, is Joe. But he's always been square to me. . . . No, Quetch, I'll stay with the caravan, with the Romany folk. Once a vagabond, always a vagabond, they say. I'll miss you. But, well . . . Good luck to you, Quetch. . . . Better be going now. If Joe once lays hands on you you'll never get away till he sells you, you can be sure of that.'

"So, very sad at heart—for I had grown very fond of the strange

"Mudge shook his head."

Mudge, the gypsy mongrel, the dog of few words—I left the fair and struck out along the road again, the Road of Fortune, alone.

"Dear me, what an unsatisfactory world it was! When one did find a nice kind of life, something or somebody always seemed to shove you out of it just as you were beginning to enjoy it.

"Still, I had much of the world to see yet. And after all, my experiences so far had not brought to me that ideal independent sort of life that I was looking for. I was sorry I had not been able to have my fortune told. I looked at my paw again. I was sure it must be a good one. It was a nice sunny day. I soon threw aside my gloomy thoughts and trotted forward, eager to see what every new turn in the road might bring."

The Acrobat

HAT DAY I HAD VERY BAD LUCK IN THE MATTER of food. I hardly got anything to eat all day. By the evening I was positively ravenous. I came to a town. Hoping to pick up bones or scraps that other dogs had left, I searched several backyards. But all I got was two or three fights with wretched, inhospitable curs who objected to my coming into their premises.

"Then, famished and very bored with life, I wandered through the streets. At a corner I came upon an acrobat performing. He was standing on his hands and doing somersaults and things like that. He was all alone. There was a hat laid on the curb-stone in front of him, and from time to time people threw coppers into it.

"This set me thinking. The man was evidently making his living this way. In my life with the gypsies I had often seen dog-acts in the circus ring. Some of the tricks I had practiced myself when I had had a notion to go in for a circus career, and I had become skilled in quite a few of them. I could stand on my front paws, beg with a lump of sugar on my nose, throw a back somersault, and

"I came upon an acrobat performing."

so forth. Very well then, I said to myself, why shouldn't I give a one-dog show on the streets of this town the same as the man was doing? But I needed a hat for the people to throw money into—only in my case I hoped they would throw cutlets and sausages instead. Yes, the first thing to do was to get a hat.

"I knew that hats were to be found in shops and on garbage heaps. I set off and hunted round the backs of houses. The garbage heaps of this town had everything on them *but* hats. Most annoying. Where could I find one? I *must* have a hat. I passed a hat shop. The shopkeeper was busy writing in a book. There were lots of hats on the counter and many more, in boxes, on the floor. I was desperate. He could easily spare me one—he had so many. I dashed in and tried my luck. Bother it! I couldn't get the hat out of the box quick enough.

The shopkeeper threw his book at me and chased me out.

"I went on down the street.

"'Never mind,' I said to myself. 'I'll get a hat, somehow, yet.'

"As I turned the corner into another street I saw an old gentleman crossing the road. He was all muffled up and full of dignity. And on his head he had an elegant high hat—just the kind of hat I wanted for my performance.

"'Ah!' I said to myself. 'If I can only trip that old gentleman up, his hat will roll off and I can take it to another part of the town and begin my show.'

"No sooner said than done. I leapt out into the road and ran between his feet. He stumbled and came down with a grunt on his stomach. His hat rolled into the gutter. I grabbed it and shot off down the street. Before the old gentleman had time to pick himself up, I was round the corner and out of sight.

"I didn't stop running till I got to an entirely different part of the town, quite a distance away. Here I felt I was safe from pursuit. I found myself at a busy street corner.

"'Now,' I thought, 'the next thing is to collect a crowd.'

"I set the top hat on the curb-stone, got inside it and started barking for all I was worth. Very soon passersby began to stop and wonder what it was all about. I went on yelping—I was sorry I hadn't a drum, that's what I should have had. Then I got out of the high hat, bowed to the audience and began my show. I begged, stood on my front paws, threw somersaults, etc. It was quite as good a show as the acrobat had given—better in fact.

"The audience didn't know quite what to make of it. They gaped and gaped. Then they began asking one another, 'Where's his master?' ... 'Who's he with?'

"I got inside it and started barking."

"The silly people couldn't believe I was my own master, giving my own show. After a little they came to the conclusion it was some new trick, that my master had hidden himself somewhere near and was just proving how wonderfully I had been trained by not appearing on the scene himself till after the performance was over. Then pennies began dropping into the hat. That was all very well, but I couldn't eat pennies.

"However the crowd finally did realize that I was entirely on my own. And some old ladies in the audience, instead of giving me coins, took their money into a butcher's shop nearby and bought some meat to give me. This I gobbled up with great relish and they went and got some more. The crowd grew bigger and bigger meanwhile. And pretty soon, eating between somersaults, I was as full as an egg and

I couldn't have done another trick if you had given me a kingdom.

"Well, my act earned me a very square meal, but it also nearly cost me my liberty. Why is it that people just can't seem to understand that a dog may be satisfied to be his own boss? Before my show had gone very far, many well-meaning people among the audience decided they ought to adopt me.

"'*Such* a clever little dog!' cried one old lady. 'I think I'll take him home with me—that is, if no one really owns him. Did you see the way he ate those sausages I gave him? He must be starving. He ought to have a good home, such a clever dog.'

"At that I made up my mind to close my act in a hurry. But it wasn't at all easy to get away, I found. By this time I had attracted such a crowd at the corner that the traffic was held up. People were jammed in around me like a solid wall. Several persons in the audience began to argue as to which of them should adopt me. I should have been flattered no doubt but I wasn't. I looked around frantically for a means of escape.

"Then suddenly the old gentleman whose hat I had stolen came up on the outskirts of the throng and recognized his topper, filled with pieces of meat and calves' liver, sitting on the curb-stone. Furious with rage he began milling his way in through the mob. While he was picking up his hat and emptying the meat out of it—I hadn't been able to eat more than half of the crowd's contributions—I scuttled out through the lane he had made coming in. The people's attention was suddenly turned to his lamentations and the story of how I had stolen his hat. And while they were listening I got through into more open country in the middle of the street.

"But the crowd was not long in missing me.

"'Stop him! Grab him! He's getting away!' someone called.

"And then as I bolted round the corner I realized that I had the whole town chasing me.

"I had eaten so many sausages and veal kidneys and pork chops that running at all was no easy matter. However, I saw plainly that if I was going to keep my treasured liberty, I had to put my best foot forward.

"Luckily it was quite dark now. And as soon as I got off the main thoroughfares, away from the shops and into the dimly lit back streets, I soon gave the crowd the slip.

"Ten minutes later, when I slowed down on the open road again outside the town, I said to myself—

"'Well, I earned my own living tonight, all right. But next time I do it I'll try some other way.'"

HUGH LOFTING

"Emptying the meat out of it"

The Monastery

UETCH'S STORY HAD NOW BEEN GOING ON for some hours. And the attention of the audience had not slackened in the least. For my part, while my fingers felt a bit stiff from writer's cramp (for you must remember I was taking down all these stories in shorthand, to be put into the book, *Tales of the Home for Crossbred Dogs*), I was still too deeply absorbed in the history of this strange little terrier to bother about the time. Neither had it occurred to the Doctor to look at his watch. And it is quite likely that we would all have sat there listening till the roosters crowed if Dab-Dab had not suddenly appeared and told us that it was long after midnight and high time that the Doctor was abed.

So the rest of the Story of the Dog Who Set Out to Seek His Fortune was put off till the following night.

But when the next evening came, I could see by the eager way the crowd got ready to listen that the delay had only made them that much keener to hear the remainder of it.

HUGH LOFTING

"Dab-Dab suddenly appeared."

"The next chapter in my story," Quetch continued, "was rather odd—peaceful but odd. The colder weather was coming on—for it was late in the year. When I felt that I was well beyond the reach of pursuit of the angry old gentleman and the townsfolk, I began to keep an eye open for a decent place to sleep. The best I could find was a haystack, into which I burrowed a sort of hole and curled myself up inside. I was just about to drop off when a biting cold wind sprang up in the east and began blowing right into my little den. I soon realized that I had to make a move. I tried the other side of the stack but it wasn't much better. So I decided to go on down the road and find another place.

"I hadn't gone very far when I heard a bell tolling. I peered into the darkness off to the side of the road and saw a large stone building. At one end there was a sort of chapel with stained glass windows, dimly lighted. It was the only habitation in the neighborhood, standing in the midst of its own grounds, apparently. I went up closer and saw that there were men dressed in robes solemnly gathering in the little chapel. It was evidently a monastery. I knew, because there had been one near our home farm. These monks would be going into vespers, the evening service.

"Well, I was never what you would call a religious dog. On the other hand, no one could call me bigoted or intolerant. Among my friends upon the Scotch farm I had had Episcopalian, Presbyterian, Methodist, and Baptist dogs. One of my closest chums had been an Airedale who belonged to a Jewish rabbi. The little chapel looked warm and inviting compared to the cold night outside. The doors would soon close. I joined the procession and went in to vespers.

"Well, it seemed that some of the monks were not as broad-minded about matters of religion as I myself. They objected to my coming in. I suppose they thought I wasn't a Roman Catholic dog and hadn't any business there. Anyway, I had no sooner found an empty pew, free from drafts and curled myself up to listen to the service in comfort, than I was grabbed by one of the lay brothers, carried to the door and put out.

"I was greatly shocked by this. I had always understood that monasteries were famous for their hospitality. What sort was this, when a gentleman of the road, taking shelter from a windy night within their walls, was grabbed by the scruff of the neck and shoved out into the cold? While I was wondering what I would do next, the organ started playing and the monks began singing psalms. Such voices, my gracious! I could do better myself. I would show them. I leaned against the chapel door and joined in the chorus. Of course I couldn't sing the words. But I had no difficulty in following the general lines of the tune quite as musically as they were doing.

"To my surprise, my joining the choir seemed to stop the organ. Next I heard whisperings behind the closed door of the chapel.

"'Perhaps it is the Devil, Brother Francis,' I heard one monk say, 'trying to disturb us at our devotions. Do not open the door on any account.'

"This wasn't very flattering, nor in the least helpful. But presently the abbot, that is the head of the monks, came down to the

HUGH LOFTING

"I joined in the chorus."

door of the chapel to see what all the disturbance was about. The abbot was a very fine man. He became, afterward, a great friend of mine. Devil or no devil, the abbot believed in facing the problems of life. He ordered the door to be opened at once. He smiled when he saw me sitting on the step outside.

"'Come in, stranger,' said he, 'and take shelter from the wind and cold.'

"I didn't wait for any second invitation but trotted in at once and made myself comfortable in one of the pews. Several of the monks looked kind of shocked and scandalized. But as it was their own abbot who had let me in, there wasn't anything they could do about it. Then they went on with the service.

"After it was over they all started to troop out again. They were very solemn and serious. I joined the procession, sticking close to the abbot, who was, I realized, a good person to keep in with. From the door of the chapel, two by two, with our eyes on the ground, we traipsed along a stone-paved cloister and entered another door. Beyond this, I was delighted to discover, lay the dining room, or refectory, as it is always called in monasteries. Good cooking smells greeted our nostrils. With the cold, nippy wind I already had a great appetite again.

"Well, I followed the monastic life for several months. It wasn't half bad. The monks were a very nice lot of men when you got to know them. And as soon as I was accepted into the order I was allowed to go everywhere and do pretty much as I pleased. In that respect it was one of the freest, most agreeable chapters in my whole career. The old abbot was lots of fun. Naturally of a very cheerful disposition, he often had, I could see, very hard work keeping up the solemn dignity that seemed to be expected of his position as head of the monastery. I am sure that he found in his friendship with me a chance to let off steam and be natural. Many was the jolly run we had together, down in a hollow of the monastery meadows where no one could see us, in pursuit of an otter or a hare.

"Of course it *was* quiet, there's no denying that. Prayers, digging in the garden, farm and house work, were all we did; and day followed day in peaceful sameness. But for my part I managed to get a good deal of fun out of it. In return for my board and lodging, I kept the monastery and the farm buildings free from rats. That gave me plenty to do. And it was about this

"Many was the jolly run we had together."

time that I first became a collector. The abbot was a geologist and he used to collect stones and pieces of rock. I helped him in digging for them.

"Yes, I had a very peaceful life while I was a Monk Dog. I would probably have stayed with it much longer if it had not been for my desire to see more of the world. This finally led me to bid farewell to the monastery and its nice abbot and set forth once more upon my wanderings."

THE EIGHTH CHAPTER

The Shepherd
in Distress

THE WINTER WAS NOW IN FULL SWING AND IT was not a good season to be homeless. For a week or two I spent about the hardest time that I have ever gone through. Icy blizzards were blowing most of the time. When I wasn't nearly frozen I was almost starved to death. I could well understand then, I assure you, why it was that we dogs, as a race, had remained dependent upon man. Many a time I was tempted to get adopted by any master or mistress, no matter how stupid or severe, so long as I got one square meal a day and a warm bed in return for my bondage.

"One day when I was down to a very low level of misery and want, trudging along the road wondering where my next meal was coming from, I saw a shepherd having a hard time rounding up his flock. He had a sheepdog with him, but the animal was a fool and no good at the business.

"I was awfully weak for want of food, but I saw here a chance of something worthwhile. The shepherd was in despair. The wind was blowing like a crazy hurricane, now this way, now that. Darkness was coming on. The sheep were scattered in all directions, scared by the gale. The man's dog was more a nuisance than a help. He tried hard enough; but he just didn't know the business of sheepherding, and that was all there was about it. Having helped my father on the home farm—he was one of the best sheepdogs that ever barked, even if he was only a terrier—I did know something about it.

"After a little while the poor shepherd saw that his dog was worse than useless and he whistled and called him off the job. That was my chance. In less time than it takes to tell, I shot round that flock and herded it up through the gate that I saw the shepherd was trying to pass it through. Once I had the sheep in the fenced enclosure the job was done and the shepherd was happy. I came up to him wagging my tail. He fell on my neck and almost wept. If that flock had been lost in the night storm, I suppose he would have got into serious trouble.

"That was how I started two friendships that lasted a long while—one with the shepherd, the other with his dog. I went home with the two of them that night and was rewarded with a good hearty meal of stew and a warm bed. While supper was being prepared I heard the shepherd telling his wife how, when it looked as though the flock would be surely lost, I had appeared on the scene and saved the day.

"But the curious thing about this incident was that the shepherd, by no means an educated person, never tried to take advantage of me, restrict my liberty or capture me as his property. I suppose, being a sheepherder himself, he recognized in me an expert in his own trade who was entitled to respect. In other words, I had, for perhaps the first time in dog history, hired myself out as an independent specialist and could leave or stay with the job as I pleased.

HUGH LOFTING

"Telling his wife that I had saved the day"

"Poor though he was, the man gave me splendid meals, in every way as good as his own. I took his dog in hand—he was a collie, a decent fellow even if he was a bit stupid—and taught him over several weeks how sheepherding should be done under varying conditions of weather.

"You know, that game is not quite as easy as it looks to the man who passes by. Sheep are a herd animal—very much a herd animal. If the weather is fine they behave one way; if it is rough they behave another; if it is hot they do this; if it rains they do that, and so forth. Now, if you're a sheepdog—a good sheepdog—you've got to know these things and act accordingly.

"Well anyway, I put the shepherd's dog through a regular course. I enjoyed it myself—as one always does when teaching the other fellow. By the end of a fortnight poor Raggles, as he was called, was a really good sheepdog and could be trusted to take care of a flock even if a blizzard sprang up at twilight, which is perhaps the hardest thing that a sheepdog is ever called upon to do."

THE NINTH CHAPTER

City Life

B UT MY YEARNING TO SEE THE WORLD LED me to drop that too, just as it had the peace of the monastic life. And the day came when I said good-bye to the shepherd and his dog and set out once more. It had been kind of lonely on the sheep farm and I thought I would like to try city life for a while. I journeyed on till I came to a big town. You see, being still pretty inexperienced, I thought it would be quite a simple matter for a dog to go to a city and take up his residence there like a person. But I discovered it wasn't.

"Firstly, finding a place to live was hard. I solved that problem eventually by taking up my quarters in an old packing case that I found in an empty lot. It was one of those places where people dump rubbish. The packing case, as a kennel, left a good deal to be desired, but it might have been worse. The wind and the rain blew in through the holes of it. But it was much better after I had stuffed it and lined it with some straw and rags that I found nearby among the rubbish.

HUGH LOFTING

"The packing case as a kennel left a good deal to be desired."

"Another problem was the food. This was always sort of hard. But I had supposed it would be easier in a city where so many had to be fed and such a lot of food was on sale. But, on the contrary, I never met with such extraordinary difficulty in getting enough to eat.

"However, the worst thing of all was the dogcatchers. In cities, I discovered, homeless dogs are not allowed. By homeless they mean ownerless. An office called The Department of Public Health is responsible for this. It is not supposed to be healthy for a town to have ownerless dogs knocking around its streets.

"Of all the inhospitable, unfriendly institutions, that of town dogcatchers is I think the worst. The idea is this: a man with a wagon goes round the streets. And any dogs he finds who haven't collars on, or who appear to be without masters, or lost, get grabbed by the dogcatcher and put into his wagon. Then they are taken to a place and kept there to see if anyone wishes to claim them or adopt them. After a certain number of days, if no one has come forward to give them a home, they are destroyed.

"Dear me, what a time I had keeping out of the clutches of those dogcatchers! I seemed to be always getting chased. Life just wasn't worth living. Although I managed to get away, I finally decided that a town was no place for me and that I didn't care for city life at all.

"And then just as I was preparing to leave one evening I *did* get caught. Goodness, how scared I was! As the wretched old wagon rumbled along over the cobbled streets I cowered inside, thinking that the end of my career had surely come. At the home or whatever it was called where we were taken, we were treated quite kindly, as a matter of fact—fed well and given decent beds. Well, there I waited in the greatest anxiety, wondering whether I was going to get adopted or not.

"On the third day, which I believe was the last day of grace allowed, an old lady called at the home. It seemed it was a habit of hers, calling to see if she could rescue any stray dogs from destruction. Her keen old eyes picked me out right away.

"'Oh,' said she, 'he looks like a nice dog, that Aberdeen over there. I think I can find a home for him.'

"Then she asked the man in charge to keep me till the next day, when she hoped to be able to bring someone along who would adopt me.

"This she did. He was a funny sort of man, harmless enough. He took me away with a piece of string tied around my neck. And I assure you I was glad enough to go with him.

"An old lady called."

"After I got to his home I decided that he wasn't very anxious to have me, really, after all. I felt that most likely he had only taken me to oblige the old lady. He was one of those fussy bachelors, worse than any old maid—had to have everything in his house in apple-pie order and nearly had a fit if I jumped onto the chairs or left hairs on the hearth-rug.

"After staying with him a week I made up my mind that he would probably be greatly relieved if I ran away and freed him of my company. Which I did, choosing the nighttime for my departure so that I could get out of the town without running into those wretched dogcatchers again."

THE TENTH CHAPTER

The Hermit Dog

THIS TIME I DETERMINED TO REMOVE MYSELF from the haunts of man completely. I must confess I felt considerably disappointed in humankind—disappointed and a good deal annoyed. It seemed to me that man took far more than his share of the good things of this world and that he bossed the rest of creation much more than he had any business to. So I was now going to live independently of him. I think part of the idea was proving to myself, as well as to mankind, that a dog could be really self-supporting.

"To find a piece of country that was wild enough for my purpose was not easy. I made inquiries of dogs whom I met along the roads. They told me of certain big forests and heaths where they reckoned that a dog could live, hidden away in peace, if he wanted to. These districts were all quite a distance off. I chose one that sounded the best and started out to get there.

"It took me three days of steady travel. On the way the countryside grew less and less peopled; and when at last I came to the part

I was making for, it certainly was lonesome and desolate enough for anything. Some of it was mountainous. For the rest, wide expanses of forest and brambly rolling heath sheltered only the timid native creatures of the wild. One couldn't find a better place for a dog to lead a hermit's life.

"I began by making a thorough exploration of the whole section till I knew every dell and thicket in it. Then I found a fine old hollow tree, like a bear's den, which made the snuggest home you ever saw. No winds or storms could reach me there, and it was as dry as any house or kennel. It was situated in one of the remotest and thickest parts of the forest where no stray traveler would be likely to

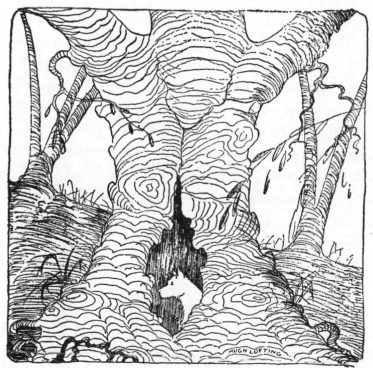

"I found a fine old hollow tree."

find me—even supposing that any stray travelers ever passed that way. Quite near there was a splendid little mountain brook where I could always get a drink. Rabbits seemed plentiful, partridges and woodcock too; and there were a few squirrels and small game. Even in the winter season the woods were full of wonderful smells and looked very attractive.

"'So,' I said to myself the first evening when I brought home a rabbit to my lair and prepared to turn in for the night. 'So! What do I care now for man and his silly civilization? Here I will settle down, a wild dog, independent and self-reliant, living on the wilderness as did my forefathers before me. This is the life! Let man go hang!'

"Well, I stuck to my experiment long enough to prove it could be done. Entirely self-supporting and independent, I lived in the woods through the rest of the winter. Hardships I had in plenty; but I did it. Of course my diet was almost always raw meat, occasionally fish when I managed to catch the big trout drowsing in the rocky pools of the mountain brook. But that wasn't often. They were clever customers and were seldom off their guard. But I did get one or two a week—after I had secretly watched how the otters managed it, lying on the banks among the bracken, motionless for hours, and then, when the chance came, plunging right into the icy waters like a fish myself and battling with them in their own element. I learned a lot of hunting dodges from the otters—and from the weasels too.

"In many ways it was indeed a great life. But suddenly after a while I found I wasn't really contented. True, I had all I wanted, liberty and independence included. But, there was no denying it, I wanted something else besides. I found myself wandering off to

"Battling with them in their own element"

the few lonely little farms whose pastures bordered the heathlands beyond the edge of the forest. I didn't know why I did this at first. But soon I realized that I wanted to see and talk with other dogs. One farm dog I persuaded to leave his home and come and live with me. Together we had a very good time and he enjoyed it no end when I showed him how the independent wild life could be lived and taught him a lot of the hunting lore I had learned from the otters and foxes. And then too, hunting with a partner was of course much easier than hunting alone.

"But after a few weeks we both got sort of mopey. It perplexed us a good deal till finally we talked it over together and came to the conclusion that perhaps we wanted to be among people again. At first we would neither of us accept that idea at all. Still, we had to admit it in the end. Human company could give us something we couldn't get here. We both started remembering what good times we had had with this farmer, or that shepherd, or those children, going for walks, playing games, ratting together and so forth. One evening my friend said to me:

"'You know, Quetch, the trouble is we *can* live alone the same as the wild animals. But I don't believe we want to—not for long, anyway. Our ancestors have lived for so many generations as part of the human household that now we miss the things that mankind's company has provided us with. There was a small boy back on that farm I left—as funny a little tow-haired scrub as ever you laid eyes on. I never thought I'd miss him, never. He used to take me with him when he went to look for mushrooms in the fall—or for birds' nests or water lilies in the springtime. And now—it's funny—I find myself longing to see him again. . . . Would you mind very much, Quetch, if I left you, and went back?'

"Well, what could I answer? When he asked me that question I realized at once that the end of the experiment had come for me as well as for him. Life in the wild alone, after I had shared it with him, would have been quite unbearable for me.

"'All right,' I said. 'Maybe I'm more independently inclined than most dogs. But there is a great deal in what you say. Nevertheless, if I go back to man and his civilization I will only do it on certain conditions. I must be allowed to be my own boss. I will *not* be chained up and made to keep a whole lot of rules.'

"'In that case, why don't you go and try to get into the Doctor's club?' said he.

HUGH LOFTING

"Why don't you try to get into the Doctor's club?"

"'Doctor? Club?' I asked. 'I don't follow you. What doctor? What club?'

"'Well,' said my friend, 'I don't just know where he lives, but almost any dog you meet seems to have heard of him. Dolittle is his name—lives somewhere down in the West Country, as far as I can make out. Must be a very remarkable person, from all reports. Has a club for dogs that is run by the dogs themselves. Certain rules of course, but only those that the members realize are necessary and lay down. Why don't you try and find him?'

"So that was how I first heard of Doctor Dolittle and his Home for Crossbred Dogs. Right away I realized it was the kind of place I had been looking for all my life up to this—where dogs were allowed to be themselves, and yet where they could enjoy human company, on a proper footing, as well.

"When my friend set out I went with him. I had no regrets over leaving my woodland home, in spite of its being such a wonderful spot. At his farm we parted and I went on. As yet of course the neighborhood was very wild and lonely; and there were not many dogs to ask directions from. But soon I came to villages and towns. All the dogs I questioned seemed to have heard of John Dolittle, all right, but none of them could give me very definite instructions as to how to reach his home. Some said he might be abroad because he traveled a great deal. I avoided the larger towns as I was still afraid of the dogcatchers. Most of the information given me spoke of the Doctor as living in the West Country; and I kept traveling in that direction all the time.

"In my wanderings I eventually came to a town that was neither very large nor very small. In the market square I saw a Punch-and-Judy show going on. This form of entertainment had always amused me and I stopped to watch it. Presently another dog came up to me from behind and called me by name. Turning, I was delighted to find my old friend Toby. He had been watching the performance with a professional interest.

"We got chatting and I asked him if he had ever heard of this John Dolittle. You can imagine how glad I was to learn that not only was Toby living with the great man himself but that this town which I had come to was none other than Puddleby-on-the-Marsh, where the Doctor had his home. Toby volunteered to take me round there to see if he could get me into the celebrated club.

"And so there came an end to my wanderings. I had been a

HUGH LOFTING

"I saw a Punch-and-Judy show going on."

tramp dog, a performing dog, a gypsy dog, a monk dog, a professional sheepherder and a hermit wild dog. Not a very exciting career perhaps, but at least it had plenty of variety in it. I can assure you I was very glad to settle down in these pleasant surroundings"— Quetch waved an expressive paw toward the wide dining room and the gymnasium that lay beyond the double doors—"which are certainly my idea of a comfortable independent life. I hope the club continues to flourish for many years and I thank you for the attention with which you have listened to my story."

The Topknot Terriers

P ROFESSOR QUETCH WAS GIVEN QUITE AS much applause as any storyteller who had gone before him. When it had subsided ,Jip, as president of the club, got up to thank him formally on behalf of the audience.

This over, Jip went on to say that since no story had yet been slated to follow Quetch's, he would like to know if any members had suggestions to make about filling out the remainder of the evening's entertainment.

Then one dog got up (he was a cross between a St. Bernard and a mastiff) and said that he thought a story about the Doctor would be a good idea. These stories that they had heard were very good of their kind, but he felt that the members would like to hear one about John Dolittle himself.

Jip agreed that this was a good idea. Then he started to count off the dogs, besides himself, who had lived a considerable time with the Doctor. There was Swizzle the clown dog; Toby the Punch-and-Judy dog; Kling the detective dog; Blackie the

retriever, and Grab the bulldog. Each of these in turn was asked
if he could think of any incident in his life with the Doctor that
would make a good story.

But none of them seemed to be able to remember on the spur
of the moment anything that could be considered complete enough.
Then the Sea Dog (who had already told us a thrilling yarn out of
his own adventures at sea) got up and said:

"I think that Jip himself, who has after all known John Dolittle
longer than any of us, ought to tell us a story about the Doctor."

At this there were many "Hear, hears!" from the members.
And Jip felt that he had to get up and make some reply.

"All right," said he, "in that case I think I'll tell you the
story of how John Dolittle invented the Topknot Terrier. You
know then of course that the Doctor has never cared very much
whether a dog was what is known as a purebred. Whether a dog
had a nice personality, or was intelligent, was far more important
to him. Well, some years ago there was a certain rich and high-
born lady, known as the Dowager Countess of Battlebridge,
who realized that the Doctor was a great man. This was curious;
because people as a class usually think him something of a crank.
That, as many of you know, has always had the effect of making him keep very much to himself and the animal world. But
the Dowager Countess of Battlebridge was an exception—an
exceptional woman all round, in fact. She was extremely interested in, and fond of, animals and she had a great admiration for
the Doctor's knowledge of animal medicine. She did not, any
more than the rest of the world, believe that he could talk animal languages. But she saw that he certainly had a great gift for
communicating ideas to them and getting them to understand

what he wanted. She had a whole lot of dogs of her own and was a great authority on breeds, attending all the shows, where she was very often one of the judges.

"Whenever any of her animals were sick, she always got the Doctor to attend to them, maintaining that he was the only veterinary surgeon in the country worthy of the title. Among her dogs she had one very jolly little poodle called Juanita—frightfully purebred, prizewinner and all that.

"One day Juanita was missing. The dowager countess was in despair. She put advertisements in all the papers, hired detectives to hunt for the dog, and everything. All to no purpose. Juanita the

HUGH LOFTING

"The dowager countess was in despair."

prize poodle had disappeared as completely as though the earth had opened and swallowed her up.

"One evening when the Doctor and I were in the study, we heard a tapping at the window. I knew that tap. I had heard it before. It was Cheapside the cockney sparrow knocking on the glass with his bill.

"'Well, Doctor,' says he as soon as he was let in, 'where do you think Juanita the prize poodle is hiding? In your stable.'

"'In my stable!' cried the Doctor. 'What a place to choose when she had the most luxurious home in the country to live in!'

"'Yes, but listen, Doctor,' says Cheapside, coming closer

"It was Cheapside knocking on the glass with his bill."

and lowering his voice. 'That isn't all. She's got puppies—five of 'em, the strangest little things you ever saw. They've got topknots on their heads like Fiji Islanders. Look like a cross between a weasel and a pincushion. I reckon she's ashamed of 'em, is Juanita—being they're so odd-looking—and that's why she has kept in hiding.'

"'Oh well,' said the Doctor, 'let's go down and take a look at them right away.'

"Thereupon we all proceeded to the stable with a lantern. And under an old manger, among some straw and autumn leaves, we found Juanita and her family. I am bound to say that Cheapside's description had not been in the least exaggerated. They *were* strange. At first I could scarcely believe they were dogs at all. It was only by the smell of them that I was sure.

"'My goodness, Juanita,' said the Doctor, 'why didn't you let me know you were here all this time?'

"'Well,' said she, 'for one thing I didn't want to put you in an embarrassing position with regard to the countess. And for another I—er—I—er—'

"She looked at the unusual puppies and paused. She seemed dreadfully awkward and ill at ease.

"'They're hardly purebred, you see, Doctor,' she said at last. 'I didn't know what my mistress would say or do about them. Frankly, I was scared. The countess, as you know, only has dogs of the highest pedigree in her kennels.'

"'Well,' said the Doctor, '*I* think they are a very jolly-looking lot. These topknots are quite unique—and very smart in my opinion. Are they intelligent?'

"'Oh yes, indeed,' said Juanita brightening up and showing

no end of motherly pride. 'They're the cleverest lot of puppies I ever had.'

"That, as you can imagine, got the Doctor more interested than anything she could have said. And finally he became tremendously keen on these unique puppies—so keen that he took them across from the stable to his house, where they made themselves a great nuisance to Dab-Dab the housekeeper. They ran all over the place and you stumbled on them everywhere you went.

"Nevertheless, there was no denying that they were, as the Doctor had said, distinctly unusual. 'Clever' wasn't the word for them: they were positively uncanny. I have never seen anything like it. Usually it takes a dog years to learn anything about human speech and what it means—if indeed he ever does. But these little beggars seemed to catch on to all that was happening or being said in any language right away. Dab-Dab continued to storm and insisted that they be put back in the stable; but the Doctor said:

"'No, Dab-Dab. These pups are an extraordinary case of animal intelligence. They must stay. I want to study them. Why, they have real brains, Dab-Dab—*real brains!*'

"'They're mongrels,' she snapped. 'Homely mongrels at that.'"

"'I don't care,' said the Doctor. 'They represent a distinct advance in animal intelligence.'

"Juanita, who had up to this been scared and ashamed about how they would be received, now began to put on no end of airs as the mother of the most intelligent puppies on record. The Doctor gave them all sorts of tests to demonstrate how clever they were. I do believe that he had hopes of someday getting them to take up mathematics and science—if not to run for Parliament. He was quite excited and worked up over it.

HUGH LOFTING

"Why, they have real brains, Dab-Dab!"

"Not a great while after Juanita's presence in the stable had been announced by Cheapside, the Doctor felt that he ought to notify the Dowager Countess of Battlebridge; for she was still very disturbed over her prize poodle's disappearance. The good lady was overjoyed at the news and immediately asked that Juanita be restored to her home. But the poor puppies, since they were not purebred, she was not in the least interested in. Then the Doctor took two whole hours trying to explain to her that she was wrong.

"'Don't you see,' said he, 'how much more important it is that Juanita has brought an unusually intelligent kind of a dog into the world than that her children should carry on some set type of breed?'

"Well, the Doctor, after talking very enthusiastically for quite a while about the brilliant intellects of these puppies got the countess herself interested too. She asked to see them. And the Doctor took her over to the house at once to show them to her.

"And it didn't take those pups long to win the countess's heart. But after she had raved over them a while she seemed a bit ashamed of herself.

"'Oh, but just *look* at them, Doctor,' she cried, 'with these delightfully absurd, woolly mops on their heads! They're darlings; but they're mongrels. I'd be ashamed to have them in the house.'

"'Yes, I know. But after all,' said the Doctor, 'breed in dogs is a very artificial thing. Hardly any of the breeds that are popular today are pure native dogs. The bull terrier, the Pomeranian, the black-and-tan: they have all been produced by crossbreeding in the first instance. The only true original breeds are the Alaskan sleigh dog, the dingo of Australia, and one or two more. Now what I was going to suggest is this: you are a famous authority on dogs with society and the Kennel Club. It is within your power to popularize this new breed that Juanita has given to the world and make it the vogue of the day. Why, only last month Sir Barnaby Scrogley produced a new breed, which he called the Bob-Tailed Bolivian Beagle. It has since become quite fashionable. His breed hasn't the wits of a cockroach—I know, because I've talked with them. Whereas these puppies of Juanita's surpass anything in dog intelligence I ever met.'

"This set the countess thinking. As a matter of fact, she was quite jealous of Lady Scrogley, Sir Barnaby's wife, who was another well-known woman authority on dogs and frequently acted as judge at the Kennel Club shows. The idea of producing a new breed that could outshine, as the fad of the moment, the Scrogleys' Bolivian beagles appealed to the dowager countess immensely.

"'Humph!' she said at last. 'And what, Doctor, would you call this breed? It doesn't look like anything that has ever been registered so far on the Kennel Club's books.'

"'We'd call it *The Topknot Terrier*,' said John Dolittle. 'A smart name for a very smart dog. I'm sure they would be popular.'

"'Humph!' said the countess again. 'Perhaps you're right. They certainly are awfully attractive mites. . . . Well—er—you must give me a little time to think it over.'

"The next day the countess called on the Doctor and told him

HUGH LOFTING

"We'd call it the Topknot Terrier."

that she had decided to follow his suggestion. The puppies were all brushed and combed and their topknots were trimmed (by a French barber) into a very smart shape. They were then taken over to the countess's mansion and adopted into the household with all due ceremony and honor.

"The result of this was exactly as the Doctor had predicted. They became the rage in a week. The dowager countess took one or two with her everywhere she went. And since she was such a very important figure in sporting society these unusual dogs were remarked upon, talked about, and written up in the papers. Everyone wanted to know what the breed was. He was told: *The*

"Their topknots were trimmed into a very smart shape."

Topknot Terrier. It was repeated everywhere. But the countess went the Doctor one better. Seeing that the Scrogleys had produced a race of beagles from Bolivia, she wove a wonderful story about the *Topknots* coming from some remote island in the South Seas. And they finally became known as the *Fijian Topknots*. And if you claimed to be in the fashion, *not* to have a Fijian Topknot just put you outside the pale instantly. The countess was besieged with letters inquiring about the breed—Where could they be obtained? What were they fed on? etc., etc.

"She was delighted—because not only did her new breed entirely outshine the Scrogleys' Bolivian beagles, but it earned its popularity by real brains and natural charm. The Fijian Topknots were known to be able to do anything short of bookkeeping and astronomy. Also, for the present anyhow, they were nearly priceless—because there were only five of them and all the fashionable ladies in the land were falling over one another to buy them.

"The shah of Persia, who happened to be visiting London just then, simply insisted that he wouldn't be happy unless he could take one back to Teheran with him. The dowager countess refused outright, saying she didn't know what sort of treatment they would receive in Persia. But a special request arrived from the prime minister that this whim of the foreign monarch should be gratified. And one of Juanita's children sailed away in the shah's suite. We learned afterward that the pup was treated very well—but got dreadfully fat eating too many sweetmeats in the shah's harem.

"The Doctor was very pleased, for, in its way, this was a great triumph.

"'That just shows you, Jip,' said he to me one evening, as he was reading his newspaper in front of the fire, 'how utterly absurd is this idea of purebredness in dogs being so much more desirable than crossbreeding. Here we have made a regular mongrel into the last word of up-to-dateness. And all because we called in the aid of a few *society* people. The whole thing is just a question of fashion, Jip. Just fashion—nothing more.'"

THE TWELFTH CHAPTER

Dogs' Jobs

A FEW NIGHTS AFTER JIP HAD ENDED HIS
story about the Topknot Terriers, the Doctor happened to be present again at one of the after-dinner
storytelling sessions at the Home for Crossbred
Dogs. And, as usual, he was asked to tell a tale himself.

He rose and said he was sorry he could not think of any at the
moment, but he had been greatly interested in what Quetch had
said about the business of sheepherding.

"This," he went on, "is an example of something that dogs can
do better than anyone else. Now there are other things that dogs
can do—I mean in a professional way. Their experiences, even if
they did not form very long stories, would be, I think, well worth
hearing—and instructive. Will all those dogs present who have ever
worked professionally please stand up?"

At that, to our considerable surprise, a good dozen or more
dogs rose among the audience and waved a paw or something to
attract attention. There were some who had been watchdogs; one

had worked in an Inuit sleigh-team; another had done duty as a lifeguard at a children's swimming beach; one, a St. Bernard, said he had been employed at the famous monastery in the Alps and rescued lost travelers from mountain snowstorms; another got up and told us he had led a blind man through city streets and helped him earn a living; a funny old veteran of a bloodhound said he had been employed as a tracker by a prison to hunt down prisoners who ran away; two others said they had worked in Holland pulling vegetable barrows around like horses; another had been a collector for charity, going through the city with a tin box on his back into which people put pennies for the cause of the Prevention of Cruelty

HUGH LOFTING

"These I took down."

to Animals; several sporting dogs had spent years at the various jobs dogs do in retrieving, tracking, and pointing with the guns. And there were many more.

"Well, now you see," said the Doctor, "we have here a great many members who have worked for their living. If some of them would tell us of their experiences and a little about the job which they were employed in, I'm sure it would be most interesting."

This was eventually done. Each dog gave us a short talk on the profession he had followed, sometimes about the job itself and sometimes part of his experiences while employed in it. These I took down and made into a separate chapter called "Dogs' Jobs" in my book entitled, *Tales of the Home for Crossbred Dogs.*

PART TWO

The First Chapter

Insect Languages

HERE WERE TO HAVE BEEN TWO VOLUMES TO that book, *Tales of the Home for Crossbred Dogs*. But it was around this time—when I was finishing the first of them—that I was asked by the Doctor to assist him in another department. This kept me writing so busily that everything else was laid aside for the time being.

It was the study of insect languages. For years and years the Doctor had been patiently working on it. He had, as I have told you, butterfly-breeding houses where the caterpillars of moths and butterflies were hatched out and liberated in a special enclosed garden, about the size of a room, full of flowers and everything needed for butterfly happiness.

Then hornets, wasps, bees, and ants—we had other special apparatus and homes for them, too. Everything was designed with one foremost idea in view: to keep the insects happy and in normal conditions while they were being studied.

And the water-born creatures, like the dragonflies, the stone

"The moths and butterflies were liberated in an enclosed garden."

flies, etc.—for them he had hundreds of small aquarium tanks with plants and grasses growing in them. Beetles, the same way. In fact, there was practically no branch or department of insect life that the Doctor had not at one time or another studied with a view to establishing language contact with it. He had built many delicate machines, which he called "Listening Apparatus."

About this time, too, Morse's experiments in electricity and telegraphy were attracting a good deal of public attention. And John Dolittle had been very hopeful that these sciences would aid him in some way. Bumpo and I had built him a shed especially for this, and he had entirely filled it with electrical batteries and things that he felt confident would eventually solve some of his problems in connection with insect languages.

But in spite of a tremendous amount of patient labor, trial and experiment, he had admitted to me only a week or so ago that he felt he had accomplished nothing. So you can imagine my surprise when, just as I was finishing the last chapter to the first volume for the mongrels' club, he came rushing into the dogs' dining room, grabbed me by the arm, and breathlessly asked me to come with him. Together we ran across to the insect houses. There, over the various listening apparatus, he attempted to explain to me how he had at last achieved results—results which, he was confidently sure, would lead to his dream being realized.

It was all highly scientific and frightfully complicated; and I am afraid that I did not understand a great deal of it. It seemed mostly about "vibrations per second," "sound waves" and the like. As usual with him on such occasions, everything else was laid aside and forgotten in his enthusiasm.

"Stubbins," said he, "I shall need your help for the secretarial work and the note-keeping—there's a tremendous lot of recording to be done. I am overwhelmed by my results. It all came at once—so suddenly. In one swoop I established what I believe are the beginnings of language-contact with five different kinds of insects: a wasp, a caterpillar—or rather a maggot—a housefly, a moth, and a water beetle. If I am right in my surmises, this is the greatest moment in my whole career. Let us go to work."

And then for many days—and most of the nights too—we labored. Goodness, how we worked! Dab-Dab was in despair. We were late for all meals—for some of them we didn't turn up at all. A large part of the time I was asleep, or half asleep, because the

Doctor not only worked regularly far into the night, but he was up early in the mornings as well. It reminded me of the time when he had met his first success in shellfish languages on the ship going to Spidermonkey Island.

He brought insects into the house in pails, in biscuit tins, in teacups, in everything. You never saw such a mess. His bedroom, the kitchen, the parlor, the study—everywhere you went you found pots of maggots, glasses full of wasps, bowls full of water beetles. Not content with that, he kept going out and getting more. We would walk miles and miles across country, armed with collecting-boxes, in search of some specially large beetle or some new kind of wasp,

HUGH LOFTING

"Gub-Gub was continually getting stung by the wasps."

which he felt sure would be better for experimenting purposes than any he had used so far.

Poor Gub-Gub was continually getting stung by the wasps—indeed the house seemed full of them. As for Dab-Dab, her indignation every time a new lot of maggots was brought in was quite indescribable. She threw several lots out of the window when the Doctor wasn't looking; but she was always brought to account for it. Because John Dolittle, no matter how many messy little cans he had placed around the house, knew immediately if a single one was missing.

Foreign Insects

OR MY PART, I CANNOT TRUTHFULLY SAY THAT I ever got into real, personal, conversational contact with the insect world. But that John Dolittle did there can be no doubt whatever. This I have proof of from things that happened. You cannot make a wasp stand up on its front legs and wave its other four feet in the air unless you know enough wasp language to make him do so. And that—and a great deal more—I have seen the Doctor accomplish.

Of course it was never quite the free and easy exchange of ideas that his talking with the larger animals had come to be. But then insects' ideas are different; and consequently their languages for conveying those ideas are different. With all but the very largest insects, the "listening," as it was called, was done with these quite complicated and very delicate instruments.

All drafts and vibrations had to be carefully shut off. Later on, Bumpo and I made a second building specially for this, with a floor so solid that no footfall or shock, no matter how heavy, could jar the apparatus. It was also equipped with a very fine system for heating the atmosphere to exactly the right temperature. For the Doctor had found that most insects are inclined to go to sleep immediately when the temperature falls below what is for them the normal climate of their active season. As a general rule, the hotter it was the more lively they were and the more they talked. But of course the air could not be allowed to get much warmer than full summer heat.

We called it *listening* for convenience. As a matter of fact, it more often consisted of recording vibrations, the pitch of a buzz, the velocity of the wing stroke, and other slight noises and motions that insects make. With some of the very largest ones it was possible to hear the sounds given out with the naked ear. The clearest results that John Dolittle obtained were with imported insects, such as locusts and cicadas of different kinds. How he procured these foreign specimens was rather interesting. He asked several birds to make special trips abroad for him and to bring back the grubs and eggs of grasshoppers, crickets, etc. For this of course he employed insect-eating birds who would know where to look for the specimens and could recognize them when they found them. Then in his incubating boxes at home he hatched out the eggs and grubs into the full-grown insects.

Most of the information that the Doctor gathered from this new study of insect languages was concerned with the natural history of the various species and genera. With this I filled over sixty thick notebooks for him. But we learned from certain cases, with which he was able to get into closer touch, many interesting personal stories of insect life and society. These, I think, might be more entertaining to the general reader than the purely scientific material

"He asked several birds to make special trips abroad for him."

that we gathered and stored away during the seven or eight months we spent on this work. We found that several kinds of butterflies had considerable imagination; and some of the yarns we were told I strongly suspect were made up out of whole cloth for our amusement. Others sounded as though they had the ring of truth to them. However I will shortly narrate one or two and then you can judge for yourselves.

All of the Dolittle household, with the exception of the harassed Dab-Dab, were greatly interested in this new departure of the Doctor's. And as soon as I had gotten a new section written into my notebooks, we were at once besieged by

Chee-Chee or Polynesia or Too-Too or Gub-Gub to read it out loud. And that is how most of the following anecdotes came to be told round the kitchen fire in the manner of the good old days when the Doctor had amused his family every night with a fireside yarn.

Tangerine

ONE OF OUR MOST INTERESTING INSECTS WAS a wasp. The Doctor had of course experimented with a considerable number of wasps. But with this one he had achieved better results than with any. The tiny creature seemed highly intelligent, was much given to talking, so long as the room was kept warm; and, after he had gotten used to John Dolittle, would follow him around the house like a pet cat wherever he went. He allowed the Doctor to handle him without apparently ever dreaming of stinging him and seemed happiest when he was allowed to sit on the Doctor's collar about an inch from his left ear. Gub-Gub it was who christened him with a name of his own—*Tangerine*. This was because when the Doctor had been making inquiries of the wasp as to what foods he liked best, he had said a certain yellow jam was his favorite. We tried apricot, peach, quince, Victoria plum. But we finally discovered that what he had meant was a marmalade made from tangerine oranges.

He was then presented with his own private jar of marmalade—

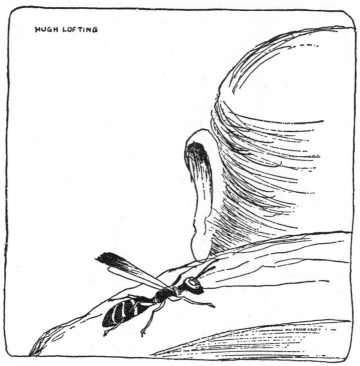

"He seemed happiest when allowed to sit on the Doctor's collar."

with which he seemed greatly delighted. But we saw almost right away that we would have to limit his allowance. He would eat such enormous quantities at one sitting. Then he'd fall asleep and wake up in the morning complaining of a dreadful headache. One evening he ate so much that he fell right into the pot and lay there on his back fast asleep, blissfully drowning in his favorite marmalade. We had to fish him out and give him a warm bath, because of course his wings and everything were all stuck together with the jam. In this the white mouse assisted us, as no one else's hands were small enough to wash a wasp's legs and face without doing damage.

This passion for marmalade was Tangerine's only vice—

"No one else's hands were small enough to wash a wasp's legs."

otherwise he seemed to have a very nice disposition, not one that could be called waspish in the least. Gub-Gub, having been stung by wasps before, was dreadfully scared of him. But for the rest of us he had no terrors, beyond a constant anxiety that we might sit on him—since he crawled over all the chairs and sofas and beds in the house as though he owned them.

Among the anecdotes and stories of the insect world that Tangerine related to us, that of "*How I Won the Battle of Bunkerloo*" was one of the favorites. And this is how he told it:

"The battlefield of Bunkerloo was situated in a pleasant valley between rolling hills covered with vineyards and olive groves. Many battles had been fought in this historic spot. Because, for one thing, it formed a naturally good place for battles; and, for another, it was at an important point where the territories of three countries touched upon one another. In the fields and the boles of the olive trees round about there were several wasps' nests—as there naturally would be in a district of that size. They had always been there—though of course not the same wasps. Yet the traditions and folklore had been handed down from one generation to another. And the thing that we feared and hated most was battles. Dear me, how sick we were of war! For, mark you, even in my mother's lifetime there had been two battles fought out on that same ground.

"Yes, indeed, war to us was like a red rag to a bull. It seemed such a stupid waste. From either end of our beautiful valley armies would come with cannons and horses and everything. For hours they would shoot off evil-smelling gunpowder, blowing some of the trees right out of the ground by the roots and destroying simply no end of wasps' nests—some of them quite new ones, which we had spent days and weeks in building. Then, after they had fought for hours, they would go away again, leaving hundreds of dead men and horses on the ground, which smelled terribly after a few days—even worse than the gunpowder.

"And it never seemed to settle anything. Because in a year or two they'd be back again for another battle and ruin the landscape some more.

"Well, I had never seen any of these battles myself, being a young wasp. Nevertheless, I had heard a whole lot about them from older relatives. But one evening, just as we were putting the finishing touches to a brand-new nest, one of my uncles came in and said:

"'Listen: you can all save yourselves the trouble of any further work on that job. There's going to be another battle.'

"'How do you know?' I asked.

"'Because,' says he, 'I've seen them getting ready, up there at the mouth of the valley, digging in the big cannons on the hillside just the way they did last time. And that same general is there who was in charge last time too, General Blohardi, as they call him. His battles are always more messy than anybody else's.'

"Well, when I heard this I was fired with a great ardor to do something. Our nest, which we had just finished, should be defended, I felt. The next day I went out to look over the situation. I flew down to the south end of the valley, and there, sure enough, were men in red coats bringing in enormous cannons and making no end of a mess. Behind them as far as the eye could

HUGH LOFTING

"'How do you know?' I asked."

reach were tents and tethered horses and ammunition wagons and all the other paraphernalia of war.

"I went down to the other end of the valley and there was another army doing the same thing. When they were ready, the two armies would come forward into the middle of the valley and fight out their silly battle.

"On the following day, early in the morning, we were awakened by a great blowing of bugles and beating of drums. Still hopeful that I might do something on behalf of my fellow wasps—though I had no idea what it could be—I left the nest and started out again to reconnoiter.

"About the center of the valley, up on the hills to one side, there was an especially high knoll. On this I saw the figures of horses and men. I flew over nearer to investigate.

"I found a group of very grandly dressed persons gathered about a man on horseback who seemed to be a highly important individual. He kept looking through fieldglasses this way and that, up and down the valley. Messengers were arriving and departing all the time, bringing him news from every quarter.

"I decided that this must be the famous General Blohardi himself. Now about these names I am not very certain. They were names that we wasps gave and they may not be the right names at all. We called him General Blohardi because he was always blowing so hard through his long red mustache, which puffed out before him when he spoke like the whiskers on a walrus. The two armies were the Smithereenians and the Bombasteronians—but those also may not be the regular names. General Blohardi was the field marshal of the Bombasteronian army.

"It was clear that the general had come up to this high point so he could get a good view of the fight—also no doubt because he wanted to stay in a safe place himself. Evidently, from the way in which he kept blowing out his mustaches, he expected a very fine battle—one of his messiest. Before he was done with our beautiful valley it would be just a howling wilderness full of broken trees, dead and wounded men, and maimed horses.

"I felt so furious as I watched him there, snapping out his pompous orders, I was ready to do anything. Yet what could I do? I was such a tiny creature. A mere wasp!

"Presently a bugle blew far down the valley. It was followed almost immediately by the roar of cannon. All the horses moved

"His long red mustache puffed out like the whiskers on a walrus."

restlessly, and the general and his officers leaned forward in their saddles to see the show.

"The battle had begun!

"Now the whole object of the Battle of Bunkerloo was to gain what is called possession of this valley. What either army would do with the valley after they got it I don't imagine either of them knew. But that was what the battle was for: to win the valley. To us it didn't matter at all which side won it, because they would both make a nasty mess in getting it. What we wasps wanted was to stop the battle.

"As I noticed the horses move restlessly at the first roar of the cannon, an idea came to me. It would be no use my going and stinging General Blohardi on the nose—though I would dearly have loved to do so. But if I stung his horse, I might possibly accomplish something. The animal was a lovely steed: cream-colored, groomed to perfection, high-spirited, and as nervous as a witch.

"Well—no sooner thought than done. I hopped onto the horse behind the general and stung the poor fellow in the flank. It was a dirty trick to play on the horse and I wanted to apologize to him afterward, but he was much too far away.

"The results were instantaneous and astounding. The horse gave one bound and shot off down the hill with me and the general, as fast as he could go. By this time the armies were on their way toward the center of the valley. I had to cling for all I was worth not to be blown off by the rushing wind. I crawled along his flank and stung him in another place. Then he went faster still.

"When we reached the level in the bottom of the valley where the cavalry were already charging, I feared he might turn and join the other horses. So I stung him a third time. At this he put on such speed that I was blown off and had to fly behind—where I had great

"The horse gave one bound."

difficulty keeping up with him. On and on and on he went, straight across the flat and up the other slope.

"Now, as I have said, Blohardi was the commander-in-chief of the Bombasteronians. And when the cavalry of that army saw their famous general in full flight leaving the battlefield at goodness knows how many miles an hour, it completely disheartened and demoralized them. They too took to their heels. And that was the end of the battle.

"The general of the Smithereenians got no end of decorations and honors for the victory of Bunkerloo. But," Tangerine ended modestly, "it was, as you see, really I who had won the battle. . . . Now I'd like a little more marmalade, please."

Domestic Insects

I HAVE NEVER SEEN POOR DAB-DAB IN SUCH A state of fuss and annoyance in my life as she was these days.

"It was bad enough," she said to me one evening on the brink of tears, "when the Doctor used to fill the house with lame badgers and rheumatic field mice. But this is a thousand times worse. What's the use of my trying to keep the house clean when he does nothing but ruin and smother it with bugs and insects. The latest is he is making friends with the spiders in the cellar. Their webs, he says, mustn't be brushed away. For years I've been working to get the place free of cockroaches; and last night he was hunting everywhere with a lantern.

"'Surely, Dab-Dab,' says he, 'we have *some* cockroaches?'

"'Surely we have *not*,' says I. 'It took me a long time to get rid of them, but I succeeded at last. Not one roach will you find in my kitchen!'

"'Dear, dear!' he mutters. 'I wanted one to talk to. I wonder if Matthew Mugg would have any in his house!'

"'Surely, Dab-Dab,' said he, 'we have some cockroaches.'"

"And off he goes to get that good-for-nothing Matthew to supply him with cockroaches. Of course once they get back in the house they'll breed and be all over the place again in no time; and all because he wants to talk to them, mind you. And who cares, I'd like to know, what a cockroach might have to say—or a spider, either? That's the worst of the Doctor, he has no—er—sense in some things."

"Well, Dab-Dab," said I consolingly, "this present study may not last very long, you know. There are so many fresh branches of natural history continually claiming his attention, it's quite possible that by next week he will be off on a new departure entirely and you will be able to get your house in order again."

Dab-Dab shook her head sadly.

"I haven't much hope," said she. "There's a whole lot of different bugs he has still to listen to, as he calls it. Why, do you know, Tommy, what I heard him saying the other day?"

The housekeeper dropped her voice and glanced guiltily over her shoulder.

"I heard him asking Jip if he thought *fleas* could talk!"

"And what did Jip say?" I asked. I confess I could not help smiling at the look of horror on her face.

"Well," said she, "happily Jip gave him very little encouragement. 'Fleas?' he growled. 'All they can do is bite. Don't have anything to do with 'em, Doctor. They're a dirty lot!'"

"'Well,' said she, 'happily Jip gave him very little encouragement.'"

At this moment John Dolittle came into the room bearing a small tray of maggots.

"Stubbins," said he, "I want to do some experimental work with these. If you will come with me we will begin with listening machine number seventeen."

"Ugh!" grunted Dab-Dab, glancing into the tray. "What gooey, messy-looking things!"

Without further delay the Doctor and I proceeded to our apparatus sheds and set to work. We had quite good results. It seemed that several of the maggots—particularly one large and lively white one—had somehow got the drift of Dab-Dab's remark and were considerably offended by it.

"She has no right whatever to call us gooey and messy," said the maggot. "Personally, to me ducks and people are much more gooey and messy than nice, clean, athletic maggots. And we would be glad if you would tell her so."

"And you know, Stubbins," said the Doctor after I had written this down into a notebook under the heading of *Experiment No. 179,* "I quite sympathize with their feelings in the matter. This idea of—er—revulsion and dislike on the part of one member of the animal kingdom for another is quite baseless and stupid. Myself, I've never felt that way toward any living thing. I won't say that I'd choose a maggot or a snail to make a warm personal friend of. But certainly I would not regard them as being unclean or less entitled to respect than myself. I will certainly speak to Dab-Dab. Now we want to get some information from these maggots about their geographical distribution. I would like to know roughly over what parts of the world their species is to be found. This big fellow seems quite lively and intelligent. Just raise the temperature another five degrees, will you? And turn on a trifle more humidity. Then we will question him."

The subject of how various insects got scattered over the different countries and continents was one that greatly interested John Dolittle about this time and he was engaged in writing a pamphlet on it.

Well, the maggot told us a very entertaining story of travel and adventure, but he was not very helpful on the question of geographical distribution. He had not on the journey he described observed any of those things that would have been of scientific value to us.

"It's too bad, Stubbins," said the Doctor. "I fear we can't get any further on this experiment for the present. However, I have a water beetle in one of my glass tanks who, I think, can give me a much more definite record of his travels—a record that may help us to show pretty exactly how his species comes to be found on the American side of the Atlantic and on this side also. If you will come to the study with me we will see what we can do."

The Water Beetle

THIS NEXT EXPERIMENT THAT WE MADE IN insect language was entirely different from any we had conducted so far and turned out to be one of the most successful. It was much more like our research work in shellfish speech than anything else. By perfecting and extending the apparatus we had used for aquatic and marine creatures, we managed to establish very good contact with the water beetle. His conversation was quite plain, and John Dolittle seemed to have very little difficulty in following what he was trying to say. This surprised me somewhat because he never seemed to stay still an instant, but was forever flying and shooting around this glass jar in which the Doctor kept him; now swimming freely in the clear water; now burrowing into the mud at the bottom; now perching on a water plant and polishing his nose with his front feet.

After the Doctor had conveyed to him what it was he wanted to know, he told us the following story:

"It is about our traveling you want to know, huh! Well, of

HUGH LOFTING

"He was forever shooting around this glass jar."

course being able to swim and walk and fly, we do a good deal of touring. But this, I fancy, is not what *you* would call traveling. It is all short-distance work, though much of it is very interesting. We water beetles are very fortunate, I suppose, since there are hardly any animals that care to fight with us. The big pickerel and pike are about our only dangerous enemies; they have to be quite hungry before they will consider us good eating. I have occasionally had to leave the water and take to my wings when being chased by these ferocious fish, and have even had to leave one pond or stream altogether when they had become too numerous, and seek other water homes. But those times were happily rare. The first occasion that I took a really big journey was on the foot of a duck."

At this point the Doctor stopped the proceedings, fearing that he might not have heard this right.

"A journey on the foot of a duck?" he asked. "I don't quite understand. Would you mind explaining that?"

"Certainly," said the water beetle. "It is quite simple. You see, when we are not out swimming freely in the water in search of food, we usually work our way down into the mud below, to the depth of, say, half an inch to two inches. This often enables us to hide away from the fish of prey who cannot dig for us. We are really very safe. Few water beetles ever fall victim to their enemies in their own element.

"But I and a friend of mine were once carried off from our native pond and transported an enormous distance—well, as I told you, on the foot of a duck. Our pond was away out in a lonely, marshy stretch of country where few people ever came. Those who did, came in the fall and winter to shoot ducks. Of ducks there we had plenty, also every other kind of wild fowl—snipe, geese, plovers, redshanks, curlews, herons and whatnot. Even of these we water beetles were not afraid. We only had to burrow into the mud an inch or two and we were usually safe. But we didn't like the ducks. They used to come in from the sea and descend upon our pond in thousands at nighttime. And such a quacking and a stirring up of the water they made! They'd gobble up the weeds like gluttons and any small fish such as freshwater shrimp or other pond creatures they could lay hold of.

"One night I and a friend of mine were swimming around peacefully and suddenly he said:

"'Look out!—Ducks!—I saw their shadow crossing the moon. Get down into the mud.'

"I took his advice right away. Together we burrowed into the mud without any further argument. The water over us was barely above three inches deep. In hundreds the ducks descended. Even below the surface of the mud we could hear their commotion and clatter. How they paddled and stirred around!

"Then suddenly—*Bang! Bang!*

"Some sportsmen nearby who had lain in wait for them had opened fire. We had heard this happen before; and we were always glad because the sportsmen drove the ducks away and left our pond in peace.

"For part of what happened next I have to rely on another water beetle who chanced to return to our pond just at the moment when the sportsmen opened fire. Because of course, I and my friend, being below the mud, could neither see nor hear anything.

"Ducks were dropping in all directions, splashing into the water—some wounded, some killed outright. It was a terrible slaughter. Some of them who had been cruising in the water near where we were rose instantly on the first shot and were killed a few feet above the surface of the pond. But one, it seems, was sort of late in getting up and that very likely saved his life; for while the sportsmen were reloading their guns, he got away. The water, as I have told you, was very shallow just there and he was actually standing on the muddy bottom, wading. As he gave a jump to take off, his broad webbed feet sank into the mud an inch or two. And he took to the air with a big cake of mud on each foot. I and my friend were in those cakes of mud.

"Now, this species of duck, which was not an ordinary or

HUGH LOFTING

"He took to the air with a cake of mud on each foot."

common one, was apparently about to make its migration flight that night. The flight was in fact already in progress, and the flock had stopped at our pond to feed on its way. With this alarm the remainder of the ducks at once headed out to sea.

"As for me, I had no idea for some moments of what had happened. And I could not communicate with my friend because he was on one of the duck's feet and I was on the other. But with the rushing of the wind and the quick drying of the mud, I soon realized that something very unusual was taking place. Before the mud dried entirely hard I burrowed my way to the surface of the cake and took a peep outside.

"I saw then that I was thousands of feet up in the air. And from the shimmer of starlight on wide water far, far below, I gathered that I was being carried over the sea. I confess I was scared. For a moment I had a notion to scramble out and take to my own wings. But the duck's enormous speed warned me that we were probably already many miles from land. Even supposing that I could tell which direction to go back in—I knew of course nothing of this big-scale navigation such as birds use in their long nights—I was afraid of the powerful winds that were rushing by us. In strength, my own wings were not made for doing battle with such conditions.

"No, it was clear that whether I liked it or no, I had to stay where I was for the present. It was certainly a strange accident to happen to anyone, to be picked out of his native haunts and carried across the sea to foreign lands on the feet of a duck!

"My great fear now was that the mud might drop off in mid-night and go splashing down into the sea with me inside it. As a precaution against this I kept near to the hole I had made to look out through, so that I would be able to take to my own wings if necessary. Through this I nearly froze to death. The rushing of the cold air was terrific. My goodness, what a speed that duck kept up! I drew back into the inner shelter of the mud cake. I knew that so long as I could hear that droning, deafening whirl of the duck's wings that I was still attached to my flying steed.

"Pretty soon the mud got so hard that any further drilling through it was out of the question. But as I had already made myself a little chamber runway by turning round and round in it before it hardened completely, I was quite comfortable so far as that was concerned. I remember as I peeped out of my little window—nearly freezing my nose—I saw the dawn come up over the sea. It was a wonderful sight; at that great height the sun's rays reached us long before they touched the sea. The ocean stretched, gloomy, black and limitless, beneath us while the many-colored eastern sky glowed and reflected on the myriads of ducks who were flying along beside mine, necks outstretched, glowing golden and pink—all headed toward their new homeland.

"I was glad to see the day arrive for more reasons than one. It made the air warmer. And I could now see if any land were to come in sight.

"I was still very anxious about getting dropped into the sea. Once we got over land of any kind I would feel happier. The ducks started honking to one another as they saw the dawn. It almost seemed as though they were exchanging signals as conversation of some kind, because I suddenly saw that they somewhat changed direction following a leader, a single duck, who flew at the head of the V-shaped flock."

THE SIXTH CHAPTER

The End of
the Journey

T HE CHANGE OF DIRECTION CAUSED ME TO
wonder why the leader of the flock had made it. I crept
to the edge of my hole in the mud-cake and craned my
neck out as far as I dared so as to get a view ahead.

"And there a little to the left of where the sun was rising lay a
low line of something sitting on the sea. The morning rays made it
glow like molten silver at one end; and at the other, where the light
had not yet reached, it was dark and black.

"Land! The flock was heading for it. Would they rest there, or
just take their bearings and pass on? My bird, at all events, didn't
seem in need of a rest. After a whole night's going he seemed as
fresh as a fiddle and was whacking away with those great wings of
his as though he had only just started.

"It didn't take the leader long to make up his mind. He came
sailing over the low-lying islands with his gallant band. He circled
a couple of times while the others hung back, quacking. Then he

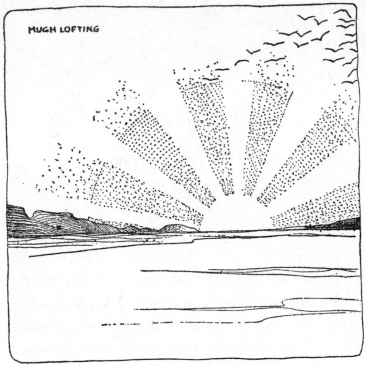

*"To the left of where the sun was rising lay a low line
of something sitting on the sea."*

shot off again, headed once more for the open sea where no land
bounded the horizon.

"'Goodness!' I thought. 'How long is this life going to last?'

"But now the sea was all lit up and bright with the risen sun.
It seemed to put new heart into the fliers, for their quacking and
honking broke out louder than ever as they swung off in the new
direction after their leader. I began to wonder how many other
small creatures like myself had thus shared the flight of migrating
birds. It was certainly an extraordinary experience. Also I wondered
how my friend was getting on in the mud on my duck's other foot.

"I had a notion to crawl forth and go and see. But the moment I found my nose out of the hole in my mud-cake I realized that that would be madness. The rush of the air past the duck's stomach was enough to blow your eyes out, and besides, if the bird should feel me creeping up one leg and down the other it was quite likely he would scratch his feet together to knock me off. I decided I had better not try to get into communication with my friend till we were on solid ground. Indeed it was lucky that the duck kept his feet tucked well back against his feathers. It was that, I am sure, that kept the mud from falling off and sending me to a watery grave in the wide sea below.

"Well, at last we came to the land the ducks were making for. We sighted it on the evening of that second day. Great rocky headlands jutted out into the ocean, some high, some low. The chief of the flock led his followers over it and then swung to the left. I imagine it was southward. It looked as though he now meant to follow the shoreline down till he came to the exact region he was seeking.

"Anyway, I felt more at ease. If I got dropped now—the ducks still maintained a considerable height—I could crawl out of the mud-cake before it struck the earth and on my own wings land safely in some sort of territory where I'd stand a chance of surviving.

"Not only did the ducks keep up at a great height, but they also kept up their perfectly incredible speed. And very soon I noticed that the climate was changing considerably. It got warmer and warmer. I became quite lively. And now I could look out of the hole in the mud-cake and watch the changing landscape below without any fear of getting frostbitten. And my gracious, how that landscape did change! One moment we were over flat marshy fen-land that stretched away as though it would never end; and the next it was mountains, range upon range, with here and there a glimpse of the sea, where great crested capes stretched out into the surf; and you could see the waves breaking against the feet of high cliffs.

"The greenery also changed—now sparse, nothing but scrub shrubbery that barely covered the big expanse of smooth rock. Then came park lands where I could spy deer grazing and still larger creatures. And finally we flew over dense, deep jungles where the trees were so thick and close-packed you felt you would alight on a velvet carpet if you just sailed down and landed.

"At length some signal seemed to be sent back from the leader up ahead. Because all the flock stopped and started circling and eddying away in the wildest manner. We had arrived over a wide, wide bay on the shoreline. The coast seemed low; and behind it were many ponds and lagoons. I could tell from the dizzy singing in my ears that my duck was descending—like the rest—in widening circles to the flat marshlands they had come so far to seek."

The Colony of Exiles

YOU CAN IMAGINE HOW GLAD I WAS TO reach real solid ground again. The duck's plump body came to rest in the marshy ground without noise or fuss. It seemed almost as though he had merely flown from one pond to another, instead of crossing those leagues of wild ocean and thousands of miles of land. He just shook himself, grunted, and began to look about for something to eat.

"Of course, as soon as he moved, the cakes of dry English earth that had clung to his feet all the way came off in the wet mud of this foreign land. And poor little me with them. Oh, such a relief! At once I crept out of the hole and swam forth into the cool, oozy mud of the lagoon. I was hungry myself. I too bustled around to raise some food.

"But for me the territory was new. The ducks had been there before. It was their winter home. They knew all the grasses, all the shellfish, all the water life fit to eat. But I! I suddenly found myself swimming about in a tropical lagoon full of large, strange enemies and small new creatures that might be food or might be poison.

"I swam for hours before I dared act. I was taking no chances after coming through that long journey of danger and adventure. At last I met an insect that looked familiar. I maneuvered about him for a while. The water was kind of muddy, stirred up from the paddling and wading of the ducks. Then I recognized him. It was my friend who had made the journey on the other foot of the same duck. We almost fell on each other's necks.

"Tell me,' I said, 'where can I find something to eat. These waters contain nothing but strange sights for me.'

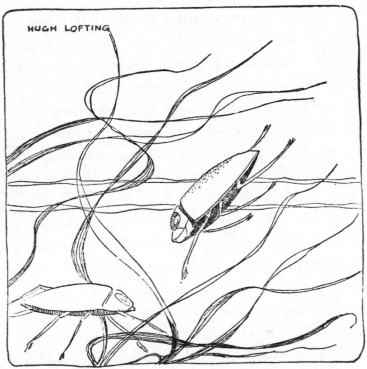

"I maneuvered about him for a while."

"He laughed.

"'Why,' said he, 'I've just had the grandest meal of my life—fish eggs in plenty. Come with me. I'll show you.'

"'But what about those dangerous-looking fellows?' I said. 'It seems to me we're surrounded by nothing but enemies.'

"He glanced back at me and chuckled over his shoulder as he led the way.

"'Don't forget that we are just as strange to these fellows here as they are to us,' said he. 'They don't know what to make of us—as yet anyway. They're just as scared of us as you are of them.'

"Now pond life is, as you probably know, a very strenuous business. All kinds of creatures—fish, beetles, worms, salamanders—every species has its enemies. And if you want to live to a ripe old age you've got to look out. And so as I followed my friend, and everything from great pike to ferocious-looking turtles, came up and glowered at us through murky waters, you may be sure I felt far from comfortable.

"But in a little I realized that many of the larger species who in our own waters would not have hesitated to attack us, here were by no means so bold and seemed almost, as my friend had said, to be scared of us.

"After we had had something to eat, we crept out of the lagoon onto the muddy bank to take a look around. The ducks were still feeding. All kinds of other water fowl, too, many of which I had never seen before. Some of them were quite curious and beautiful: long-legged fellows like great cranes with scarlet bills and wings; flat-headed smaller kinds like snipe, built for speed with tiny beaks and mincing gait; geese and wild swans of various sorts; and great big-mouthed pelicans that dived for fish

"Came up and glowered at us through murky waters"

with a mighty splash and gobbled up their prey by the bushel.

"It seemed a regular paradise for birds; no sign of human habitation in sight. On one side, lagoon after lagoon led outward to the sea; on the other, flat marshland lay between us and the mountains.

"'This,' I said to my friend, 'seems like a very nice place we have come to.'

"'Yes,' he replied. 'I don't think we have done so badly. I wonder if any more of our kind ever came to these parts.'

"'You never can tell,' said I. 'Let's look around and find out.'

"So off we swam together down the lagoon to see if we could

find any others of our own kin who had been exiled on these foreign shores.

"After about an hour's search—the lagoon was several miles long and had many lesser lagoons running off it in every direction—we came upon one or two solitary specimens of our own kind. They were very glad to see us and at once asked for news of the homeland. We told them what we could. But the information they could give us was much more important. They had been here some time and had already got acclimatized. Familiar as they were with the dangers and the advantages of the waters, they told us what parts to avoid and where the best feeding was to be found. The temperature of the water was of course, generally speaking, very much higher than that of our native haunts. But they had discovered that by seeking certain very shallow places at night, when the wind regularly blew down from the mountains, cooler territory could always be found. While by day special spots where rocky creeks ran into the lagoon afforded some relief from the tropical heat.

"Well, with these few fellow beetles whom we discovered here (it seems they had probably been imported the same way that we had), we formed a regular little colony. That is, it was little to begin with. But very soon we had large families of young ones growing up, and after a few months we felt that we formed quite an important species in the pond life of that region. That, I think, is about all I have to tell you of how I went abroad."

"Oh, but listen," said the Doctor, "you haven't told us yet how you got back here."

"That is quite simple," said the beetle. "I came back by the same means as I went out: on the feet of some waterfowl. Only on the return journey I am not so sure what kind of bird it was that carried me. As soon as I realized I had been returned to England it did not take me long to find my way back to my own particular pond. My case was of course peculiar. I know now that quite a few small water creatures get carried abroad—sometimes in egg form only—in that same way. But it is exceptionally rare, I fancy, for one individual to get back to the waters that he started from. I was given quite a wonderful reception. The beetles in my native pond turned out to do me honor. And I felt like a great traveler who had done something wonderful."

HUGH LOFTING

"The beetles in my native pond turned out to do me honor."

THE EIGHTH CHAPTER

A Lifetime of
Twenty-Four Hours

T THE CONCLUSION OF THE WATER BEETLE'S
story the Doctor, as he had done with the other insects,
put many questions to him by which he hoped to get
some practical natural history out of his strange tale.

"Could you describe to me," he asked, "the appearance of that
duck that carried you abroad on his feet?"

Thereupon the beetle told us what he remembered of this species of wild fowl that regularly visited his native pond—a splash of
pink on the cheeks; gray wing feathers, etc.

When he was done the Doctor muttered to me:

"It wasn't a duck at all, Stubbins, I fancy. Sounds to me much
more like one of the rarer geese. I had suspected that the feet of a
duck could hardly accommodate a cake of mud big enough to carry
him without discomfort. I think I know the bird he means. Only
visits certain parts of England in the early fall. Now we'll see what
we can find out about the geography of the trip."

John Dolittle then asked him certain things about the winds on the voyage, the appearance of the islands the birds flew over, and of the coastline down which they traveled before they reached their final destination.

The beetle's answer to these questions seemed to please the Doctor a great deal. For before they were ended he suddenly grabbed me by the arm and said:

"It's Northern Brazil, Stubbins. I'm sure of it. This is quite valuable information. I had often wondered how that species got out onto the American side. Everything points to it: the bird that carried him, the islands, the coastline—everything. This will complete a very important chapter in my pamphlet. My gracious, if I could only train some of those insects to note the things I wanted to know! The whole trouble is of course that they only observe those things that are of value to themselves. But maybe—er—perhaps later on—"

He paused, silent.

"Why, Doctor," I laughed, "are you going to make naturalists out of beetles now?"

"If I only could," he replied quite seriously. "For mark you, Stubbins, there are many things in natural history that *only* a beetle gets the chance to observe."

After he had thanked the water beetle for his kind services, we carried him down to the old fishpond at the bottom of the garden and let him go.

Our next experiments in insect language were extremely interesting. They were concerned with a family of flies that, John Dolittle told me, were called the *Ephemera*. These creatures lived their whole life circle within the space of one day.

"I am very anxious, Stubbins," said he as we were beginning, "to learn what it feels like to be born, live a whole life and pass away, all in twenty-four hours. A dog lives from ten to twenty years; men from sixty to ninety; the mountains last many thousands before they crumble away. But these little fellows are content to pack all the joys and experiences of life into twenty-four hours. Some of their philosophy, their observations, should, I think, be very valuable to us."

And so with a pale, gossamer-like, green fly on the platform of our most delicate listening machine, we set to work. The poor little creature was already middle-aged, because he had been born early that morning and it was now two o'clock in the afternoon. He seemed very frail; and one could easily understand that so unrobust a constitution wasn't made to last very long.

We worked on him for half an hour and our results were very meager. He had things to say, we felt sure. But it was a language new to us. Clearly anyone who has to pack his whole life into one day must talk very fast. We soon got the impression that he was really pouring out hundreds of words a second. Only we weren't catching them quick enough.

"Look here, Stubbins," said the Doctor, "we are being entirely heartless. We can't let this poor fellow spend more than half an hour talking to us. Why, half an hour out of his life is a forty-eighth part of the whole. That would be nearly eighteen months for us. What must he think of us? Imagine anyone talking to you for a year and a half without stopping! Let him go at once. We must do this on a different system. We will catch several singly and only keep them in the apparatus for five minutes at a time, If we are swift enough with our note-taking, we shall perhaps be able to gather a little from what each one says and piece it all together afterward and make something of it."

And so by catching a number of ephemera and listening to each for a very short period, we went on with our experiment.

This wasn't easy. Because not only did the kind-hearted Doctor refuse to keep his captives in the listening apparatus for more than five minutes, but he would not on any account restrict their liberty, before or after the listening experiments, for a single moment. Consequently we were obliged to go out after each specimen singly, catch it, and bring it back to our work sheds with all possible speed. Fortunately, at that particularly season of the year, spring, we were able to get those flies in abundance—for a week or so, anyhow.

The results of our labors after ten or twelve days were really quite good—in the circumstances. By very exhaustive and continuous work we learned to follow the extraordinary language of this species with fair ease. It was the most tiring task I think I ever did as the Doctor's secretary. The speed of the flies' statements was positively staggering. We had to invent a sort of extra-rapid shorthand of our own, in which a single sign sometimes stood for a whole sentence. After each specimen was released, we went over the notes together and put them into such form as would be later understandable, while what had been said was still fresh in our memories.

This chapter in the book that John Dolittle later completed on insect language was perhaps the most interesting in the whole work. For not only had this species a tremendously swift and condensed way of speaking, but its powers of observation were correspondingly quick. In any life that lasts only twenty-four hours your impressions of this world must of course be taken in at great speed. More than that, these impressions proved to be very original— quite different from those of any class of insects that we had so far studied. I think it is safe to say that the ephemera wasted less time in forming their opinions and making their decisions than any other class of animal life.

"You know, Stubbins," said the Doctor, "it is really too bad that these creatures have not a hand in many of the affairs that we humans think we are so good at. Imagine a cabinet minister or the postmaster general making all the decisions of his whole career within twenty-four hours! I know lots of cabinet ministers and heads of government departments that ought to be made to try it. One thing must be said for the poor little frail ephemera: they certainly know how to make up their minds—and act—quickly."

THE NINTH CHAPTER

Dab-Dab's Views on Insect Life

AFORTNIGHT LATER WE WERE ALL GATHERED round the kitchen fire after supper. I had been working pretty hard at my secretarial duties and the Doctor had insisted that I take an evening off. But he of course, who never seemed to take, or need, a rest, was busy outside in his sheds, on some new phase of his studies in insect language.

"I wonder," said Chee-Chee, looking dreamily into the fire, "how much longer he is going to occupy himself with these miserable bugs. Seems to me a sort of a dull study. It should be getting near the time for him to take a voyage, don't you think so, Tommy?"

"Well," I said, "let us see: How long is it since he went on one?"

"Five months, one week, and three days," said Chee-Chee.

"We got back on the twenty-third of October—in the afternoon," Polynesia put in.

"Dear me! How precise you are!" said I. "I suppose you two old globetrotters are hankering to be off again. Homesick for Africa?"

"Well, not necessarily Africa," said Chee-Chee. "But I admit I would like to see him get started on something more exciting than listening to cockroaches."

"The next voyage he goes on," said Gub-Gub, "he must take me with him. I haven't been abroad since he visited the Land of the Monkeys, and the Kingdom of the Jolliginki. It's my turn to go. Besides I need it in my education. There must be a chapter in my *Encyclopedia of Food*, on African Cooking."

"Humph!" grunted Dab-Dab, who was clearing away the dishes from the table behind us. "I don't know where the funds are coming from if he does go on another voyage. There is precious little left in the money box."

"Thirteen pounds, nine shillings, and twopence-halfpenny," put in Too-Too the accountant, "and the baker's bill for last month not paid yet."

"If you think you are going to get the Doctor to drop bug language for a long while yet, you are sadly mistaken," said Dab-Dab. "What do you think he was talking of last night?"

"I've no idea, Dab-Dab," said I.

"Well," continued the housekeeper in a weary voice, "he mentioned—just mentioned in passing, you know—that he thought it would be a good thing if he did something for— for"—she seemed to have great difficulty in bringing herself to pronounce the fatal word—"for *houseflies!*"

"For houseflies!" I cried. "What on earth was he going to do for them?"

"The Lord only knows," groaned Dab-Dab, her voice full of patient weariness. "That's what I said to him: 'Doctor,' I said, 'what in the name of goodness can you do for houseflies, the greatest pest on earth—creatures that do nothing but carry disease and ruin good food?'

"'Well,' says he, 'that's just the point, Dab-Dab. The house-flies have no friends. Perhaps if some naturalist, and a really great naturalist, Dab-Dab—one who could look far, far ahead—were to take up their cause and see what could be done for them, they could be made into friends for the rest of creation instead of enemies. I would like to start a Country House for Houseflies. I think it might lead to some very interesting results.'

"There," Dab-Dab continued, "I flew right off the handle. I admit I don't often lose my temper." She swept some cheese-crumbs savagely off a chair seat with her right wing. "'Doctor,' I said, 'that is the last straw. You've had a home for lost dogs; a rat and mouse club; a squirrels' hotel; a rabbits' apartment house, and heaven only knows how many more crazy notions. But the idea, *the very idea*, of a *Country House for Houseflies*!—well, that to my way of thinking is about the end. Can't you see,' I said, 'that this encouragement of other animal species—without more, er—er—discrimination, I think you call it—will lead to the ruin and destruction of your own kind and mine? Some creatures just can't be made friends of. Encourage the houseflies and man disappears.'

"'Well,' he said, 'I've been talking to them. And I must confess there is a good deal to be said on their side. After all, they have their rights.'

"'Not with me, they haven't,' said I. 'They are a nuisance and a pest and cannot be treated as anything else.' Such a man! What can one do with him?"

"Still," put in Gub-Gub, "it *is* a wonderful idea—a Country House for Houseflies! I suppose they would have a boy-swatter for swatting boys who came in and disturbed them—the same as people have a flyswatter to kill flies. . . . And maybe have papers full of sticky goo near the door, in which people would get tangled up and stuck if they invaded the premises. It's quite an idea. I'd like to see it started."

"You'd like to see it started, would you?" screamed Dab-Dab, rushing at poor Gub-Gub with outstretched neck as though she meant to skewer him against the wainscot. "You haven't the wits of a cockroach yourself. You get started on your way to bed at once—or I'll get out the frying-pan as a pig-swatter."

Gub-Gub retired into a corner.

"Just the same, it's a good idea," he muttered to Too-Too as he settled down where the irate housekeeper couldn't see him.

HUGH LOFTING

"'Just the same, it's a good idea,' he muttered to Too-Too."

I am glad to say that the Doctor did not, as a matter of fact, attempt this wild plan for the encouragement of houseflies. Heaven only knows what would have happened if he had. He mentioned it to me once or twice, however.

"My idea was, Stubbins," he said, "that flies with a house of their own to go to—or several—would not bother to enter people's houses. This eternal war between the species—man against rats, rats against cats; cats against dogs, etc., etc.—there is no end to it—must lead finally to some sort of tyranny. Just now man is on top as the tyrant. He dictates to the animal kingdom. But many of his lesser brothers suffer in that dictation. What I would like to see—and indeed it is my one ambition as a constructive naturalist—would be happy balance. I've never met any species, Stubbins, that did not do some good— general good—along with the harm. Houseflies, for example: I've no idea what good they do, but I'm sure it exists. By making them our friends we ought to be able to get together and improve conditions all round, instead of making war on one another. War gets us nowhere."

"But there were other insect species that you thought of investigating, were there not?" I asked, hoping to side-track him away from the houseflies, which to me sounded like a rather hopeless direction.

"Oh yes, yes—to be sure, to be sure," said he hurriedly. "I've only just started. There are the moths and butterflies. From them I hope to learn a great deal. It is hardly the right season yet for the natural hatching out of butterflies and moths. But I have been working on my artificial incubators. We have a splendid supply of chrysales. I think I can turn out in the next few weeks about any kind of moth and butterfly I want—that is, of those varieties that are naturally found in these parts."

The Giant Moths

THE FOLLOWING EVENING CHEE-CHEE, BEFORE the Doctor returned to his sheds outside the house, broached the subject of a voyage. This, rather to our surprise, had the effect of keeping the Doctor in the fireside circle for several hours later than was his custom.

"Well, Chee-Chee," said he, "I'd like to take a voyage—it's quite a while since I went abroad—but you see, there is so much work yet to be done on insect language here at home. I never believe in leaving anything unfinished—if I can possibly avoid it."

"Yes, but listen, Doctor," said Polynesia. "You will learn a whole lot more about insects and their languages abroad. It never seemed to me that traveling ever interrupted *your* studies. On the contrary, the farther you were from home, and the more difficult the conditions that faced you, the more you got done—so far as I could see."

"Humph!" muttered the Doctor. "That's quite a compliment, Polynesia, I wonder if it's true."

"In any case, Doctor," said I, "it's a long while since you were on a voyage. And you know one does miss a lot if he does not go abroad every so often."

"That's so," said he. "That's true enough. But then the trouble is: Where to go? You know, Stubbins, I'm afraid that in my old age I've got very hard to please in the matter of travel. All the big and important exploration has been done. If there was a job like that which Columbus did, or Magellan, or Vasco da Gama, still left to be accomplished, that would be different."

"What did Vasco da Gama do?" I asked.

"Oh," said Bumpo, "he was the man who sailed around the Cape of Good Hope, and had the cheek to think he'd discovered it."

"Hmm," said John Dolittle, considering this. "But the point is, Stubbins, that most of the big, important exploration is already carried out. Why should I worry about mapping the details of the smaller geography when there is the languages of the insects, with all they may have to tell us, still misunderstood, still a secret to mankind? Why, I heard from some moths whom I questioned this afternoon the most extraordinary things that no one would believe if you told them. This study of insect languages may seem very unimportant to you when mentioned alongside a voyage to foreign shores. But I assure you it isn't. No one who hasn't studied insect language can have any idea what it may contribute to—er—modern thought and philosophy."

"Yes, but, Doctor," I said, "abroad, as Polynesia suggests, you might accomplish still better results in your studies."

"Abroad!" John Dolittle's voice sounded to my surprise almost contemptuous. He walked over to the window and threw back the curtains. The light of the full moon poured into the room.

"Stubbins," he said suddenly in a strange, intense voice, "if I could get to the moon! That would be worthwhile! Columbus discovered a new half of our own planet. All alone he did it, pitting his opinion against the rest of the world. It was a great feat. The days of big discovery, as I said, are gone by. But if I could reach the moon, then I could feel I was truly great—a greater explorer than Columbus. The moon—how beautiful she looks!"

"Lord save us," whispered Polynesia. "What's come over the good man?"

"Humph!" muttered Bumpo. "It seems to me the Doctor is just being foolish, as it were. The moon! How could he get there?"

"It is not such a wild notion, Stubbins," said John Dolittle, leaving the window and appealing to me with outstretched hands. "Someone will do it—someday. It stands to reason. What a step it would be! The naturalist who first reached the moon! Ah! He will be the one to make strides in science—maybe to give all investigation a new start."

"Listen, Doctor," said Polynesia, evidently anxious to call him back to earth and practical matters, "we haven't had a story from you in ever so long. How would it be if you told us one tonight?"

"Story—story?" mumbled the Doctor, in a faraway sort of voice. "My head is too full of problems. Get one of the family to tell one. Tell one yourself, Polynesia, you know plenty—or Chee-Chee, yours are always worth hearing."

"It would be better, Doctor," said Chee-Chee, "if you told us one. It isn't often, lately, that you've been home evenings."

"Not tonight, Chee-Chee, not tonight," said John Dolittle,

going back to the window and looking up again at the moon. "I told you: my head is full of problems—and moths."

"What do you mean, your head is full of moths, Doctor?" asked Dab-Dab in rather an alarmed voice.

"Oh," said the Doctor, laughing, "I just meant the study of moth language—and its problems. I've been at it now for several days and nights and my head is full of it."

"You should take a rest," said Chee-Chee. "A voyage would be a fine change for you—and all of us."

Now the Doctor had put in a good deal of time on the moths already, I knew, without my assistance. I was naturally keen to hear if he had made any special discoveries. I had become so much a part of his research work that I felt almost a bit jealous now if he went off on his own and left me out.

"Had you heard anything of unusual importance, Doctor," I asked, "in your work recently with the moths?"

"Well, yes," he said. "I hatched out one of the hawks last night—a beautiful specimen. I put her—she was a lady moth—in a glass dome with a small light in it on the windowsill. Great numbers of gentlemen hawks came to call on her. How they gathered so suddenly when their species has never been seen within a hundred miles of here goodness only knows. I caught a few and experimented with them in the listening machines. And—er—"

He hesitated a moment with a puzzled look on his face.

"Well," I asked, "what did they tell you?"

"It was most extraordinary," he said at length. "They didn't seem to want to let me know where they came from, nor how they had found their way here. Quite mysterious. So I gave up that line of inquiry and asked for general information about their history and traditions. And they told me the wildest story. Perhaps it has no truth in it whatever. But—er—well, you know most of the members of the hawk family are large—that is, for this part of the world. So I got on to the subject of size, and they told me of a race of moths as big—well, I know it sounds crazy—*as big as a house*. I said at once of course, 'No. It can't be. There's some mistake'—thinking that my scanty knowledge of the language had led me astray. But they insisted. There was a tradition in moth history that somewhere there were moths as big as a house, who could lift a ton weight in the air just as though it were a feather. Extraordinary—mysterious! The moths are a curious race."

Otho the Prehistoric Artist

"OH WELL, COME ALONG NOW, DOCTOR," SAID Chee-Chee, "tell us a story, do."

"Not tonight," John Dolittle repeated. "You tell them one, Chee-Chee."

"All right," said Chee-Chee, "I will. But I am by no means sure this crowd will understand it. I'll tell you one that my grandmother used to tell us—in the jungle—a tale of long, long, long ago."

"Good!" grunted Gub-Gub, coming forward to the table. With the Doctor present he was no longer afraid of Dab-Dab the housekeeper.

"Thousands and thousands and thousands of years ago," Chee-Chee began, "there lived a man. Otho Bludge was his name. He had a whole country to himself, in those far-off days when there weren't so many people in the world. He was an artist, was Otho. He lived to make pictures. Of course there wasn't any paper then and he had to use such materials as he could get. Reindeer horn was what he used mostly. There were plenty of reindeer about. For a pencil he used a stone knife. And with this he would cut his pictures on the flat part of the horn. Sometimes he used rocks, cutting and chiseling into the stone the ideas that occurred to him as worthwhile.

"He had made pictures of deer, fish, butterflies, bison, elephants, and all the creatures that abounded around him. His one great ambition was to make a picture of man. But man was scarce. Otho himself was the only specimen in that district. He looked at himself and tried to make a picture of arms and legs. But it wasn't much good. Then he went down to a pool in the stream and tried to draw his own reflection. But he had to lean away over the water to see his image, and that was hard too.

"'No,' he said, 'I've got to find another creature like myself and make him stand still. Then I'll draw my best picture—a portrait of man.'

"So he set out hunting. And for days and weeks he wandered over the wide country, which he had all to himself, and went outside and beyond it in search of a fellow man. But not one could he find. Many interesting new animals he saw—many of whom fought him and chased him across the landscape. Trees, too, that he had never seen before gave him many fresh ideas for pictures. But man he could not find. As a matter of fact, he had only a very vague idea of ever having seen another human. That was his mother. How she had become separated from him he could not remember—nor how he had managed to survive when left alone.

"So, quite disconsolate and miserable, Otho returned to the place where he usually did his drawings and tried to make his picture of man without anyone to draw from. But it didn't go any better. He could get a leg or an arm or a head to look pretty right, but the whole body didn't seem to fit together at all.

"Trees which he had never seen before gave him ideas."

"Then he said to himself aloud—he often talked to himself because he had no one else to talk to—'Oh, how I wish someone would spring out of the ground and stand on that rock over there so I could finish my portrait!'

"And then, what do you think? You could never guess. While he was looking at the rock there he saw a sort of pink fog gathering on top of it. Otho Bludge brushed the back of his hand across his face thinking that perhaps the glare of the sun was doing strange things with his eyesight. But the pink fog seemed real. Presently it began to clear away like the valley mists before the winds of dawn. And when at last it was gone, he saw kneeling on the rock a beautiful woman, just the way he wanted for the picture, a bow and arrow in her hands. About her right wrist, which was drawn back to hold the arrow on the bowstring, she wore a bracelet of blue stone beads.

"Otho was so delighted with his good luck that he didn't dare speak a word. He took a fresh piece of reindeer horn and set to work at once. He carved and carved and carved. Never had he drawn so well in all his life. He knew he was cutting his master picture. The little girl kept perfectly still like a statue for two whole hours. Otho knew afterward that it was two whole hours because of the shadows that the rocks threw. He used to measure his time by the length of the shadows—having no watch, of course.

"Finally he finished his picture. It was good. He knew it was. He held it out to look at it. But when he glanced back at the rock, he noticed that the pink fog was beginning to return.

"'Good gracious!' said he to himself. 'Can it be that she is going to fade away again?'

"Yes, it seemed like it. The pink fog was growing and she was disappearing. Only a sort of shadow of her now remained. Otho was terribly upset.

"'Listen,' he called out, 'why are you going away? I've got a whole country to myself here—and it's much too big for just one. Why don't you stay and play at housekeeping with me?'

"But she only blushed all over, shook her head, and went on disappearing.

"'At least you can tell me who you are before you go, can't you?' cried poor Otho, tears coming into his eyes.

"By this time she was nearly gone. Very little remained of her except her voice, which said faintly but musically:

"'I am Pippiteepa. I am sorry, but I have to go back into the

Unseen World. I have a very busy life before me. For I am to be the mother of all the Fairies. Farewell!'

"Nothing was now to be seen but just a thin ribbon of the pink fog curling slowly upward. Poor Otho rushed to the rock and clutched it as though by sheer force to keep her in his world where he wanted her so much. But she was gone. And lying on the place where she had stood was the bracelet of blue beads. That was all that was left of her. It must have fallen off while she was doing the disappearance magic. Otho put it on his own wrist and wore it all his life.

"For a long time he was dreadfully miserable, wandering around the rock for hours and hours, hoping she might change her mind and come back. But she never came. It's a kind of sad story, but my grandmother swore it was true. Otho at last got into a fight with one of the big grazing beasts that lived in those times, a sort of cross between a giraffe and a giant lizard.

"This creature came up and wanted to crop the grass that grew around the now sacred rock, and Otho tried to drive him off. He got nasty and put up a fight. This kept Otho so busy that it put Pippiteepa out of his mind for the rest of the day. And after a while he went back to making pictures of animals and trees. He carefully kept the portrait he had made of Pippiteepa, but never again attempted to make a picture of man. He went on hoping, always, that someday she would change her mind and come back."

"The Days Before There Was a Moon"

I DON'T KNOW THAT I HAVE EVER SEEN THE Doctor more interested in anything than he seemed to be in this story of Otho Bludge and Pippiteepa.

"Tell me, Chee-Chee," said he, "you say your grandmother told you this story, eh?"

"Yes," Chee-Chee replied, "it was one of her favorite ones. I must have heard her tell it at least a dozen times."

"Humph!" the Doctor grunted, "very curious—most peculiar. Did she ever say anything which might give you an idea of when—how long ago—this took place?"

"Well," said Chee-Chee, "of course to me it only seemed like a—er—a legend, I think you call it—something that might have never happened but that was believed by almost everyone."

"But the time?" the Doctor repeated. "You have no idea about when this was supposed to have happened—I mean anything else that was spoken of as belonging to the same period, which might give us some clue?"

"No, I don't think so," Chee-Chee answered. "And yet, wait, there was something. I remember she always began the story this way: 'In the days before there was a moon,' though I could never understand why. It didn't seem to me very important."

Doctor Dolittle almost leapt out of his chair.

"Did your grandmother ever speak of the moon further, Chee-Chee—I mean, anything more than just that?"

"Yes," said Chee-Chee, evidently cudgeling his brain to remember things long past. "It seems that in monkey history, which was of course always a mouth to mouth business, there was a belief that the moon was once a part of the earth. And there came a great explosion or something and part of it was shot off into the skies and somehow got stuck there. But how it became round like a ball I could never understand, nor find anyone who could explain it to me. Because they used to say that the piece of the earth that got shot off was the land where the Pacific Ocean now is and that isn't round at all. But of course the whole thing is by no means certain. Myself, I've always had grave doubts about the truth of any part of the story."

The household was quite delighted over Chee-Chee's story, not only with the entertainment of the tale itself, but because the Doctor became so absorbed in the subject of the moon and the legends of monkey history that he kept us all up till long after midnight.

"You know, Stubbins," he said to me, "no matter how wild this story may sound, it is curiously borne out by several things. For instance, I remember that in my conversation with the giant sea snail he told me of a belief that was firmly held by the older forms of sea life that some such shooting off of part of the earth's surface

"I must have heard her tell it at least a dozen times."

made the deep ocean and accounted for the moon. Also my geo-logical observations when we were traveling across the floor of the Atlantic certainly pointed to some such violent cleavage—only Chee-Chee says his grandmother spoke of the Pacific Ocean, not the Atlantic. You know it makes me almost want to go back to Africa and question some of the older monkeys there. I might get other versions and more details of this strange story of Otho Bludge and Pippiteepa."

"Well, Doctor," said I, scenting a chance to get him off on a voyage after all—for I felt he sorely needed one—"why not? Last time when you were in Africa, according to Polynesia anyway, you were so busy with hospital work and getting away from the Jolliginki army that there must have been a great deal of interesting work that had to go undone."

"Oh, but," said he, shaking his head impatiently, "I mustn't be tempted. One would never get anything accomplished by just running off after every attractive idea that pulled one this way or that. I must stick to this insect language game till I feel I have really done something worthwhile with it. I want to follow up the story the moth told me about a giant species. It is funny, these legends in animal history—the monkeys and the moon, the moths and the giants. There is something in that, I feel sure. The moths are a very mysterious race. I don't believe that one tenth part of what they do in the general economy of the animal and vegetable kingdoms is appreciated. And imagine what a moth the size of a house might do!"

"But surely," said I, "if there were such enormous flies flopping about the world somewhere, other people must have seen them. I confess I can hardly believe the story."

"It sounds incredible enough, I know," said he. "But I'm sure that if there were not something in it, the story would not exist among the moths."

Memories
of Long Arrow

F OR ME, ONE OF THE MOST INTERESTING THINGS
in the Doctor's study of insect language was the hatching out of the moths and butterflies from the caterpillar
or chrysalis forms. Throughout the previous autumn and
part of the winter I had assisted him in the collection of caterpillars
and chrysales and we had a fine stock in the hatching houses. The
care of these required considerable knowledge and experience—
of which I had not a great deal, though I was always learning. They
had to be kept at the right temperature and moisture and each
caterpillar had to be fed on a special kind of leaf till he had spun his
web and retired into his chrysalis shell. But the Doctor, who had
studied butterflies ever since he was a boy of nine, had a positively
prodigious knowledge of the subject. He never seemed to make
a mistake and in his hands a moth or butterfly could be made to
hatch out with just as much ease and comfort as it would in the
wild state. In fact, conditions in the Dolittle hatching houses were
rather more fortunate for these insects than those of the open, for

they were protected from their enemies, which very frequently in the wild would devour a butterfly or moth almost as soon as it was born into the world.

With some of the rarer and more beautiful flies it was quite a thrilling thing to watch for their hatching. The Doctor usually gave each specimen at least a day's freedom in the little indoor flower garden, which was prepared for his reception, before experimenting on him with the listening apparatus.

But one of the early discoveries we made was that the language, such as it was, had been apparently known to the insects before they were born into the fly state.

"Each caterpillar had to be fed on a special kind of leaf."

"I imagine, Stubbins," said the Doctor, when we were discussing this curious fact one day, "that one of the reasons for this is that the insects already have some life experience in the caterpillar form. Then the methods of conveying their ideas, which we call a language, cannot be called after all actual talking, in which the tongue has to be trained to make sounds. And for the rest there is no doubt that this form of life inherits a lot more experience and training than we or the larger animals do. Their memories go further back, beyond the short term of their own life, and carry over impressions and ideas that really belong to the herd—to the species."

This knowledge of things that lay outside their own experience in the moths and butterflies interested the Doctor a great deal. The case of the gentlemen visitors who mysteriously found their way to the Doctor's house to call on the lady hawk was not by any means the only example of the astonishing things these creatures could do.

When it came to trying to find out *how* they accomplished these mysterious feats we discovered we were against a hard problem. They themselves did not seem to know how they found their way about as soon as they were born; how they knew the way to the kind of leaves and food they wanted, even.

They seemed to be born also with a quite unexplainable store of legends and history about their own species and a knowledge of the enemies that they must avoid if they wished to survive. All they could tell us when we came to question them on *how* they got this knowledge was that they *knew* it.

"You know, Stubbins," said the Doctor, "that is what is called intuitive knowledge, by the philosophers, knowledge you are born with. With humans it is pretty small. As babies we know enough to cry when we want a bottle and we know enough to suck the bottle when it is given to us. That's about all. It isn't much. But it is something. Chickens, on the other hand, are born with a knowledge of how to walk and peck and how to run to their mothers when she gives the call of alarm if danger is near. That's better than we can do. But these fellows! Their intuitive knowledge is tremendous. Their mothers are nowhere near them when they come into the world. Yet they know how to fly, how to set about the whole business of life right away. But the part that fascinates me is their knowledge of legends and history belonging to their own race. That's something quite new, as far as I know—and also the main thing that makes me so hopeful that we can learn a great deal of real scientific value from them. It is the intuitive knowledge that we humans are so short on—especially the so-called civilized humans."

He paused a moment, thoughtful and silent.

"You see, the native people," he presently went on, "are much better. You remember Long Arrow?"

"Yes, indeed," I said. "Could I—could anyone—forget him?"

"Nearly all," said the Doctor, "of that perfectly wonderful botany work that he did was accomplished by intuitive investigation. The same with his navigation and geography. I used to question him for hours trying to find out how he had done these things. He didn't know. He just began along some line of instinct and followed it till he got results. Long Arrow! My gracious, what a wonder he is! The greatest scientist of them all. And the big wigs up in London, the Royal Society, The Natural History Museum and the rest, they hardly know his name! When I tried to tell them about him they thought I was cracked, a sort of Münchhausen romancing about his voyages—Ah, well!"

This recalling of Long Arrow and our days on Spidermonkey

Island put us both in a serious reminiscent mood. Chee-Chee, who had shared those days and adventures, had come into the study a moment or two before and was listening intently. I saw an expression on his face that told me he had the same thought in mind as I had. I turned back to the Doctor, who had moved over to the window and was once more gazing up at the full moon, which flooded the garden outside with a ghostly light.

"Listen, Doctor," I said, "supposing you sought out Long Arrow again: Isn't it quite possible, with his great knowledge of this intuitive kind of investigation, that he might be able to help you with your study of the moths—the language of insects? He has probably already done a great deal in the same direction himself."

I saw from the quick manner in which the Doctor swung away from the window and faced me that my dodge to get him again interested in the idea of voyages had had effect. But almost at once he frowned as though a second thought had interfered.

"Oh, but, Stubbins," said he, "goodness only knows where Long Arrow may be now. He never stayed many months, as you remember, in any place. It might take years to find him."

"Anyhow," said Chee-Chee, speaking up for the first time, "I don't see why you shouldn't go to Spidermonkey and take up the trail. You hadn't any more idea of his whereabouts last time you set out to seek him. And yet you found him."

Again the Doctor paused. I knew the wanderlust was on him— as it was on me, Chee-Chee, and Polynesia. Yet he evidently felt that in following his impulse he was running away from a serious and important work.

"But, Chee-Chee," he said, "last time I had something to go on. Miranda, the Purple Bird of Paradise, had told me he was somewhere in the neighborhood of Northern Brazil or Spidermonkey Island. While now?—No one on earth could tell us where to begin looking for him."

"Listen, Doctor," I said. "You remember the way we decided last time? You had given up all hope of finding him, when Miranda came and told you he had disappeared."

"Yes, I remember," said John Dolittle.

"So we played Blind Travel, the Atlas game, you remember that?"

"Yes, I do," said the Doctor.

Chee-Chee shuffled along the floor and drew a little nearer.

"Well," said I, "why not play it again? You don't know where he is. Last time we had good luck. Maybe we'll have as good—or better—this time. What do you say?"

For some moments John Dolittle hesitated. He went back to the window, drew aside the curtains, and again gazed up at the moon.

"How beautiful she looks!" he muttered.

"Well?" I repeated. "What do you say? Shall we play Blind Travel?"

This appeal to the boy in him was evidently too strong. The frown disappeared from his face and suddenly he smiled.

"I think it might be quite a good idea, Stubbins. It is supper-time, I fancy. Bring along the atlas and I'll meet you in the kitchen."

Blind Travel Again

CHEE-CHEE WAS OVERJOYED. AS THE DOCTOR left the study to go to the kitchen, I moved toward the bookcase. But the agile monkey was there before me. Scaling up the shelves as though they were a ladder, he had the big volume down off the top in less time than it takes to tell it. Together we carried it to the table and laid it down.

"Oh my, Tommy," he whispered, "we're in luck!"

He began opening the pages. The first—how well I remembered it!—title page: *ATLAS OF THE WORLD. Giving the Latest Discoveries in Africa, the Arctic and Antarctic Continents, etc. Published by Green and Sons, Edinburgh, in the year, etc., etc.* Then came the astronomic page—the signs of the zodiac; phases of the moon; precession of the equinoxes . . .

"The moon!" muttered Chee-Chee. "Poor old Doctor! He seems to have gone almost balmy about the moon. My, but look at all the lands we might visit! Come on, Tommy, let's get to the kitchen and make him begin before he changes his mind."

Grabbing a sharp pencil off the Doctor's desk, I took the heavy volume under my arm and followed Chee-Chee out of the room.

In the kitchen we found all the family seated about the table waiting for us: Bumpo, Gub-Gub, Too-Too, Jip, and the white mouse.

"Ah," said the Doctor, "you have the atlas, Stubbins—and a pencil? Good! Just hold back the dinner a moment, Dab-Dab, will you, while we see where we are to go?"

"Go? Go? What does he mean?" asked Gub-Gub of Chee-Chee in an excited whisper.

"He has consented to play Blind Travel with us," Chee-Chee whispered back.

"What on earth is that?" asked Gub-Gub.

"Oh, you open the atlas with your eyes shut and put a pencil down. And whatever point it hits, that's the place you've got to go. Goodness, I'm all of a flutter! I do hope it's somewhere in Asia. I want to see the East."

Well, if Chee-Chee was in a flutter, as he called it, Gub-Gub was even more agitated over this momentous game we were about to play. He kept running around to a different place at the table, jumping up on someone else's chair, being sat on, upsetting people, overturning furniture and generally getting the whole gathering frazzled and confused.

Not that any of us were what you could call calm. A very great deal depended on this strange game that the Doctor had invented when he was a young man. Then it only affected him. In those days he was a free, unattached bachelor and this odd method of determining his destination meant very little difference so far as preparations were concerned. But now (I did not yet know how many of the household he meant to take with him) its outcome might mean much for several of us.

"Listen," said the Doctor when he had the big book laid in the center of the table. "Last time Stubbins held the pencil. How would it be if Bumpo did it this time? He is a lucky individual, I know."

"All right," said Bumpo. "But I hope I don't send you all to the middle of the Pacific Ocean." (He was turning over the first few pages and had paused at one illustrating the proportions of the globe in land and water.)

"That's all right," said the Doctor. "One of the rules of the game is that if your pencil falls on water, you have a second try. And the same thing applies if you touch a town or a district where you have been before. You keep on trying till you strike land, land that you have never visited. Then you have to go there—have to—somehow."

"Very good," said Bumpo, taking up the pencil and closing the book. "I hope this is one of my lucky nights."

"I hope so too," whispered Gub-Gub, nosing up his snout onto the table between the Doctor's elbow and mine. "I would like a warm country where there is plenty of sugarcane. It's years since I tasted sugarcane. In the Canaries it was, when we were hiding away from those wretched pirates. You remember, Polynesia?"

Gub-Gub Halts
the Game

I T WAS QUITE A PICTURE, THAT GROUP AROUND
the table—and it will never fade from my memory while life
lasts. Bumpo was the only one standing. He held the pencil
in his enormous right fist. His left hand grasped the atlas,
closed, and resting on the back of its binding, ready to let it fall
open at whatever page Fate should decide. The rest of us were
seated round in a circle, tense with excitement, watching him.
Four candles burned on the table in brass sticks. For a moment
you could have heard a pin drop, so perfect was the silence.

"Are you quite ready, Bumpo?" asked the Doctor in a strangely
steady voice. "Remember, you close your eyes, let the book fall
open, and then stab down with the pencil point."

"Yes, Doctor," said Bumpo. "I'm quite ready."

"Splendid!" said the Doctor. "Go ahead."

Bumpo let go his left hand. The heavy book fell open with
a *bang*. His right fist, describing circles in the air with the pencil,
slowly lowered the point. . . . Then—*Crash!*

Gub-Gub in his eagerness to learn where we were to go had rocked the table as he lurched forward, and all four candles toppled over. The room was in darkness.

At once a babel of voices broke out everywhere. Everyone shouted advice at once. But the Doctor's was too emphatic to be drowned.

"Hold it, Bumpo!" he cried. "Don't move your pencil. We will have a light here in a moment. Keep your pencil where it is."

Of course, as is always the way, the matches were *not* handy. Dab-Dab, whacking poor Gub-Gub over the ears with her wing, started out to find them. She was quite a long time about it. But soon we began to see dimly anyhow. For the full moon that flooded the garden outside the windows made it possible to make out the general shape of everything in the room. One of the curtains had not been completely drawn across.

"It's all right, Doctor," said Bumpo. "I'm hanging on to it. Get a match and let's see where we are to go."

The excitement, as you can imagine, was tremendous. The moonlight in the room was enough to see one another by, but not enough to read by.

"I'll bet it's Africa," said Polynesia. "Well, I don't know as I shall mind. It *is* a good country."

"It isn't Africa," said Too-Too. "I know it."

"What is it, then?" we all cried, remembering that Too-Too could see in the dark.

"I shan't tell," said Too-Too. "But you can take my word for it, it's a surprise! Yes, it's certainly a surprise. We shall need all the money we can raise for *this* voyage."

"Oh, do please hurry up with the matches, Dab-Dab!" cried

Gub-Gub. "I shall burst if I don't know soon where we're going. And this moonlight is giving me the jim-jams."

So intent was he on getting a light, he left the table and groped his way out of the door to assist the housekeeper in her search. All he succeeded in doing, however, was to bump into her in the dark as she came in with her wings full of a fresh supply of candles and the much needed matches. Completely bowled over by her collision with the portly Gub-Gub, Dab-Dab dropped the matches, and in the scuffle they were kicked away into some corner where they couldn't be found.

Among us who remained in the kitchen, the general excitement

"Tripped over a mat and fell into a pail"

was not lessened by the sounds of Gub-Gub getting spanked and pecked by the indignant duck. Squeaking he ran for the scullery, where from further noises that followed, he apparently tripped over a mat and fell into a pail.

At last the Doctor himself went to the rescue. He succeeded in reaching the larder without mishap, where he found another box of matches and came back to us with a light shaded in his hands.

As the first beam fell across the open atlas my heart gave a big thump. Bumpo rolled his eyes toward the ceiling in horror. Polynesia gave a loud squawk. While Chee-Chee hissed beneath his breath a long, low hiss of consternation.

The book had fallen open at the astronomic page. Bumpo's pencil had landed on a smaller illustration down in the left-hand corner. And its point still rested in the center of the moon!

PART THREE

THE FIRST CHAPTER

Bumpo's Concerns

THE DOCTOR HIMSELF WAS, I THINK, THE ONLY
one who made no remark at all. Silent and thoughtful,
he stood gazing down at the atlas over which Bumpo's
huge fist still hung, holding the pencil point into the
heart of the moon.

"Shiver my timbers!" growled Polynesia, hitching herself along
the table with her funniest sailor gait. "What a voyage, my lads,
what a voyage! Yes, it's the moon, all right. Well, I suppose he might
have hit the sun. Its picture's there and all the other blessed heavenly
bodies. Could be worse."

"I wonder," said Gub-Gub, who had returned from the scullery and was now also leaning over the page, "what sort of vege-
tables they have in the moon."

"Tee-hee!" tittered the white mouse. "Such a joke I never
heard!"

"I don't see why there shouldn't be rats," said Jip. "The moon
always looks to me as though it was full of holes."

—• 671 •—

"'Shiver my timbers!' growled Polynesia."

"It should be a cheap place to live," said Too-Too. "I don't suppose they use money there at all."

"Yes, but it would cost a pretty penny to get there, don't forget!" muttered Dab-Dab.

Bumpo's feelings about the strange outcome were quite curious. He seemed dreadfully worried. I noticed his big hand was trembling as it still grasped the pencil in place. Yet Bumpo was no coward, that we all knew. It was the unknown, the source of all human fear, that now shook his courage. Gently John Dolittle leaned over and took the pencil from his paralyzed hand.

"I don't like it, Doctor," he said in a weak voice at last.

"I don't like it a bit. Why, only last night you were saying you wanted to go to the moon. And now when we play this game, and with eyes shut, I hit it! Right in the center! The moon itself!"

"Oh, it's just a coincidence, Bumpo," said the Doctor. "It is odd. I admit—most odd. But—er—well, it's a coincidence, that's all."

"All right," said Dab-Dab, finally breaking into the discussion with a more practical voice, "coincidence or not, in the meantime the supper is getting cold. If you'll take that wretched book off the table, Tommy, we will bring in the soup."

"But shouldn't we play it over again, Doctor?" asked Jip. "That's a place no one could get to, the moon. We are entitled to another try, are we not? According to the rules of Blind Travel."

"Maybe," snapped Dab-Dab, "according to the rules of Blind Travel, but not according to the rules of this kitchen—not before supper anyway. The food's been delayed half an hour as it is. Sit down, everyone, and let's begin before it is ruined entirely."

We all took our places at the board, and the meal was begun in rather an odd general silence that was broken only by Gub-Gub's noisy manner of drinking soup.

"Well, anyway, Doctor," said Bumpo after a few moments, "you couldn't get there, could you? To the moon, I mean."

"Oh, I wouldn't go so far as to say that, Bumpo," replied the Doctor. "On the contrary, I'm convinced someone will someday get there. But of course for the present, until science has provided us with new methods of aerial travel, it is pretty much out of the question. As a matter of fact, in a way I'm glad the game turned out in the fashion it did. I was already beginning to regret that I had promised Stubbins and Chee-Chee we would play it. I really should stick to my work here. I am awfully keen to get to the bottom of this story the moths told me about a giant race. The more I think of that, and the further I follow it up, the surer I become that it has a foundation of truth."

"You mean you won't take another try at Blind Travel, Doctor?" said Chee-Chee in a sadly disappointed voice.

"Well," said John Dolittle, "I have fulfilled my promise, haven't I? The pencil struck land, which no one could reach for the present anyhow. If you'll show me some way I can get to the moon, we'll go. In the meantime—well, we have our work to do."

THE SECOND CHAPTER

The Tapping on
the Window

ND SO THERE FOLLOWED ON THE GENERAL
feeling of consternation one of acute disappointment.
The whole household, with the possible exception of
Dab-Dab (and I'm by no means sure she too would
not have welcomed the idea of a voyage at this time) had been
keyed up to the promise of departure for foreign shores. Now with
the prospect of remaining home indefinitely, there was quite a let-
down all round. Promptly remarks began to break forth.

"Well, but, Doctor," said Chee-Chee, "how about Long
Arrow? You agreed that he might be most helpful in this study of
insect language and er—What did you call it?—intuitive investigation. Are you going to give up the idea of consulting him, just
because Bumpo struck the astronomic page in the atlas?"

"Chee-Chee," said the Doctor, "didn't I tell you that I don't
know where he is and that I know of no way of finding out? I agree he
might be most helpful—and perhaps the only scientist in the world who
could aid me. But if I don't know where he is, how can I get at him?"

This argument convinced me and, I must confess, saddened me quite a little. For I had really set my heart on a voyage with John Dolittle, which was an experience, I knew, like nothing else in life. But to my great joy another ally came to the aid of Chee-Chee and myself.

"Doctor," said Polynesia suddenly and severely, "you know you are just trying to fool us. Do you mean to say that with *your* knowledge of the animal world you couldn't find out where that man is—with all the birds and the beasts and the fishes of the seven seas more than anxious to assist you in anything you want? Tut-tut!"

The Doctor for a moment looked almost guilty. And I suddenly realized that he had taken advantage of the outcome of our game of Blind Travel to put off any voyage for the present, deliberately, because he felt he ought to stick to his work at home.

"Oh well, Polynesia," he said finally in some confusion, "you must admit I have fulfilled my promise. We have obeyed the rules of the game. The land we hit on was an impossible destination. I repeat: if you can show me a way to get to the moon, I'll take you there."

The shrewd old parrot, who had given John Dolittle his first lessons in animal language, was not easily fooled. She put her head on one side, dropped the piece of toast she had been chewing, and regarded him with a very knowing expression.

"You haven't answered my question, Doctor," said she. "Do you, or do you not, believe it is impossible for you to find out where Long Arrow is now?"

"Well," said John Dolittle, "you remember what a dickens of a job we had in finding him last time we set out to hunt him?"

"Yes," said Polynesia, "but that was because he had got trapped in the cave by the falling rocks. If he is free now, as he probably is, it would be no great matter—for you."

For a moment the Doctor squirmed in his chair. Polynesia was the best arguer I have ever known.

"But don't you see," he said at last, spreading out his hands in front of him, "I have such a tremendous lot of work here still unfinished. I told you this legend the moths spoke of, about a race of giant flies—moths as big as a house, who could lift a ton weight as though it were an ounce. That is something that must be looked into. Goodness only knows what it might lead to."

"And goodness only knows what your going abroad might lead to either," said Polynesia. "But the truth is, I suppose, you just don't want to go. You're tired of ordinary exploration and voyaging. The moon is the only thing that would satisfy you—like a baby."

A little silence fell on the assembly. Dab-Dab had not yet begun to clear away. Everybody seemed to be thinking hard.

And then there came the most mysterious tapping on the window, an odd, heavy, muffled sort of tapping.

"Boo!" grunted Gub-Gub. "Spookish!" And he crawled under the table.

"I'm not going to pull back the curtains," said Bumpo, "not for a fortune. You go, Tommy."

I was after all the nearest to that window. I guessed it was Cheapside, as usual, asking to come in. But I should have known. No sparrow ever made a noise like that. I swung aside the curtains and gazed out into the moonlit garden. Then I clapped my hand to my mouth to stop the yell of surprise that rose to my lips.

THE THIRD CHAPTER

The Giant Race

I SHALL NEVER FORGET THE FEELING I HAD AS MY eyes made out the strange picture there on the lawn beneath the eerie light of the moon. It wasn't so much that I was frightened but that I was astonished, overwhelmed—so overwhelmed that for some moments after I had stifled my first impulse to yell, I could not speak at all. Presently I looked back at the Doctor and opened my mouth, but no words came.

"What is it, Stubbins?" said he, rising and joining me at the window.

Used as John Dolittle was to strange sights and unusual things, this vision outside the glass for a moment staggered even him. There was a face looking in at us. To begin with, it took one quite a while to realize that it *was* a face. It was so large that you did not take it in or see the connection, at first, between the various features. In fact, the entire window, at least six feet high by three feet wide, only encompassed part of it. But there was no mistaking the eyes—strange and very beautiful eyes. Anyone but those who, like the Doctor and myself, were intimately familiar with the anatomy of insects, would quite possibly have taken them for something else. But to us, in spite of their positively gigantic size, they were unmistakably the eyes of a moth.

Set close together, bulging outward, shimmering like vast iridescent opals in the pale candlelight from the room, they made us feel as though we were gazing through a powerful magnifying glass at an ordinary moth's head.

"Heaven preserve us!" I heard the Doctor mutter at my elbow. "It must be the giant race. Snuff the candles out, Stubbins. Then we'll be able to see the rest of him better."

With trembling hands I did as I was told—then sped back to the window and the fascination of this astonishing apparition. And now, when the candlelight did not interfere with the moon's rays in the garden, it was possible to see more. The moth positively seemed to fill the whole garden.

His shoulders behind the head, which was pressed close against the panes, towered up to a height of at least two stories. The enormous wings were folded close to the thick furry body, giving the appearance of the gable end of a house—and quite as large. The enormous foot that had softly struck the window still rested on the sill. The great creature was quite motionless. And even before the Doctor spoke of it, I got the impression that he was injured in some way.

Of course, the excitement among those in the room was terrific. Everyone, with the exception of Gub-Gub, rushed to the window and a general clatter broke forth that the Doctor at once hushed. Gub-Gub preferred the safety of his retreat beneath the table to any moonlight encounters with the supernatural.

"Come, Stubbins," said the Doctor, "get some lanterns and we will go out. Chee-Chee, bring me my little black bag, will you, please?"

Followed by Jip, Polynesia and Too-Too, the Doctor hurried out into the back garden. You may be sure I was not far behind them with the lanterns—nor was Chee-Chee with the bag.

That whole night was one long procession of surprises. As soon as I got out into the garden I became conscious of something funny happening to my breathing. The air seemed unusual. As I paused, sniffing and half gasping, Chee-Chee overtook me. He too seemed to be affected.

"What is it, Tommy?" he asked. "Feels like sniffing a smelling-bottle—sort of takes your breath away."

I could give him no explanation. But on reaching the Doctor we found that he also was suffering from some inconvenience in breathing.

"Give me one of those lanterns, Stubbins," said he. "If this moth is injured I want to see what I can do to help him."

It was a curious, fantastic sight. The Doctor's figure looked so absurdly small beside the gigantic form of his "patient." Also it was very hard to see at such close quarters and by such a small light where the patient left off and where the garden began. One enormous thing, which I had at first thought to be a tree he had knocked down in landing, turned out to be his middle left leg. It was hairy and the hairs on it were as thick as twigs.

"What do you reckon is the matter with him, Doctor?" I asked.

"I can't tell just yet," said John Dolittle, bending and peering around with his lantern. "His legs seem to be all right and I should judge that his wings are too. Of course I couldn't get up to examine them without a good big ladder. But their position seems natural enough. It would almost appear as though exhaustion were the trouble. From the general collapsed condition of the whole moth he looks to me as though he were just dead beat from a long journey."

"What is this business that keeps catching our throats, Doctor?" asked Chee-Chee.

"The air is surcharged with oxygen," said the Doctor. "Though what the source of it is I haven't yet discovered. Possibly the creature's fur, or maybe his wing powder. It is quite harmless, I think, if a bit heady and exhilarating. Bring along that second lantern, Stubbins, and let's take another look at his head. How on earth he managed to land down on a lawn this size without ripping himself on the trees I have no idea. He must be a very skillful flier in spite of his great size."

With the aid of the two lights, we carefully made our way toward the creature's head, which was almost touching the side of the house. We had to pull bushes and shrubs aside to get up close.

Here we found the peculiar quality of the air on which we had already remarked more pronounced than ever. It was so strong that it occasionally made the head reel with momentary fits of dizziness, but was not otherwise unpleasant. Lying on the ground beneath the moth's nose were several enormous orange-colored flowers. And the Doctor finally detected the oxygen, as he called it, as coming from these. We were both nearly bowled over as we stooped to examine them. The Doctor, asking me to accompany him, withdrew into the house, where from the surgery he produced cloths soaked in some chemical liquid to counteract the effect of the potent perfumed gas from the flowers. With these tied about our noses and mouths we returned to our investigations.

"I don't think it's pure oxygen," said the Doctor as he examined one of the enormous blossoms. "If it were, I don't imagine we could stand it even as well as this. It is a powerful natural scent given out by the flowers, which is heavily charged with oxygen. Did you ever see such gigantic blooms? Five of them. He must have brought them with him. But from where? And why?"

Bending down, the Doctor placed one of the flowers under the moth's nose.

"He couldn't have brought them for nothing," said he. "Let's see what effect their perfume has on him."

"'I don't think it's pure oxygen,' said the Doctor."

THE FOURTH CHAPTER

The Awakening of the Giant

A T FIRST IT APPEARED AS THOUGH THE Doctor's experiment was going to have no result. The huge head of the moth rested on the ground almost as if dead. But knowing how long even our own kinds of moths could stay motionless, we did not yet have any fears on that score.

"It's the position that's curious," muttered the Doctor, still holding the huge bell of the flower over the moth's nose. "The head is thrust forward in quite an unnatural pose. That's what makes me feel he may have actually lost consciousness from exhaustion—oh, but see, wasn't that a tremor in the antennae?"

I looked up at the feathery palmlike wands that reared upward from the head (they reminded you of some fantastic decorations in the turban of a rajah), and yes—there was no doubt of it—the ends were trembling slightly.

"He's coming to, Doctor," I whispered. "Hadn't you better stand farther away in case he struggles to get up? To be stepped on by one of his feet would be no joke."

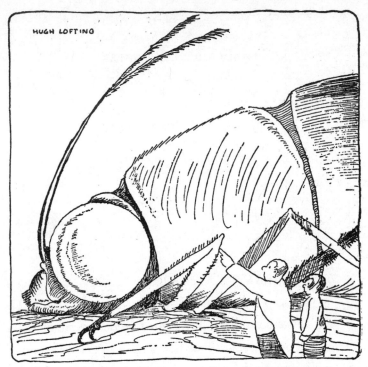

"'Wasn't that a tremor in the antennae?"

The Doctor's utter fearlessness in the presence of this unbeliev-able monster was quite typical. The animal kingdom had no terrors for him. And a moth the size of a large building disturbed him no more, so far as his personal safety was concerned, than a newborn lamb. And that strange trust was always shared by the animals them-selves. I have never seen any creature that was afraid of the Doctor or disposed to fight him. It was this perhaps, above all things, that set him apart among mankind and made him the naturalist he was. Every living thing appeared to have confidence in him from the moment it set eyes on him.

And so it seemed to be with this great insect that looked as though it belonged to some other world than ours. You could not say it opened its eyes—because a moth's eyes, having no lids, are always open. But presently, when by various little signs—like the increased trembling of the antennae, small shiftings of the legs, and a slight raising of the head—it showed us that it was really alive and conscious, it seemed quite unalarmed. I noticed those enormous eyes, now glowing with newer, more conscious, light, turn and take in the figure of the Doctor busying himself with various little jobs for the comfort of his patient. The giant moth made no struggle to get up. On the contrary, he gave a sort of deep sigh, which indicated he was almost pleased on waking to find the Doctor fussing round him. As I looked at them, John Dolittle and his gigantic patient, I began to wonder what would have taken place if this creature had fallen into another garden and into other hands. Fear, on account of his great size, superstition, and ignorance, would most likely have brought about some violent attack upon him, leading to his unnatural death.

But with the Doctor, no. Size, foreign characteristics, and qualities did not incur fear or distrust. On the contrary, anything new attracted him, always, rather than scared him. And by being with him I, in a lesser measure, had grown to share something of this confidence—even if I had not yet learned to impress the same feeling of trust on creatures I met with.

I was sharply reminded of what the Doctor had said about intuitive knowledge as I watched these two. The moth of course could not speak one word of the Doctor's language, nor the Doctor, so far, a syllable of the moth's. And yet, without language, they seemed to be conveying certain things to one another with fair ease. For example, the Doctor evidently wished to climb up and examine the moth's wing muscles, which he expected had been overstrained in the long flight. Somehow, goodness only knows by what means, he conveyed this idea to the patient. Anyway, it suddenly contracted its chest and let its front pair of legs spread apart, so that the summit of its shoulders was lowered a good ten feet. Then very carefully, lest he hurt the moth's skin, the Doctor clambered up in the deep fur that covered the middle trunk (I think he called it the *thorax*) until he stood where the enormous wings were joined to the body.

Up there where no rays from the lamp could reach him he was quite invisible to Chee-Chee and me. But presently he called down to me to open his little black bag and throw him up a bottle of liniment.

Keeping a Secret

O F COURSE ON AN EXCITING OCCASION OF this kind the Doctor, who always seemed to be able to do without sleep if necessary, outstayed all of us in the garden. Polynesia was deeply interested also, but by three o'clock in the morning she retired to the house and took a nap on top of the grandfather clock on the stair-landing. Chee-Chee finally fell asleep under the bushes. I, by pinching myself at five-minute intervals, managed to carry on till dawn showed over the roof-ridge of the house. Too-Too, of course, could always stay awake with more comfort during night hours than in daylight. He and the Doctor were, I think, the last left on deck. He told me the next day that John Dolittle had not gone to bed before six in the morning.

Staggering around the garden with one eye open and the other shut, I had managed to act the part of the Doctor's assistant almost as long as that. When I woke up (about two o'clock the following afternoon) I found myself on the hall settee with the carpet drawn over me for bedclothes. I learned, when I went to the kitchen and found Dab-Dab frying eggs, that John Dolittle had made the giant moth comfortable in the garden and was planning to see him early the following day.

Luckily the night had been mild. I took the cup of tea and piece of toast that Dab-Dab offered me and went out into the garden. Here of course I discovered the Doctor, who after a couple of hours' nap somewhere between six and nine in the morning, was continuing his study of the strange visitor. He had evidently been trying out various foods, because great quantities of different edibles lay about the lawn. What strange instinct had guided the Doctor finally to honey I do not know, for certainly this giant specimen did not look like any of the honey-sucking moths with which we were familiar. But certainly John Dolittle had hit upon a food agreeable to the creature, even if it was not his natural one. When I came up to them, the creature was just starting on a new comb while the frames of six others lay around him on the grass.

The Doctor had managed by this to get the moth to move back somewhat from the house. He now stood, or sat, comfortably on the lawn; and while he occupied most of the turf, we could approach him from all sides and get a much better idea of what he looked like.

In color he was a light brown in the body with very gorgeous wings of red and blue. His legs were green, the rest of him black. In shape he was of the type that keeps the wings closely folded to the body when at rest, though, to be sure, his general lines and appearance were only vaguely suggestive of any species we knew among earthly moths.

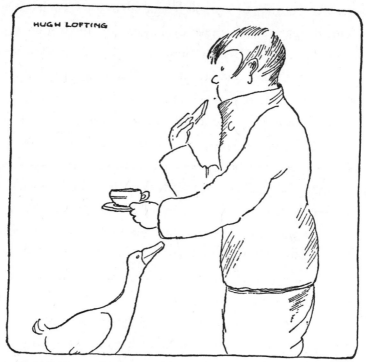

"I took the cup of tea and piece of toast that Dab-Dab offered me."

"I moved him over here," said the Doctor, "so that there should be less chance of anyone seeing him from the front garden."

"But how did you manage to make him understand you wished him to move?" I said. "Can you speak his language already?"

"Oh no—not a word," he said. "But—well—I suppose I really don't know just how I did it. I moved over there and beckoned to him and put the food down. And—well—anyhow, he seemed most well disposed toward me and anxious to cooperate in any way."

I laughed.

"That, Doctor," I said, "is the thing that has made you succeed in animal languages where so many naturalists have failed. I'm not so sure that Long Arrow was much better than you when it comes to doing things by instinct rather than by science. But why are you so afraid the people will see the moth?"

"Why, Stubbins," said he, "if the townsfolk get wind of this extraordinary creature being here, we would be besieged, just besieged, by visitors. He doesn't like strangers. Of that I'm sure—naturally timid, you know, in spite of his size. No, whatever happens, his presence here must be kept secret. And by the way, if Matthew should call—and you know he usually drops in almost every night after supper—don't let him come into the back garden, whatever you do. We will have to bind Bumpo and the animals to secrecy in this. Because while Gub-Gub and Jip can't talk with Matthew, they might easily give the moth's presence away. And the one thing Matthew can't do is to keep a secret."

And so that afternoon we called the household together and swore them all to absolute secrecy. More than that, the Doctor was so afraid that someone might discover the moth's presence and spread the news abroad, he instituted a system of sentries. Bumpo, Jip, and I took it in turns to stand guard at the front gate to make sure that no one strayed in by accident. We did duty in three-hour shifts, night and day. To make extra sure, Too-Too and Polynesia, who were both good hands at keeping awake, watched alternately from the ridge of the roof where they could see anyone approach from any direction.

And it was a good thing that we did take those precautions. I had never realized before how many people ordinarily came to our quiet establishment in the course of a day. Tradesmen's boys delivering groceries; animal patients calling at the surgery; people dropping in to ask the way; the man from the

HUGH LOFTING

"Too-Too and Polynesia watched from the ridge of the roof."

water company to look at the meter; peddlers who wished to sell things, and so forth.

But with our system of sentries, no one ever got a glimpse of the giant moth nor a suspicion that he was hidden in the Doctor's garden.

"Have you any idea, Doctor," I asked one evening, "where this creature has come from?"

"As yet I have not," said he. "I have been trying to find that out, as you can easily imagine, ever since he arrived. I have examined his feet most carefully, hoping that that might give me a clue. But so far it has led to nothing. I even put some particles of dust I found under a microscope. But I am sure, from my examination, that they were picked up after his arrival here in the garden—while landing, no doubt. What I hope to do now is to get into communication with him through some form of vibration record, just as we did with the ordinary moths and flies. But of course it isn't going to be easy with a creature of this size. We will have to devise a special apparatus to fit the job. I fear it may take a lot of work. But it doesn't matter. I feel I am on the eve of discovering big things. I am quite content to spend a long time on this. It is worth it."

The Butterflies' Paradise

ND THUS WE SETTLED DOWN, WITH OUR sentries to keep the world out, to try and get in touch with this strange creature who had visited us from parts unknown.

To begin with, of course, the Doctor, with his extraordinary knowledge of the moths and butterflies of almost every part of the civilized world, was able to eliminate a great deal of territory as an impossible source for the moth to come from. He had one theory, which he followed for quite a time, and that was that it had come from what is called the Subarctic Regions. Very little was known so far, he told me, about insect life in those parts.

Then he got another idea, very far removed from the first. He had noticed that the giant moth was very cold at night. John Dolittle was quite upset over this. He made all sorts of arrangements about warming the garden. He worried Dab-Dab to death by buying oil stoves by the dozen to set around the garden, and supplemented these with hot-water bottles actually in hundreds.

We had the most terrible time getting them in secretly, because of course the dealers insisted on delivering them by wagon. But we had to be just insistent and bring them up to the house ourselves. They of course wanted to know what on earth we were going to do with so many hot-water bottles. A small town is a difficult place to keep a secret in.

Then the Doctor, following up the idea that the moth might have come from the tropics, started to question Chee-Chee. He asked him if he had ever heard his grandmother speak of giant insects at any time.

Poor Chee-Chee thought very hard for quite a while. He could not seem to remember any occasion on which his grandmother had referred to such creatures. But presently he said:

"Oh, wait now—yes, I remember, there *was* something."

"Good!" said the Doctor. "What was it?"

And all the animals, hoping for another of Chee-Chee's stories of the ancient world, gathered about him to listen with attention.

"Well," said he, "there is no record that I know of, of any such insects belonging to the tropics—I mean especially to those parts—either in past times or nowadays. But I do remember my grandmother saying that in those days before there was a moon, the world had no end of perfectly enormous creatures running about it, and that man had a terribly hard time to survive. This was particularly so at certain times when various species like the dinosaurs and some of the more dangerous animals multiplied in such quantities that they crowded everything else out of certain sections. It wasn't only by chasing man and destroying him that they had made life hard for him. But for instance, when a swarm of these giant lizards descended on a farm where he had been growing corn and raising a few goats, they would eat up the whole crop, roots and all, in a few minutes, or clear off all the natural turf down to the bare ground so that there was nothing left for the goats to feed on."

"Yes, yes," said the Doctor, "but the insects, Chee-Chee. Do you recall your grandmother speaking of any giant moths, beetles, or butterflies?"

"Yes, I was coming to that," said the monkey. "She used to tell us of one time—again in the days before there was a moon—when a certain valley lay for a considerable time undisturbed by most creatures. You see, although there was occasional crowding in some areas, the world at that time had lots and lots of room in it. And, as I

"A swarm of giant lizards descended."

was saying, in this quiet, forgotten valley a giant race of butterflies is said to have flourished. Of course my grandmother never saw them, they were millions of years before her time, and she only handed on the story to us as she had heard it. But she said it was still believed that these butterflies with their wings outspread were a hundred paces across from tip to tip."

"Had your grandmother ever spoken of other giant insects, Chee-Chee," asked the Doctor, "of moths, for example?"

"Oh well," said the monkey, "when I called them butterflies I was merely thinking of the general term in our language for all big flies of that sort. It is quite possible that the insects she spoke of were really moths. In fact I think it is more likely, since they appear to have been exceedingly strong; and moths would be stronger than butterflies, wouldn't they?"

"Er—yes—generally speaking," said the Doctor, "they would. But how do you know they were strong?"

"Well, it seems," said Chee-Chee, "that when man first came into the valley he found it full of extraordinary flowers and vegetation of all kinds. The soil seems to have been very, very rich there. It had been a lake up in the hills many years before, simply filled with fish. Then suddenly, through an earthquake or something, all the water drained away through a crack in the mountains, and the fish of course died in the mud that was left. The smell of the rotting fish at first drove every living thing away. But it also seems to have fertilized the valley in a very extraordinary manner. After a while seeds from the ordinary wildflowers and weeds began blowing in across the mountains. They took root, sprouted, bloomed, and died down. Then *their* seed was blown about and did the same thing. But the new seed was very much better than the old, for the plants from which it came had grown strong in the most fertile ground in the world. And so it went on, each spring bringing forth finer and larger plants until, they say, many little wildflowers that in other parts were no bigger than a button, had become here gigantic blossoms growing on bushes as high as an elm tree.

"And of course where there are flowers, butterflies and moths and bees and beetles will always come. And thus in time this deserted valley, once a dried-up sea of mud, stinking of rotten fish, grew into a butterflies' paradise. It was set deep down in a canyon whose walls were sheer and unscalable. Neither man nor beast came to disturb this flower-filled playground where the butterflies and bees led a happy gorgeous life of sunshine, color, and peace."

Chee-Chee's story of the Butterflies' Paradise—as did most of his yarns of the ancient world—got us all deeply interested. From Gub-Gub to the Doctor, we were all listening intently as the little monkey, squatting tailor-fashion on the corner of the table, retold the legends of prehistoric times that his ancestors had handed down to him.

"Well," he went on, "as it was with the flowers that fed and grew larger on the rich soil of the valley, so it was with the butterflies and bees who fed on the flowers. They became enormous. The honey they got from the blossoms made—"

"Excuse me," the Doctor interrupted. "Honey, did you say?"

"Yes," said Chee-Chee, "that was the food they got from the flowers, of course. So it was believed that it was the honey, peculiarly rich in that district, which made them so big."

"Humph! Yes, yes. Pardon me. Go on," said the Doctor.

"But naturally sooner or later such an extraordinary valley, filled with such extraordinary creatures, would have to be discovered and disturbed by strangers. There was a tradition among the monkey people, my grandmother said, that a party of baboons was the first to enter it. They, however, when they had finally scaled the rocky heights surrounding the canyon and looked down into the valley filled with gaudy-colored flies as big as ships, were so scared that they bolted and never went back there again. But some men who had watched the baboons climbing up made a note of how they reached the top, and followed over the same trail. Among this party there was one very bold spirit who often led the others in attacks upon the large animals. While the others hung back in hesitation, he descended the break-neck precipices, determined to

"A party of baboons were the first to enter it."

investigate those lovely giants. He reached the bottom and there, from the ambush of an enormous leaf big enough to hide a regiment under, he suddenly sprang out onto one of the butterflies as he crawled over the ground in the sun. The big insect, thoroughly frightened, took to his wings at once; and with the wretched man clinging to his shoulders, he soared away over the mountaintops. Neither of them was ever seen again."

THE SEVENTH CHAPTER

The Home of
the Giant Moth

A GENERAL CHATTER OF COMMENT AND criticism broke out around the kitchen table as Chee-Chee brought his story to an end.

"It's a good yarn, Chee-Chee," said Gub-Gub, "quite good. But I don't like it as well as the one about Otho Bludge."

"Why, Gub-Gub?" the Doctor asked.

"Oh well," said the pig, "Otho's story was more romantic. I have a natural preference for romantic stories. I liked that part about the bracelet of stone beads which Pippiteepa left on the rock behind her—which Otho took and wore on his own wrist the rest of his days. That's a very romantic idea. It is dreadfully sad that he never met her anymore. I wish Chee-Chee would tell us that one over again."

"Some other night perhaps," said the Doctor. "It is getting late now and we should be thinking of bed."

The Doctor was almost as interested in the great orange-colored flowers that the moth had brought with him as he was in the moth himself. To begin with, he had almost immediately on discovering them taken the greatest pains to preserve the great blooms. Huge quantities of ice (which was quite an expensive luxury in Puddleby) were procured from the fishmonger to keep the flowers fresh as long as possible. Meantime John Dolittle experimented with one specimen to find out what gases its perfumes contained.

The work apparently proved very interesting for him. He was quite good at analytical chemistry and he told me that the flowers presented problems that he felt had never been encountered by chemists before.

When he was done with this he turned his attention again to the moth himself, but took precautions in the meantime that the remaining flowers should be given the best of care and made to last as long as possible.

In his study of the moth, progress was slow. If it had not been for the fact that the giant insect itself was most kindly disposed toward his investigations and did his best to help the Doctor in every way, I doubt if he would have gotten anywhere. But one day I gathered from the fact that John Dolittle had stayed out on that particular subject for nearly twenty-four hours at a stretch, and had missed his night's sleep altogether, that he was most likely achieving something important.

Well, the outcome of these long sessions of study on the Doctor's part was that one very early morning he rushed into my room, his eyes sparkling with excitement.

"Stubbins," he said, "it's too good to be true. I'm not certain of anything yet, but I think—I *think*, mind you—that I've discovered where this creature comes from."

"Goodness!" I said. "That's news worth a good deal. Where?"

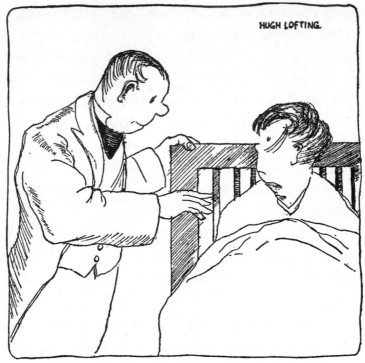

HUGH LOFTING.

"One very early morning he rushed into my room."

"I guessed," he said, "that it couldn't be Europe. The more remote corners of the world, like the subarctic and the tropics, didn't quite—well, they didn't exactly fit in either."

"Anyway, you know now," I said. "Tell me quick, I'm dying to hear."

"I have every reason," he said, looking sort of embarrassed lest I should disbelieve him, "to suppose that *he comes from the moon!*"

"Heaven preserve us!" I gasped. *"The moon?"*

"I have very little doubt," he answered. "I managed to rig up some sort of apparatus—after a good many trials and a good many failures—which should convey his vibrations. If it had not been that he was just as anxious as I to get in contact I could never have done it. He came as a messenger, it seems. You remember Polynesia has told you, I know, of the time when the monkeys in Africa sent word to me by a swallow that they were suffering from an epidemic—that they had heard of me and wanted me to come to the rescue?"

"Yes," I said, "Polynesia has told me many times."

"Well," said he, "this is something of the same kind. It seems unbelievable. And every once in a while I wake up, as it were, and pinch myself for fear I am trying to believe in some extraordinary and delightful dream—something that I have conjured up myself because I wanted it so to be true. And yet I think I have real reason to believe it. If so, this is by far the greatest moment of my career. To be called to Africa by the monkeys on the strength of my reputation, to cure them in the hour of their distress, that was a great compliment. To let loose Long Arrow, the naturalist, from his prison in the cave, that was a moment well worth living for. But to be summoned to another world by creatures that human eyes have never seen before, that, Stubbins, is—"

He waved his hand without further words. His voice sounded strangely chokey. It was not often that I had seen John Dolittle overcome by emotion.

Flowers of Mystery

NYONE CAN VERY READILY IMAGINE INTO what a condition of extraordinary excitement this statement of the Doctor's would be likely to put me. All sorts of visions and possibilities passed before my mind. But so anxious was he that no false alarm should be spread abroad till he was certain of his facts, that he strictly forbade me to whisper a word of the matter to anyone before he gave me permission. He said nothing annoyed him so much as the half-baked announcements of scientists promising all sorts of wonders that never come true. And it must be said for John Dolittle himself that he never published a word that he was not prepared to stand by and prove. But then he very seldom "talked for the newspapers," as it is called, anyway.

Before many days had passed we decided that the flowers the moth had brought with him were almost as complicated a mystery as the great insect himself. The Doctor was, as I have said, in constant anxiety lest they should wither. It was not to be hoped of course that they would last more than a few days. His progress with the moth's "language" continued to be tantalizingly slow; and every morning he would go to the little special greenhouse where he kept the blossoms, expecting to find his treasures had wilted and passed away. But morning after morning they seemed as fresh as ever; and he was greatly puzzled. The ice and spraying and other care we gave them could not account for such extraordinary endurance.

The Doctor was pretty good at botany, as he was in all branches of natural history. He found on careful examination that the flowers had certain bulbous knobs just where the stem joined the bell of the blossom itself. These he told me were something quite different from the anatomy of any flower known to the earth's vegetable kingdom. Of course he had long since supposed that if the moth came from the moon, he brought the flowers also from that world. He was sure that these knobs or glands, as he called them, accounted for the flower being able to endure so long in a state of perfect freshness after it had been plucked from its plant. He wondered if all moon flowers had the same quality.

But what mystified us a great deal more was that the flower apparently had the power actually to *move* itself—not only to change its position from that in which it had been laid down, but also, we finally proved, to shift itself from place to place.

The way the Doctor discovered that peculiar quality of the Moon Bells, as we called the flowers, was this: he was in the habit of bringing one of the blossoms twice a day to the moth to smell. He had discovered that the insect derived great benefit from this daily tonic. He told me he was sure that the moon moth found our earthly atmosphere entirely too sluggish and lacking in oxygen. If we left him for more than about twelve hours without a sniff he got sleepier and sleepier and would finally almost collapse.

At nighttime, after the moth had had his final sniff, the Doctor always took the blooms back to the special ice-cooled conservatory to be stored till the next day. Of the five blooms, he used each one conscientiously in turn—thinking thus to economize the precious perfume. But that, by the way, proved to be unnecessary. For the flowers were as good a tonic at the end of the week as they were when we first discovered them. This treatment, with vast quantities of honey for food (which we actually supplied to the insect in barrow-loads), was practically the only treatment that we gave our strange visitor.

Well, as I said, the Doctor would with the greatest care take the flowers back to the greenhouse and lay them down on a thick bed of asparagus fern. But the following morning, as regular as clockwork, he would find the flowers in different positions.

In the beginning, he had not laid any importance to this. But one evening he had put a bloom down almost touching the door of the conservatory because the others were occupying almost the entire space of the small house with their enormous bulk. When he came in the morning, expecting to find the flower he had used the night before close against the door, he was astonished to see that it and all the blossoms had rolled away toward the far end, and that last night's one had swung right around so that the stem instead of the bell was facing the door.

At first he thought someone must have been in during the night and shifted the flowers. But the same thing occurred the following day. As usual he didn't speak of it to me till he was sure of his facts. We sat up one night and watched with a lantern, and both of us distinctly saw the flower nearest the door roll over and change its position.

At first, for my part, I wasn't satisfied.

"Why, Doctor," I said, "that could have been an accident. The way the flower was laid on the uneven bed of fern could account for its rolling a short distance like that!"

"All right," said he, "we will watch again tomorrow night. I am convinced—and I think I can prove to you—that the flowers do not like the draft from the door. They move away from it of their own accord, by rolling."

So the next night we repeated our watch. And this time I was completely convinced. We put two flowers close against the door. After about an hour one of them deliberately began to roll away toward the other end of the conservatory, A little later the other followed, both crowding in on the remainder of the specimens, huddling like sheep that wished to escape a storm. I could hardly believe my eyes. There was no question of accident here.

On our way back to the house the Doctor said: "You know, Stubbins, I feel we are here presented with an almost entirely new problem. There are flowers in our own vegetable kingdom that catch flies and close up at night and things like that. But one that can move itself after it is cut off from its plant is something quite new. You know, Stubbins—er—of course—" (The Doctor hesitated a moment in one of his moods of half-embarrassment, which had been pretty common of late.) "Er—this whole thing is so new and perplexing—but, well, I've had a notion for some days now that those flowers can communicate with one another."

"You mean that *they can talk!*" I cried.

"Just that," said he. "The way that they arrange themselves when they crowd up together at the far end of the conservatory— and—and I have even thought I could detect some exchange of conversation. But of course, as I said, it is all so new. I may be wrong."

"Goodness!" I said. "That's a new idea, with a vengeance, isn't it?"

"It is," said he. "But in the moon? It may be the oldest idea there is—that flowers can talk. Certainly you and I have evidence already that they can think—and move."

Smoke on
the Moon

THE NIGHT FOLLOWING THAT ON WHICH WE had finally determined that the Moon Bells could move of their own accord, I came into the Doctor's study about nine o'clock. At first I thought there was no one in the room and was about to go out to the kitchen. But presently I heard Polynesia whisper:

"Is that you, Tommy?"

And then I made out Chee-Chee's form also squatting on the floor by the window.

I must confess that by this time I was getting sort of prepared for anything. I had even told my parents that I might leave any day on a voyage for parts unknown. The Doctor had become so . . . so secretive. Try as hard as I might to keep track of what was going on, I still had an uncomfortable feeling that John Dolittle was making discoveries and plans of which he was telling to no one—at least not to me. That feeling had disturbed me a great deal.

"Yes, Polynesia," said I. "This is Tommy. What's going on here?"

"Oh," said she, and I knew at once from the tone of her voice that she was on her guard, "the Doctor is just taking a few observations through his new telescope."

I realized right away that the Doctor was doing nothing of that kind. He *was* looking through his new telescope, it was true—an instrument that had cost him just pots of money to buy. He had even kept its purchase a secret from Dab-Dab, who always scolded him whenever he laid out large sums on scientific instruments. But I saw at once that he wasn't taking observations.

"He was looking through his new telescope."

"What are you doing, Doctor?" I asked, coming up to where he handled the telescope in the dark.

"Oh well, Stubbins," said he, "I'm—er—I'm trying to see if they're signaling."

"What do you mean—they?—signaling?" I asked.

"Well, you see," said he, "I thought that if they sent down this moth with some sort of a message to me—which I really believe they did—that maybe they, those folk in the moon—I have no idea yet what sort of creatures they are of course—would possibly give out some sort of signal to get in touch with him and see how his expedition was getting on. . . . There! Did you see that? I'll swear I saw a puff—a sort of puff of smoke coming out from the moon's left side. You look in, Stubbins. Maybe I'm dreaming again!"

I looked into the telescope. But I must confess I could see little beyond the ordinary map of the moon. This I was already somewhat familiar with. The Doctor had several pamphlets issued by various astronomical observatories that gave details and maps of that side of the moon which was the only one we earthly people had ever seen. He and I had during the last few days studied these with a good deal of interest and attention. The Doctor himself was very familiar, I knew, with everything that had been learned and published on moon geography up to that time. He seemed disappointed when I told him I could see nothing unusual in the moon's appearance tonight.

"Strange—very strange!" he muttered. "I could have sworn I saw something—like a cloud, suddenly appearing and then fading away like smoke, on the left side. But there! This is all new. So much of it is guesswork as yet. And I'm always afraid that I'm being carried away by my own ideas and hopes."

I must confess that I felt he had on this occasion been misled, until I happened to meet Too-Too later in the evening, coming off duty from his post on top of the roof. He and Polynesia still took it in turns to watch for intruders visiting the Doctor's premises who might hear of the moth's presence in his garden and carry the news abroad before the Doctor wished it known.

The little owl whispered that he would like to see me alone a minute. I took him onto my shoulder and proceeded upstairs to my room. There, with his usual accurate behavior in the complete darkness, he found the matches for me, carried them to the candle, and rattled them till I found my way to him.

"Shut the door, Tommy," he said mysteriously as soon as I had struck a light, "and take a look outside to make sure no one has followed us."

This I did.

"Well," said I, coming back to where he stood blinking beside the lighted candle, "what is it, Too-Too? Has anyone heard about the moth being here?"

"No," said he. "So far, I think I can say with absolute certainty the moth's presence here is a secret. Though I have serious fears about that gossip Gub-Gub. If he tells any other pigs, you can be sure we'll have all the porkers in the neighborhood nosing round to see what's going on. But as yet I fancy he hasn't had a chance. That's not the point. What I wanted to see you about was this: Did you happen to look at the moon at all this evening?"

"Yes," I said, "I looked at it through the Doctor's new telescope. Why?"

"Did you see anything—er—unusual?" he asked.

"No," I said, "I did not. The Doctor asked me the same question. He was sure he had seen something out of the ordinary."

"Ah!" grunted Too-Too. "There you are. I thought so."

"Why, what happened?" I asked.

"Well, you know," said he, "we owls are pretty familiar with the moon. Her phases are, I suppose, more important to us than to almost any animal family. The light, you understand, for hunting and traveling by night is very important. Well, tonight happened to be the full moon—exactly full at ten o'clock. I was looking up at it thinking how bright it would be in the woods for hunting—too bright in fact—when suddenly I saw a small cloud puff out from the left side, like smoke it was. It didn't last more than a couple of seconds and then it was gone. But—well, I'm sure it was done deliberately."

"How do you mean?" said I. "By someone in the moon itself?"

"Well, of course," replied the owl. "I know it most likely sounds crazy to you. But after all, there's no use you and I pretending to each other that we haven't guessed where this moth comes from, is there? We don't have to let the world in on this secret. But—well, after all we *know*, don't we? If he hasn't come from the moon, where else could he have come from? And what's he doing here, hanging around in very uncomfortable circumstances? He has come for some purpose, hasn't he?"

Too-Too's Warning

THE DIFFERENCE BETWEEN TOO-TOO AND Polynesia in this matter, as far as I was concerned, was very noticeable. Polynesia had seemed as though she wanted to keep things from me; Too-Too was for taking me into his confidence. I had had an uncomfortable feeling that the old parrot was looking toward some occasion where—as I mentioned before—the Doctor also might wish me to be left in ignorance regarding his plans. How far John Dolittle himself was in agreement with her in this, and how far she was acting on her own, I did not know. But it had caused me a good deal of anxiety.

To find that Too-Too was willing and anxious to be quite frank with me cheered me up considerably.

"You mean," said I, "that this moth is staying here in the hopes that he may take the Doctor back with him to the moon?"

"What else?" said Too-Too, spreading out his wings in a funny argumentative gesture. "After all, you know the great man's reputation. There's nothing very surprising in that it should have reached the moon. No one can say yet what their civilization up there may have grown into. But naturalists like John Dolittle are not born every day—nor every century. They want him, I suppose, to solve some problem. And you may be sure that the Doctor will not be slow to answer their call for help. And what is more, he will certainly keep his going a secret till the last possible moment."

"Humph!" I muttered. "You think then that he might hop off any minute?"

"I don't know," said Too-Too. "There is no telling. They certainly haven't let *me* in on any secrets. But I'm sure that giant moth came with some orders about bringing the Doctor back with him.

"'What else?' said Too-Too."

How long it may take the Doctor to learn enough of the insect's language to know what they want, I cannot tell. But if you are interested, I would advise you to keep a very close watch on John Dolittle's movements for the next few days. A word to the wise, you know—"

I pondered a moment before answering.

"All right," I said at last. "Thank you, Too-Too, for warning me."

"It was not only on your own account," said the owl, "that I dropped this word of caution. If he goes, we animals would be much happier if he had some other human with him. Getting to the moon is—well—a risky business, to say the least—and it is my guess that he will avoid taking any more company than he can possibly help, on account of the risk."

It was only very shortly after that conversation with Too-Too that I made it my business to question the Doctor about his plans.

"So it is true," I said, "that you have hopes of getting to the moon with the help of this moth?"

"Well," said he, "it will depend of course on how things pan out. But yes, I think I can certainly say that I have hopes in that direction. As I told you, it seems pretty certain now that this moth was sent down specially to fetch me."

"It is a very thrilling idea," said I. "But to be quite honest, I don't see how you're going to manage it. They say there is no air there, don't they?"

The Doctor shrugged his shoulders.

"There is animal life there anyway," said he. "These moths can manage very well. It is probably a different kind of air, that is all. I am faced with the problem of finding out what sort of atmosphere it is they have there. Once I've done that I shall be in a very much better position to say whether or no the earthly human can subsist in the moon. I am beginning to come to the conclusion that up there the vegetable kingdom is relatively much more active and important than the animal kingdom. Of course that's only guesswork so far. But everything points to it. I believe that the atmosphere, whatever air they have, is created or influenced very largely by the vegetable kingdom. That is why the moth brought along with him those flowers whose perfumes seem so important to him."

"But," said I, "scientists have said there is no water there, haven't they? That if there were there would be clouds?"

"Oh well," said the Doctor, shrugging his shoulders, "how do they know—without having been there? Perhaps the moon water is of a different kind—one that does not volatilize and go off into clouds—the way it does with us. Perhaps the air, the heat, is of a different kind. Who shall say? The only way to know is to go there and see."

"That's all very well," I replied. "But in the job of finding out you could, so far as I can tell, very easily give your life without anyone thanking you."

The Doctor pondered seriously a moment.

"Yes," he said at last, "I admit it may sound sort of crazy to most people. But I have a confidence in animals. The lunar animal kingdom wants me up there for something. As yet I haven't been able to find out exactly what it is. But so far all my life, as you know, I have trusted the animal kingdom and I have never had that confidence imposed on. If the moon animals want me, I'll go. And I have no fear about their finding a way to get me there—and a way to get me back."

"Humph!" I said. "But even if there should be air—of a sort—on the moon itself, there is none in between, is there? My understanding of this situation is that when you get away from the earth a certain distance you come to the end of the air envelope. How can anyone fly when there is no air for his wings to beat against?"

Once more John Dolittle shrugged his shoulders.

"The moth managed it," he said. "I imagine that so far as a medium for flying is concerned, the gravity of the earth, being stronger than the gravity of the moon, pulled him down here without much effort on his own part, as soon as he got outside the moon's attraction. That would make it look as though it were easier to get here *from* the moon than from here *to* the moon. However, the most important thing would seem to be carrying enough atmosphere with you to support life on the voyage."

"Is it far," I asked, "to the moon?"

"Far enough," said he. "But only about one fourteen-hundredth part of the distance to the sun. As soon as I am convinced that they, that is the moon's animal kingdom, wants to have me come, then I'll go. I'm not afraid. They will take care of me. If they can get one of their people down to me, I should be able to get up to them. It is merely a question of knowing conditions and making provisions for perfectly natural, if new, conditions."

Of course when the Doctor put it in that way there was after all very little to be said. That sublime confidence of his in the animal kingdom, whether it was of the moon or the earth, overcame all difficulties in a manner that left you almost gasping. If the moon creatures wanted him, he would go. That was the end of the matter.

For the rest, everything now depended on the development of conversation between himself and the giant moth. We had

"'Is it far?' I asked, 'to the moon?'"

successfully kept the secret of its presence with us from the outside world—so far.

"You know, Stubbins," said he to me one evening when we were talking this over, "I am not even telling the animals, my own household, I mean, about any plans I may have for a possible journey to the moon. One cannot be too careful. If it ever leaked out that I was contemplating such a thing we would have a reporter from every paper in the country clamoring at our gates for an interview within twenty-four hours. The world may call me a crank. But anything sensational like this can start an avalanche of publicity that nothing will stop. Polynesia is about the only one I have taken into my confidence.

I suspect of course that Too-Too, Chee-Chee, and Jip have some idea of what is going on. But I haven't discussed the matter with them and I know I can trust them to keep their suspicions to themselves."

"Have you," I asked, "decided yet, if you do go, whom you would take with you? I presume you hadn't thought of going entirely alone?"

"Um—er—" the Doctor murmured, "that is a bit hard to settle yet. The—er—well, the risks, you know, Stubbins, are great. There is no sense in trying to hide that. It is something so entirely new. Sometimes I feel I should take no one with me at all—that I haven't the right to. If I go alone and I fail to get back, well, I'll have given my life in a cause worthwhile. As I said, for my own safety I haven't much fears. But I'm not so sure that the same protection would necessarily be given to the rest of my party. I have made no final decisions yet. Polynesia I would like to take—and Chee-Chee. I feel they both might be very useful; but for the rest, much as I would like to have them with me, I think they are better off where they are—at home."

And now of course the most important question for me was: Would I, Tommy Stubbins, be of the Doctor's party on the voyage to the moon? I was almost afraid to ask the question of him directly. Never have I been so divided in my feelings about anything. One minute I was just crazy to go. The next I realized what a mad, wild expedition it was and felt that the chances of anyone returning alive from such a voyage were too slight to be worth mentioning. Then followed the picture of how I would feel if I let him go alone and stayed behind myself. That finally decided me. Scared blue as I was of the whole scheme, I knew I just had to do my utmost to accompany him. I *couldn't* let him go without me. The following evening I broached the subject.

"Doctor," I said, "you are of course counting on taking me with you on this trip?" (I felt it best to begin by supposing that he was.) "You would find it hard to do without a secretary, wouldn't you? There is bound to be an enormous lot of note-taking to be done, eh?"

I watched his face keenly as he pondered a moment before answering.

"Well—er—Stubbins," he began at length, "you know how I feel about taking anyone with me—even those animal friends of mine, members of my household, who have no one to mourn over their loss if they should not come back. And—er—in your case, Stubbins, you must realize that it is—quite difficult. Please do not think that I don't appreciate the fact that you want to share the dangers of this entirely new enterprise with me. I admit I would be more than glad of your company. I expect to be faced with situations when the companionship of another human might be a tremendous comfort and help. But—well, you know, Stubbins, as well as I do, how your parents would feel if I took you with me on such a trip. To the moon! Compared with that, our other voyages look like a twopenny coach ride to the outskirts of London. Then again, remember, Stubbins, I am flying in the face of all scientific authority. Whatever my own doubts may be, the fact remains that all astronomers, from Newton down, who have studied the moon, emphatically declare that no life can exist there—that the moon is a dead world. I am gambling, like Columbus, on my own opinion pitted against the rest of mankind. . . . No—I'm sorry. But nothing would excuse me, in my own eyes—let alone the eyes of your mother and father—for taking you with me. You—you must stay behind. You will be needed here. I—I can't take you, Stubbins."

I felt crushed. It seemed as though there was nothing more to be said. And yet his final decision left me a little unsatisfied. When I had warned him of the dangers for himself in going to the moon he had argued one way, making light of the risk; and when I had asked to be allowed to come along he had argued the other way, and laid stress upon the dangers of the enterprise.

Resolving to make just one more try, I pointed this out to him and ended by saying:

"If the flowers the moth brought, Doctor, grew on the moon, there must be water there. Isn't that so?"

To my surprise he did not seem embarrassed by my stroke of logic at all.

"Probably, Stubbins, that is true. But do not forget that we are facing the problems and natural history of a life wholly unknown to us. The chemistry of these plants is something utterly new to our own science. That I know by pretty thorough investigation of them. To us the idea of producing plants without water is something quite impossible. But on the moon, again, who shall say? They may be air plants, parasites like our orchids, living on the moisture of the atmosphere. Or anything. No one can tell how they get their nourishment or carry on life till he has seen them growing in their native surroundings. Listen, Stubbins: if I had ever seen *a tree growing on the moon* I would feel I could answer your question better. But I haven't. And I have no idea whatever as yet from what source these flowers derive their life."

He paused a moment, then rose and approaching my chair where I sat gloomily scowling at the table with my head in my hands, he clutched my shoulder in a kindly grasp.

"Good friend," said he in a funny, chokey sort of voice, "let's not discuss it anymore. You know, don't you, how much I'd love to have you. But I can't, Stubbins—I just can't take you."

THE ELEVENTH CHAPTER

Our Midnight Visitors

OFTEN, WHEN I LOOK BACK ON THE PAST, I realize that the Doctor's answer to my request to let me accompany him had the opposite effect to that which he hoped for—or expected. I made no answer whatever to his decision that night. I went to bed. But there I lay awake thinking.

What might happen if I let him go alone? I recalled what Too-Too had said: "We, the animal members of his household, would be much happier if he had some other human with him." And then, I suppose, just the fact that my coming was forbidden made it seem all the more desirable and put me on my mettle.

Anyhow, after many hours of sleeplessness, I decided that I would say nothing, lie low, and remember Too-Too's advice about keeping a very close watch on John Dolittle's movements for the next few days.

And as it turned out, it was a good thing that I did so. It is without question the proudest thing that I can boast of in my whole record that this determination, which the Doctor's refusal of my company bred in me, led to my eventually going with him.

From that night when I made up my mind, I hardly let him out of my sight. No detective ever played a game of closer shadowing than I did. Whenever he sent me off on an errand, I pretended to go, but sent Jip or Chee-Chee instead. From moment to moment I did not know when he might depart; but I knew where he was and exactly what he was doing. For I was quite determined that when he went, he would *not* go without me.

In this Too-Too was the only one who helped me. There were hours of course when I could not be on the watch myself. I had to sleep. At such times the little owl did duty for me. I don't think that the Doctor ever realized how closely shadowed he was.

The hour came at last. I was fast asleep. Too-Too woke me by gently pulling my hair. In a second I was wide awake.

"Tommy!" I heard. "Get up! Tommy! Tommy!"

"What is it?" I whispered. "What's happening?"

"Get your clothes on," whispered the owl. "The Doctor has gone out into the garden. He has his little black bag with him—and his overcoat. I have a feeling that things may be happening. Come down into the garden. Don't strike a light. Better be on the safe side. I can see. I'll guide you. But hurry—for goodness' sake!"

My bedroom was so small, and I knew the exact position of everything in it so well, that it was no great feat for me to dress myself in the dark. I remember, as I felt for my clothes and finally drew them on, wondering what I had better take with me for this strange new voyage. What would one need most on the moon?— Who could say? For who had been there? I had given this problem some thought already and decided that the freer we were of luggage the better. That had always been the Doctor's principle; and considering how impossible it was to make a choice in these circumstances, it seemed here a particularly good rule to follow.

My new big pocket knife! Yes, I must take that. I got it out of the bureau drawer. It, with a box of matches, was all the luggage I took. Many a time afterward I laughed at the solution. And yet of course I did not know for certain that night, as I hunched on my overcoat in the dark, whether or not I was leaving the house and the earth for the great voyage. Still, something told me that the little owl had probably guessed right. I could hear him fidgeting and muttering somewhere near the door, impatient for me to be going. He gave a grunt of relief when I finally felt my way toward him and whispered that I was ready.

Hopping down the pitch-black stairs ahead of me he led the way, by means of his funny little grunts for signals, to the kitchen. Here I very stealthily undid the bolts of the back door, which led into the garden.

I had not the vaguest notion what time it was. I knew Too-Too could tell me, but I was afraid to call to him. The moon was visible, but only by fits and starts; because the gentle wind was blowing clouds across the sky in a constant procession.

Too-Too waited a moment for me to get used to the dim light of the garden. He knew that my stumbling or stepping on a cracking twig might easily give us away. He whispered that he would go forward alone and reconnoiter. I saw him crouch for a spring as though he meant to take to his wings. Flying he could see more than walking and be less likely to be noticed himself.

But he did not leave the ground. Suddenly, sharply, he turned his head. Then he came back to me.

"Tommy!" he whispered. "There are strangers in the garden. Two men have just come in at the front gate."

As I bent down to listen to him, he hopped onto my knee, and from there to my shoulder, a favorite traveling place of his when we went about together. From this lookout he could easily whisper into my ear.

"Who do you reckon they are, Too-Too?" I asked.

"Goodness only knows," he replied. "We've got to keep a close watch on them anyway. Then we'll soon know, I fancy. They're behaving mighty strangely—evidently anxious not to be seen."

"Do you think they might be burglars trying to get into the house?" I asked.

"Not the slightest chance of that," said the owl promptly. "No one in his senses would pick out the Doctor's establishment as a house to rob. Everybody knows he is almost always penniless. Everything in the house of real value John Dolittle sold long ago. We must watch these birds and see what their game is. But it isn't plunder."

So, under whispered orders from the owl, I crept along in the shadow of bushes and hedges and tried to find out what our strange visitors had come for.

Very soon we saw it was a case of spying on spies. The two men, for the present at all events, wanted nothing more than an opportunity to find out what the Doctor was doing. There was no question now that the secret of the giant moth's presence in our garden was out. His gigantic form, lit up by the moon's waning light, occupied the greater part of the back lawn. The black figure of the Doctor could be plainly seen scouting around it.

As a matter of fact, I found myself playing a double part and watching both the Doctor and the men. I very soon saw from John Dolittle's movements that Too-Too had guessed right and that tonight was the date that the Doctor had decided on for his departure. Several suspicious-looking packages lying about the lawn, besides the black bag, showed me that John Dolittle had made preparations of a more extensive kind than he usually did for his voyages. The question now that seemed most important was: Would these men try to interfere with his departure before he got away?

Altogether it was for me a strange and crazy night of adventure. At no time could I make up my mind whether it was more important to watch the Doctor than to keep my eye on the men. The men, I felt, were a menace, a danger, which at any moment might interfere with John Dolittle and with plans that could very possibly mean a great, great deal to the advancement of science and knowledge for the human race. On the other hand, if I neglected to watch the Doctor himself, he might quite possibly take flight with the moon moth and leave me behind.

While Too-Too and I were trying to make up our minds which we should give our best attention to, the men, to our great astonishment, came out from their concealment in the shrubbery and boldly walked up to the Doctor on the lawn.

"Good evening, Doctor Dolittle," we heard them say. "We represent the *Slopshire Courier*. We understand that you are interested in certain experiments and natural history research of a novel and sensational character. Would you be so good as to answer a few questions?"

"There you are, they're reporters!" whispered Too-Too. "I had expected as much. I wonder how on earth they heard of the moth's being here though."

"Well—er—" the Doctor began, "this is a very unconventional hour for you to call on me. But perhaps if you came back in a few hours—say at ten or eleven in the morning—I might find time to give you an interview. Just now I am very busy."

The reporters, who were clearly anxious to get the information they wanted right away (so as to be ahead of the other papers in their announcements), conversed together a moment before replying. Then they turned back to the Doctor. Neither Too-Too nor I heard exactly what they said. But whatever it was it seemed to be agreeable to the Doctor and in keeping with his wishes. For immediately after, the two men retired and the Doctor disappeared into another part of the garden.

It is quite certain that without Too-Too's aid in this night's work, things could never have turned out as successfully as they did. I have often thought since that if the little owl had ever wanted to enter the profession of animal detective, the great Kling could have been easily surpassed.

For Too-Too certainly had a gift for seeing things without being seen. Directly the men parted from the Doctor, he parted from me.

"Listen," said he before he left my shoulder: "I don't trust those gentlemen. We have a double job tonight. The Doctor should be the easier of the two, because he will be less suspicious. You watch him. I'll keep an eye on the newspaper fellows. It may be that they'll clear out, as they said they would. And then again they may not. We can't afford to risk it. You go ahead and watch John Dolittle and I'll let you know if the *Slopshire Courier*'s men do anything out of the ordinary. Remember, whatever happens, the Doctor must *not* go on this voyage alone."

"All right, Too-Too," I said, "I'm ready for all emergencies. Go ahead."

With a little flirt of his wings, the owl left my shoulder and soared away into the darkness of the night. Then very, very stealthily and cautiously I made my way along the garden, keeping always in the shadow of hedges and shrubs, toward the great figure of the moon moth squatting on the lawn.

It wasn't easy work. For one thing, I could not locate the Doctor himself for quite a while. And I was scared that any minute I might run into him and have to confess that I'd been spying. I didn't feel at all guilty about that. If Too-Too, speaking for the animal household in general, felt it necessary that he should be watched, I was very willing to do it without any qualms of conscience at all. What might not depend on my vigilance and skill? He must *not* go alone.

What was that? Yes, the Doctor's figure coming out from behind the shadow of the moth. In his hands he held two packages. I wished that I had Too-Too's trick of seeing clearly in the dark. Dare I move a little closer?

As a matter of fact I did not have a chance to, before I found Too-Too back on my shoulder. With a gentle fanning of wings he dropped down beside my right ear as gently as a butterfly landing on a leaf.

"They haven't gone, Tommy," he whispered. "Never had any intention to, I imagine. They clattered down the front steps, making a great noise, but almost immediately came back again on tiptoe. They are now hanging around the front garden close to the wall."

"What do you think we had better do?" I asked.

"Well, as far as I can see, it's a choice of two things," said he. "Either we continue to watch them and see how much they find out;

or we wake up Bumpo and get him to chuck them off the premises. Myself, I'm all for throwing them out. I think it can be done without the Doctor's realizing that you've been watching him. That's important, of course."

"I think you are right," said I. "Suppose you take a spell at watching the Doctor while I go and wake Bumpo. I don't imagine they'll hang about long after he has recommended an early departure to them."

To this the owl agreed. And I wasted no time in getting to the business of rousing Bumpo.

I found His Highness the Crown Prince of the Jolliginki snoring away in a dead sleep. With much effort, I managed finally to get him to sit up.

"Is it a conflagration, Tommy?" he asked, sleepily rubbing his fists into his face. "It can't be time to get up yet. It's still dark."

"Listen, Bumpo," said I shaking him. "It's important, serious. I'm awfully sorry to disturb you but it just couldn't be helped. Two men have come into the garden. They're newspaper reporters, it seems, spying on the Doctor. The Doctor himself is still working with the giant moth. We didn't want to disturb him. But these strangers must be gotten out, off the premises, you understand. You're the only one who can make them go. Get up and dress— quick."

PART FOUR

Bumpo Clears
the Garden

A FTER BUMPO WAS FULLY AWAKE, HE WAS not slow in coming to the rescue.

"Why, I never heard of such cheek!" he said as he climbed into his clothes. "What do they think the Doctor's home is, I'd like to know—a sort of general information bureau, open all night? Where was it you saw these miscreants last, Tommy?"

"Too-Too said he saw them down in the front garden hiding in the shadow of the wall. But listen, Bumpo: it is most terribly important that we don't raise a row. If you can grab them quietly and make them understand that they've got to go, that's what we want. We *can't* have a rumpus, you understand?"

"Of course I understand," said Bumpo, jerking on his coat and reaching for a club that stood in a corner by his bed. "They'll understand too. Such cheek! I never heard anything like it. This, after all our watching! Well, well! Come with me. We'll soon make them shift along."

In the game of moving in the dark, of seeing without being seen, Bumpo was almost as good as Too-Too himself. His African upbringing had brought him a gift that all his college education had not dulled. Ahead of me he went down the stairs, feeling his way without a light, till he reached the ground floor. There without hesitation he made his way to the front door, opened it, and passed through almost without sound. He signaled to me to hang back a few paces in the rear and then slipped across the gravel path to the wall.

In spite of his instructions I was not far behind him. I was pretty sure the Doctor could hardly hear us here unless we made a great lot of noise. Bumpo felt his way along the wall and presently from the jump he gave I knew he had met his quarry. Stealthily I moved a little nearer, and in the dim light I could see he had the two men by the scruffs of their necks.

"Listen," he whispered in a curious, fierce hiss: "Get out of this garden as quick as possible and never come near it again. There's the gate. Go!"

Beside the two shadows near the wall, his great bulk towered up like a giant. Not waiting for an answer, he conducted or shoved them toward the head of the steps that led down to the road.

Here at the gate I saw, for the first time, the faces of our visitors by the light of a streetlamp. They certainly looked scared—for which they could hardly be blamed. To be grabbed unexpectedly from under a hedge by a man of Bumpo's size was enough to upset anyone.

They did not wait for any second orders to depart but bundled down the steps as fast as they could go, only too glad to escape with whole skins.

His job finished, the good Bumpo was immediately overcome with a desire to finish his night's sleep. I thanked him for his assistance and he at once returned to his room. As I wished him a very late good night I noticed that the dawn was beginning to show, a faint gray behind the poplar trees to the eastward. This I felt must mean that John Dolittle would either hurry up his departure before real daylight appeared, or else give up the project till the following night. I wasted no further time in speculation but made my way, as quickly as I could without being heard or seen, round to the back lawn to find out what was happening.

I discovered the Doctor in a state of considerable excitement conversing with the moth. He appeared to have made great advances in means of communication with the giant insect since I had last seen him so engaged. The apparatus he was now using was little more than a tuning fork. Indeed, it almost seemed as though he had found a way of speaking with his guest directly. When I first got a glimpse of him he had his head down close to that of the moth's and held his left hand on one of its antennae. Once in a while he would consult the tuning fork grasped in his right hand.

From the moth's movements, little jerks of the head and tremors of the legs, it looked as though he was busily engaged in getting some message to the Doctor. I guessed the argument was over whether the start should be made tonight or postponed on account of the approaching daylight. I crept nearer to the back end of the giant creature to be ready in case the decision were made for departure right away.

Of course, in describing that whole night, it is very hard to give a proper idea of the difficulties that beset me. The hour before dawn is generally supposed to be the darkest. Be that as it may, the moon

certainly hung very low and the light was faint enough. I had no idea
of how prepared the Doctor was. I knew from what I had seen, and
from what Too-Too had told me, that he had moved certain baggage
out into the back garden. But it was almost impossible to determine
under the circumstances how far he had perfected his plans.

However, after a few moments more of watching him, prepared
at any moment to spring onto the moth's deep fur if he should make
a move to fly, I decided that they had both given up the project for
tonight. For presently I saw the Doctor's dim figure move away
from the moth and conceal some packages beneath the shrubs.
Also I got a vague impression that there was a hurried conversation
between the Doctor and Polynesia, who appeared to be perched
somewhere in the direction of a lilac bush.

As you can imagine, I was weary with the long watch and
the excitement and everything. As soon as I saw the Doctor start
toward the house I felt I was relieved from further need of watch-
fulness for the present, at all events. Bleary-eyed for want of sleep,
I waited till I heard the Doctor enter the house and lock the door.
Then I made my way to a window that I knew was not latched, slid
up the sash, and crawled in.

I knew my trusty lieutenant Too-Too was somewhere abroad
still and that I could rely on him to let me know if any occasion
should arise requiring my presence. My head had no sooner touched
the pillow than I went off into a dead sleep.

My dreams, however, were soon disturbed by all manner of
dreadful visions of myself and the Doctor flying through the air
on the back of a dragon, landing on a moon made of green cheese
and peopled by a giant race of beetles and other dreadful fantastic
insects whose one ambition was to gobble us both up.

Again I was awakened by the good Too-Too.

"What is it now?" I asked. "Don't tell me the Doctor's gone!"

"No," said he. "He's asleep—for once in his life. Seeing how he has worked the last weeks, I wouldn't wonder if he didn't wake up for a fortnight. But we're having visitors some more. I don't know what to do about it. Those wretched newspapermen must have told the whole town, for all sorts of people are peering in at the garden gate. It is now about ten o'clock. And ever since daybreak, children and nursemaids and every kind of folk have been hanging round as though they expected a balloon to go up or something. Bumpo of course is still dead to the world. And no one else is stirring but Dab-Dab and Chee-Chee. I think you ought to get down and take a look at things. It seems to me as though we'll have the whole town around us before long. And some of them are so cheeky! You never saw anything like it, coming into the garden and picking the flowers as though the place belonged to them."

"All right, Too-Too," said I. "I'll get up. You might go and see what you can do toward getting Bumpo under way, will you?"

Too-Too, promising he would do what he could in that direction, left my room: and only half-rested as I was—for it had been little more than five hours since I had gone to bed—crawled out and started to dress.

Arriving downstairs I found that he had not exaggerated matters in the least. I peered through the study windows and saw that there was a large group of people gathered at the front gate. Most of them had not dared to come in. But there were a few bolder spirits who were already wandering about the front garden, peeping round the corners of the house and whispering together as though they expected some strange performance to begin any minute.

"Peeping round the corners of the house"

While I was cudgeling my brains for some means of dealing with the situation Bumpo happily arrived on the scene.

"Don't let them think we're hiding anything, Bumpo," I said. "But they must be kept out of the back garden. The moth must not be disturbed or scared."

I must admit that Bumpo did very well. He began by herding out those who had strayed inside the gate. A few who were more obstinate he assisted by taking them by the coat collar or sleeve and showing them where the private premises left off and the public highway began. But for the most part he conducted the clearance with great tact and politeness.

It was quite evident, however, from the remarks of the people that the wretched newspapermen had blabbed their story in the town. Also, though they had not of course guessed the Doctor's destination, they had, it seemed, announced that he was about to take a voyage on the moth's back. This of course was natural since they had seen John Dolittle preparing and gathering his baggage in the garden.

"When is he going to start?" the crowd asked. "Where is he going?" ... "Will he really fly on the big moth?" ... "Can't we see the creature?" ... "Where are you keeping the animal?" etc., etc.

Bumpo, in his best Oxford manner, was very discreet and most courteous.

"Sh!" said he. "Doctor John Dolittle will make his own announcements to the press in due course. In the meantime, be good enough to leave the premises. He is sleeping after many hours of heavy work and study. He cannot be disturbed."

A large fat man climbed over the wall beside the gate. Bumpo took two strides, pushed him gently but firmly in the face with his hand, and the man fell heavily to the roadway.

"It is not polite," said Bumpo, "to force your way into a gentleman's garden without invitation."

The Mounted Police

BUT OUR TROUBLES BY NO MEANS CAME TO an end with clearing the garden of our inquisitive visitors. I have often thought since that some means of distracting their attention in other directions would have been a better way for us to deal with the problem than turning them off the premises.

Because they did not go away. They were surer than ever now that something extraordinary was going on that we did not wish known. And while we had the right to forbid their trespass on the Doctor's premises, we had no authority to prevent their gathering in the road. And they *did* gather, without any question. I suppose that when I came downstairs there must have been about fifty persons. But when these had hung around the gate talking for about an hour, their number was multiplied by ten.

The bigger the crowd became the faster it seemed to grow. Every tradesman's errand-boy, every carter going into town, every peddler—in fact, every passerby, stopped and inquired what was the matter. Heaven knows what tales they were told. The Doctor's reputation was fantastic enough for anything already. It only needed a whisper that he was going to fly away on a moth to make any country yokel want to stop in expectation of a show.

John Dolittle himself had not yet woken up. I was in the deepest despair. The road was now jammed; and farm carts, carriages and delivery wagons, utterly unable to pass, were lined up on either side of the crowd that thronged about the gate. Anyone coming down the Oxenthorpe Road now just had to stop whether he was interested or not, simply because he couldn't get by.

"Tell me, Too-Too," I said, "what on earth do you think we

"Every tradesman's errand-boy stopped and inquired."

had better do? If this goes on we'll have to get some assistance from outside. I never saw anything like it."

"Look," he said, peering out of the window beside me. "Here come some police—mounted police, too. They'll soon clear the crowd away."

"I hope so," said I. "Two—no, three—four of them. It will keep them busy to get this mob scattered."

Well, the arrival of the police did clear the roadway, it is true. But that is all it did. So far as the people's interest was concerned, however, it made the situation worse rather than better. It was a little added excitement and sensation. The crowd obeyed orders and gathered on the pavements, leaving the roadway clear for carts and carriages to pass. But still it stayed.

Presently I saw one of the policemen come up to the foot of our steps. He dismounted, tied his horse to the lamppost and started to ascend.

"You'd better go and see what he wants, Tommy," said Too-Too. "I suppose he'll ask what has caused the disturbance."

I went to the front door and opened it. The constable was very polite. He asked if I could tell him what had brought the crowd around and if there was anything I could do to make the throng go home.

For a moment I couldn't think of a thing to suggest. Finally Too-Too, who was sitting on my shoulder, whispered, "You'll have to wake the Doctor, Tommy. We've done all we can."

I asked the constable to come in and went upstairs to John Dolittle's room. I hated to wake him. He was sleeping like a log and I knew how much he needed his rest. Very gently I shook him by the shoulder.

"What is it, Stubbins?" he asked, opening his eyes.

"Doctor," said I, "I'm terribly sorry to disturb you. But we felt it just couldn't be helped. It seems that the moth's presence here has leaked out."

"Yes, I know," said he. "It can't be helped. These wretched newspaper fellows—you can't keep them out. Two of them came to see me in the garden last night."

"But the truth is," I said, "that they have blabbed their story to the whole of Puddleby, it seems. The road is just blocked by the crowd who have come to see you fly to the moon. The police have finally arrived on the scene and they want to know if there is anything

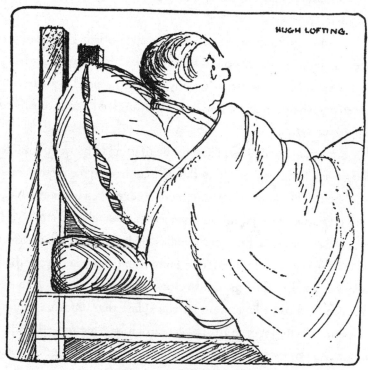

"'What is it, Stubbins?' he asked."

we can do to make the throng go home. They are quite polite. But we couldn't think of anything to suggest. So I came to ask you what you thought should be done."

The Doctor's handling of the situation was, I decided afterward, extraordinarily good.

"Well," he said, climbing out of bed with a yawn, "I suppose I must speak to the crowd. Just let me get my clothes on and I will see what I can do."

I left him and returned to Too-Too downstairs.

"Keep an eye on him," said the owl, when I had explained what had passed between us. "You see his hand has been forced, as it were. And—well—anything might happen now, you know, any moment."

I didn't quite understand what he meant. But I realized the need of keeping an eye on John Dolittle. I had no opportunity to ask the owl further what exactly he had in mind, because the Doctor at that moment came down fully dressed and interrupted our conversation.

After a few minutes' talk with the policeman he went out into the garden and from the top of the steps addressed the crowd in the road below. He began by giving them a general chatty sort of lecture on natural history, touching on various branches of study with which he had lately been occupied. This had the excellent effect of getting the crowd into a good humor and dismissed from their minds a good deal of their suspicions that he was keeping things from them. Presently he went on to explain that unfortunately he could not invite them in to see the garden and his collections just now as he was particularly busy at the moment and things were not in order for public exhibition. They would realize, he said, that by blocking up the road and causing a disturbance they had—quite unintentionally, he felt sure—interrupted his work. If they would be so good as to retire peacefully they would confer a great favor on him and the police. And possibly at some future date, if they would call again, arrangements could be made to show them over his establishment in which they had shown so kind an interest.

To my great amazement the simple speech had precisely the right effect: the crowd actually seemed to realize for the first time that its behavior had been discourteous; and in almost an apologetic mood it at once began to break up and disperse.

"There's no doubt about it, Tommy," sighed Too-Too, as together we watched the throng fade away down the road. "They may call him a crank—but he's a great man."

The Errand

S O FOR THE PRESENT WE WERE RELIEVED OF *that* worry. But it was not very long after the crowd had gone that I almost wished it back again. The people, while they were a nuisance and one did not know what they might do if they continued to gather, were at all events a protection against something that both Too-Too and I greatly feared. And that was the Doctor's escaping alone with the moon moth. We felt that there was little danger of his making an attempt with all that mob present.

But when, shortly after lunchtime, John Dolittle came and asked me to go off on an errand for him to Oxenthorpe, which would keep me away from the house, I knew, till after nightfall, I got really alarmed. Stuttering and stammering, I made all the excuses I could possibly think of on the spur of the moment. I said I felt tired and asked if Bumpo could not go in my place. But Bumpo, it seemed, had already been sent away on another errand. All my other efforts to get out of the trip failed likewise. There was nothing to do but accept the job. But as soon as I parted from the Doctor I went and sought out Too-Too.

"Tommy," said he, when I had explained matters, "you just can't go. That's all there is about it."

"But what am I to do?" I said. "I'm his assistant, after all. I can't refuse to obey orders."

"No," said the owl, putting his head on one side and winking a large eye knowingly. "You don't refuse—that would be most unwise—but you don't go. It is very simple. You just keep out of sight."

"But what can I say," I asked, "tomorrow, if he is still here, and asks me about the errand?"

"Tomorrow's tomorrow," said Too-Too. "And it can take care of itself. Even if he hasn't gone he's not going to kill you for disobeying orders. We can think up some excuse. But *don't go off the premises.* The fact that he is so urgent about this trip he is sending you on—and I don't know of any really pressing business he has had in Oxenthorpe for years—makes me suspicious. Also, Bumpo's being already gotten rid of on some other job looks to me like clearing the decks for action. No, don't worry about tomorrow. By that time, if I guess correctly, John Dolittle will be on his way to the moon."

I finally decided the little owl was probably right. So with some excuse for reentering the back garden, I bade the Doctor goodbye and with all appearances of dutifully obeying orders started off down the road, presumably bound for the little inn about half a mile from our house, where the coaches stopped on the way from Puddleby to Oxenthorpe. But as soon as I was well out of sight I loitered about till the coach went rattling by. Then I made my way round to a narrow lane that skirted the Doctor's property at the back. There I scrambled up the wall and dropped down on the other side.

This part of John Dolittle's grounds was nearly all dense shrubbery. Of recent years he had found it hard, with all the studies that claimed his attention, to keep the whole of his garden in good order; and on this side there was an acre or two of tangled orchard and overgrown bushes that had been allowed to struggle and survive as best they could. It was excellent cover. Through it I noiselessly made my way till I was within a few yards of the back lawn and the tail of the moon moth himself.

And then began several hours of waiting. I was well concealed, and from behind some high laurels could see all that took place on the lawn. For a long time nothing seemed to happen at all and I began to wonder if Too-Too had guessed wrong. Once in a while I'd see the Doctor's head through the windows of the house as he passed from one room to another. But finally, somewhere about half-past six, when the sun had dropped well down to the horizon and a coolness in the air spoke of coming darkness, John Dolittle opened the back door and hurried out onto the lawn. With him were Chee-Chee, Polynesia, and Jip. As he came up to the side of the moth he was talking in a quick, businesslike way to Jip.

"I'm sorry," he was saying. "I *can't* take you, Jip. Please don't ask me any more. It takes so long to explain and I've only a few minutes. Remember those letters I've left on the study table. There's one for Stubbins, one for Bumpo, and one for Matthew. Show Stubbins where they are when he gets back and ask him to explain to everyone how sorry I am to rush away in this sudden sort of manner without saying good-bye. But I'm so afraid of those townsfolk and newspaper people coming back and stopping me if I don't get away now while I can. Stubbins will look after the zoo, and Bumpo and Matthew everything else. Get those packages out from under the lilacs, Chee-Chee. And, Jip, you'd better go off and keep Gub-Gub amused while we slip away. I sent him down into the kitchen garden to dig up some radishes."

"Yes, Jip," put in Polynesia, "for goodness' sake, keep that wretched pig occupied. If he knows the Doctor is leaving for the moon he'll bawl the whole town around us in five minutes. What about the flowers, Doctor?"

"I've got them," I heard the Doctor whisper. "They're hidden behind the privet hedge. I'll get the packages up first, and then we'll attend to them. Where did I put that ladder? I wish Chee-Chee would hurry up. Keep an eye open, Polynesia, and let me know if you hear any sound."

The Doctor seemed much more upset about the possibility of being disturbed before he got away than he was over embarking on this perilous expedition. For me, my heart was thumping like a sledgehammer, for I realized that Too-Too had been right and there was every chance that the flight would be made immediately. With the greatest care, lest my movements be detected by the watchful Polynesia, I crept a foot or two nearer and measured with my eye how far I'd have to spring to get hold of the deep fur on the moth's tail. Once I had gotten a grip, I felt I could easily manage to haul myself up his spine to the wider spaces of his back. These were now covered by his folded wings; but I knew that as soon as he took flight, provided I hang on at the take-off, I could scramble up later.

Finding the ladder, the Doctor placed it against the great insect's right side and climbed a few rungs. Then he waited till

Chee-Chee emerged from the lilacs with the packages in his arms. These John Dolittle took from him and stowed away somewhere up on the shoulders—though what method he used to fasten them by I could not see.

When this was done he came down and with Chee-Chee's help brought the big moon flowers out and stowed them away also. One, however, he laid down in front of the moth's head. This was grasped by the insect and drawn in close by his two front legs.

At length the Doctor descended again and took a final look round.

"Is there anything we've forgotten, Polynesia?" he whispered.

"You've left a light burning in the cellar," said the parrot.

"No matter," said the Doctor. "Stubbins or Bumpo will find it. Good! If we're all ready we'll go aboard. You follow me up, Chee-Chee, and we'll push the ladder down from the top."

The Stowaway

JOHN DOLITTLE WASTED NO TIME IN sentimental farewells. It wasn't his way on ordinary earthly voyages; and one might be sure that his manner would be equally free from theatrical gestures when he was leaving for the moon. As soon as Chee-Chee had climbed up behind him he thrust the head of the ladder away with his hand and it fell gently into the shrubbery. That thrust was, as it were, the breaking of the last tie that bound him to the earth, yet he made it as though he were merely brushing off a crumb from his coat.

As the moth's wings began to lift, I knew that the moment had come. The great creature was facing down the long sward of the lawn and he had some hundred yards to rise in before he would have to clear the willows at the south end. I was terribly anxious. I did not know this insect's particular flying form, whether he rose steeply or slantingly, suddenly or slowly. Yet I was terribly afraid of jumping too soon; for if the Doctor or Polynesia should see me, I would certainly get put off. I must not be discovered before we were well on our way to the moon.

I finally ended by deciding that it was better to be too soon than too late. If I should be caught and turned off I might still stand a chance of persuading the Doctor to take me or of stowing away a second time. But if I jumped too late then there was nothing to be said or done.

Luckily, both Chee-Chee and Polynesia started talking at the exact moment I hit upon to spring. This covered up what noise I made in leaving the laurels. I was in great fear, as I took hold of huge handfuls of the moth's deep fur, that the insect would make some complaint to the Doctor—with whom, as far as I could make out, he had now established pretty complete conversational communication without the use of instruments or apparatus of any kind.

But my fears were unnecessary. I imagine the moth took my invasion of his fur coat as merely some more packing on of bundles. The hair was so deep that I found myself almost buried, as I drew closer to his body. This was a good thing, because there was still a little twilight left; and had the Doctor or Polynesia come astern of their flying ship to make a final inspection, I need have no fear of being seen.

And so I clung expecting every moment to feel my feet leave the ground.

I'm sure, on thinking over it afterward, that not more than five seconds could have passed from the time that I grasped the moth's furry coat to the moment he started. But it felt like an hour.

I could just see the outline of the trees and the house roof against the darkening sky when those great wings beat the air for the first time. The draft was terrific and, despite the covering of deep fur in which I was half buried, my cap was torn off my head and sent flying into the laurel bushes behind. The rest of what happened was for quite a while entirely confused in my mind. The sensation of going up and up; the need to cling on in a very perilous position; the rush of the air as the moth gained speed, altogether the experience, for one who had never known it before, was bewildering to say the least.

I remember vaguely hoping that the insect's hair was strong enough to hold my weight, as I saw we were over the willow tops, with a hundred feet to spare and still mounting, mounting! It required all my courage not to scramble up right away to the more level ground of the moth's back where I could find the comforting company of the Doctor and Chee-Chee. I admit I felt very lonely back there when I realized we had actually left the world behind and the lights of Puddleby began to twinkle so far—oh, so far!— below me.

Up and up, and up! My head reeled when I looked down. So I decided it was better *not* to look down. We were in for it now, as the schoolboy says, and the most sensible thing was to make the best we could of the situation.

I shut my eyes tight and just held on. How long I remained so I can't say—probably about an hour. Then I began to feel cold. My hands were numb with clutching tensely. Some part of my confused mind decided that this was the time for me to climb to the level of the moth's back where I could lie down and rest. Glancing upward I saw that the big wings were beating the air well away from the moth's body. I need not fear that my ascent would interfere with the machinery of flight. I kicked my shoes off and let them fall thousands of feet—to the earth we had left. Then, grasping as best I could the moth's hairy body with hands and feet, I started. I must reach level lying soon or my strength would give out.

I suppose it was a good thing for me that I could not see the earth swimming and disappearing below me as I made that crazy climb. It didn't take so very long. But when later I did gaze down on the earth, a round ball with little lights stuck all over it—I realized that I might have been a great deal more scared than I had been.

I had not found either the Doctor or Chee-Chee yet. For the first few moments when I felt I didn't have to cling, I was quite satisfied to stretch myself out on this level part of the moth's back and

"I kicked my shoes off and let them fall."

just rest. Indeed I was sorely in need of repose. My arms and hands were so stiff from clutching, that the muscles were numb and sore.

I was still somewhat unhappy about speaking to the Doctor. After all, I had deliberately disobeyed orders. Presently, when I rose and looked about me, I saw him. I made out first the shape of his high hat, surely the most absurd thing that mortal eyes ever met with in such circumstances. But I don't remember ever having caught a glimpse of anything that was more comforting and reassuring. It was pressed well down on his head and next to it Chee-Chee's skull, sharply ape-like, stood out against the blue-green moonlit sky.

"Next to it Chee-Chee's skull stood out against the moonlit sky."

Yes, I admit I was very much afraid. You see, I had never disobeyed the Doctor before. It is true he was no stern disciplinarian. To me, as to everyone, he had always been the most easygoing, indulgent of employers.

But this was something new and different. In everything he had been the leader whose orders were obeyed without question. Here for the first time I had acted on my own in a matter of serious moment and importance. What would happen when he knew?

Very slowly I crept still farther forward through the moth's deep fur. Then, gently, I touched the Doctor on the shoulder. At the moment he was looking earthward through his telescope. He started violently as though some supernatural hand had grasped him.

"What? Who is it?" he asked, peering backward into the gloom behind.

THE FIFTH CHAPTER

The Doctor's Reception

I T IS I, DOCTOR—STUBBINS," I SAID. "I COULDN'T let you go alone. I got on at the last minute."

"Stubbins!" said he, lowering his telescope. "Stubbins! Why, I thought you were in Oxenthorpe."

"I didn't go, Doctor," I said shamefacedly. "I—well, I wanted to come for myself and I did feel that you shouldn't be allowed to make the trip all alone."

For a moment there was silence broken only by the steady hum of the moth's wings. I wondered what was coming, what he would say or do. Would he ask the moth to go back and land me on the earth? I noticed Chee-Chee's head turn, and in the pale moonlight a sickly grin of pleasure spread over his scared face as he realized there was more company on this perilous trip.

"Well," said John Dolittle at length, and my heart sank at the cold, almost stern ring in his voice that he had never so far used on me, "I don't quite see why you should begin now, Stubbins, to take it on yourself to worry about my safety and—er—disobey me."

HUGH LOFTING

"'Stubbins!' said he, lowering his telescope."

"I'm sorry," I said. "But—"

I stopped silent. After all, there wasn't anything more to be said. For a minute or two I sat wondering gloomily if this was the end of our relationship. It was, I had to admit, an enormously cheeky thing that I had done. I suppose as a matter of fact I might not have embarked on it without Too-Too's support.

But my anxious thoughts were agreeably interrupted. Suddenly in the gloom the Doctor's strong big hand gripped my arm in a friendly comforting grasp.

"Just the same, Stubbins," I heard him say (and in the dark, without being able to see it, I could imagine the typical smile that accompanied his words), "I can't tell you how glad I am to have you with me. At the very moment when you touched me I was thinking how nice it would be if you were here. Heaven send us luck, Stubbins! Did you tell your parents you were coming?"

"No," said I. "I didn't have a chance. There was no time. Besides, I was so afraid that if I left the premises, you'd slip away without me."

"Oh well," said John Dolittle, "let's not assume the worst. No doubt we'll muddle through all right."

"You usually do, Doctor," said I. "I'm not afraid so long as you're with me."

He laughed.

"That's a pretty good reputation to have," said he. "I hope I deserve it. Look, you see that big patch of lights down there?"

"Yes."

"Well, that's London," he said. "And the white streak running away from it to the eastward is the River Thames. This bunch of lights over to the northwest is Oxford, I imagine. Look, you can see the moonlight reflected on the river all the way up from London. And that big white area is the sea, the Channel."

The map of the British Isles was indeed at this height almost completely revealed to us. It was a cloudless, windless night. And the moth's flight was steady, smooth, and undisturbed as his great wings purred their way upward, putting goodness only knows how many miles between us and Puddleby every minute.

Suddenly I realized that from being scared to death with the newness of this situation I was, as usual with the Doctor's comfortable company, accepting the adventure with a calm, enjoyable interest. I found myself looking down on the world we had left behind and picking out geographical details as though I were merely gazing from a coach window.

He himself was like a child in his delight at the new experience. And he kept pointing to this and that and telling me what it was, as our great living flying machine lifted us further and further and made more and more of the globe visible.

But presently he panted and coughed.

"Air's getting thin, Stubbins," he said. "We are approaching the dead belt. Must be close on twenty thousand feet altitude up here. Let's get those flowers out and fasten them on. We've got one for all of us, luckily—five. Hulloa there, Polynesia!—And Chee-Chee! The flowers! Remember what I told you. Keep your noses well into them. Come, Stubbins: we'll get them unstrapped."

As I moved in answer to the Doctor's summons, I became conscious myself of how thin the air was. The least effort made me breathe heavily.

Somewhere amidships on the moth's body the flowers had been fastened down to a long belt that went about his middle. I joined the Doctor and Chee-Chee in their efforts to get the blossoms loose. The rush of wind made this difficult; and in the dim moonlight I realized that John Dolittle was asking the moth to slow his pace down till we had the work done. As far as I could make out, he did this by means of the creature's antennae. Those long whisker-like arrangements were laid down flat along the back in flight and within easy reach.

It gave me a much greater feeling of security as I saw that the Doctor thus had his ship in control. It only took him a second to communicate his wishes to the insect. And then we hovered. The great wings still beat the air with giant strokes. But the ceasing of

"He did this by means of the creature's antennae."

the rush of wind past one's ears told me that he was merely holding his position and, as it were, treading air.

"All right, Stubbins," said the Doctor, handing me one of the great blooms, "here's yours. Chee-Chee, you take this one. And we'll put this further up toward the shoulders for Polynesia. Now remember, everybody, life itself may depend on our keeping these within reach. If you have the least difficulty in breathing take a deep sniff of the perfume. Later we'll probably have to keep our heads inside them altogether, when we reach the levels where there is no air at all. Is everybody ready? Get the flowers well down into the fur so they are not blown away when I give the order to go ahead."

In a moment or two Captain Dolittle was satisfied that his crew was prepared for the rest of the journey. And reaching for the antennae communication cord, he gave the order for full steam ahead.

Instantly the wings above us redoubled their speed and the whistle of rushing air recommenced.

I found it not so easy now to look over the side, because I was afraid to leave my moon flower lest it be blown away. I gave up studying the map of the disappearing world and fell to watching the moon above and ahead of us.

Crossing
"the Dead Belt"

HROUGHOUT I TRIED VERY HARD TO REALIZE and remember every detail of that night's voyage. For I knew that later on, if I survived, I would want to write it down. After all, it was the great chapter in John Dolittle's astounding and eventful life. Also I knew the practical Doctor would never bother to remember those things that were not of scientific value to the world. Yet he and I were the only ones to see it who could write—though, as a matter of fact, both Chee-Chee and Polynesia remembered what they were able to see better than either of us.

Still I must confess, for me it was not easy. The moon moth put on his greatest speed when the Doctor gave the order to go ahead the second time. The noise, the rush of air past our ears, was positively terrific. It actually seemed to numb the senses and make it almost impossible to take in impressions at all. Soon I found the air getting so thin that I had to keep my head almost constantly buried in the blossom; and communication with the Doctor became an impossibility.

But worse was to come. We finally reached those levels where there was no air at all. Then what happened is entirely confused in my mind and, for that matter, in the Doctor's also. Moreover, no amount of questioning of the moth afterward enlightened us on how he had performed the apparently impossible feat of crossing that "dead belt" from where the air of the earth left off and the atmosphere of the moon began. I came to the conclusion at last that the giant insect did not himself know how the deed was done. But of course it may very well have been that the moth's lack of scientific knowledge and John Dolittle's faulty acquaintance (good though it was in the circumstances) with the insect's language, accounted between them for our never learning how an apparent impossibility had been overcome.

It is indeed no wonder that we, the passengers on this strange airship, saw and realized little enough of what was taking place during that phase. As we got further and further into the parts the Doctor had described as the dead belt, the moth's pace slackened till he was hardly moving at all. He kept working, in fact his great wings beat harder and faster. But the trouble was, there was nothing there for him to beat against. And soon the gravity of the earth itself, which was what he relied upon to maintain his position, seemed to grow fainter.

The result of this was that our flying ship seemed entirely to lose his sense of balance; and we, the passengers, all got desperately seasick. For hours, as far as I could make out, the great creature turned over and over, apparently helpless to get himself into any kind of position at all, utterly unable to go up, down, forward or backward.

For our part, we were occupied with only one thing; and that was making sure we got enough oxygen into our lungs to go on breathing. We hardly dared now to bring our noses out of the flowers for more than a glimpse. There was very little to see anyway.

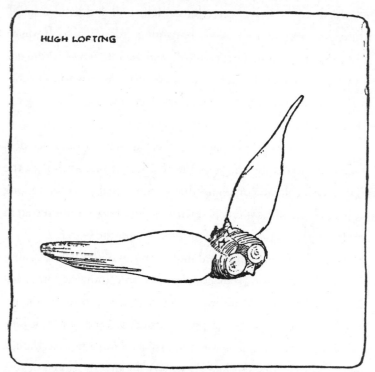

HUGH LOFTING

*"For hours and hours the great creature turned over and over,
apparently helpless."*

The moon appeared to have grown much larger; and the earth was just a tiny round pebble away, away off in space.

One curious thing was that we now had to make very little effort to stick on. It didn't seem to matter a great deal whether our heads or our heels were pointing to the earth. The force of the gravity was so faint it seemed you could stay clinging to the moth's fur as long as you did not actually push yourself off. And even if you did that, you felt you would merely move away a few yards into space and stay there.

We did not however, you may be sure, try any experiments of this kind. We just sat tight, breathed in the perfume of the flowers

and hoped for the best. Never have I felt so ill and helpless in all
my life. The sensation was something quite indescribable. It was as
though gravity itself had been cut off, and yet enough of it remaining to make you feel ill in your stomach every time you went round.
Finally I just shut my eyes. My nose was bleeding like a running tap
and there was a dreadful drumming in my ears.

How long we stayed wallowing there in space I have no idea.
I felt as one sometimes does in bad weather at sea, as though the
end of the world had come and that it didn't really matter so long
as it hurried up and got finished with the job. I wasn't interested in
anything. I just wanted to die—and the sooner the better.

At last, after what appeared like eternities of this helpless, aim-
less turning and tossing, our craft seemed to calm itself somewhat
and I opened my eyes. Withdrawing my head a little from the depths
of the moon flower, I took a peep outside. I could not look long
because the lack of air made that impossible. It was almost as though
someone were holding his hand over your mouth and nose—a very
curious sensation in the open. But before I ducked my head into
the flower again, I had from that short survey of my surroundings
drawn great comfort. I had seen that the positions of the earth and
moon were now reversed. The world we had left was *over* our heads,
and the moon, to which we were coming, was *beneath* us.

Of course this only meant that our moth had turned himself
about and was headed toward the moon, instead of away from the
earth. But, much more important than this, I realized that he now
seemed steadied in his flight. And while he still had only a poor
atmosphere to work in, he was going forward and was no longer
turning around helpless and out of control. As I popped my head
back into the moon flower I congratulated myself that the worst

HUGH LOFTING

"I took a peep outside."

stage of the journey was probably over and that very soon we should for the first time in human experience be able to feel and breathe the atmosphere of the moon world.

Also, with our ship once more in control and flying forward on a level keel, I suddenly found that I felt much better inside. I could open my eyes and think, without feeling that the end of all things was at hand. I wondered how the Doctor and Chee-Chee were getting on; but as yet of course I could not get into communication with them.

Little by little I felt the gravity of the moon asserting itself. At no time did it become nearly as strong as the earth's, which we had left. But you cannot imagine what a sensation of comfort it was to be held by gravity at all. That feeling—happily past—that you were tied to nothing; that there was no "up" and no "down" and no "sideways"; that if you got up too suddenly you might never get seated again, which we experienced going through the dead belt was, beyond all question, the most terrible experience I have ever known.

My sense of time on this expedition was just as completely destroyed as my sense of direction and, indeed, of anything else. Later when communication became easier, I asked the Doctor how long he thought we had taken over the trip. He told me that during the passage of the dead belt his watch had stopped. Gravity—or the lack of it again—we supposed accounted for it. And that later when we got within the moon's influence and were steadily, if feebly, pulled toward her surface, his watch had started itself again. But how many hours it had remained without working he could not say.

He told me that probably our best instrument for reckoning how long we had been on the voyage was our stomachs. Certainly we were both desperately hungry shortly after we had passed the dead belt. But since we had all been seasick for many hours, that is not to be wondered at; and it did not help us much in determining how long we had taken over the trip.

The Doctor also later went into long calculations about the light: when the earth was illumined by sunlight; when it grew dark; when the moon ceased to show sunlight and began to show earth-light, etc., etc. He covered pages and pages, calculating. But the fact remained that during the passage of that dreadful dead belt we had all been so ill and confused that no observations had been taken at all. The moon might have set and the sun risen and the earth both risen and set a dozen times, without any of our party knowing the difference. All we were sure of was that the Doctor's watch had stopped going as we passed beyond earthly gravity and recommenced when we came within lunar gravity.

Moreover, with the weaker strength of the lunar gravity, his watch probably went at an entirely new rate of speed after we left earthly influence. So, all in all, our calculations on the trip were not of much exact scientific value. Seasickness is a nasty thing.

From the time that I took that first glimpse out of my moon flower I began to keep a much more definite record of what was happening. As the moon air grew stronger, I felt more and more myself. It wasn't the same as earth air. There was no question about that. It was much more, what should one call it?—"heady." This apparently was because it contained more oxygen than ours did.

I could see, as presently I grew bolder and took more frequent glimpses, that both John Dolittle and Chee-Chee were also picking up and generally taking notice. Polynesia, I found out afterward, was the only one who had not been badly disturbed by the dead belt. Swirling in midair was to her, as it was to all the flying creatures, mere child's play. If she had only been scientifically educated, she could have told us how long we had taken over the trip. But the old parrot had always had a curious contempt for human science, maintaining that man went to a whole lot of unnecessary trouble to calculate things that birds knew by common sense, just as soon as they were born.

After a little the Doctor and I began to exchange signals. We did not yet attempt to leave our places as we still felt a bit unsteady on our legs. But, like seasick passengers in ships' deckchairs, we smiled encouragingly at one another and endeavored to show by gestures and signs that we thought the worst of the weather was over.

THE SEVENTH CHAPTER

The Two Sides
of the Moon

I N ONE OF THESE PASSAGES OF MIMED CONVER-
sation between the Doctor and myself, I got the impression that he was making remarks about the quality of the
moon air on which we were now being carried. There was
no doubt that it was changing at enormous rate. Finding anything
outside my flower that I could breathe in at all, I was becoming
quite adventurous and independent. I even went so far as to leave
the flower entirely and walk, or crawl, down to where the Doctor
squatted. But a violent attack of coughing just as I was about to say
something to him made me beat a hasty retreat.

"Still," I said to myself as I dropped down with my head in
my own blossom, "it is something to have got to him. Back there a
little while ago I felt as though I could never see or get to anyone
any more."

Presently the Doctor paid me a flying visit. He too had to make
it short. But we had the satisfaction of feeling that we were in contact.
We had not been sure up to this that we could *hear* one another's

voices in moon air. The Doctor had often spoken in Puddleby, when the voyage had first been contemplated, of a danger from this source.

"The ether," he had said, "is what carries sound with us here on the earth. We can by no means be sure that up there there will be any ether at all. If there isn't, ordinary speech will be impossible."

And with this in mind he had perfected between himself and Chee-Chee a kind of sign language. Too-Too had told me of this, and I had secretly watched their practice and gained some knowledge of the system.

So you can imagine how glad we were to find that up here also there was ether that could carry our voices. We found presently, however, that it carried them much more easily than it did on the earth. As we approached the moon and its new atmosphere became more apparent, we found that we had to speak lower and lower. It was very peculiar. Finally, if we did not want to break one another's eardrums, we had to talk in the faintest whispers—which could be heard at quite a long distance.

Another very peculiar thing was the light. The Doctor and I had the longest arguments later on trying to settle whether we landed on the moon by earthlight or by sunlight. It would at first seem of course that there could be no question whatever on such a point. One would suppose that on the moon earth-light would be very little stronger than moonlight on the earth; while sunlight would be a hundred times as brilliant. But not at all. Something about the lunar atmosphere seemed to soften the sunlight down so that up there it appeared very little stronger than the light thrown by the earth This had a very peculiar and definite effect upon colors.

Presently, as the moon gravity became stronger, the Doctor and I were able to get up from our lying positions. We still carried our flowers with us so that we could take a "whiff" every once in a while if we felt we needed it. But we could talk together in low tones and, in a fashion, make observations. It wasn't long after we thus "came to life" that John Dolittle asked the moth through his antennae communication cord to slow his pace down a little. We felt that it would be easier for us if we got used to this moon air slowly. It certainly had a very invigorating and exciting effect upon the human system.

Another point over which the Doctor and I argued a great deal afterward was on which side of the moon did we land? The earth people have, as everyone knows, only seen one side of the moon. Maps and careful examinations have been made of that. Now, in spite of bringing with us the latest moon maps, it was not easy to decide on which side we were landing. Close-up, the mountains looked very different from what they did through the telescope from the earth. I always maintained—and do still—that the moth deliberately went round to the far side before he attempted to make a landing. The Doctor swears he didn't.

How can I describe the last moments of that voyage? To say that I felt like Columbus first sighting a new world does not convey the idea at all. I must admit I was scared to death. And so, I know, was poor Chee-Chee. As for the Doctor and Polynesia, I can't say. I don't believe that hardened old adventurer of a parrot ever got a real scare in her life. With Polynesia one always had the feeling that she dictated to Life, instead of having Life dictate to her. But that may have been partly due to her look of complete independence.

The Doctor?—Well, I doubt if he was scared either. He had often told me that he had many times been mortally afraid in the course of his career. But I imagine it was never at moments such as this, when the lure of scientific discovery shut out every other feeling.

That he was thrilled it is certain. Even the tough worldly-wise Polynesia admitted afterward that *she* had the thrill of her life when the droning wings of the giant moth suddenly shut off their mighty beating and stiffened out flat, as we began to sail downward toward the surface of this new world that no earthly creature had yet set foot upon before.

The Tree

I MUST HERE SPEAK AGAIN OF THIS QUESTION OF light. At no time, as I have said, was it very powerful. And one of its effects was to soften the colors in a very peculiar way. As we descended we found that the moon had a whole range of colors of its own that we had never seen on the earth. I cannot describe them because the human eye, being trained only to the colors of the earth, would have nothing to compare them with and no way of imagining them. The best I can do is to say that the landscape, as we slowly descended upon it, looked like some evening landscape done in pastels—with a tremendous variety of soft new tones that became more and more visible the closer we got.

I think there can be no question that the Doctor and I were both more or less right in our argument about which side of the moon we landed on. In other words, we landed between the two. I know that looking backward as we came down I saw that both the earth and the sun were visible. The earth pale and dim in the heavens—as one sees the moon often by daylight—and the sun brighter but by no means as glaring as it appears when seen from the earth.

We were still at a great height from the surface. But already the roundness was beginning to fade out of the eye's grasp and details were taking on greater importance. The Doctor, after again asking the moth to make the descent as slowly as he could, so that we should have a chance to grow gradually accustomed to the new air, had his telescope out and was very busy pointing to this crater and that mountain and the other plateau as features that were already known to us from the astronomers' moon maps.

From a certain height it was easy to see the night-and-day line,

"The Doctor had his telescope out."

on our side of which the moon's surface was only dimly lit by the earth's pale light, and on the other more brilliantly illuminated by the rays of the sun.

Of course I suppose anyone trying to land on the moon by mechanical means could quite easily have lost his senses and life itself in the attempt. But with a living airship that could accommodate itself to one's needs, we had a tremendous advantage. For example, as we dropped lower and found the air more difficult to deal with, the Doctor again grasped the antennae communication cord and asked the moth to hover a few hours while we got accustomed to it. The great insect immediately responded to this demand and hung motionless in midair while we prepared ourselves for the final descent.

Captain Dolittle then called the roll of his crew and found that we were all at least alive and kicking—also terribly hungry. Sandwiches and drinks had been put aboard before we left. But these were long since used up. I have never felt so hungry in my life.

Over that last lap of the descent we took a long time. With the communication cord constantly in his hand, the Doctor approached the moon at his own pace. The night-and-day line moved of course very rapidly. Moreover, how much of that was confused with our own movement (we did not descend in a straight line by any means) it is hard to say. This accounts largely for the difference of opinion between John Dolittle and myself as to which side of the surface we actually landed on. Close-up, the details of all the moon maps no longer meant much, because those details that we had seen through telescopes as mere fractions of an inch were now become mountains and continents.

I suppose the greatest anxiety in the minds of all of us was *water*.

Would we find it on the moon? Moon creatures might exist without it: but we must perish if it was not there.

Lower and lower in circles slowly we sank. At first prospects looked very blue. The landscape, or moonscape, immediately beneath us was all, it seemed, volcanoes, old craters, and new craters—mile upon mile.

But toward that night-and-day line that showed round the globe, we turned hopeful eyes.

I have seen the Doctor enthusiastic many times—when for example he discovered something new in any of his unnumbered branches of natural history research. But I never remember his getting so excited as he did when watching that ever-moving day-and-night line on our slow descent, he suddenly grabbed me by the shoulder. Forgetting for the moment how the moon atmosphere carried sound, he nearly deafened me with—

"Stubbins, look! A tree! You see that, way over there at the foot of the mountain? I'll swear it's a tree. And if it is, we're all right. It means water, Stubbins, *water*! And we can manage to exist here. Water and *life*!"

The End

Looking for another great book?
Find it
IN THE MIDDLE.

Fun, fantastic books for kids
in the in-beTWEEN age.

IntheMiddleBooks.com